Penguin Books
Dear Hearts and Gentle People

Born in New Zealand, Ruth Park came to Australia to take a job
as a journalist. Here she married D'Arcy Niland and travelled with
him through outback Australia working in a variety of jobs from
shearers' cook to fruit packer – all of which provided a rich source
of material for her later writing.

Her reputation as a writer was established when her first novel
The Harp in the South was published in 1948, and its sequel,
Poor Man's Orange in 1949, neither of which has been out of print
since their first publication.
She has written almost forty books, including ten novels and
twenty-seven children's books. Her many prizes include the
prestigious Miles Franklin Award for *Swords and Crowns and Rings*
(1977) and the 1981 Australian Children's Book of the Year Award
and The Boston Globe Award for *Playing Beatie Bow* available
in Puffin.

Other books by Ruth Park

Novels

Missus
Poor Man's Orange
The Witch's Thorn
A Power of Roses
The Harp in the South
The Frost and the Fire
Good Looking Women
Serpent's Delight
Swords and Crowns and Rings

Children's books

The Muddle-Headed Wombat Series
Callie's Castle
When the Wind Changed
Playing Beatie Bow
My Sister Sif
Things in Corners

Non-Fiction

The Drums Go Bang (with D'Arcy Niland)

Ruth Park

Dear Hearts
and Gentle People

PENGUIN BOOKS

Penguin Books Australia Ltd,
487 Maroondah Highway, P.O. Box 257
Ringwood, Victoria 3134, Australia
Penguin Books Ltd,
Harmondsworth, Middlesex, England
Viking Penguin Inc.,
40 West 23rd Street, New York, N.Y. 10010, U.S.A.
Penguin Books Canada Limited,
2801 John Street, Markham, Ontario, Canada L3R 1B4
Penguin Books (N.Z.) Ltd,
182-190 Wairau Road, Auckland 10, New Zealand

First published under the title *Pink Flannel* by Angus &
Robertson Ltd, 1955
Published in Penguin Books, 1981
Reprinted 1982, 1986, 1989

CIP

Park, Ruth.
Dear hearts and gentle people
First published as Pink flannel. Sydney: Angus & Robertson, 1955
ISBN 0 14 005854 0.

I. Title.

A823'.3

Dear Hearts
and Gentle People

I was born on an enchanted island. Like a green lizard it clings close and crooked to the underside of the world, and the seas around it are the colour of jasper.

The dark voyagers who first found the island called it The Big Fish. They could see it in their minds, vast and streaming, dragged from the depths by a godlike angler. Thus it has always been most singularly a creature of the sea, dwelling aloof from the rest of the world. This quality of singularity, of dispassion towards the anxious complexities of the continental civilizations, looks out from the eyes of its people. Their reserve and silence is as self-contained as the sunlight that dawdles in its golden, butterfly-haunted gullies.

Many of these people have forgotten, or never comprehended, that their island was once enchanted. As a land is built upon, its contours mutilated, its rivers broken to saddle, its aborigines torn from their secret law and language, it withdraws its primal magic into itself. But there is always someone who can touch that magic, or recall it as it was.

Some folk look back to their childhood and find it was always summer weather. I remember mostly the immaculacy of frost, a river running deep and mumbling under ice watermarked with mud; fluffed-up linnets; hoofs striking bell-sounds from stony roads.

In fact, weather when I could wear my pink flannel petticoat, which was threaded through the yoke with a narrow black ribbon, because my Auntie Barbara, who made it, was a dressmaker with towny ideas.

One thing I deplore about the diminution of families is that every child's quota of aunts is accordingly reduced. I even know some children with no aunts at all. Now, my childhood was different. It was rich in aunts. Lavish and bounteous were the aunts thereof. Looking back at it all, I can hardly believe there were so many. There were querulous, woolly aunts who came out at Christmas, like mistletoe; brisk aunts who had mysterious boxes full of old dresses and hat-veils lendable to nieces on rainy days.

My most remarkable aunt was Uncle Olga, who lived at Waitomo. Uncle Olga's husband, Uncle Ray, was notable for two things. His cousin Gilda invented the shimmy, and he hoarded newspapers. Why, that poor woman couldn't as much as get the outside pages of the *Star* to wrap up the fish-heads without Uncle Ray going to market about it. He would rescue papers from trains, football grandstands, and public lavatories. You may think he was a little jelly-headed, but this was not so. Uncle Ray merely had a passion for self-education.

Uncle Olga was one of those fragile little women who look like clothed twigs. This wee, repressed thing would open her ladylike mouth and out would roll a voice like Chaliapin's, causing iron bullock-drivers to cough uneasily into their rum and Bovril. This of course was why, in my literal mind, she was irrevocably Uncle.

Best of all my relatives were the Four Radiant Aunts, with whom I lived. They ranged from seventeen to twenty-three, exquisite giggly creatures with swathes and waves and kiss-curls of brown and flaxen and bright bay hair. They wore their waists round their hips and their hems round their knees; fuji dresses with elbow sleeves and stripes running round the wrong way; slave bangles and beads shaped like little persimmons, hats that came down snugly, like cosies, to their lovely eyebrows.

And the way they smelt...Orris root, and rose sachet, and Koko-for-the-hair!

We all lived together in a little weatherboard house which used a vast walnut-tree as an umbrella. This was canny of the little house because in the King Country the rain turns to mud even before it hits the ground. Later on, when I went to school, the walnuts provided me with endless bargaining power.

The Radiant Aunts were as thick as thieves and loved each other tremendously. They never fell out, and they always looked after each other, which they are doing to this very day. When I got to know them I could understand very well how, when their eldest sister, my mother, died in Australia, and my distraught father, Tom Hood, was all for putting me in an orphanage, they instantly wrote a letter hardly readable for tear-stains, asking if they could have me as their very own. So, at the age of three, I travelled back to my native shore in the care of a New Zealand Shipping Company stewardess, my only souvenir of Australia being a large spider shell, with an interior polished to pink silk by the warm waters of the Barrier Reef.

Barbara had not been twenty-one at the time, and had defied her father, old Grandpa, in order to take me. After begetting five girls, he felt he couldn't bear another one, and in a cold black storm of Scandinavian temper he packed his gear and got out, and went to live at Kawhia by himself. There he spoke of his daughters as 'dem broddy vimmin', and told everyone they had sent him away because he always left the toilet seat up. A bad old man he was, coarse and frightening, smelling of the whaleships in which he had spent most of his life. Still, his daughters had to thank him for giving them a beautiful name.

He was born Albrechtsen, and so were they, but when the Great War came, canny old Syver saw that the New Zealanders wouldn't be able to distinguish between German and Dutch or Swedish names. So he changed his right smartly, for he had no wish to have his windows kicked in, or to be beaten up by some patriot in the belief that he was a German. Particularly as he hated the Huns as much as he hated the Rooshians.

Naturally he wanted his new name to indicate his long service on the sea. Boatswain, he considered, and Mariner, but then he thought dommit! Vy not go to the top?

The name looked good on the window of the girls' little dressmaking establishment.

MISSES ADMIRAL, ROBES AND MANTLES

Ailie, the youngest, most romantic sister had wanted to call the business THE LITTLE SHOPPE, but after grave consideration the other sisters turned it down on the very good grounds that people in Te Kano took most things seriously. It was true that when the new bootmaker put up the sign REPAIRS WHILE U WAIT, passers by always stopped and gawked. And when some poor, ambitious pastrycook called her shop THE KAKE KOTTAGE, customers always looked away from the sign in well-bred embarrassment, thinking that she couldn't spell.

Well, there they were, a houseful of girls who had fallen heiress to another who was credulous, literal, and very young, believing all adults to be infallible and divinely inspired.

There was scandal and humiliation, grief and wickedness in that little town of Te Kano, but looking back life there seems to have had all the smiling delight of a piece of light music. So that is what this story must be – a piece of light music.

One of the most marvellous things about New Zealand is the fact that you have only to knock on the door, and there you are in the past. Events have moved so fast that there is a curious sense of historical foreshortening. My grandfather, old Syver, made his first visit to New Zealand as a ship's boy during the Maori Wars. Why, the old rogue, he said he used to stand up against a hardwood door and Colonel von Tempsky, that great romantic commando, would throw bowie knives pang between his fingers. Lie or not, the dates are right, and he could have done it.

In the same way the little town of Te Kano was full of history, not the sort in books, but the sort which sits round on verandas in rocking chairs, or squats on the marae before the Pa, or goes to Church and kneels on faithful, rheumaticky knees and thanks God for each hour of grace and favour.

Our neighbour, Mrs Cuskelly, who kept a boarding house and was known locally as Old Frosty Eye, had been one of the dozen children of a dour-lipped Irish immigrant who had taken up land miles out in the dreary scrub beyond Te Kano. Mrs Cuskelly, then Mollie Toohey, had been put to the scrub-cutting. By the time she was eleven she had cleared forty-five acres, and was old enough and strong enough to take the other end of the cross-cut saw in the heavy timber. Mrs Cuskelly had a pair of hands like snow-shoes. Her children would say that one whack alongside the lug was enough to knock you out the kitchen door. But she never raised her hand to her husband, more's the pity. Nor to her son Cocky Cuskelly, her sorrow, and in some inverted way, her pride.

When I was five Cocky Cuskelly was twenty, but he was little taller than me, with the face of a mischievous old fairy, and a two-storey head. When the rest of her children wore patched and outgrown clothes, Mrs Cuskelly dressed Cocky in warm tweed knickerbockers. How the tailor got them to fit Cocky was a miracle. He probably shortened the knicker and lengthened the bocker.

As far as one could see there was nothing whatever the matter with Cocky's brain, but he had never gone to school. There must have been some arrangement between the truant inspector and the medical authorities. However, Cocky was keen as a whip and could read, write, and figure much better than his parents. When Cocky was young Mrs Cuskelly, poor soul, tried to keep him under cover. Yet in her brave, outright Irish way she would refer to him as 'my poor afflicted, God mend his suffering heart', which so affected other women in the town they would go home and promise their children mayhem if they didn't let poor Cocky Cuskelly join in their games. The children did their best, but their instincts put a brake on their charity.

You know the way dogs look out of the corners of their eyes when they spot some new kind of animal? That is the way the Te Kano children would look at Cocky Cuskelly, uneasy, astonished, their calloused brown feet itchy to be going. And then they would slink away, ears flattened, tails down, creeping into their homes with such sickly looks that their mothers would reach for the ipecacuanha bottle.

Cocky ignored me until I was old enough to do the messages, then he took to following me round. He said nothing, made no approaches of any sort, but prowled noiselessly along behind me at a distance of three or four feet. When I turned round he would stop still and stare. I tried to be friendly, but he wouldn't answer. Then in a trembling voice I tried to bribe him with a penny to go away. His child's hand advanced to take the penny, then he put it into his mouth and swallowed it. I burst into screams of terror and ran away home as fast as I could, but no matter how fast I went Cocky's laughter kept pace with me.

He did the same thing to his father, an inoffensive little man in shirt-sleeves and a hard-hitter, who wanted nothing of the world except to be left alone, especially by Mrs Cuskelly. Cocky followed him round docilely until the very sight of a shadow across his path was enough to make the father choke nervously on his Adam's apple.

'And why shouldn't the lad be with his own father, and him so dependent upon you?' Mrs Cuskelly would demand, and the poor man had no defence. Then he discovered how to get rid of Cocky without any trouble at all.

The only weakness in the inhuman little creature's makeup was his queer deformed head. Not that he was ashamed of it. On the contrary, he was a complete extrovert and did everything he could to draw the amazed attention of the world to it. But he could not bear water on it. The merest hint of a rain shower was enough to send him scampering down the street like a fleeing bantam. If he were caught in the rain he would tear off most of his clothes and swathe them round his gigantic head like a turban, making at the same time the terrified sounds of a child in a bad dream.

So Mr Cuskelly kept a water pistol in his pocket. Just the sight of it was enough for Cocky. Whimpering, he would flee to his mother, and she never understood why.

In the curious cabal of silence which children can so perfectly create, the rest of the Cuskelly clan ignored the existence of their elder brother. I do not recall my special friend, Pola Cuskelly, ever mentioning him. Heaven knows what sort of a life he gave them within the privacy of the home circle. Most likely they all ended up by carrying water pistols, as did the boarders, who liked Mrs Cuskelly's cooking too much to be frightened away. Yet Cocky was not wicked. It was just that his soul had pointed ears.

For a time the watermelon paddock down our road was continually raided by gangs of big happy Maori lads from the Pa. They would choose deathly dark nights, and the only way you could tell they were crying havoc amongst the melons was the sound of rich, carefree schlooping and an occasional honey-soft chuckle. But Cocky always knew. He even knew which melon-vine they particularly favoured, with the result that during the next raid one of the Maoris felt round amongst the cool unseen leaves and discovered a melon with hair on it.

One can easily imagine that big young fellow standing there, fingers glued to the melon, his brown colour rapidly ebbing to a dirty grey, his eyes falling out of his head. Finally the warrior spirit of his ancestors comes to his aid, he explores further, and his fingers come to a pair of ears. At that they crumple away with a bad case of nervous paralysis, and their owner gives a screech like a morepork.

11

The shocking news is babblingly communicated to his friends, and most of them streak away from that ghastly paddock at once. However, one of them, with half-white blood and consequently a terrible inquisitiveness, creeps back and tremblingly flashes a torch round amongst the melons. And there he sees Cocky's bodiless head lying huge and awful amongst the vines, eyes staring and mouth open...

Mrs Cuskelly couldn't for the life of her imagine how Cocky got so much mud on his clothes.

'You'd of thought he'd been standing in a hole,' she said.

Then came that frosty night in early August, when the town like a small gloomy galaxy had vanished, as was its habit, into the vast country darkness. In cities, where men have filled the air with a thousand unwaning moons, you forget the blind quality of natural darkness. This is the way it fell over the old King Country, mysterious, positive, complete, and as never since would you realize that the world had spun its face away from the sun and you were looking out into spacial wastes which had never known the dayspring.

The girls were working very late that night, and when I woke myself with a cough and came wandering out to find some butter and sugar for it, I found them weary and languid, the fire dying down and the bitter cold already creeping in under the door and round the window frames. Then my Auntie Barbie looked old, and Francey half-asleep...but I was still too young to know how hard they worked. I rubbed a patch in the steam on the window. The moon had risen, and the house was in a thick furry shadow. Only the edge of the roof shone as if wet.

'You've left the washing out,' I observed drowsily.

'Darn it!' groaned Louisa, whose duty it was.

She crunched out over grass that was already frozen into exquisitely sculptured spikes. A few minutes later she came in with the sheets, frozen stiff as boards. She and Francey had a desperate struggle at the doorway to bend them into hoop shapes in order to get them through into the room. Finally Louisa cantankerously bashed the corners flat and squeezed them through. The door was hardly shut before Barbie said 'Hush!'

All of us heard the strange, soft footsteps on the roof. Worse than that, they went down the wall, hesitated a moment, and then crawled up again. Then there was silence, and the silence was more terrifying than the sound. I can still see those four pale faces, the large startled eyes, and little Ailie starting to tremble.

'Oh, Louisa!' gasped Barbie, 'And you were out there by yourself.'

Now the footsteps did a little jig on the roof, slid down the corrugated iron with a noisy glee and shot off into space with a skid. We stared at the window, expecting a face to plaster itself against the pane. But nothing came. Then the feet walked up the wall again.

'It can't be a man,' began Barbie, 'and there's no animal as big as that.'

'I wish Pa was here!' wailed Louisa.

I began to bawl loudly, and the feet bounced up and down the wall in eerie recognition of my distress.

Barbie tremulously picked up the poker.

'Barbie,' ordered Francey, 'you're not to go out. Pa wouldn't let you!'

Like one sister the four rushed to the window, threw it up and shrieked, 'Mr Cuskelly, help, help!'

The footsteps hopped on top of the chimney, and a spatter of soot rained down on the fire. Then they did a derisive tattoo on the roof.

In the country the sound of someone yelling carries a very long way. Doors flew open and windows banged up, cowbells jangled in a fright, and dogs began to bark. Lamps flared up all over that side of town. Little Mr Cuskelly was to be seen peering doubtfully from behind his wife's massive silhouette.

'Dear God in heaven, what is it, darlin's?' she called.

Then we discovered what those terrifying aerial footsteps were. Cocky Cuskelly was perched up in our walnut-tree. He held in his hand a long pole with a fork, each prong being padded like a boxing glove. With this he had cavorted at his pleasure upon the resonant iron roof.

Cocky was not abashed when the torches were turned upon him. With a calm ironic gleam he looked down upon his spluttering father and incredulous mother. Finally he spat down upon the upturned faces.

That finished it. By the grace of God Mr Cuskelly's garden tap was the only one in Te Kano that night not bearded with an icicle, so he turned the hose on Cocky.

If Cocky had had a nervous system he would have had a nervous breakdown. As it was he disappeared in a nocturnal ambulance and his mother spread it about that he had been sent to Wellington to 'a place of restraint'. Mr Cuskelly blossomed like a rose, but he still never got round to chopping any stove-wood.

But Cocky came back. Two years later the defunct People's Palace, a vast ghost-house of a theatre, was bought by some company with more money than sense. As the cleaners went through it they said you could see the rats jumping out the windows like fleas off a Maori dog. They swept out the garlanded clots of dust, slapped some gilt on the pillars, and replushed the sagging seats.

Allan Wilkie brought *Merry Wives* there, but it scandalized the Te Kano populace. A few local productions tottered along, and a vaudeville show, or, as it was known then, 'A Fuller's', came through from Auckland. The trainload of gaudy scenery, weary sequinned girls, mind-readers, trained dog-troupes, and iron-faced ushers arrived in a winter dawn, but most of Te Kano was there to meet it, so rare was such a visitation.

14

Imagine then that theatre full of the false glamour of dim light, a palpitating crowd of country people, unsophisticated and delighted, some of whom had ridden many miles to see the show. Imagine the romantic music, the gorgeous velvet curtain sweeping aside without a sign to show a glittering scene of night, speckled with stars that had the faces of girls, and centred with a descending crescent moon.

And who should be perched on the inner bend of the moon but Cocky Cuskelly, the man in the moon?

Mrs Cuskelly gave a piercing shriek and fainted, and in the rest of the theatre was a shocked and embarrassed silence.

Cocky became a circus acrobat and died many years afterwards of a broken neck.

'Somebody pushed him, and not before time,' said his father, tolerantly.

Something else of import happened that week Cocky Cuskelly was up in our walnut-tree. I found out about love.

It was an astonishing discovery. Like a little caterpillar I crept to the edge of my Lifebuoy-haunted, buttonhook-ridden life, peeked out the door and realized apocalyptically that one day I, too, would be a woman.

Two doors from MISSES ADMIRAL, ROBES AND MANTLES was a fruit-shop, and twice a week their scraps and rotten un-sold fruit and vegetables were put out in a big drum for a being called the Pig Man. For a while I thought this referred to his looks, but after lurking for a long time in the high sorrel at the back of the fruit-shop's backyard, I was fortunate enough to see him in person. He was built generally on the lines of a kauri, in that it was a long way up to the first branch, and even further to the second. This enormous person lifted the big drum of old cauliflowers and ex-potatoes with an easy swing, and hurled the contents on the back of his wagon. I was awed.

'Here, sis,' he said. I looked cautiously round, saw that he could be referring to no one but me, and went a little closer. He had a nice coral-pink face, bright-blue eyes, and a veranda of flaxen hair with a smear of pumpkin on it.

'You tell your auntie she'd better or else,' he said.

'Which auntie?' I quavered, being unused to conversation with men.

'The pretty one,' he replied, as he and his wagon clip-clopped off.

Possibly my faithful rendition of this tactless remark was what started Grandpa Admiral's furious hostility to the Pig Man. I can't say it put Ailie, Barbie, and Francey on his side, either.

But the Pig Man couldn't be expected to know he had put his great pumpkin-stained hoof in it. He was a person of spectacular simplicity of soul. He looked the world straight in the eye, and if it peered down its long nose at him, he knocked it flat.

At the time he met my darling Auntie Louisa she was eighteen and he not much older. Two years previously his dad had died and left him a hundred acres of swamp and fern-tangle out on the flats a little south of town. The Pig Boy, as he was then, spent all his savings on a few sows and a good dog, and set up house in an old Maori shanty on the property.

In the way of boys then he could and did do everything, He cleared and drained, burned off and fenced. The sows were frequently seduced by wild boars, returning repentant to his doorstep. But the litters seemed to benefit by the change of air, and the Pig Boy's pork was peculiarly succulent, gaining a quick reputation even in that district where everyone's plate spilled over, and I have heard my Auntie Francey apologize for a lunch which consisted only of a 'bit of old hashed pheasant'.

Strong, willing, hard-working, smart enough to pick up

cheap buttermilk from the dairy factory and free vegetables from the fruit-shops, the Pig Man, you'd think,
would be an acceptable suitor for any girl. But no. He
came under the heading of Forbidden Aliens.

The whole of the white population of Te Kano went
round trembling indecisively on the verge of what was and
what was not Nice. This varied from class to class, and on
the whole the fourteen-bob-a-day man was a darned sight
more proper than his medical or solicitorial brother. His
taboos were steely.

The Admiral girls freely borrowed from all classes. With
Grandpa in their background like an evil old spook, they
adopted every taboo in sight and felt safe. One of these
by-laws was: No Nice Girl shall go with a young man of
unsuitable occupation.

A pig-keeper was improbable.

A garbage man was impossible.

A night-cart man did not exist.

My Uncle Olga was in love with a night-cart man once.
His name was Vern.

Very often, probably just after Uncle Ray had snatched
the last pages of the *King Country Chronicle* from her hands
and left her with half a hundredweight of tea-leaves and
nothing to wrap them in, Uncle Olga's little face would
shrivel up sad and sour and I would know she was thinking of Vern.

He was a fine, upright young fellow with not a thing
against him except that in order to earn some money
quickly he had put on the white overalls of the County
Council and become one of the furtive shadows who
dodged through the moonlight – a clanker of cans and a
rider on that mysterious and nameless vehicle which like a
tumbril rumbled through the deafening silence of the King
Country midnights.

Uncle Olga had not known his occupation. She thought
he did something respectable like driving the steam-roller.

17

Then one day the secret came out. For days Uncle Olga couldn't speak. For weeks she couldn't look anyone in the eye without bursting into tears. She allowed, in her weakness, her elder brother Syver to ribaldly bombast her out of ever seeing Vern again.

Vern was proud. He did not even try to persuade her to change her mind. He resigned from the Council, moved to another town, bought a men's outfitters and made a small fortune selling mighty bottle-green sombreros to the Maori boys. He had become perfectly respectable, and the only deplorable thing about it was that he was now married to someone else.

Uncle Olga never forgot Vern, especially when Uncle Ray was around. She referred to him as her Bus, and it was left to one's imagination to assume she had missed him.

When it came out, therefore, that Louisa Admiral was seriously going with the Pig Man, Uncle Olga stuck up for him in passionate baritone rumblings, but no one else did.

'Oh, Louie,' wept Francey, 'when you're married you'll be called Mrs Pig Man, and your children will be the Pig Kids, and we'll be the Pig Aunts.'

With this the remaining aunts went off into shrieks of laughter, while Louisa bowed her delicate white neck and wept, softly, gently, like spring rain falling.

Anyone with half an eye could see that Louisa didn't want to be known as the mother of Pig Kids.

'You are a beast, Francey,' said Barbara reproachfully.

Louisa lifted her head. She looked like a dewy young tree.

'No, Barbie. Francey is just being cruel to be kind.' she whispered.

Then Francey seized her sister, and their two bright chestnut heads came close together while the elder girl cried, 'Oh, Louie, it's just that I don't want you living out there in that awful shack with no water laid on and mud

18

everywhere and...and...oh, Louie, you're so pretty, you could do so much better for yourself!'

'Yes, you could, Louisa,' said Barbara lovingly, 'Why, you've got the flattest chest in town.'

It must be remembered that this remarkable statement was made when bosoms were wanderers upon the face of the earth and brassières were constructed vertically. We all looked with great admiration and interest upon Louisa's reed-slim forum, which was exactly the same size all the way up from her belted hips to her shoulders.

'There's no one better than *him*,' said Louisa, softly, dreamily.

'Well, he hasn't proposed yet,' said Francey sharply.

'And I hope he doesn't!' added Barbara.

'Send the child outside,' said Ailie instantly, and I was bustled outside, gagged with an apple, for they thought that word was one I well might know. I didn't, but I put it away for reference and when opportunity offered I looked it up in a dictionary at Mrs Cuskelly's. By then I had forgotten the true word and looked up 'suppose' instead.

My aunts were under the common illusion that a very small child is part of the furniture and doesn't notice. The truth is, of course, that children miss nothing and understand almost everything. What they don't understand they store away in their memories for future reference, and many a mother would blush if she realized what her children will comprehendingly recall about her in five years' time.

At the moment, however, I rushed round and stood under the kitchen window to see what else I could hear.

'You see, girls,' Louisa said in a low, tense tone, 'I've got to face pigs, but he's got to face Pa.'

There was an instant silence, then bedlam. The Radiant Aunts were sharply divided on this point. Barbara, in all dignity of her elder sisterhood, thought Pa, bad and all as he was, better than pigs. Ailie and Francey, rash creatures, were strongly pro-porker.

I can imagine the Pig Man, in his spectacular innocence, puzzling out the proper way to Suppose to Louisa. Diamond rings were out of the question, and his natural inclination to give her a litter of shocking-pink sucking pigs he had just sufficient good sense to suppress.

So he Supposed with a La Gloria.

It must have been tantamount to giving a present-day girl a TV set. Heaven alone knows how many sides of bacon it cost. Looked at in terms of pig-mash the price must have been astronomical.

It was the first phonograph seen in Te Kano without a horn.

I can see it yet, immensely tall, so that my nose came level with the wonderful fretwork on its front. In fact there was a particular curlicue where I once got myself painfully suspended by a nostril.

It was a colour known as bright oak, the shade of a cosh-boy's tan shoes.

What glory there was in those old phonographs! The green baize of the turntable, those undustable little compartments that held old and new needles! The haughty jut of the handle! The lid lifted on a sort of dislocated metal elbow, beautiful to behold, and if you didn't have it up properly it would come down with a bang and cut Al Jolson off in the middle of a bleat. You could hear him fuming away *sotto voce* under the lid.

For the first week of the La Gloria we had so many visitors that the ten records which came with the machine imprinted themselves so irrevocably on my brain I can to this moment burst into the identical strains of 'In the evening by the Moonlight' complete with the guk-guk-guk in the middle where Mrs Bedding of the sweetshop dropped her teacup.

Maoris lurked under our hedge to hear, smiling bashfully when I rushed out and pompously sooled the dog on to them.

How can I explain the terrible starvation for music which afflicted us all in those days? Perhaps the towns had their fill, but Te Kano never. If the Salvation Army ever had come there it would have had a thousand conversions, just for the sweet sake of the good raucous music it provided. We chased visiting bands down the main street, looking with inexpressible delight upon the curly golden mouths of the big wind instruments. On New Year's Eve we stood silent, hypnotized, watching those solitary Scotsmen who strutted back and forth like roosters as they played proud and piercing upon the beribboned pipes. And on Anzac Day at the soldiers' memorial our hearts, unspoiled by radio, talking pictures, or any mechanical music whatsoever, unbearably sensitive to the cold chaste notes of the bugle, broke clean across as the Last Post shivered the air.

Yes, the Pig Man very nearly made his alley good with the La Gloria. One could see Barbara, Ailie, and Francey hovering, as it were, above the abyss. One moment they were blown this way by the wind of their own conservatism; the next tossed stormily upon the tempestuous emotions which argued down all opposition with the statement that any man who Supposed with such a magnificent instrument was worth considering.

It was, anyway, regarded as a firm enough basis for one of those formidable family gatherings which occurred in the days when problems were discussed by the Relations. Nowadays as far as I can see Relations are avoided like the itch, but then there was no avoiding them. If you had Relations you had 'em, like six toes on one foot.

The Radiant Aunts had them.

Aside from Grandpa, there was his sister, that Uncle Olga who lived at Waitomo with Uncle Ray. The latter emerges fully blown from the half-formed shadows of my memory as a distraught type. Aside from collecting news-papers, he was a sensitive, gentle person with all the qualities of a poltergeist. It was almost impossible to approach him without being injured. Consequently my Uncle Olga was always bandaged somewhere. I have myself seen the little woman, delighted over some birthday gift, fling herself into his arms and a second later retire screaming. In his emotion he had dropped his cigarette between her corset and her stomach. If he kissed her he poked his moustache in her eye. Once, in their honeymoon days he had absentmindedly tossed his boiling shaving water into the bath, forgetting that Uncle Olga was already in it.

Physically Uncle Ray was small and pink and a little dazed, like a shickered goldfish. I loved him.

There were also, at that La Gloria conclave, an aunt and some distant cousins known as the Hen and Chickens. Aside from their hoots of pain as they were greeted by Uncle Ray, I can just recall them as being richly and blackly garbed.

The cousins had perpetrated a sentimental fraud common to those times. Irretrievably on the shelf even before the outbreak of the Great War, they had, in the course of it, one by one appeared in deepest mourning. They had 'lost someone'. Thus they joined the sad throng of genuine mourners, deftly cashed in on all the unspoken sympathy, and gradually moulded their faces into comely expressions of gentle resignation.

For the rest of their lives they were to remain faithful to these nameless soldiers who had died so nobly.

The youngest Chicken even had a photograph of the Unknown Warrior's Tomb above her washstand, a piece of chicanery much resented by the other Chickens, who hadn't thought of it quickly enough.

Mysterious women! Ceremonially I was pressed to each pouting beaded bosom, smelling strangely of dusty laven-

der, eau-de-Cologne and tea and scones. Hardly would I
have my nose scratched by a cameo breast-pin than my
alarmed cheek would be indented by a brooch of plaited
gold. And there were little sighs and gasps like the rustling
of wings ...

'Dear child!'

'Not like her mother!'

'So sad!'

'Ssssh!'

Yes, I remember them swimming down the front path,
a stately and jetty fleet. A comparison eluded me for years
until one evening on an Australian river I saw five black
swans. There they were, even to the red beaks.

What could have happened to the Hen and Chickens in
the end? The shadows have closed softly round them: their
restrained and everlasting grief is no more substantial than
the faded perfume of their good black silks.

It must not be thought that the Radiant Aunts sent
forth a summons to the family caucus. On the contrary the
Relations, conferring secretly and gustily by letter, decided
that 'they really must go down to Te Kano and try and
put poor dear Louisa straight'.

As for Grandpa, his consent would be required for the
marriage not only because Louisa was under age, but because she was a daughter and he was a father.

'Right's right,' said the Relations, shuddering.

It was a time of teapots and the finding of rich little
harvests of crumbled Madeira cake under the dining-room
table. Pola and I waxed both fat and bilious. Pola's real
name, of course, was Vi'let, but she had renamed herself
after Miss Negri, whom we had heard was a creature of
transcendent beauty, which Pola thought she was, too.

Most of the time I was not allowed to be present at the
family discussions. I was sent outside to play with Pola.
Usually, however, being of a free and roving turn of mind,
I went right through the Cuskelly backyard and out on the

other side, with the intention of playing with the Maoris, instead.

Let no grown-up fool herself into the belief that her child's mind or her child's life is an open book to her. The secret life of children is perhaps inexpressible, and is thus guarded by a natural silence. Acute and patient observers of adult life, children learn early to keep their own counsel about anything doubtful or unknown. They have not enough words to justify anything, therefore the adult art of false rationalization is barred to them. They have no authority, therefore they are rarely listened to attentively. Silence is their chief refuge and defence.

Silence, therefore, was to obscure the fact that most of us white children knew a good deal more about Maoris than our mothers and fathers.

The Radiant Aunts always knew I had been visiting the Maoris because when I stepped inside the house the fleas jumped off me in millions. After I found out the manner in which they knew, I always visited Cuskelly's first and allowed the fleas to bale out there.

Maoris were *common*.

Who knows the idiomatic meaning of this word now? Yet it demonstrates exactly the attitude once, and perhaps still, held towards the native New Zealanders. Colour prejudice, so different from any other country's colour prejudice, was not exactly because the Maori had a brown skin, but because he had a rough manner of living.

Because of this attitude, it was extremely difficult for him to have any other manner of living.

Civilization took away from him his raw and natural manliness; it also raised a forefinger and forbade him gentlemanliness. He was taught that his savage life must be a thing of the past. He must be a white man in all ways except in those customs and crafts which were picturesque enough to amuse or entertain tourists. At the same time it was demonstrated quietly, modestly, and lucidly that he could not expect pakeha social privileges. Ah yes, he would, in due course, receive the old age pension, but in the meantime he must not anticipate that his daughters might marry white men without comment, nor his sons marry white women without scandal.

There are many quotable exceptions to this generalization, but not in Te Kano.

I remember chiefs riding in from their ancestral holdings accompanied by their dark squires. The hoofs of their shaggy horses slipped on asphalt where only thirty years before the raupo grew. Noble men in ragged shirts and dungarees, who were born for splendid nakedness; their massive women smothered and ludicrous in gaudy blouses and long black skirts, hems stiff with dirt and bidibids. I remember the old lords, heads white as thistles, faces tattooed in bold and sweeping patterns – bend of the breaking wave, curve of the knucklebone, clockwise spiral of the unfurled fern. They rode with a ponderous shyness. They had not changed, but their world had.

Drunken white men stood along the kerbside and laughed at them.

I recall the dark eyes of the young Maoris turned upon those guttersnipes, angry, self-conscious, and resentful. But the dark eyes of the old men were sad with the knowledge that the day of the Maori was already gone. His sun began to set when they denied him dignity.

It was not like that amongst the children. In our secret life the Maori children were exactly like ourselves except that they were mostly superiorly gifted. Anything that could be done with the hands they did well, sometimes superlatively. They sang and recited, played football and cricket better than anyone else; good-humoured and always laughing, they were immensely popular, not because they were Maoris or in spite of it but because they were nice kids.

When they left school, however, they discovered they had put on social inequality along with the long trousers.

In the tranquil, soft-voiced, restrained atmosphere of Te Kano, with its unexpressed subsidiary layer of shame, defiance, snobbery, and inferiority, an occasional Maori through sheer greatness of soul rose to a position where he ceded nothing of his national ethos yet wore civilization as a graceful garment. One of these was Mr Hana.

I knew him mostly through his daughter, Huriana, who was eight when I was eight. She had the silence and exquisite submissiveness common to some Eastern women: there was, in fact, the gazelle look of the Arab about Huriana. Her hair was not curly but straight as water, and it had in it the copper streak which told of far-back Moriori blood. No matter how you combed that hair it fell instantly into fluid shapes; it could no more be dishevelled than could a waterfall. Huriana's older brother, Donald Hana, had a similar face. Unfamiliar in its contours, completely unrelated to any racial type I have ever seen, Donald's face was the best evidence I have ever seen for the anthropological theory that the Polynesians are shipwrecked survivors of some sea-swallowed continent. He was prince of a city that lay many fathoms deep, its towers tilted in the ooze, its temples filled with swinging veils of water, its avenues but passage-ways for whales, idly rubbing against the knees of stony gods and emperors who knew the world when Europe was the southern fence of the ice-pack.

Donald had the same kind of self-contained silence as a tree or a rock. I stared at him, awed, and did not know why I stared.

Perhaps it was some premonition of the time when I would stare at him again, in astonishment and grief.

I was playing with Huriana in a little 'house' under the macrocarpa hedge when my friend Pola Cuskelly came to tell me that Grandpa had arrived from Kawhia. Now, Grandpa's voyage from the west coast had not been without its incidents. He attracted hazards like a lightning con-

26

ductor. The announcement of his intention to come to the marriage council had been treated as a storm warning, the Relations fastening down their spiritual shutters, and scurrying hastily round in their consciences to make sure no private or scandalous business had been left lying about.

For Grandpa was a perfect devil at digging out embarrassing facts and dwelling on them pungently and lengthily.

He arrived in his own inimitable way, in a microscopic buggy held together by bits of fishing line and stolen fence-wire. It was drawn by a frayed, neurotic pony, which always looked as though it needed a good strong cup of tea. Grandpa drove right through the front gate, across the lawn and ten bob's worth of red-hot pokers, and actually got the pony's front hoofs on the top step where he could conveniently reach across and hammer on the front door with his stick. The charge to open the door was won by the Hen, who, finding herself confronted by the agitated countenance of a horse, had to be taken away by two Chickens to have her corsets undone.

Unluckily I had missed this dramatic entrance, but Pola had seen it all, even to the swipe Grandpa had taken with his hammerheaded stick at Uncle Ray's hard knocker, left undefended in the hall. Grandpa had some sort of inexplicable liking for my friend Pola, remembering her from one far-apart visit to another, and addressing her as Wi'let.

I recall beating it home that autumn afternoon, with the amber haze creeping out from under the thick damp hedges, and far and clear as blackbirds' voices the sound of Maoris scooping gravel down on the river bar. From every chimney uncurled a long blue plume of smoke like a cat's tail. Our own little house had already lit up its front windows with sunset. They looked like the celluloid panes in a doll's house.

And, you know, Grandpa's personality had already

penetrated even to the front gate. Always tidily shut, it hung open, creaking alarmedly. Pola and I, mouths open, hands clammy with excitement, followed Grandpa's trail across the lawn, through the ruin of the red-hot pokers and on to the grey-painted veranda boards which Francey kept polished to a degree guaranteed to toss any commercial traveller on the back of his cheeky skull. Now that glossy surface was dented circularly by the hoofs of the pony at present having a nervous breakdown in the back paddock.

The front door was closed, but we listened there and all the way round under the windows, to the electric, shivering silence, which was suddenly shattered by a harsh voice shouting rude Scandinavian words.

The next moment Uncle Ray rushed through the back door crying; 'Olga! Olga!'

Quivering with rage, flaming pink, his blond moustache piteously tousled, he had all the appearance of an uncle who has been pulled feet first through the sound barrier. The next moment Uncle Olga joined him, arms half in and half out of her coat, weeping bitterly.

'Don't you mind, Ollie!' said Uncle Ray, taking her in his arms and kissing her in a passion of sympathy. Uncle Olga sprang away with a screech. He had forgotten to take the cigarette out of his mouth.

This mysteriously woeful pair hurried past us, climbed into their vast, funereal tin Lizzie and jerked out of the paddock without so much as a 'Hooray!' At the gate Uncle Ray got out, raced after a fleeing piece of newspaper, captured it, and leapt back into the motor-car.

Now, what with her brother Cocky, and her mother's ancestry, and the fact that her father never did so much as a hand's turn round the place, Pola was quite used to volcanic eruptions in the home, but in my tranquil feminine environment a voice was rarely raised.

Thus it was with real fear that I tiptoed into the kitchen

to find my Aunt Francey crying into the stewed rhubarb, and a horrible air of tension pervading the entire house.

Nowadays it is difficult to imagine the grip a man like old Syver Admiral had on his family. He was one of the vast number of moral incompetents who found that the physical fact of fatherhood gave them authority over a number of people. That the fatherhood was accidental, incidental, and impatiently resented had nothing to do with the authority, which was eagerly accepted and furiously defended. He had, during their childhood, driven his family like a whaling crew. His wife, that nameless Grandma whom the girls barely remembered, had died young and gladly, and it was a miracle that the docile, bullied girls had grown up as delightfully as they had. That miracle was my Auntie Barbie, innocent, gentle, and brave, who had bowed like a tree to the blast of his dirty temper and savage unreasonableness, but never broken.

'Oh, poor Louisa!' sobbed Francey, deserting the unresponsive rhubarb for me. 'He's a beast, that's what he is.'

Then she smoothed back my hair, looked earnestly into my alarmed eyes and said, 'Oh, Jenny, I hope you never have to call your father a beast!'

Of course I could not remember him well enough to call him anything. Nor could I remember my Grandpa clearly as anything except a roaring voice and a big smell of old salmon tins. It had been at least three years since his previous visit, and to a child that is almost half a lifetime.

I timidly inquired why Uncles Olga and Ray had left so hastily, and was told I wouldn't understand. As a matter of fact, Uncle Olga had rashly endeavoured to put in a good word for the Pig Man, quoting as evidence the misguided shattering of her romance with the Ben Hur of the night-cart, whereupon Grandpa had cruelly recapitulated the whole thing for the shocked and tittering benefit of the Hen and Chickens, playing both roles with gusto and ad-libbing, I believe, in a manner calculated to make the water on Uncle Olga's knee boil.

It was characteristic of my affable Uncle Ray that he had loyally stood by his wife during this episode, which could be construed as highly satisfactory to a husband widely publicized as a poor second choice.

The Hen and Chickens were in the terrible predicament of being frightened to death of Grandpa, and at the same time determined not to go home until with their own eyes they had seen the liquidation of the Pig Man.

This was scheduled for after tea.

For some reason I could not fathom the Radiant Aunts decreed that I should not be taken in to see Grandpa until they had wrought their wonders and I could shine at my absolute best.

Though it was only autumn, warm weather left Te Kano with a bang like a slammed door, and there was a certain D-Day for all of us kids when we were put into our winter underclothing. For some rich and unlucky ones this meant a marvellously intricate piece of engineering known as 'combs'. Some combs (short for combinations) had long limbs, others were truncated. They all were of that thick, mottled-looking wool which appears to have some skin disease of its own. Fortunately I could itch even without the help of combs, and so my winter uniform consisted of a singlet and a great big pair of bloomers exactly like Sir Walter Raleigh's. So far I had avoided them, but when Barbie was dressing me to meet Grandpa, she found them in the drawer, and with the sudden impulse which so characterizes youthful aunts, decided that I might as well break them in. No one can say I did not fight. The old Viking spirit was not dead in me, either. But eventually I was forced into the cavernous depths of the bloomers, and the elastic was pulled snugly about my knees, just at the right height to show every time I bent over.

'There! Aren't they warm and comfy?'

I surveyed myself in the glass, my skinny torso above this vast billowing of stiffish wool. From the rear I looked like twin pumpkins. Then I glanced at the aunts, a quick, glaring look calculated to catch them out in a giggle. But every pretty face was anxiously approving.

I loved my aunts. Heaven knows I wanted to break in my bloomers just to please them, but they picked a darned bad time for it. Even Walter Raleigh can't have enjoyed the process. It was a business which needed endurance and concentration, in which one's energies should not have been deployed on grandpas from Kawhia. From that moment my awe and terror of Grandpa took second place to my grim preoccupation with my bloomers.

They pulled the dress over my head. It was a lovely dress with the waist round my hips and a skirt made of broad flat pleats about four inches long. It was a strange colour known as crushed strawberry, with little black scallops edging simply everything. Even through the dress the contour of the bloomers was visible.

The Aunts exchanged congratulatory glances.

'Just as well we got her to break them in early,' they told each other. 'Whatever Pa notices, it won't be *that*.'

They listened for a moment at the door of the sitting-room, which had been converted into a boudoir for old Syver. Then with a convulsive gasp which spoke of fear, Barbie ushered me into the room. For a moment I could hardly recognize the place, it was in such a mess. That curious lack of symmetry known in the New Zealand vernacular as skew-whiffness was so prevalent it seemed impossible that one old man had achieved it in the space of four or five hours. One curtain was tied up in a knot, the other dragged half off its rod. A split cushion protruded a great helpless tongue of sateen lining. Shoes were on the mantelpiece, and a pair of socks lolled out of a vase from which the flowers had been removed and flung to drip on the hearth-rug. 'Cupid Awake' had Grandpa's peculiar hat hooked over his gilt frame, and 'Cupid Asleep' lay on the floor with his glass cracked. On the sofa, enthroned in a rat's nest of blankets, his malicious gnarled toes plucking effectively at the upholstery, easefully reposed my Grandpa.

Brought thus face to face with this legendary personage, and hearing the uncontrollable gulp in my auntie's voice as she said, 'Pa, here is Jenny', I forgot for a moment the intolerable itch of my under-garments and just gaped.

I was brought up on the Brothers Grimm, and Grandpa was most certainly a character from one of the more un-pleasant stories, such as that one where a stepmother cuts off a little boy's head and uses it for fertilizer in a flower-pot. Grandpa was a robber chief, or a large elf. He had been constructed with a broad solid base, probably to save him from tipping over on a tilting deck. He was the colour of strong tea. What a face that old man had! The years had achieved nothing but an emphasis on the prowlike jut of the nose, the slanting keyhole nostrils, the cruel flat lips which split to show a mouthful of crowded, yellow, de-cayed teeth. Unlike most old gentlemen he had not decently retired behind a faceful of whiskers, and his chin and throat showed strong and massive. His spiky unkempt hair even yet retained a little of that fox colour he had been noted for in his youth. I found myself touching my own hair, for it was ruddy too, and an astonished shame filled me to think that I had thus proclaimed my relation-ship with this shockingly unorthodox old man.

Grandpa had noticed it, too, and his grin flattened. He bawled, 'Vot? Vot, vot, vot?'

'Thora's little girl,' said Barbie tremulously.

'Vot, vot, vot?'

It was thus his habit to confuse people before they had a

chance to say anything, probably part of a softening-up campaign.

It seemed to me that he glared hatefully, but I suppose he was only trying to find in my smudgy features some sign of my mother's almost forgotten face. He jerked a thumb at Barbie.

'Get out of here, you. I want to speak mit Yannie.'

I could hardly believe it when Barbie actually left me alone with this dragon. I was too paralysed with shock to gallop after her, and when my muscles did start to function I found his twisty brown fingers had hooked themselves in my dress. It was either go closer to him or get the dress torn, and economy won.

Very often one reads in stories of children gazing clear eyed into the accusing faces of their elders, but that wasn't the fashion in my childhood. Adults had more steeliness in their faces, perhaps. I was petrified when Syver Admiral gripped me. I thought he was going to blame me for the death of my mother, or something equally incomprehensible, and I would not have had a word with which to defend myself. I fixed my horrified gaze upon the dark freckles that blotched his lips. If I had been a weepy child I would have broken into tears of sheer fright.

Actually what he said was, 'Hey, you know how to vork der ting?'

Der ting! I went on gaping adenoidally.

'Der ting, der ting, der musicker!'

He shook me sharply, leapt off the sofa and pushed me towards the La Gloria, which the sisters had carefully hidden under yards of table-runner in the darkest corner.

Though I had never been allowed to put on a record by myself, I knew perfectly well how to do it. Now, as the old man shoved the phonograph squealing out into the light, I stammered, 'My aunties wouldn't allow me to—'

'Broddy vimmin!'

He scooped the paper envelope off a record, gave it a rub across the seat of his pants and thrust it at me.

A moment or so later a musical-comedy soprano, wonderfully thin and sharp like a darning needle, floated out through the closed door to the women who waited full of anxiety and curiosity on the other side. What could they have thought? The old man had ears like a hawk. He heard something, for he shuffled over to the door and turned the key.

'*Broddy vimmin!*'

He listened spellbound to the record. His face was so still it seemed to have turned into a hunk of carved timber. Indeed, it had that appearance, a queerly shaped knot of wood, hair like a winged shadow, eyes slitted into darkness.

No matter how little music we had had, he had had less.

What music there had been in his Swedish fishing village behind the sea-wall I cannot imagine. Perhaps enough for him to notice the silence of those sub-Antarctic latitudes where he had spent nearly all his young manhood.

When I look back, and regard Grandpa as the foreign stranger he always was, I see two pictures. One is of the young ship's boy, his body covered with sea-boils, his bleeding hands daubed with Stockholm tar, asleep in all his sodden steaming clothing in a pig-pen fo'c'sle. Sometimes I see far beyond that stumbling vessel, to the grim and gleaming pinnacles standing like tusks of iron in a spouting sea. They are those islands Grandpa called Dago Rammer Eeze (Diego Ramirez). Here he was almost wrecked on his first rounding of the Horn.

The other picture was one I found in some nameless settler's letters when, years later, I was preparing to write a book about the New Zealand goldfields. Listen to this. 'I saw in a grogshop beside the Molyneux, a man playing a comb with a rag over it, while a drunken miner covorted with a woman in tawdry muslin to *this abominable music*.'

34

When I read that I thought, yes, there's Grandpa on the other side of the coin.

At the moment, of course, all I did was gape at Grandpa in chilly fright and scratch myself.

I must say I managed the La Gloria in a very expert way. We rushed through 'Bells of Moscow', 'In the Twilight, O My Darling', 'Gimme Jazz Or I'll Die', and had just started on a new and raucous masterpiece by Al Jolson when both Grandpa and myself became aware of a steady tapping on the door.

With a yell of frustration Grandpa rushed over to it. He walked on the sides of his feet like a parrot, a curious rollicking gait.

'Vot, vot, VOT?'

'Pa,' I heard Louisa faltering, 'it's...it's...Mr Hilder.'

This name made no imprint on my consciousness until I saw the Pig Man, towering amongst the Hen and Chickens like a tall tree amongst a lot of scrub.

'VOT?'

'Oh, Syver, really,' squealed the Hen suddenly, 'you know, Louisa's intended.'

All at once the whole room was full of people. Skirts were everywhere. The smell of old salmon tins was practically dispersed by a great blast of eau-de-Cologne. I saw the Pig Man come stooping shyly under the doorway. Though I was in utter torment I stopped scratching for a moment to admire him. He had that cleanliness only country boys can manage. I think they use washing soda. He shone. I can still see the way the light was reflected from his cheekbones and the bridge of his nose. The crystallinity of his eyes, the fine yellow bulge of his hair, the kindness and capability of his big awkward hands...oh, they were beyond reproach. I believe for a moment even the Radiant Aunts, who had only seen him in his Pig Man's uniform, were softened.

Now all this time Al Jolson was kicking up an awful noise. He sounded as though he were singing down a kerosene tin.

'Maaaaaameeeeee!'

I wish you could have seen the Pig Man's face when he realized that we had been playing the La Gloria. Delight, pride, and modesty rushed over it like waves on a pool. It went at least two shades more coralline.

Louisa looked lovely, too.

She was wearing one of those outfits in a defunct fabric called stockinet. It clung to the figure like a leech and made Louisa look like a pale-blue culvert. But the Pig Man loved her. You could seee that even through all his shyness and awkwardness.

Well, there they all were, stuffing that little room to bursting point. Grandpa stood by the phonograph, glaring. I furtively edged a finger under the elastic in my bloomers and scratched madly.

Grandpa said, 'Dat child has worms.'

'Maybe she needs a drench,' said the Pig Man, kindly and naturally. The Radiant Aunts all blushed passionately, because worms were a disgrace and medicine was not usually mentioned in mixed company.

I was insulted. I bent my flaming face against the phonograph, where Al Jolson, having faded away in the manner of old records, sounded as though he were singing from an immense height.

'Please, Pa, won't you turn the machine off while we talk?' asked Barbara. Grandpa snarled out a grin.

'Vy should I turn off mein phonograffer for dis pig fella, eh?' he inquired.

I am sure the Pig Man did not immediately comprehend that significant possessive of my Grandpa's. He was suffering from that paralysis caused by extreme good manners, which can practically demobilize the brain.

The song whanged to an end. The record went

PIRru-PIRru-PIRru, as the needle whizzed round on that waste-land between Al Jolson and the hole in the centre. Louisa leapt to turn it off, but Grandpa fended her away.

'Yannie does it,' he commanded.

And to me, 'Play it again.'

So we played it again.

That lovely young man sat there, knees outspread, face pink with innocent dismay, giant boots Nuggeted to within an inch of their lives. A personal interview with the Pa of the girl he loved, he very well understood, but you could see he was wondering what the blazes all these other people were here for. He sneaked bashful looks at the crow-like circle of the Hen and Chickens. They sat well forward on their chairs, bending upon him looks which ranged from tender sympathy to a sort of sorrowful glee. His ears had buzzed with so much confusion he hadn't understood Louisa's agitated introductions, and to him these mysterious and funereal figures had no bearing upon the matter at all.

Added to this, he could see the soft lips of Louisa's three sisters pressed firmly in what even an artless Pig Man realized was a disapproving expression.

And, of course, there was Al.

But almost at once Grandpa took charge of the room. Barbie made no more than a tremulous movement to straighten it up a bit before he bent a terrible glance upon the Pig Man.

'How mootch money you got?' he inquired.

The Pig Man cast a desperate glance at the avid faces of the Hen and Chickens.

'Good year I can make maybe three hundred profit.' he roared above the music.

'Vot, vot, vot?'

'Oh, Pa,' implored Louisa, 'please turn the La Gloria off!'

'Vy I turn out my musicker, heh?' He returned to the attack. 'Vy you want to marry mit my Louisa?'

The Pig Man flamed. Even the whites of his eyes turned pink.

'I sorta like her.'

'Vot, vot, vot?'

'Mammmmmee, my mammmmeeeeeee!' butted in Al.

One of the Chickens, who had a tendency to slight hysteria, gave a hoot and buried her face in her hanky. Not a sound escaped her. She was socially impeccable, but it's a wonder she didn't blow the back of her head off.

'Oh, please, Pa,' said Barbie in distress, 'how can you expect to hear Mr Hilder above that noise?'

'And besides,' said Louisa tearfully, 'I don't think it's fair . . . before everyone like this . . . it should be private —'

'Shoot the mouth!' bellowed Grandpa.

Louisa subsided, pale and trembling. I think she was more frightened of Grandpa than any of the others. Ailie quickly put her little hand comfortingly over her sister's.

The Pig Man had dignity, the same sort of large, unselfconscious dignity as a draught-horse.

'If you don't mind, Mr Admiral, I'll wait until you've finished playing the phonograph,' he said gently.

Old Syver's eyes glinted with delight. His lips flattened in a devilish grin. From my worm's-eye view I could see the yellow teeth jumbled and criss-crossed like old clothespegs.

'Huh!' he snorted. 'Maybe I play mein musicker all the broddy night!'

The look that came over the Pig Man's face must have turned many a mutinous backfatter off its swill. I quailed. The giggling Chicken stopped in mid-cackle and looked wide-eyed over the black-edged hanky.

'What do you mean, Mr Admiral, your music . . . er, your phonograph? I gave that La Gloria to Louisa for a present.'

The old man paused, and enjoyed the pause. He sneered. 'Mein musicker. I take it back to Kawhia mit meinself.'

The Pig Man rose. Puzzlement, disbelief, and a ponderously growing anger were on that frank young face. Louisa said, fluttering, 'Oh, Desmond, don't... don't say anything...'

Old Syver glared up at him, a crusty ball of hate and contempt.

The phonograph, unattended, slowly wound itself down, uroo, uroooo, uroooooooo!

'Oh, no you don't,' said the Pig Man, his vast fists gripping the back of his chair. 'That machine belongs to Louisa, and you're not taking it away from her.' He looked with a very appealing protectiveness at Louisa, who was by now openly crying. 'Don't you fret, Louie, I won't let him.'

Louisa, did you not gif me der musicker?' cooed the old man.

There was silence. Louisa was too overcome to reply. The Pig Man's face was fiery was dismay and disappointed pride.

'Louie, you didn't give it away?'

'No, of course she didn't!' snapped Barbara suddenly, putting her arm round her weeping sister. 'And I must say, Mr Hilder, it's not very nice of you to come here and make this fuss about a present.' She glared over her sister's bowed head.

'I take it to Kawhia,' said Grandpa, looking at the La Gloria with vengeful triumph. With one stride the Pig Man had ranged himself alongside the machine. He whipped the needle off the record and slammed down the lid. He may have been only a boy, but he had authority.

'Nobody's going to take Louie's phonograph away while I'm here,' he said.

Grandpa swelled.

'It's only Pa's manner of speaking,' said Barbie quickly. 'Now, I'll just go and get us all a cup of tea, and—'

'Big stinker!' shouted Grandpa suddenly. 'You stink, you pig-yard.'

'Look who's talking,' retorted the Pig Man with spirit. 'If ever anyone was as high as a fish, that's you.'

'Mr Hilder, really!' exclaimed Francey.

Now occurred the puzzling incident which was never referred to again in the Admiral family except indirectly. The Pig Man always maintained that Grandpa suddenly attempted to wooden him out by butting him in the chest. Grandpa swore many a time that the Pig Man grabbed his head and tried to rub off his (Grandpa's) nose against a lot of sharp waistcoat buttons. I alone can tell the truth. Grandpa, suddenly emboldened by what he thought was support from his daughters, reached across to wheel the phonograph out of the Pig Man's clutches. The Pig Man pushed him off. It was a gentle push considering the lad's vast dimensions. Grandpa, cunning old gnome, made the most of it. He rushed sideways across the room, his left foot stepping in the neatest way over the right one, then down he went like a row of pine-trees. Oh, what a chorus of shrieks and screams! The two devoted Chickens bore off their mother to undo her corsets once more, the other Chickens screamed, 'Oh, you beast! Hitting an old man! Oh I never did! Shame, you wretch!' and such like, and the Four Radiant Aunts stood paralysed. I don't suppose they had ever seen their father prone before.

Then I gasped, 'Oh, Auntie Barbie, he's all bleedy!'

That tore it. The sight of the Admiral's blood on the carpet dispelled any doubts they may have had of the Pig Man's murderous intentions. With shrieks of horror they sped towards the fallen Pa, quite disregarding the fact that the bleediness in question came from a small wound 'Cupid Asleep' had inflicted with his broken glass upon the back of his enemy's rocklike skull.

'Aaaaaaaah!' groaned Grandpa, turning up his eyes and groping feebly.

Now, all this time the Pig Man had stood beside his

La Gloria, simply dumbfounded. Now he took a step forward, his guileless pink face all aglow with shame and distress.

'Shall I get a doctor...how was I to know...honest to goodness, Louie dear, I didn't–'

'How *dare* you call my sister dear when all the time her father lies there bleeding from a head wound, you...you ...*article!*' hissed Francey.

The Pig Man, appalled, looked pleadingly at his loved one.

'Louisa, you don't think I hit him, not really you don't, do you, Louisa?'

Barbara stepped neatly between them. 'This is the moment you must choose, Louisa,' she said passionately. 'If he hits your old father he'll hit you. You'll be a beaten wife, Louisa!'

'What?' bawled the Pig Man.

He snatched up his hat. 'You're mad, mad as meat-axes, every one of you!' he yelled, and, stepping on a Chicken as he went, rushed from the room. The three Radiant Aunts converged with consolatory cries on poor Louisa, who bawled heartbrokenly into her hanky, not looking at anyone. As for me, I was peering fascinatedly at the old man, who had opened his eyes within the spiky shelter of his eyebrows and was glaring vindictively at his daughters.

'*Broddy* vimmin!' I heard him mutter.

Well, a child of eight can't go on indefinitely being sorry for an aunt who has just lost her intended. There were, of course, all sorts of thunderings going on above my head, but I had more interesting things to think about. Grandpa disappeared one day, and with him disappeared the La Gloria. It seemed very silent when it went, and I missed it very much. So did the aunts, I think, but they behaved as though it had never lived in our little house with us. Louisa often looked a bit pinky-nosed, but she said it was indigestion. Pigs were never mentioned in her presence, and early in the piece Auntie Francey took me aside and cautioned me never to mention that nasty Mr Desmond Hilder to Auntie Louisa or I'd catch what-for.

And so, I suppose, what with the aunts thus working on her, and the Pig Man never coming to see her any more. Louisa's love simmered down. But I didn't know it had died until one day I heard Barbie saying triumphantly to Francey that Louisa had decided to get her teeth out.

'So she must be over it, thank goodness for that.'

It may not be clear to the present privileged generation why teeth extractions should have such a bearing upon romance, but in the twenties (and especially, I suppose, in such backwaters as Te Kano) getting the teeth out was a major adventure. People went round in a gummy state for months and months, and such a state is not conducive to romance. Courting was difficult enough in Te Kano with the mosquitoes bleating round nocturnal couples begging for a bite, and Pola told me that she was the actual witness of a scene concerning her older sister which will probably horrify the sentimental.

'Vera kept growling about the mosquitoes and saying, 'Wait a bit till I swat this one on my neck,' every time he wanted to kiss her, so Wilf said, 'Ah, darn this for a turn-up!' and he scouted round for some cow manure and made a real beaut smoky fire. And *that* kept them away.'

So when Louisa voluntarily took the step into gumminess the sisters knew she had cut herself off from all thought of love. And they rejoiced in their affection for her, for they truly thought a Pig Man was no suitable match for their darling Louie.

To keep Louisa company we all ate soft foods for ages. Francey, who kept house for us, cooked so many custards and squashy puddings she began to smell of nutmeg and vanilla.

'I'll never look a blancmange in its good nourishing face again.' she complained.

We had lemon sago for pudding the day I discovered about the Fantocinis.

It happened one autumn day. Francey suddenly looked up at the lunch table and said. 'I forgot. The Fantocinis are going. They're shifting.'

I trembled with excitement. The house with the harp was going to be empty! Its Victorian bow-windows would be stripped of the impenetrable net curtains and lie bare and blazing in the westering sun; the big room where the harp had stood would be revealed; its wallpaper patched with unfaded squares, and its vacant floor like a plain wooden picture framed in a border of dark varnish.

At that time I had an illusion that if I stayed very still and concentrated terribly hard on whatever I was doing, I should merge as it were with my surroundings, and the adults wouldn't notice that my ears were flapping to catch every word. So I spiritually melted into my lemon sago and was rewarded by some cryptic and intensely grown-up conversation.

'Now whatever does *he* want to leave Te Kano for?' asked Louisa.

'What in the world would they want to stay for?' answered Barbara cynically, and indeed no one could say that Mr Fantocini had made a fortune out of his piano lessons.

'She's gone already,' observed Francey, reaching for my plate. 'Don't leave your mouth open like that, Jenny. Do you think she could have adenoids again, Barbie? Well, this morning just after you'd left for the shop Mr Fantocini came driving back in a terrible state. He could hardly speak he was so tired and upset, Jenny! Do shut it, dear!'

'But where had he been?' breathed little Ailie.

'I didn't like to ask,' said Francey. 'He just said abruptly that Mrs Fantocini had had a turn in the night

43

and he'd taken her to Hamilton. He's put her into an institution. I'll bet.'

'Not before time,' said Barbie, then they all shot looks at me, and I left my mouth open quickly in self-defence.

As soon as I could I crawled through the fence to see Pola, who was just as batty about exploring empty houses as I was. Once, at another empty house we had found a prism from a chandelier, and had fought bitterly over it. I had knocked out a loose tooth in the front of Pola's mouth, but Pola had remained loyal and told her irate mother the fairies had taken it, thus hoisting Mrs Cuskelly with her own romance. We would walk blocks and blocks so that we might enter boldly through some unlatched, heedless gate, and tiptoe about the hollow verandas and uninhabited fowl-houses.

No one had ever been inside the Fantocini garden, because Mrs Fantocini was so funny. Pola and I accepted her as a fascinating and logical phenomenon. We liked to watch her going along the street, often waving her dirty hand to people we couldn't see, no matter how we peered. Once, too, she had whipped up her skirts and showed us the tops of her stockings, which were pink lace. I recall being very shocked when I told Barbie about it because Barbie cried furiously, 'It's a disgrace! It's a pity she doesn't go right off her head and be done with it, poor old gentleman!'

When Pola and I came home from school the next afternoon Mr Fantocini had already driven away in the wake of a great furniture van. Francey was very thrilled. Mr Fantocini had come over to say good-bye. A poor, mean-suited little man, he bobbed up the path on his bandy legs, his face blotched with fatigue and age, and his soft helpless hands so knobbly one would never have believed them capable of stroking powerful music out of the strong strings of the great harp.

'I came straight out with it and told him how sorry I

44

was,' she said excitedly. 'I just couldn't help it, Louisa, so it's no use looking at me so sniffily. I said, "It's been a long weary time for you, Mr Fantocini, and you've done the right thing, I'm sure," and then I said, "She must have been like a mosquito at you, Mr Fantocini, with her queer tormenting ways."'

'Oh, Francey!' said Barbie, shocked.

'I know,' confessed Francey gloomily, 'it wasn't the right thing to say, because he just burst into tears, and I didn't know which way to look.'

With that she burst into tears herself.

'Jenny!' said Barbara severely, 'don't you dare go over to the Fantocini place!'

'Of course not,' I said instantly.

I tore round the fence and there was Pola waiting. Without a word we went down the road a little and crossed over where our overseers couldn't see us. There was a loose wire in the Fantocini fence and we wriggled through it with urgent agility, for perhaps other children had noticed the furniture van and were at the house before us.

'I don't care, as long as it isn't Nora Bedding,' said Pola. 'You remember last time she got there first and found those kittens in a sack,' she added surlily.

We were too timid to go straight up the path to the house. We circled amongst the lush rotting undergrowth. There was a rich autumnal smell of overgrown shaggy chrysanthemums and wet decaying leaves. How quiet it was! When we stood still we could hear our own hearts beating, heavy and a little alarmed. It was almost as though a spell lay on that empty, forgotten garden.

'That's where she used to sit, often,' observed Pola. We carefully avoided stepping on a huge flagstone beside the dry, thistle-crowded pool. It was warm there. A lizard brown as silk ran and poised, its throat throbbing. As long as we could remember (which wasn't more than two years or so) Mrs Fantocini had sat there and combed her thick dark treacly-looking hair with her fingers, her eyes looking sulkily at nothing. We bent and stared concentratedly at the slab. It was marked all over with deep scars, as though someone had sat there and stabbed fiercely at it with something sharp.

There was not even a cat to be seen, yet the house had a curiously unlonely air. It was like a house from which the owners have departed only for an hour or two. At any moment I expected to see the bent form of Mr Fantocini come hurrying up the path; he always had an air of hurry upon him as though he regretted leaving his wife alone, and was anxious about what might have happened to her in the meantime.

'Nora will be here soon,' urged Pola.

Yes, we would have to be quick. We went boldly up to the house. I shinned up the weatherboard wall and rested my chin on the blistered window-sill. Silence, emptiness, and the dull-golden sunlight pouring in through the blank panes, striping the floor diagonally and turning the lofting motes into a microscopic galaxy. I remembered that this was the room where they said the harp had stood. I remembered things they had said, my aunties and their friends... 'It was as tall as a man... Mrs Fantocini hated it and he only played it after she had gone to sleep... she's so queer.. funny... he played in the orchestra for Anna Pavlova.'

The laundry door was unlatched. We pushed it open and stared in the half light. There was a scrubbed smell of wood-smoke and Sunlight soap. Mr Fantocini had swept everything very clean, and a stub of Manila broom leant beside the copper.

I pulled open the copper door. It gave a complaining yelp, startling in the stillness. But there was only a heap of dark ashes and a charred, screwed-up ball of paper. When we opened it out we found it was made of a great number of strips with music scribbled on them in pencil. They had been jagged up and down with scissors. They were no good to us at all.

There was a little white-painted window high up in the wall. It was a bathroom window, for through the crack we could see the dim shape of a shower.

'I could climb up there,' I boasted.

'So could I,' said Pola sharply. We dared each other for a moment, and then Pola clambered onto the dirt-clotted shelf and pushed at the window. It opened with a squawk. She clung to the sill' and wormed her way through, and there was a resonant clang as she fell into the bathtub. I cautiously followed. Beyond the bathroom door was the dark, quiet passage.

'Wow, won't Nora Bedding be mad!' cried Pola jubilantly.

Now I felt afraid. Much as I loved empty houses, I had never been inside one before. An uneasiness pressed on me. How was I to tell Mrs Fantocini wasn't hiding in one of the rooms? *I* hadn't seen her go, or Mr Fantocini, either. Perhaps he was sitting in there behind the closed door with the golden harp tilted upon his shoulder, his hands raised to bring the aqueous ripples out of it.

But there was nothing in any of the rooms, not a forgotten picture, or a candlestick or a cup without a handle. Nothing but the dirty sunlit windows, and beyond them the drowsy oblongs of the tangled garden. Mr Fantocini had cleaned everything up very thoroughly.

I poked in the narrow crack beside the skirting board, looking for lost threepences or buttons, and I found something. It was a pearly blue bead, jammed in the crack.

'*She* used to wear beads like that,' said Pola jealously.

Now I was so pleased I flung the drawing-room door open with a bang. In the big low-ceilinged room the sunlight had a strange yellow tint as though smoke obscured it. Pola was cross because I had found the bead, and looked round to find something she could vent her anger on. She pulled a stick of red chalk out of her pocket and started to write Violet on the wall. Then she changed her mind and rubbed it out.

'Look, someone's washed the wall,' she observed. There were faintly noticeable patches here and there on the paper near the floor. They were not wet, but the bloom on the paper had disappeared. On the floor were damp blotches, too. And there were several beads, blue like the other one. I found them all, and ostentatiously put them in my pocket, saying, 'This is a good house, after all.'

Pola said sulkily, 'I'm going now.'

I gave a yelp and bolted after her. I knew as soon as Pola had gone all the bogies of the house would come out to chitter and whimper at me.

Pola, too, had been afraid, for as soon as she had reached the outside of the house she became garrulous with relief.

'My mother said that Mr Fantocini was a famous harpist somewhere on the other side of the world, and when Mrs Fantocini turned out queer he had to give it up and come and live here where no one knew them.'

'Grown-ups are screwy,' I said.

We looked carefully in the flower-bed which ran along the side of the house. Once in a similar bed we had found a brass doorknob and a tin half full of bewhiskered polly-wogs. But there was nothing in this one except a tangle of overgrown whitened stems and a few sodden flowers that crept up against the wall and sagged away again.

'Look, Pola, you can get under the house here.'

We could plainly see a loose board, almost hidden under the dark fall of leaves that were tacked neatly into place on the wall. The tack was an old rusty one, with a silvery half-circle on its face as though someone had but recently given it a whack with a hammer. Pola unhooked the vines, and they collapsed in a mass. She levered at the board, and it moved easily, leaving a dim dusty aperture just asking to be climbed through.

'There might be an old bike under there,' she suggested excitedly.

Underneath, I stood up cautiously. The top of my head nearly touched the dust-clotted beams. The ground was hard, grey, and caked, like the floor of some strange cave, stretching off into the narrow slanting darkness. Something glittered like a shell on the ground. Pola darted past me and picked it up triumphantly. It was another pearly blue bead. I looked feverishly round for some discovery for myself, but there was nothing. There was not even anything hung from the beams, like old chains or brushes or bunches of strung onions, though they were scraped clear of dust here and there, as though someone had recently passed.

I explored as far as I could without crouching, and then I came to a spot where the ground was soft. It was quite a big patch that had been dug all over, and then stamped hard again. But to my bare feet the difference was noticeable.

I poked about in the dirt with a stick. It went down quite a long way and struck something. Maybe it was a rock. The stick caught, and I tugged hard. When it came out I looked at the end curiously. In amongst the dirty fibres were a few white cotton particles and a hairlike thread of blue silk.

Nothing interesting. I threw the stick far away under the house in disgust. Pola saw something glistening in the wan light. It was thin and metallic. She tugged and tugged but it wouldn't budge.

Suddenly it gave, and out of the earth came a thin metallic wire that coiled as she pulled.

'What's that?' I was jealous as I craned over her shoulder.

'It's a wire. It looks like a silly old string from his silly old harp,' said Pola crossly.

We stretched it out between us, and Pola twanged it with her teeth. It gave out a shivering ghostly breath of music.

'I wonder how it came out of the harp?'

'Maybe Mrs Fantocini pulled it out. When she was angry.'

He wouldn't like that,' said Pola.

We wandered back towards the opening in the wall, contented. We had found our share of loot. No matter what Nora Bedding found, she wouldn't find this. We pushed the board back carefully, and draped the vines and leaves over the tack. Then we stood on the path and dusted each other, for in some things grown-ups were very observant.

I noticed that the gravel, in a wavering line which led round to the back of the house, had been raked very neatly over. I thought with a faint pang of Mr Fantocini working so hard, and in such a hurry, to get the house tidy.

'We won't tell Nora about the place under the house,'

'We won't tell anyone.'

'And we'll keep the harp-string and the beads in our cubbyhouse in the willow bank.'

'And they'll be our secret.'

Agreed, we walked off through the hot, silent garden, holding the harp-string between us and twanging it as we went.

We never did get to play with that harp-string, because a day or so after we had hidden it in our secret place, a kingfisher's hole in the river bank, a sudden flood rose and swept it away. And as for the beads, they fell through a hole in my pocket somewhere on the way to school, and I never saw them again either. Nothing but our pact to keep silence, and this we did, mostly because life was so full we forgot the entire incident almost at once.

My meeting with Blackleaf Forty seemed very much more important. She was a terrible and terrifying old Maori matron who lived down on the river bank. She had a name, but since it was always mentioned in lowered tones I never caught it. I gather she was Te Kano's Bad Lady, but no shadow of impropriety ever touched her friendship for me and a dozen other kids who shot in and out of her shack, devoured her smoked fish and scones, and raided her plum trees. Her profanity was remarkable. As poetry fell naturally from the lips of Shakespeare, so did bad language from Blackleaf Forty.

I can see her yet, long coarse black hair down her back like a horse's tail, a greenstone pendant in one ear and a shark's tooth attached to a narrow black ribbon in the other. She wore a long black skirt and a bright blouse. Bottle green, she favoured, and what we unkindly called Maniapoto pink. She had bare feet and a man's felt hat with a pheasant-feather tip stuck in the ribbon. But that face! Brown chamois-leather, the chin and lips boldly traced in blue. Cruel, arrogant lips, and eyes like black water . . . that was Blackleaf Forty. She would have been meet wife for Te Rauparaha, and companion for Kupe on the isle-less sea.

What first drew me to Blackleaf Forty was her pirau pit. Of course even a nasal cripple can smell pirau, but I had a nose like an anteater, and the first introduction to this shocking delicacy of the old-time Maori was one which left my sense of smell scarred for life.

In a wet and soggy gully behind her house Blackleaf Forty had dug a shallow trench. She tramped about six inches of fern into the bottom, and then stacked in corn cobs, husk and all. The trench was already filling with water by the time she had finished. She stacked more fern on top, to keep the rats from getting at the corn. I think it must have lain there, decomposing, for about six weeks, when she fished it out, scraped the corn off the husk, and rolled it into balls about the size of eggs. It looked like rotten pumpkin, but smelled more like bad eggs. These little H-bombs were then roasted in the hot coals.

Just about the time my poor Auntie Louisa was getting her teeth out, Blackleaf Forty asked me a favour. She wanted me to take a kit of pirau corn over the hill to an old friend of hers, Pou.

'Who's he?'

'You know old Pou! He is Huriana's old grandfather
...Huriana Hana.'

'I don't care,' I said in my lovably candid way. 'I'm
not going to carry that stinkpot stuff through the street for
anyone.'

I remember that strong, vital woman turning into a
little old Maori lady before my very eyes. She shrank and
shrivelled, her lip bulged out into a pout of unutterable
sorrow. Her eyes went in a long way and became filmed
with tears. To think that I, Henia, her——, ——, ——!
To think that I wouldn't do this——, ——, —— little
favour for her, and here she was dying of consumption,
bronchitis, and ingrowing toenails and couldn't move a
step to help herself. And there was Pou...all alone...the
poor old—— ——, and these stuck-up Hanas wouldn't
even own him, the ——, ——, ——! And there was I, her
friend, her very own little ——, ——, ——! And I
wouldn't do this for her.

She was wonderful. I was out of the house and half-way
up the hill clutching my kit of awfulness before I knew
where I was.

The last mile to the Big House was familiar to me. Only
last Saturday matinée I had seen a powerful picture where
Monte Blue, wrongly condemned to fry on the hot seat,
had to march the above mile, suffering intensely every
inch of the way. Monte knew nothing, though. If he had
had a kit of pirau in his hand, the hot seat would have
seemed like a haven. I had hardly reached the crest of the
hill, moving in my own little aura of intolerable stench,
before I met a loathsome ginger family known as the Kirbys. Great husky beasts they were, with knees like horses'
hoofs, and glittering little eyes.

They began their usual hullabaloo of greeting,
then, as one Kirby, reeled backwards, screeching
"POOOOOOH!"

Nearly consumed by shame and humiliation, I cut and ran, with all the Kirbys strung out behind me like the tail of a comet. Sometimes I outstripped the smell and they got it, and then there were reelings and spittings, and renewed outcries of shameful things. Other times the smell billowed up for me and me alone, thick and viscous, and I hung out my tongue and was nearly sick. Faint and uncaring, I glanced back and saw that the Kirbys had given up the chase. Distant and eerie, the cry of 'Poooh!' came floating to me. I staggered along the gully, ducked through the tea-tree and there was the solitary, apparently uninhabited whare of the old man Pou.

A dog with the looks of a starveling fox slunk about the door. She lifted a lip in melancholy fashion and hid under the water-tank.

At first I thought that Pou must have gone away. Then I noticed the thinnest filmiest thread of smoke drifting from the roof. It was nothing more than a tatter of gauze against the tender autumnal blue.

Did I say roof? Yes, there was no chimney.

Timidly I knocked. The tall tea-tree whined and whispered, and all at once I was overcome by fear. I was going to put the kit of pirau down on the doorstone and run, when the knock was answered by a voice from within.

How can I put it? My flesh comes up in goose lumps when I think of it. A human voice calling from a pit? From a vast height? It called from the distance of a past time.

Thin, tenuous, ghostly, it called: 'Haaaa-ereeee-mai!'

I stood there still as a stone.

Twice more the voice called, the last time with a thinner, more fluctuating sound, and suddenly I pushed the door open and looked into the house.

There were so many holes in the roof it was quite light, and I could discern beside the fire that was smouldering in the middle of the earthern floor the humped-up figure of the oldest Maori I had ever seen. The strong broad-planed skull seemed too heavy for the corded bird's neck that falteringly swung towards me. At first I thought he was blind, but a blue spark still glimmered in the hollow shell-shaped pits of his eyes.

He wore nothing but half a grey woollen blanket; it was charred and ragged round the edges, for it was his habit to scrape away the fire at night and lie down on the hot earth.

What complete and utter poverty was the lot of this old man Pou! There was no object in all the whare except a cooking vessel of some sort, and a pile of firewood. A few potatoes lay in a hollow in the floor.

What he could have thought when he saw the strange pakeha child standing there I cannot imagine. His tattooed lips moved slowly, stiffly, and the faint thread of a voice said, 'Ka hemo ahau i te hiainu.'

I dropped the pirau and taking the cooking pot ran outside to the tank. The starved dog whimpered at me. She had a litter of puppies there.

It was only when I was giving the old man a drink that I realized I had actually understood what he had said . . . 'I am dying with thirst.' Brought up with Maoris, I had been constantly familiar with their language, its sound and modulation. My vocabulary was large, my grammar almost non-existent, yet now for the first time I understood the essential meaning of sentences. As often with young children and very old people, some sort of intuitive comprehension was present.

I built up his fire and he put the pirau corn to roast in the coals he raked out to the edge. His whole body was tattooed, a wonderful map, a decorative pattern of forgotten history, drawn over a period of years on his living skin when it was young and supple. Now it was just a parchment chart pulled over a cage of bones.

He said, 'Katahi te hari o toku ngakau!'

How happy I am!

I had never seen such comfortless poverty yet he was happy. He took no further notice of me, but sat there watching the pirau and sucking his gums avidly. I went out, carefully closing the door, which was nearly off its hinges. I said severely to the poor bag of bones that snarled at me, 'Shoot your mout'!'

Fortunately she understood only Maori. However, the unprovoked roughness of my remark rankled all the way home, and by the time I reached Cuskelly's I was soggy with repentance. I tore round to the back door of the establishment, and panted out, 'Got any scraps for a hungry dog, Mrs Cuskelly?'

I thought she looked at me a little peculiarly, but then adults are always looking at kids that way, so I didn't take any notice. She handed out a tinful of bones and scrapings and bits of cooked meat, and closed the door rather rapidly.

This time I approached the whare with a bossy sort of familiarity. It was silent as the grave. The pitiful squeakings of the blind puppies sounded quite loud. There were no birds in the tea-tree thicket. I gave the food to the slavering dog and hurried away.

This time, as I was about to enter my own gate, my friend Pola stuck her head up over the hedge and said curtly, 'My mother says you pong.'

It was not so much the unforgivable insult as the cumulative effect of the day's experiences, the galloping here and there, the pursuit of the Kirbys, the awful oldness of Pou, and most of all the hunger of the faithful dog, that made me burst into loud bawls. My Auntie Francey, all aproned and floury, rushed out of the house.

'What's the matter, dear? Did you hurt yourself... Jenny! Ooooh!'

The smell of the pirau was in my clothes and my hair. It oozed, I believe, from my skin. The more I howled, the more I sweated with emotion, the worse I smelt, and the more alarmed my dear auntie became.

She called over the hedge to Mrs Cuskelly, 'Oh, Mrs Cuskelly, Jenny's broken out into a terrible smell! Send Vi'let for the doctor, quick!'

He, poor man, recognized it instantly.

'She's been up to the Pa, that's what. Give her a bath and a good hiding and she'll be right.'

Delightful man! He gave me a wonderful idea for an alibi, for I knew that my Radiant Aunts would not only forbid me to see Blackleaf Forty, but would have ten fits if they knew I had been hobnobbing with an old Maori in a burnt blanket skirt. So I confessed, with many a repentant sob, that I had gone to the Pa, and played with pirau. And I was forgiven.

It was a long time before I forgave Pola Cuskelly, though. You may have noticed that you may criticize a friend's effect on ear or eye without noticeable umbrage being taken, but you can't tell anyone she smells.

Naturally, feeding the dog every day, I got to know old Pou very well indeed. So much so that one day gentle, stately Mr Hana took me aside and said, 'Jenny, what are you doing talking to that wicked old man?'

Wicked! I stammered out some bashful reply. Wicked! Just imagine!

'I thought he was Huriana's grandpa,' I faltered.

'Great-great-grandfather,' replied Mr Hana. 'He is more than one hundred years old, that one. You must not go there any more.'

'But he is just telling me a story about the ngarara,' I protested angrily. Red flushed through Mr Hana's brown skin.

'It is just a silly old Maori lie,' he said.

In one sense I was relieved, because the ngarara was getting on my nerves more than considerably.

The Kano, like many other places in the King Country, seemed to lie over a limestone honeycomb of subterranean channels. Put your ear to the earth and you could hear the rushing of water under the earth, the fall of unseen cascades in a deathly darkness, tumbling, spilling, fluming down ancient limestone chutes, never seen by mortal eye. Down there, in the prehistoric lake-ways, said Pou, lived a great beast, a blind monster. He drew it with a finger in the soft white ash...a lizard-like thing. He said that in the heavy rains, when the subterranean rivers filled to overflowing (and it was true that the paddocks in certain places were often flooded with a seepage from below) you could listen against the ground and you would hear the ngarara gulping for air close to the underside of the earth. And I did, many times, hear this eerie and alarming sound, probably of air bubbles bursting against the stony roofs of the caverns.

So, in another way, I was a little resentful of Mr Hana's attempt to take away the reality of the underground dragon.

'Pou is never wicked to *me*,' I said proudly.

Mr Hana looked hesitant and embarrassed. He leant closer to me and said rapidly, smiling meanwhile as though to contradict his amazing words, 'Pou is a tohunga, a...a...magic man. That is all just Maori hocus-pocus, but...some died, long ago, through Pou's words.' He sighed. 'Your aunts will think I am a fool.' He put his kind hand on my hair. 'It is not a nice place for a little girl like you to go.'

I knew that the Hanas had done all they could to make the old man comfortable. They had given him clothes and furniture, and besought him to live with others, so that he could be looked after. They had, ten years before, installed him in a little whare near their own home, but he had crawled out of it on his hands and knees and gone back to the shanty in the tea-tree. In the same way he had burnt up the clothes and thrown out the furniture. He wanted none of these descendants of his who had, as he thought, gone over to the pakeha.

He belonged to a world that had gone with the coming of the white man. He had been an old man when the Maori Wars concluded. Now he was an incredibly old man, the only tree remaining in a forest of ghosts. His mind was half a century behind the modern world; his ethics were pagan, his philosophies related more to the Oriental than the Occidental mind.

He told me many of his philosophies, but perhaps his words were too complex, for I recall none of them but this. 'Men will do anything for riches. All the evil in the world they will do for riches. But all riches are useless to man except these two: land, to grow food, and women, to grow men.'

I wrote it down with all the new Maori words I had learnt, and hid it in my secret place, which was under a loose board in our wash-house. Years later, when I left Te Kano, I took out all the scraps of paper and read Pou's sayings, and was very shocked.

Pou was indeed a tohunga, and I shall tell you how I found out, but that does not come as yet in this story, for we have arrived at Piccalilli Time, and how the big flood came to Te Kano.

Very often I feel sorry for modern children who are never sent to the grocer's shop for an ounce of turmeric.

Poor kids . . . they never have the wonderful job of making brine 'strong enough to float an egg'!

They never smell the perfumes of Araby which fill the house when their Auntie Louisa is making pickled plums with vinegar and cloves and chillies and treacle, nor admire the speckled-egg glaze on a giant earthenware jar all ready to receive the plums!

Auntie Louisa made all our preserves, even though she worked in the shop. Francey owned that she had no hand with them, and Louisa had a special talent that way. So when I was sent up to the store for the turmeric, I knew it was Piccallili Time.

Women in Te Kano bottled everything, for the winter was long and austere, and vegetables scarce. I don't suppose there was anything in our garden from Cape gooseberries to cabbages that wasn't 'put down' for the winter. But Piccalilli Time was the nicest of all.

Well, there was dear Louisa, toothless and a bit cavernous and skinny, through living on junket and sponge cake and beef tea, surrounded by bits of cauli, gherkins, onions, string beans, mustard, curry, and various spices. Something thick and glutinous and yellow was plopping in the big preserving pan on General Smuts. This is what our range was called, not after the General, but after the Smuts.

I should not do the General wrong, though. He was nowhere near as smutty as many a coal range I have met since. Large, square, and glittering black, with little sparkles of red fire showing through his strictly aligned teeth at the front, he was decorated with brass taps and damper handles, and his oven door was given the crowning touch of two wonderful curly hinges, like those on a Saxon church door. Later on the General was painted with aluminium paint, but at the time of which we are speaking it was the custom to polish him, with a great hissing and a metallic smell, with a saucer of dampish blacking and a peculiar brush with an arched handle on the top. Francey bossed him round a lot, and he often retaliated by spitting soot at her, but under Louisa's gentle rule the General was a gentleman.

It was sweet little Ailie who thought of getting Louisa to make the Indian chutney. I suppose Louisa was looking a little pale and melancholy and the Radiant Aunts instantly put it down to regretful thoughts of her shattered romance. Ailie happened to be looking through the cookery book at the time and she saw just what every girl with a broken heart requires, the job of making Indian chutney.

'Oh, Barbie,' she gasped, 'it sounds delicious – and it

takes a month to make! If you don't stir it for twenty-eight days on end it is ruined.'

It was obvious that this was exactly what Louisa needed.

I must say some pretty good things went into the preliminary round. Green apples and dried peaches, chillies and mustard seed, shallots and all kinds of Christmas-pudding fruits. Also I had to fetch a stone jar of green ginger from Jim Joe the Chinaman.

It took us all a whole evening to cut up the ingredients.

All the next day General Smuts hummed away under the preserving pan, where the chutney was turning into a dark-brown succulent fluid, speckled lucently here and there with the swollen slivers of peach.

Then it was ladled into a thick white crockery jug about two feet high. This was tastefully decorated with a blue design of vine-leaves and was the solitary survivor of a washstand set comprising jug, basin, drip-tray, and chamber-pot. The latter we pronounced strictly in the French way, and I must have been twelve before I got over my conviction that teapot should really be pronounced teapo.

Anyway, Grandma Admiral's old washstand jug was a god-send in the making of the Indian chutney. It was the very thing to set beside the General's hot feet so that Louisa could stir it throughout the day for twenty-eight of the same, as directed. Of course we stirred, too, and so did any odd Cuskellys who flitted through, but it was mostly Louisa who worried about it.

She must have been two weeks into her chutney campaign when the floods came to Te Kano.

Even without any rain at all, Te Kano was a well-watered locality. The town lay in a saucer of hills. The Koropungapunga River twisted serpentinely through a cleft in the hills, flowed through the town, and spilled through another cleft on the southern side. Aside from this, countless creeks bounced down the hills on every quarter to join the Koropungapunga. Nearly every house-holder had a spring of his own, and I can tell you that water diviners let loose in Te Kano quickly went hysterical and had to be taken away.

However, we did have the usual King Country rain, as well.

This year we had even more.

I spent the first week of the great rain in bed with a stuffy cold, and hardly noticed the weather. But the first day I was allowed outside I ran down to the nearest bridge to see the river. It was a thrilling sight. The water was as brown as tea, and it ran sucking and mumbling only a few inches below the floorboards. The clotted rafts of debris it carried on its headlong rush knocked and crashed at the bridge-piles, making submarine reverberations. But I had seen this before. What really excited me was to see the Anzac Memorial, a tall granite tooth, normally resident amongst lawns and flower-beds of the river-side park, sticking up out of a seething flood like an island.

Instantly I thought of my friend Blackleaf Forty. Speechless with excitement I tore through the hesitant renewal of the rain to that part of the river where her little shanty crouched amongst the willows. She was not washed out yet. Flashing profanity flew through the air like sheet lightning. I peeped through the willows and there was the old lady, muffled like a fence-post in her black shawl, a sack over her head, and a long dark-brown hand out-stretched like the hand of doom, directing the kindly op-erations of four muddy Maori boys who had bent at the knees under the weight of a sopping wet sofa. Like the water rats and the kingfishers, Blackleaf Forty was making for higher ground.

I tore off home.

'Oh, Auntie Louisa,' I gabbled, splashing into the kit-chen, 'the river's coming up on the road, and the bridges will be washed away, and I bet the Auckland express will be caught in a slip, and there's going to be a real *beaut* flood, Auntie Louisa!'

She looked as though she had been crying.

She hastily dabbed at her nose and snatched up a jam-jar.

Then she glared at me as though I were causing the flood all by myself.

'I don't care,' she said. 'Just don't let it think it's going to interfere with my Indian chutney, that's all!'

And she slabbed the wooden spoon into Grandma's wash-jug and stirred up the mess within with as much venom as if it had been the Pig Man, liver and lights, as we used to say.

The Four Radiant Aunts were never ones to keep me indoors. They bowed to the natural law that puddles and a kid's feet are bound to come together. Consequently, when even the hardy Cuskellys were naught but a blurred and jealous row of faces at their kitchen windows, I was voluptuously splashing round the countryside, my chest well buttered with Vicks Vapor Rub, but my feet bare.

How beautiful is a paddock of rye-grass under water, the tall stems seen as through glass, the seeds lying just below the surface, each golden assegai enclosed in a bubble of air.

So it rained and it rained, not with the turbulent explosions one associates with storms, but in a steady downpour in which sky and earth and water-filled air became all the same soft grey, and trees and buildings were but myopically seen islands of darkness. On our iron-roofed township the rain set up a hollow drumming, a breathy roar which sometimes drowned out the emboldened voice of the river.

For the Koropungapunga was now an enormous map of curly brown water rising daily towards the brim of its valley bed. The tall trees in the park wore ruffs of muddy foam and debris round their lower branches: all the little trees had been submerged for a week. Already all the bridges but one were marked dangerous. The river was pouring in a rapid glossy bulge over the first rail, sluicing across the deck and slamming through the rails on the other side.

I thought maybe it was the time of Noah come again.

On the sixth day of the flood the Radiant Aunts decided it was no use going back to the shop. Not only were there no customers, but they thought they might never get over the river at night. So they came toiling home laden with sodden groceries, and meat that left bloodstains for half a mile, and, as it were, pulled up the drawbridge and defied the flood to do its worst.

And Louisa went on stirring the Indian chutney.

In the ten-minute intervals between downpours I ventured outside, a mackintoshed mushroom with a secret terror.

I was afraid that the ngarara would get out.

I was afraid that the level of the underground waters would rise sufficiently to allow the great beast to scrabble with his claws at the inner thresholds of the caves in the hills, and he would lever himself up and waddle out into the upper world.

Again and again I pressed my ear to the soggy ground. Far below I could hear the muffled tumult of the waters, a strange, immense trumpet sound which was perhaps the subterranean river spouting through a gorge. Whoom! Whoom! It was infinitely far away, and yet the whole earth trembled to it. And many smaller sounds there were, too, a-lippering almost against my ear, and a harplike sound as droplet followed droplet in fluid *arpeggio*.

In my mind I saw the creature old Pou had drawn in the pearly ash, crouched on a limestone ledge just below me, the water running from his hard reptilian flanks. And I did not see him lizard-coloured, but bleached white as bone.

Many times my aunts asked me what I was doing so close to the ground, and I said I was looking for tadpoles.

My terror was incommunicable. Also I knew that no amount of gentle chiacking on the part of the aunts would magic away the ngarara. They just didn't know.

Pou was of no use to me, either. His Maori relatives had spirited him away to a safe place in the hills, and his cabin was empty. Even the dog was gone.

Not that my terror was a consistent thing. For hours I forgot about it altogether. And when the flood became really serious, and it became plain that we, too, might have to migrate in a hurry, I enjoyed it all so much that in retrospect it seems one long picnic.

Neither do I recall that the Radiant Aunts were ever more than exasperated. Their squeals were of excitement rather than fright, and even on that last tremendous night when we were all sitting in the rafters wearing our best hats and surrounded by jars of pickled onions – well, we shall come to that directly.

It was a legend in that house, carefully but unsuccessfully kept from my big flapping ears, that when poor little motherless Jenny arrived from Australia she was *dirty*. I believe it all boiled down to a few watermarks round my neck, but the aunts never forgave the kindly stewardess in whose charge I had travelled, nor, by extension, my absent father. Then and there, confronted by my scandalous neck, they developed a complex about Keeping the Child Clean.

So I had a bath every night.

This commonplace sentence hardly does justice to the heroic aunts. It was not a matter of merely turning on the hot-water tap and throwing the child in to soak.

To be sure, some places in Te Kano had hot-water systems, but round our way we had wash-houses, craftily placed at the maximum distance from the house, preferably across a large stretch of skilly mud. Here the bathwater was heated in the copper and lugged in a bucket up to the bathroom.

The Cuskellys had their wash-house so far from the house it was practically on another section, and if you didn't want the water to be cold by the time you reached the bathroom you had to run like billy-o. I believe that this speeding with buckets of boiling water was what gave the elder Cuskellys their fame at egg-and-spoon racing. They were pretty formidable at the Te Kano Show, I can tell you.

However, the Cuskellys, like most of our neighbours, bathed only now and then. Many of the elders declined all trifling with buckets and 'had a nice rench at the sink', instead.

But I had a bath every night, and every night one of the aunts devotedly carried water.

When the flood made it impossible to get to the wash-house without a boat, the aunts held solemn conference.

'She looks greyish already,' worried Francey.

'We must keep our standards up,' said Barbie.

Louisa said nothing, except 'ninety-eight, ninety-nine, a hundred, there! Blow it!'

The chutney-stirring had become a tyrannical ritual. She gave it a hundred stirs every hour, and if it wasn't clockwise, she didn't count it.

Ah, Louisa! She was pale, and her hands had become long and thin. She looked at least ten days older than she was.

The aunts looked at her covertly, and Louisa knew they were looking. She was brave and proud. I saw her take a long breath, and then she looked back. Is she or is she not fretting over that Pig Man article, they were thinking, and Louisa's courageous blue eyes gave them not a hint of an answer.

With embarrassed relief they seized upon the bath project. It was humiliating from the first, when they tried

me for size in the little old baby bath in which they kept
the ironing nowadays. Shameful thing, it was the shape of
a mutton pie, a dreary grey galvanized iron with a gritty
bottom, and I hated it on sight. However, I fitted it as a
trussed chook fits a baking dish.

Now for heating the water! With all the preserving pans
in use, there was nothing roomy enough. The aunts held a
hurried confabulation and decided they would risk General Smuts's boiler.

Ranges don't seem to be built with boilers nowadays.
General Smuts's was a mysterious cubical cavern on the
left side of his ebony paunch, a kind of second stomach.
On the top was a little oblong slide which you pried up
with a poker, and from the front protruded a brass tap. I
had always received most unsatisfactory replies when I inquired about this curious portion of the General's ana-
tomy, and I was delighted as the aunts prepared to put it
to use for the first time. Briskly they poured kettles of
water through the hole in the top, then stoked the General
to the tonsils with hot-burning lumps of rata.

There was a wonderful warmth and cosiness in the kitchen. I can see it yet, the glossy cherry-coloured lino, the
clock on the immensely high mantelpiece looking bene-
volently down like a sun. I sat at the table, reading a Farmers' illustrated catalogue, and occasionally looking out
through the window at the streaming world. The water
was already over the road, the gateposts forlorn and isolated. How it ran, shallow and tawny, hurrying down to
the river!

'Oh, it can't come up any higher than that,' said Barbara comfortably.

I knew our little house was safe and secure, a Noah's
ark in a curly sea of shallow water.

At sunset the clouds opened suddenly, and glaring and
sinister the sun shone out for a moment before it vanished
behind the vaporous hills. The blood-red light was both

gloom and gleam: I remember Ailie, little and gentle, shivering as she stood beside me.

The next moment Cuskelly's ducks, in an orderly procession, swam out of their residence and paddled peaceably away down the road. One instant they were level with the drowned grass-tops, the next they soared with the water to the middle of the hedge.

All four aunts shrieked together, and no wonder, for the flood had broken loose from the big gorge behind the town, where the Koropungapunga had banked up some of its waters, and the time of Noah had come indeed. It was too late to move furniture, too sudden to be alarmed. We just stood at the window gawking.

We could hear the boom in the gorge like a giant tuba . . . huh-huh-huh! and then whamm! as a fallen tree went end over end into the bottom of the limestone cliff. And the mutter of the water came from all sides, louder, louder, like an approaching multitude.

Suddenly I yelled, 'I saw a dead man, I saw a dead man!'

But it was not a man, only his bones.

There came the skulls, bobbing like white mushrooms on the tide, the brown water spilling through the eye-sockets, spouting as it might spout through the jaws of gargoyles through those long-silent mouths. Some were stained dark where they had lain in the wet: others were raddled across the crown with ochre. These were the skulls of kings and queens.

The tumultuous waters had ravished the ancient burial ledges of the old Maoris in the gorge, and chiefs who had been alive when Captain Cook visited their kingdom now were borne willy-nilly down the main street in Te Kano. The Maoris were afraid to touch them, so sacred were those bones, and many were salvaged for the fun of it by the jovial white man.

Later I remember one of these skulls, its thick bone cut as clean as a whistle by a tomahawk wound, perched on a gatepost with a candle burning inside. On a dark night it was sight enough to turn a Maori white.

It was just when the last of these gruesome voyagers had danced past, and the Radiant Aunts had sufficiently recovered from their paralysis to turn to each other with frightened squeals that General Smuts blew up.

His first indication that all was not well was a coarse burp in the chimney. Then there was a metallic reverberation which was probably a burst of military language, followed by a loud explosion and a cloud of steam.

'The boiler! The boiler!' screamed Louisa.

'It's burnt through!' raved Francey.

'Turn the tap on and run off the water,' gasped Ailie, and she dashed at the stove and obeyed herself in the most heroic way.

The brass tap gave with a squawk, and what appeared to be coal-black soup poured out all over the hearth. In my excitement I had climbed up on the table and was beating a tattoo on the Farmers' catalogue with my feet. Although at the time we were too excited to think, what really happened must have been this: there must long have been a hole in the wall between boiler and fire-box, and when the water boiled it fizzed up and shot through the cavity, sending the General into spectacular fits of indigestion.

'Oh, Ailie, you *are* a cretonne!' wailed Francey as the black soup lagooned all over the kitchen floor. Louisa darted at Grandma's washstand jug and, flaming-eyed, clutched it to the flattest chest in Te Kano.

'I've got to save the chutney!'

The wild cry rang over the swelling waters, and was answered most eerily as by shipwrecked mariners from the Cuskelly dwelling.

'*Thrown on life's surge, we claim Thy care* . . .'

Pola told me later that the instant life's surge came in under their back door their father led the retreat to the dining-room table, and there, on its enormous golden oak expanse, children, boarders, and chooks remained the night, drowning the sound of crashing crockery with the stirring strains of suitable hymns.

It was all right for the Cuskelly establishment, but the Admirals lived a few feet lower, and our dining-room table submerged about seven-thirty. I know because at that moment Louisa was hanging head downwards from the manhole in the ceiling and Barbara was trying to hoist me up to her. Again and again my sweaty hands slipped from Louisa's, and again and again I slid down Barbara's front as down a banister. Finally an extra arm belonging, I believe, to Francey, reached down from the manhole, hooked itself in my collar, and amidst fearful roaring I was dragged up into the thickly dusty cavity under the roof. This I had always imagined was stuffed with dead bodies, but it was really quite a fascinating place with a low peaky iron roof, a dirty little square window in the gable, and strong rafters just made for refugee aunts and nieces to sit on in their hour of peril.

The aunts had hoisted an astonishing assortment of belongings through the manhole. Clothing, blankets, favourite pictures, food, a lamp, bits of dressmaking, the Indian chutney, and all our best hats. Louisa had saved every single one of the preserves she had so recently slaved to make, and far into the night I stared fascinated into the bulging semi-luminous eyeballs of the pickled onions which occupied the rafter opposite to mine.

Barbara cast a wistful glance through the manhole at the room beneath. The lamplight shone feebly on the stealthily rising water.

'We never did like that carpet much, anyway, did we, girls?' she said with a gulp, and the girls loyally agreed.

By now it was my bedtime, and unwillingly drugged with sleep I gazed about me. How wonderful to be in this little cave smelling of mummified mice, with floodwaters sloshing all round me, and plenty of pickled onions to eat! The aunts had put on their hats, to save them from getting crushed, and even with tired pale dust-streaked faces they looked elegant. Louisa's was pale-blue georgette, stretched over a cambric frame like a pot. It came down as far as her eye-lashes, and was absolutely immovable, even in a hurricane. Barbara's was a shade vampish, with a drunken black brim and a monster hatpin like a rhomboid of coal. The other hats were tailored and globular, just the thing to wear on a voyage to Mars.

I wonder if the Radiant Aunts thought what would happen if the water rose high enough to flood the rafters and drown us against the roof. Probably they were going to bash out the gable window with their Louis heels and shoot forth into the watery wilderness as though emerging from a torpedo tube.

The hours were slow. The lack of air, the sinister suckings of the water below, the eerie voices from the Cuskellys' place, the strong smell of burnt dust as it floated down upon the lamp chimney, sent me into a half-delirious drowse. This suddenly flicked away, and I found myself entirely awake, listening to something slither and bump along the outside of the house.

I recognized at once that it was the ngarara.

Some people's memories are tied to their noses, and to this day I cannot smell pickling vinegar without feeling again some faint and sickening aftertaste of that terrible panic which gripped me when I knew the great beast of the underwaters was snuffling round the gable of our house. I saw it in my mind, with ancient sunken eyes like circles of stone. There was wet silt in the thin leathern scales of its hide, and these scales I heard rasp along the wall only the thickness of a weatherboard from my ear. I lost my head completely and began to kick and scream like a lunatic.

I suppose the noise in that confined space was terrific. Louisa jumped up in fright and gave her head an awful bang on the roof. Ailie seized the lamp and held it far away from my flailing feet.

'It's only Cuskelly's cow swimming round!' cried Barbara.

'It isn't, it isn't!' I shrieked.

The creature bumped gently along the wall and thumped against the gable.

'Get out of there, you silly cow!' roared Francey.

A row of jars crashed over and pickled onions flew everywhere. The catastrophe made me quiet for a second, and we heard the voices from Cuskellys' raised in chorus:

Hail, glorious St Patrick, dear saint of our isle,
On us thy poor children, bestow a sweet smile!

The aunts seized upon the lull to be reassuringly comic. They shrieked insults at the swimmer outside, which was now bumping gently against the window-sill.

'Go home to your mother, you big lump!' ordered Barbara.

'Leave our house alone, you dim-witted boob!' cried Ailie.

'You've frightened poor Jenny, you blue-nosed beast!' shouted Francey.

The aunts looked at each other in approving amazement.

'Why, we're almost as good as Pa, aren't we?' they said.

Only Louisa said nothing. She was holding the top of her pale-blue cloche with a pained expression. Tears filled her eyes.

I took a deep breath and let out another sound like a latter-day air-raid siren. I knew very well that any time now the ngarara would rear its pointed head and rest its pendulous jaw on the sill of the little dirt-encrusted window. The agitated trembling which is the precursor of hysteria filled my inside. I dug my fingers into Barbara's arm and almost dragged her off the rafter.

'Chase it away, chase it away!'

It wasn't the belt on the head as much as the racket I was making which made Auntie Louisa suddenly burst into tears. She crouched amongst the salvage and the scattered onions and wept silently, her poor little white, toothless face all streaked with dirt and cobwebs, and the immovable hat sitting above it in matchless elegance.

Then the window crashed in. The aunts squealed together as the black night, murmurous and sinister with the manifold voices of the flood, showed itself almost against our faces.

I glared at the broken glass with a paralysed stare of horror.

Then the Pig Man looked in.

The level of the water was about four feet down, and at the time he was standing on a ledge about two inches wide, and holding on with one hand to the sill. Yet, wonderful fellow, seeing that he was in the presence of ladies, *he raised his hat.*

It was that gesture, at such a moment, that superb indication of good breeding in spite of all, that won the aunts. It was always mentioned in awed voices, and when you get an awed voice in an aunt, you've got something.

Dear fellow, he looked in pinkly and apologetically and said, 'Good evening!'

'Oh, Desmond!' Aunt Louisa rushed at him and for a moment I could see neither window nor Pig Man.

'Oh, Mr Hilder,' babbled Francey, 'I didn't mean *you* to be the blue-nosed beast!'

'We thought it was Mrs Cuskelly's cow,' giggled Ailie.

In a few moments he was inside the house, a vast streaming figure in an oilskin as big as a tent. The water skidded off his butter-yellow hair and ran in unsullied round drops down the country clarity of his skin. The aunts looked at him with blushing embarrassment.

'I was paralysed,' said Barbara afterwards. 'Just remembered that darling Louie didn't have a tooth in her

72

head and looked awful. I was just burnt up with shame for her.'

But that Pig Man – he just looked at Louisa, and said tenderly, 'I can see you've been fretting, lovey. Why, your dear little face is quite fallen in!'

That did it. From that moment the three Admiral sisters ranged themselves on the side of the Pig Man, prepared to fight devil or Pa. It was one for all and all for one, and if that one kept pigs, well, they were pro-pig now and always.

Queer – I can't remember our climbing out the window onto that little raft the Pig Man had hastily and ingeniously constructed when he came in from the farm to rescue his loved one and his loved one's loved ones.

I do recall, of course, the Pig Man plunging his tremendous fist with a succulent sound into Grandma's washstand jug, and the wonderful look of guilt and consternation on his face.

'It doesn't matter a bit, Desmond,' Barbara earnestly assured him. 'We just hate chutney, don't we, girls?'

The girls said they loathed it.

One by one we were ferried across the road to the slopes on the other side, already becoming mistily visible in a reluctant dawn.

The rain stopped, and the waters abated.

For months they worked on the Koropungapunga, clearing it of debris which threatened to divert the course altogether and send the river straight through the Methodist Church. For miles the river-bed was like a gigantic bird's-nest of inextricably tangled tree-trunks, driftwood, snags, and ruined houses, with the shrunken and abashed river sneaking along silently beneath them. The dangerous suspension bridges, over which we children had so often dared each other to run, had been ripped from their moorings and lay like incredibly crumpled ribbons in the thick velvety-brown silt which covered the riverside paddocks. No more would we stand on their undulant middles on rotten, crumbling planks and swing to and fro, terrified but game.

Three miles below Te Kano, a good six months afterwards, a farmer who was clearing a gravel bar came across something which, like the sea serpent and the flying saucer, was never photographed, and was reported only to be scoffed at. But this is what it was; a thing decayed and mutilated, and thirty feet long. Its rib formation was the size of a sheep's, and in shape it was like an eel.

It could, perhaps, have been some ancient old-man eel that had dwelt for generations in the subterranean river, and been washed out on that night of the flood. Perhaps fleeting glimpses of it by Maoris who timorously ventured into the hill caves had given rise to the legends of the nga-rara, a creature well established in their racial memory.

Perhaps it had merely dwelt in some secret bushy back-water of the Koropungapunga, living and growing more massive year by year as the mysterious eel tribe does.

Or perhaps the farmer down at the Three-Mile imagined it all one sunny afternoon on the gravel bar.

Anyway we were all too busy to care, for Louisa was secretly engaged to the Pig Man, with two years to wait before she could marry, and to celebrate the event, the Radiant Aunts decided to get bustered.

Uncle Olga had been bustered some years previously, and it had been a searing experience. She had struck one of those fanatic hairdressers who don't know where to stop, and although she kept whimpering and jerking out of the way of those ravening scissors, he had seized her by the chin and forcibly bingled her. It was like the Rape of Lucrece, the way Uncle Olga told it. And then to make things worse she had discovered that the bingle revealed a great irregularity of some kind on the back of her skull. She could never make out whether it was a Bump of Philogenitiveness or the place where Uncle Ray had accidentally woodened her out with a hat-box a moment or two after they set out for their honeymoon journey.

So when the Radiant Aunts announced they had done with long hair, Uncle Olga was very agitated, and indeed it was only by good luck that the Hen and Chickens weren't called down from their mountain fastness to discuss it with as much solemnity as they had discussed the Pig Man amour.

'Please, please,' pleaded the little woman in a voice like a throttled trombone, 'try it on Jenny first.'

Of course I was delighted. I was the only girl in my standard with long hair, and since it was red it came in for a lot of good-humoured remarks such as would drive any sensitive adult to murder but which a sensitive child is supposed to endure with a smile.

I was all for cutting as much of it off as possible.

So with glad cries and excited giggles I was led off to the hairdresser, Mr Bonnet. We pronounced it as written, but I should think Mr Bonnet was originally Mr Bonnay. He had the only waxed moustache in the King Country.

Of course he was charmed to have four beautiful young ladies in his dim, bay-rum-ridden salon at the same time, even though they were all very cautious. And he didn't mind at all experimenting on the dog to show them what could be done with a buster cut. So in two minutes there I was sitting up on a plank on the barber's chair, surrounded by great swathes of red hair, and I was looking rather like my own freckle-faced brother, if I'd had one.

The four aunts screamed with horror. Mr Bonnet raised a protesting hand.

'Dat is noddings,' he demurred. 'Any bootcher can cut off hair. Now I show you what de real hairdresser do.'

And before I could screech he had lit a long taper and set me on fire.

I can tell you it was an experience for us all.

Aunt Barbie, always full of responsibility, leaped across

the floor to beat this madman over the head with his own wash-basin.

'No, no!' he cried, fending her off nimbly. 'If the hair is not singed the wital fluid leaks out.'

And with that he flickered the taper all over my head, lighting little fires as he went.

'Oh! Ah! Oh, no!' cried the aunts.

'Stop it this moment!' ordered Barbara, and as fast as he lit them she beat them out with her hands.

For all Barbara cared I could lose every drop of wital fluid my hair possessed. In a trice I was snatched from the chair, and Mr Bonnet was nearly crying.

'I must have been crazy to allow it,' flamed Barbara. She turned a reproachful look on Louisa. 'Louie, why didn't you stop me?'

'Precious little Jenny,' mourned Ailie, patting my bristling head that still smelt like old burnt rags. 'Whatever would Thora say?'

Thora! At the thought of how she had failed that dear dead sister Barbie's eyes grew moist. But Mr Bonnet had had enough. Snatching me from their grasp he shot lightning from both ends of his piercingly sharp moustache, and at the look in his burning eyes the sisters spiritually reeled. That brief moment was enough. In a second I was back on my plank, and the world was full of shampoo.

I must say I looked a bobby-dazzler when he'd finished with me. Like most children under twelve years of age I never looked at myself in a glass and hardly knew my face existed except that I had to feed it. Now, apocalyptically, I discovered the existence of this entrancing thing on the front of my head. Short curly hair certainly suited it. I was bemused by my own beauty. Truly, if I had been a sultan I would have been mad about me.

The aunts were delighted, too. They apologized in

quartette to Mr Bonnet for their doubts of his genius, and then one by one they submitted themselves to his clever hands.

Ah, what were you doing in Te Kano, Monsieur Bonnet? Did you run away with someone's wife and get ze chuck out of France?

I suspect it.

My aunties bore their hair reverently homewards and laid it away in glove-boxes. That night they shed a few tears about it, but brightened up the next morning when they thought of all the money they wouldn't have to spend on those ponderous tortoiseshell slides, or hair-clasps, as we called them. You could get them six inches long and an inch wide. They had coveted the wearing of such treasures for a long time, because they sold them in their shop and it's always so nice to wear the stock.

The cutting of my hair meant a great deal to me, because it precipitated me into what was a grave scandal for our respectable village. While I was not altogether innocent of thinking up thumping great lies, I can still say that much of the blame lies at the door of Te Kano's attitude towards the normal self-confidence of a child. Te Kano adults could not bear to see a child draw attention to himself in any way whatsoever: it was showing-off, it was conceit, and he needed taking down a peg. And then he would be. The pegs we were taken down, if laid end to end, would reach from Cape Maria to the Bluff.

Of course, this did not happen with the Radiant Aunts. They recalled their own childhood much too clearly. Grandpa could take down bigger and longer and more memorable pegs than anyone else in New Zealand.

For a week whenever someone noticed my new hair and exclaimed, 'Why, you've got a buster cut!' I would beam my innocent pleasure.

This beam was a mistake. It indicated I was pleased with myself. Peg-taking was indicated. I was so teased, chiacked, tweaked, tweedled, and laughed at that I wore my hat far down over my ears like an egg-cup and entered into an obstinate and embarrassed silence which was called sulking. It was, however, a deep and trembling hurt. I could not defend myself because 'answering back' was a mortal sin, too. No matter how ill bred and unchristian a grown-up was, a child had to endure it in silence.

O course, they did not know they were being unchristian. Teasing a child was considered a good social tradition and necessary for the child's proper development.

I developed into a diminished and self-conscious little blot, ready to seize upon any pretext for blowing myself up to normal size again.

It is time now to look at the world of those mid-twenties. As you know, on many a globe of the world even today, New Zealand has been left off, giving a New Zealander the dismayed feeling that he isn't anywhere. In those times the world was so much bigger that our dear isles were farther away from England than the moon is now. Travel in any degree was rare and awesome; so much so that our apothecary, Mr Freestone, who had once been to the United States and seen Gloria Swanson in the flesh, found it necessary to speak with an American accent ever after, just to prove it.

So you can imagine that Te Kano was passionately interested in transport of any sort, especially in the progress of aviation.

As a matter of fact, Te Kano had probably the first home-made aeroplane in Australasia. The two elder brothers of the Kirby family – those raucous creatures with the knees like stallions' – went to Auckland on a visit and saw there a Sopwith-Camel on exhibition. Enravished by this spavined mechanical grasshopper, the shy country lads conducted a conversation which went something like this:

'Reckon we can belt up something better 'n that, eh, Heck?'

'Too right.'

'Time we done somethin' with that old motor-bike engine, eh, Heck?'

'Too right.'

'And what about that crook old outboard motor we got down in the paddock, eh, Heck?'

'Too right.'

Well, they built their plane, towed it up to the top of a hill with a plough-horse, and took off into yonder. *And it flew*. It walloped along for a few hundred yards like an airborne egg-beater, then the engine fell out, closely followed by two Kirbys.

The tank exploded, two haystacks took fire, and Georgie Wi's brown mare threw a double-headed foal.

But the Kirbys were out of plaster in six months or so.

You can see that we were air-minded to a degree. Consequently when it became known that two flyers were going to attempt to cross the Tasman by air, Te Kano nearly had a fit. Twelve hundreds miles in one hop! Where would they carry all the petrol they needed? What would happen if the plane had to land in the middle of the Tasman? Crazy! Wonderful! Heroic!

Alas for me that the name of one of them was Hood!

At that time Te Kano had for parish priest a small apostolic block-buster called FitzPeter. He spent most of his time on a horse, mud to the hips, for his flock were pretty obdurate about dying in their own beds, fourteen miles from the nearest buggy-track. Because he said dem and dese, and spoke familiarly (as well he might) of dett's door, folk thought he was a foreigner. But he had come straight from the Irish bogs to our King Country ones.

Through his eyes like blue glass marbles looked an angelic innocence. This is what made him wage a bitter war against the inexorable rise of the hemline. Yet skirts continued to go up like roller blinds before his very eyes. It really offended him to see all those art, silk legs flashing pinkly from the shadowy corners of his church.

This was the way the three junior Radiant Aunts fell foul of him. They were not, as has been indicated, at all daring; in fact they were modest to a pre-war degree. Yet, as purveyors of Robes and Mantles, they felt it their duty to keep abreast of *la mode*.

It was with complete artlessness that they decided to wear their new satin coats to church. Auntie Barbie had hurried on ahead with me, a noted dawdler, and so no family consultation presided over by her good taste was possible.

The satin coats were strange garments with roll collars that went down to the hems, and no buttons. The wearer had to clutch the coat together in folds at the front, usually with a hand already full of pouchy purse. Francey's was black and gleaming like stove polish, Louisa's champagne, and Ailie's a dusty pink called old rose. As I watched them walking down the aisle I thought they looked frightfully like three Norma Shearers.

Unfortunately they were just a little late for Mass, and so had to sit all alone in the front seat.

The first thing Father FitzPeter saw when he turned round to give the congregation a blast about the church debt was this awful array of six glittering knees and six shameful shins above six pointy-toed black satin shoes. He plainly felt as though he had blundered into the Folies Bergères.

That was a sermon to remember, if you like.

He didn't refer to the Radiant Aunts by name, of course. He called them Certain Parties.

And there they sat, those Certain Parties, old rose all over, listening to a flamingly eloquent description of how they made Our Lady blush, St Brigid weep, and St Joseph hide his face. It was no good trying to pull their skirts over their knees: the coats had so little skirt that they stuck out like tiny verandas when the wearer was sitting down. No, the aunts had just to sit there and suffer. The fact that every other woman in the church had equally short skirts did not help. *They* were the examples. *They* were the Parties who had made Our Lady blush.

If anything my Aunt Barbara suffered even more than her sisters.

She kept mumbling in agony, 'Oh, they're not! Oh, it isn't! Oh, it wouldn't!'

Suddenly Father FitzPeter dragged out his watch, realized he had to drive twenty miles to say Mass on the other side of the mountain, and gallopingly finished up with some advice to the Parties to look after their immortal souls rather than their poor corrupt bodies. Then, with the air of one clinching the matter, he commanded us all to say a prayer for the welfare of the brave aviators who were even then preparing to fly the Tasman Sea.

'Thank Gard,' he thundered, 'that while the womenfolk are scurrying to hell as fast as dere nedder limbs will carry dem, dese noble men are sacrificing all for progress. Gard bless the fine lads. Gard bless them, I say. Dey are names to remember, Moncrieff and Hood.'

The Radiant Aunts had hardly reached the haven of their own gate before Louisa and Ailie began to weep. They hobbled along, their poor corrupt feet already hurting in the elegant new shoes, sniffing and whimpering and blaming the Reverend Father and *haute couture* equally for their terrible mortification.

'I hope this teaches you girls a lesson,' said Barbara, her voice trembling, all the same, with sympathy.

'*I certainly won't do it again,*' vowed Francey.

And, all credit to her, she didn't. She never sat in a front seat in church again her whole life.

Meanwhile I was boiling away to myself in a respectful but bitter way. To think that they were talking about satin coats when they could have been remarking on the wonderful fact that one of the intrepid birdmen had the same name as myself! Why I thought, he might even be a relative of my father. Perhaps I, too, was an embryo birdwoman – in the egg, so as to speak – and would one day be photographed wearing mighty goggles and looking contemptuously at a cowering Puss Moth.

The idea was so remarkable that I went out and climbed the peach-tree to think about it, not coming down until I could smell dinner actually on the plates. I ate it patronizingly, but the aunts were still too pipped to notice that I wasn't speaking to anyone.

In the afternoon the Pig Man came to see Louisa, and the other three aunts spent so much time being tactfully absent it was downright embarrassing. No matter where I wanted to go I couldn't.

Finally in desperation I went out into the middle of the paddock, where the ubiquitous Louisa and her suitor were practically sure not to be, and lay down on my back amidst the odorous pennyroyal. Here there were bald patches where a child could fish for those mysterious insects known in Te Kano as penny-doctors, small pit-dwellers whose jaws would clamp on the soft white end of a grass stalk pushed down into their clay tunnels.

Do children still fish for penny-doctors on the way home from school? Do they lie motionless amidst the purple pennyroyal, watching the hawks climbing invisible stairways, and dreaming of desperate hazards in airless space?

'Desperately hazardous' were the words used by experienced pilots of that initial plan to cross the Tasman, as though that little waterway were the space between star and star. But it was more than a waterway then; it was the highway of the whale and the pasture of the mollymawk, and our grandparents, the old pioneers, had taken a month to cross it. We knew from our geography books that it was the roughest stretch of water in the world, bar the Great Australian Bight, and we knew from the newspapers that the air above it was equally turbulent. Rivers of wind followed the whirling course of the currents, and in many places were pits of emptiness called air-pockets where a plane might plunge to disaster.

And what would happen if they had to come down, those men? And how would they find their way? And if darkness came before they saw New Zealand, what then?

The deep and awed respect which fills the human heart when it beholds a venturesome heroism filled me, and I rolled over and put my face into the pennyroyal and thought, 'I wish he *was* my relation.'

Just at what stage the unknown aviator became my father I cannot say. I always knew perfectly well he was not. Neither was it wishful thinking, for I had rarely thought of my own father with anything save a vague curiosity. It must have been during those deeply embarrassed and resentful days when everyone was teasing me about my vanity and my new short hair that I suddenly conceived the fantasy. Almost at once my flattened ego revived. So great was the power of my vicarious imagination that I could stand placidly amidst a barrage of teasing, thinking such things as, 'You'll feel silly when you find out who I really am.'

Perhaps the deep unrecognized longing had been there all the time, to have a father I could be proud of, that I could boast of, even if it were only to the mossy encircling boughs of the peach-tree. My close-hugged and unreal secret ensnared me completely. I knew it was not true, and yet it could have been. I came from Australia, my name was Hood, therefore I could have been the daughter of a man destined to go into the history books.

For a long time just dreaming about it was sufficient. Then the glamorous haze faded a little, and I became hungry for more fuel to feed the fires of imagination. I remember drifting down the main street, my arms full of forgotten 'messages', and standing solitary and unnoticed behind gossiping couples and trios; I listened eagerly for even a phrase of a sentence about the fliers, and so great was the interest in them my eavesdropping was rarely un-rewarded.

They used to pin the telegraphed versions of the cable messages on the board in front of the *Chronicle* office. There was always a crowd round the board. The plane was not suitable for a long flight...the engine was untrustworthy ...there was no radio apparatus...the aviators were find-ing difficulty in financing their venture...the weather was too bad...the weather was getting worse...the flight was postponed.

'They've woken up. They know it can't be done,' said some people maliciously. But most folk in air-minded Te Kano knew it would be done. The councillors were so uni-formly confident that they met to discuss the quickest way of letting the town know the good news after the crossing. They decided to keep a long-distance line open to Auck-land, and then, when the post-office received the news, to ring the firebell.

Nobody saw me standing round listening and watching. No one guessed that all the upheaval and excitement was to me like hearing, far away, a lovely tune of which I was mysteriously a part.

Oh, the yearning to be significant which fills the heart of a little child! It is the first birth of personality, the estab-lishment of identity in an immeasurable and baffling world.

Now, all this time my dear friend Pola had been abom-inably irritated by my long silences, and my pompous refusal to tell her what was biting me. One day on the road to school we halted for a moment beside the firebell, a large red inverted bucket which hung in a steel scaffold beside the railway bridge. I stood and gawked at it. Gawk-ing was a recognized occupation amongst us, and nor-mally Pola would not have remarked on it. But now her

curiosity and her acute Celtic observation were too much
for her.

It was the day of the scheduled flight, and in my mind's
eye I could see the bell swinging already, humming, singing, beating, clanging out its triumphant message across
the little town and the paddocks, the guardian hills, and
the black furry bush beyond them.

Suddenly Pola jeered. 'You're stuck on them fliers!'

The attack was so quick I just stared at her. Normally
Pola and I settled our differences by fighting noisily and
viciously like two wild dogs, returning to being best friends
immediately afterwards. But this time I looked at her
fiercely and then blurted out with a choking triumph,
'Why shouldn't I? One of them's my father.'

At first Pola didn't believe me. She chased me all the
way up the hill with screeches of 'Liar!'

I was as affronted as if I hadn't been a liar. Something
in the outraged dignity of my indifference to her insults
touched her at last.

She said pleadingly, 'You're just kidding, aren't you,
Jen? Eh, Jenny? Aren't you just kidding?'

'It's true,' I flamed at her, and by then it practically
was.

Pola shrank pitiably. An enormous wave of jealousy
swept over her, and she almost foundered. After a deathly
silence she produced a small, piping voice, 'My mum's
uncle was hung.'

Pola's reaction staggered me. No one had ever produced
such a rabbit out of her ancestral hat as I had. Pola's
hanged great-uncle, hitherto a treasured family possession,
became as much of a nonentity as a hanged great-uncle
can become.

But she was still enraged with me. 'Why didn't you tell
me before?' she shouted.

'I was sworn to secrecy,' I answered loftily. That
finished Pola. Her faith in my veracity was pitiful. She

required no argument. The duplication of names and nationality was sufficient for her. In a moment she had entered into the thing with drunken abandon. Her jealousy forgotten, she warm-heartedly sketched out an alluring future for me. My father was coming to get me: he was making this flight specially for this purpose. He would come to Te Kano and the mayor would meet him at the railway station. There would probably be an awful big party given for the distinguished visitor, and I would be guest of honour.

By now we were standing face to face like two budgies in the middle of the road, excitedly enlarging on the theme. The Cuskellys would all be invited. Pola would be allowed, no doubt, to have that high-waisted yellow poplin dress she had yearned for so long, and we would have a whale of a time such as Te Kano had not seen since Te Kooti's era.

'Mum will be thrilled!' said the generous Pola. Instantly my blood stopped twinkling, and froze into a soggy mass of fear. I recalled too late that only a fence separated Mrs Cuskelly from my innocent aunts.

'No, you mustn't!' I gasped. 'It's a secret. I'm not allowed to tell anyone. I'll get into trouble if you tell your mother. Oh, promise you won't, Pola.'

She promised reluctantly, and in that reluctance I had the first awesome glimpse of the dark abyss over which I swung. I felt quite damp and prickly, and the sickish feeling started up in my stomach. What had I done? I looked at Pola surreptitiously. She had a queer abstracted appearance. The perspiration started to trickle down my backbone. For a second I almost told her it had all been a joke, but the moment passed, and there we were already in the school-room.

It was no use hoping for the best, for in my limited experience the best never happened, anyway.

How I underrated the loyalty of my friend Pola! While I

thought she was enviously contemplating betrayal, she was actually lost in wonderment over my revelation. Bemused and dazzled by my new importance, she missed every class question, turned mental arithmetic into a shambles, and was finally called out in front – a grim punishment – to be made a fool of.

At that time we had a teacher with a conversational style like a ping-pong ball. She could hit you six times with acid remarks while you were trying to summon up a sportsman-like grin as answer to the first one. Her name was Miss Carroll. She pinned the blushing Pola with a glance.

'And why haven't you your mind on your work this morning, Lady Violet?' she inquired.

Lady Violet drooped her head. 'I was excited,' she said, probing her toes bashfully along the crack in the floor-boards.

'About what? Is it your birthday?' stabbed Miss Carroll.

'No!' burst out Pola, 'But Jenny Hood's father is coming home, in an aeroplane!'

In the long-sustained sigh of astonishment which went up from the class I could already hear the crackling of electricity. Paralysed, I faced Miss Carroll's sharp and intelligent stare. In a twinkling she had added two and two together and didn't believe the answer.

'Jenny Hood! What have you been telling Violet Cuskelly, may I ask?'

'It's true,' persisted Pola. 'The man who's going to fly the Tasman, he's Jenny's father!'

Ah, if it had only been true! There was a gasp from the children, a sibilant wave of whispers that rose on the air and fainted and died. At the moment I could not appreciate it, but months afterwards, when I dared think about the incident without getting sick in the stomach, I felt a dim pang of pride. For you see, it proved I had been right. It *was* a wonderful thing to have a famous father.

Of course, even that moment had its distractions. Herbie Kirby, who had been eating surreptitiously under the raised lid of his desk, swallowed his orange in a lump sum, choked, and sprayed orange squash in all directions. Half a dozen bolder pupils yelled, 'Sez you!' which expression had but recently come to the King Country.

But most of them just stared. Their faces were like masks on·the ends of broomsticks, fixed in glares of astonishment, jealousy, and trepidation. For Pola's face was dark and puffy, and our classmates knew with gleeful terror that at any moment she would throw one of the celebrated Cuskelly scenes and be disembowelled by Miss Carroll in return.

'It's a dirty big lie,' croaked Herbie Kirby, recovered at last.

'It isn't!' said Pola passionately. 'Jenny told me and it's true. Isn't it, Jenny?'

'Goodness!' said Miss Carroll mildly, taking a good look at my transparent head and seeing my thoughts like hysterical goldfish flashing round a bowl. 'And what has Jenny to say for herself?'

One of the worst things that can happen to the everyday child is to have focused upon it the critical and suspicious attention of a crowd. I was crucified: even my eyeballs were transfixed. I could not pull them away from Miss Carroll's innocent stare. Burning sensations started in the backs of my legs. My hearing became as sharp as a needle, so that I could hear Henry Orpus, four seats behind me, breathing heavily through the hairs in his nose. A tiny voice squeaked out of me. 'I did tell Violet, Miss Carroll.'

Pola gave her head a proud jerk, like a wild pony. But Miss Carroll let the silence alone. Long seconds passed. They were so silent that the sound of someone practising in a nearby cottage came right inside the school. Each piano note sounded separately, like a glittering crack in the cold and deathly silence.

'I know that it can't possibly be true,' said Miss Carroll's chilly eyes, 'because if it were, it would have been all over Te Kano long before this.

That piercing, knowing stare drove me into a corner from which I could escape only with words. I had to say something. A sensation as of icy water filled my stomach, where I kept all my emotions. It was either say something or be sick. One thing alone stood out in the confusion of my humiliation and terror: discredit in the future was easier to face than instant reaction on the part of Miss Carroll and the school children. So I blurted out, 'And he *is* my father, too.'

Miss Carroll quelled the hubbub with one hand.

'Splendid,' she said. 'I must ring up your aunts after school and find out all about it.'

Until then, poor unsophisticate that I was, I had imagined that my aunts would not necessarily have to learn of my wickedness.

But that remark of Miss Carroll murdered my innocence. I sank back in my desk, barely noticing the triumphant swagger with which my friend Pola returned to her seat. What would Aunt Barbara *say*? She wouldn't believe I could be so evil. How could I possibly explain it? There was no explanation at all. I didn't know myself why I had done anything so foolhardy. I spent the afternoon in a daze, now and then stealing a frenzied look at Miss Carroll to see if she'd forgotten. Miss Carroll had one of those circular Oriental faces on which the features are little more than an occasional interruption – a scallop of red, a circumflex of dark brown, a tilt of blue, and you had Miss Carroll. She was well aware of our cruel and avid curiosity about her – her Christian name, her age, what she put on her face, the number of her sweethearts, and what she did in her spare time. She was the focus of this curiosity because she was a stranger, and while she understood this, she did not tolerate it.

Miss Carroll must have disliked us all as impersonally as she disliked the town. We were part of the tedious prison, the endless wet Saturdays and wetter Sundays, the cloddy men smelling of trucks and horses, the diffident, secretive women. We were chilblains, squelchy footballs, mud and wet skipping-ropes in the school porch, dripping taps, runny noses, lunch packets that smelt of sardine sandwiches.

I knew she disliked us, because she was happy I had damned myself with so big a lie. I could tell by the faint lift of her lip that she was pleased.

The moment we were let out of school I cut and ran, with Pola after me. She was bigger and longer-legged than I, and she quickly overhauled me.

'What's the matter? she asked, injured. Then, seeing the glare of hate on my face, she burst out, 'But you said I wasn't to tell *my mother*!'

This time when I ran away she didn't follow me, and when I got to the top of the railway bridge I glancd back and saw her far behind, dawdling along disconsolately.

And there on the other side of the bridge hung the firebell, mute and malignant. I stared at it, and all my fear and mortification melted into hatred of the cause of my downfall. I hated the Tasman Sea, and aeroplanes, and aviators, and the newspapers that had written about all these things. If I hadn't heard about Hood and Moncrieff none of these things would have happened. And that one especially, the one I had claimed as father, he had receded. No longer the centre of a cloudy dream, he was unreasonably the reason for all my grief. The sick coldness in my stomach uncoiled, and in a rage I glared at the firebell and thought passionately, savagely, 'I hope the bell never rings. I hope you never get here. I hope the wings tear off your plane.'

At this moment Henry Orpus poked me in the back.

Henry Orpus was a large mild beefy boy who wore

those very long, cardboardy shorts into which doting mothers often thrust their only sons. Henryorpus, as we called him, had been posthumous, and the centre of his poor mother's life, but she had not spoiled him. Still, he bore the imprint of his particular lot in life. He grew up with an outlook completely unorthodox for boys of that period.

He not only admitted the existence of girls and women, but he liked them.

This, of course, is a commonplace nowadays. In Te Kano of the twenties, though, if a boy under sixteen was seen talking to a girl, or indeed doing anything except beating her over the head, he lost all social status amongst his peers.

'He talks to the tarts,' was the expression, and I can tell you they were bitter words indeed.

But Henryorpus was different. His mother had told him there were lots of girls in the world, thousands of them, and they were people just like everyone else. Henryorpus had been known to open doors for ladies, and even raise his cap to schoolgirls. Naturally he was despised by the latter, who went on secretly yearning to be insulted by Henryorpus's appallingly impolite fellows.

But Henry didn't mind much. He went on being polite and gentle and conscious of a man's duty in this hard world, and he turned all the bounteous affections of his good simple heart to me.

My aunts thought this was charming. For one thing, they were tickled to death that their Jenny already had a suitor, and secondly they thought Henryorpus was a little gentleman. Every morning when he called to escort me to school they had me all ready, polished to a glimmering degree, and they were very disappointed and puzzled when I tore off and hid in the duck-house until Henry had gone on his way.

'But, Jenny,' explained Louisa, 'you could ride to school on the bar of Henry's bike!'

The idea brought me out in goose pimples. Fancy having my name linked with Henryorpus's, of all people!

So when he found me cursing in front of the firebell, and gently prodded my shoulder, I whipped round instantly and hit him a beauty on the nose.

At once it started to look like a plum, glossy and bluish and rounded on the end. A thin rivulet of blood came down over his chin and his big kind astonished eyes filled slowly with tears. But I didn't feel sorry. I felt glad and exhilarated. I looked at him with vindictive glee, hating him worse than I ever had. Henry slowly pulled out his handkerchief and carefully wiped his nose, which was already starting to puff up.

He said, ignoring what had gone before. 'I know how you feel. I got no father, either.'

These words, product of a kind and wise, uncomplicated and forgiving soul, have given me so many pangs since that day that I think Henryorpus, the almost forgotten, has had more effect upon me than many a more significant character.

But at the time I said brutally, 'Who'd want you for a son, anyway, you fat chook?'

The blood went on running down Henryorpus's fat and freckled chin, and the blood went on running from his stricken heart. Big boots, immensely long wool socks tucked over tremendous garters, awful pants, amiable cowlike face – I can see him yet. He had been stabbed illogically in his innermost soul, and only because I was guilty and afraid. It was then that I began to hate myself.

But all I did was to stick out my tongue at him and run away.

I didn't run far. Within a few hundred yards I had reached that state of mind which drives a respectable embezzler to suicide. The present had become worse than the future and the anticipation of disaster more terrible than the disaster. I rushed trembling between a decision to confess to my aunts, and a longing to run away and never see them again. But even if I did, how would I make myself forget that I had punched Henryorpus in the snout for being kind, and that I had actually cursed someone and wished him dead? In our family we believed solemnly in curses, both that they acted and that they boomeranged on the curser. The things old Pou the tohunga had told me – of the wicked ancient ones who could shrivel a green bough with a look and a wish. ...

Suddenly, as though someone had stuck a pin in me, I plunged off the road and up the hillside. Green leaves had made me think of watercress, and my aunts loved watercress.

I did not intend the watercress to be a propitiatory gift.

I wanted to give it to my aunts before they discovered my wickedness so that, looking back afterwards, no matter how sadly, they would be able to say, 'That was the night she gave us the watercress, poor child.'

My intense remorse drove me to pick it in the most diffi-cult place in all Te Kano, old Jackie Slew's spring. Not only was he a fierce old buster likely to rush out and give any marauding child a belt with a four-be-two, but he had a ferocious stallion pastured in the same paddock. The fact that neither danger was around that afternoon made no dif-ference. I would have crossed that paddock just the same. I pulled the dripping, mustard-hot stuff with passionate and prayerful abandon. Oh, God, that Miss Carroll would magically lose her memory, or the telephone break down, or anything at all that would make tomorrow unaffected by today!

When I sneaked in the back door I knew at once that my teacher hadn't yet rung up the aunts. There they were all sitting round with their shoes off, their *crêpe de Chine* bosoms lavishly snowed with coconut.

'Have a macaroon, Jenny,' invited Louisa. I took it humbly.

They continued their conversation. An open letter written in a queer draggle-tailed hand lay amongst the teacups.

'She'll regret it, girls, there's no doubt about it!'

'But Barbie, at least it's a home for her.'

'With Pa in it?' asked Barbara incredulously.

'Anyway, we can't send our Jenny there, can we, not unless... well, what do you think, Ailie, for the Christmas holidays, maybe?'

In a flash I forgot my sorrow. 'Send me where, auntie?' I asked eagerly.

'Well,' explained Barbara, 'this letter is from your grandpa's sister, the young one, Auntie Fedora.'

'She's going to keep house for Grandpa, you see,' said Ailie.

'Silly old article!'

'Francey!'

'Well, she must be. Besides, what about the f-a-i-r-i-e-s?' asked Louisa cautiously. As usual I pretended that I couldn't spell for nuts, but inside me an enormous question-mark reared up like a tree. Fairies? Not really?

'And she wants us to send you to stay with her for a few months to keep her company,' finished Barbara briskly, 'but of course you couldn't go away for such a long... oooh, what have you got there, Jenny?'

I timidly put out the watercress to drip on her skirt.

'Why, Jenny! Hooray, we can have it with our cold meat.'

'Where did you get it, love?'

'Jackie Slew's spring, Auntie Francey.'

'Erk! Throw it out to the ducks this very minute,' stormed Francey. 'Why, he washes his feet in that spring; Mrs Bedding saw him.'

'And we can't possibly eat watercress that's had old Typhoid Toes amongst it, can we?' cried the rest of the aunts, shrieking with laughter, so that they rained coconut crumbs in all directions.

How joyously I entered into their mirth! They didn't know, and maybe they would never know! I felt safer than I had for hours.

There was a brisk conversation about the possibility of the ducks transmitting the taint of Typhoid Toes to their eggs, then I ran out to put the watercress in their run.

And while I was there I climbed up the peach-tree to say another prayer. It was sunset, yellow as an apricot, and the station buildings a series of blocks of darkness against the blurry lights of the town.

'Oh, please, God,' I prayed, 'I take it all back. I didn't mean it. I didn't mean the wings to tear off the plane. I'm sorry. I was just pretending.'

But there was nothing but a cold wind springing up, and wild ducks calling far, far above.

Nobody was listening to me, a dark little blot in the dusky peach-tree.

I remembered those men had no radio, nothing but some crude instrument that gave a tick-tack signal. And I seemed to hear it, fading, fading away from the land, into the vast sign of the sea. What could I remember of that sea that I had crossed when I was young? Only the ink-blue mountains running, and the mollymawks circling, and the solitary albatross dallying on the wind. And the darkness, coming down as it was coming now, and making all quarters of the compass look the same.

'Oh, God, don't let them get in the dark, and I'll tell Auntie Barbara about the lies,' I vowed.

The firebell answered. It started up its rapid echoey song, ding-ding-ding-ding-*ding*, and the goods-train standing in the station gave a great joyous hoot. The signals glowed green, and all over Te Kano windows banged up and heads stuck out.

'They've made it,' people were saying. 'They've landed safely. The Tasman's been crossed by air! Who would have thought it! Ah, it was bound to come! Progress, eh?'

I slid down the peach-tree and ran hell-for-leather and my Auntie Barbara.

I made my confession directly to Aunt Barbara, though her sisters were standing on the veranda beside her. In some mysterious way I acknowledged Barbara as my chief authority. It may have been because she was the eldest, or even because of some subconscious recognition of her physical similarity to my dead mother.

How did the other Radiant Aunts take my sobbing revelation?

I can only remember that Barbara blushed with distress, and her sweet lips trembled with shock and astonishment. She took me quickly into the kitchen and shut the door lest any prowling Cuskelly should hear of this disgrace to the Admirals.

'Oh, Jenny!'

'She ought to be smacked!' cried Francey robustly. 'It'll be all over town, and you know what Te Kano is...we won't live it down for years.'

'Imagine that cat Miss Carrroll going to tell *us* about it,' said Louisa resentfully. 'Tell-tale-tit!'

'She did,' answered Ailie gently. She held out her hanky to me and said, 'Blow.'

I blew as ingratiatingly as I could.

'Ailie!' said Barbara severely. 'You mean to say you *knew* about this?'

Ailie nodded calmly. 'Yes, she rang up just before you girls came home. She ordered some cami-knicks, too.'

'Bother the cami-knicks!' cried Barbara. 'What did you say, Ailie?'

'I said she was silly to take any notice of what a small child said, and —'

'What colour cami-knicks?' asked Louisa.

'Black. Georgette.'

You should have asked her to ring again when I came home,' said Barbara a little coldly.

'Black,' marvelled Francey. 'I must say the school committee would hit the roof if they knew.'

'Oh, Auntie Ailie!' I sobbed, feeling myself left out of things.

'You girls simply aren't taking this seriously enough,' said Barbara soberly. 'Jenny's told some terrible falsehoods. I can hardly believe it, Jenny. After all we've taught you about truth and honesty.'

'Oh, Auntie Barbara!' I bawled. Ailie bent over me and rubbed her cheek on mine.

'Never you mind, Jenny dear.'

'Georgette. With flared legs, no doubt,' Francey was saying censoriously.

'And, besides, it was Miss Carroll's duty to report this to us; yes, it *was*,' insisted Barbara.

'Oh, fiddle!' said Louisa. 'A girl who wears black camiknicks. *She* can talk!'

'Louisa!'

I began to feel quite forgotten. I hastily produced a watery beam.

'But it's all right, isn't it?' I quavered. 'Because the curse didn't work.'

'What curse?' asked Auntie Barbara, a look of dread creeping over her pretty face.

'I cursed them,' I mumbled. 'I said I hoped the wings would rip off the plane and they'd drop into the water.'

Well, that tore it. Any sympathy Francey and Louisa had had for me melted like frost. They stared at me in authentic horror. A dark and pagan Sweden looked out of their eyes: a Druidic faith in curses, and a Christian abhorrence of them. My furtive glance wavered, and I shut my eyes to get away from those three stares of aghast belief. Out of my darkness I mumbled dully, 'And then I gave Henryorpus a bloody nose.'

But nobody cared about Henry's unlucky beak. They ignored it.

Choking and sobbing I was bundled off to bed and left in the dark with the door shut. Now and then I crept to the door and eavesdropped. Above the agitated clinking of teacups I could hear such phrases as, 'But, Barbie, curses, at her age!' And, 'Do you think she could possibly take after Pa?'

I crept back to bed and wept satisfactorily for my evil deeds. When that was finished I lay there, hungry but content, marvelling in a silent, bashful way over the uproar I had created. Had I really done all this by myself? A slow contempt built up in me for the grown-ups who could get so upset over a few lies. They told lies themselves: I knew very well they did. But it seemed to be different for children. I puzzled over this for some time, sinking meanwhile deeper and deeper into a warm, radiant pleasure that my curse had failed. I forgot the hate I had had for those airmen only that afternoon. They were friends of mine once more; successful friends, which is much better. I thanked God with vehement sincerity for His mercy.

'Oh, God,' I promised, 'if the kids tease me at school tomorrow I won't say a word. And if Miss Carroll is nasty to me I won't mind. I'll do this to make up to You for being kind.'

But this is not the way it turned out. In the morning I discovered that the airmen had never reached New Zealand at all. Their tiny plane had flown out from the shores of Australia, vanished in the sea-smoke, and was never seen again.

I couldn't, wouldn't, believe it.

'I heard the firebell ringing,' I said loudly and truculently.

'It was a false alarm, a misunderstood telephone message from Auckland,' said Louisa sadly. 'Poor, poor men.'

'It was just somebody's rotten idea of a joke, if you ask me,' cried Francey angrily.

Barbara saw the look on my face.

'Jenny, you didn't do it. It was just an accident,' she said quickly.

I went straight back into my room and got under the bed.

My life was finished. I had killed two people and dragged down an aeroplane from the sky. Shuddering and gasping, sweating and retching, I crouched down like an animal in the half-light and wished I were dead.

There was a tremendous commotion in that part of the world surounding the bed. Feet pattered this way and that, and up in the stratosphere agitated consultations took place.

'Of course she didn't do it, Francey, you silly article. How could she?'

'Oh, I wish Desmond was here!'

'For heaven's sake, Louie! Keep that great dinosaur out of this.'

'Francey, you horrid little cat, don't you dare. . . . Barbie! She called Desmond a dinosaur.'

'Barbara, don't frighten Jenny, just coax her.'

'I know perfectly well how to go about it, thank you, Ailie. Jenny, come out at once, dear.'

Dimly I heard these words, split, high-pitched, slightly reverberant. My fright was affecting my hearing. It had me by the throat so that I could neither scream nor speak. I could hear nothing clearly but that unendurable drum-like voice within me. 'You did it. You killed them.'

I saw the broken plane like a sycamore seed on the black waters, and the sea-birds circling and watching for death. These birds haunted me. More than the fish they haunted me – leathery gloss on looping necks, strong boomerang wings bent to the wind's bend, fierce and barbarous eyes, coloured like hazel and walnut, soulless and single-purposed!

'No, no!' I shouted suddenly. 'Go away! Go away!'

But it was to the birds I spoke.

Barbara spoke sharply. 'No, we won't go away, Jenny. Now, you just come out this moment or we shall have to pull you out.'

I crouched closer to the floor.

'Francey, you get over on that side of the bed and push her out.'

'I can't bend. I'm wearing short suspenders.'

Barbara wailed. 'Oh, Louisa, then you. *Please*. The poor child's hysterical, that's all. No, push the bed over first, Louisa. That's right. Now shove Jenny over towards me.'

As Louisa pushed the bed, I scuttled over with it so that I was still equidistant from the sides. I stuck my fingers firmly through the interstices of the wire mattress and braced myself. Two shingled heads bent down and poked under the bed.

Louisa tried the rallying touch. 'You *are* a funny little bunny. Come on out and I might find something nice for you.'

Barbara was firmer. 'Darling, you can't stay under there all your life. Come out and let's talk it over.'

I stiffened myself and remained silent.

'Well, we'll have to come underneath and get you, that's all.'

I gave a terrible bark which they interpreted as defiance but which was really a bit of kapok fluff in my throat, and they both got down on hands and knees and came crawling under the bed. None but Radiant Aunts would do such a thing, for adults are at an appalling disadvantage on the floor. They kept up an agitated commentary all the time, and Ailie and Francey joined in, off mike.

'Get her round the middle, Louisa. Oh, Jenny, don't be so difficult. Let go, there's a sweet little. ... Look, Louie, the little demon has hooked herself up to the wire mattress ... do you think she could have gone off her bat, Francey? ...Jenny, *let go* this moment! Louisa, you can't be trying.... Pull, Louie! Undo her fingers. Oh, Jenny. Please, Jenny darling, let go for Auntie Barbara. *Jenny!*'

It wasn't until Francey heaved off the mattress, and undid my fingers from above, an unfair and unsportsman-like move, that the two under-bed aunts managed to drag me from my moorings. By then I was so exhausted I was almost delirious. I began to shriek and kick, so that it took three of them to get me into bed, while the fourth ran for Mrs Cuskelly to send Vi'let for the doctor.

All day long I tried to die, but I felt too well. By evening, the shock had died down and I was ravenously hungry. But I knew, after the day's commotion, that it would be mean to eat. It seemed to make all the aunts' anxiety wasted and unnecessary. So, although it was an agony, I sent away untasted the glorious supper Francey brought in to me.

I felt a little better when I heard her say, out in the kitchen, 'She didn't even *peck* at it, poor little dear.'

When all was dark and quiet at last, I cried hard and silently. A tearless child as a rule, I had wept more in that twenty-four hours than in the rest of my life. My eyes ached and stung as I lifted them to see a vague light in the room.

It was a round light, halated at the edges, a gentle drowsy light from a candle, held close and sheltered by my smallest, youngest aunt, Ailie.

Whenever I read of an angel appearing to a mortal I think of Ailie as she was then, in her long white night-dress, close as a sheath, her silvery short hair giving her the look of a young boy. The candlelight shone upon the lobes of her ears, her shell-like eyelids, the brief creamy line of nose and chin.

I thought, 'Maybe Auntie Ailie is really an angel after all.'

She came closer to me. 'I had a bad dream,' she whispered. 'May I get in with you?'

I moved over silently, and this slight seraphic form, smelling of innocence like a peach-tree in bloom, puffed out the candle and slid down beside me.

In this narrative my Auntie Ailie does not often speak, and that is true of her. She had a mysterious restraint, not cold, not even aloof, an exquisite, retiring modesty that cannot be described.

There was a poem once about St Brigid. It began this way:

Brigid the daughter of Duffy, she wasn't like other young things . . .

That was Ailie, Ailie, the daughter of Syver, she wasn't like other young things.

And she was seventeen years old.

She was cold that night. Through the nightdress her skin had the firm chill of marble. Her slender feet were like arches carved in stone. But I lay there distrustfully, not even wanting to put my arms round her to warm her up. I knew adults. They came creeping subtly upon a child, and when she was least suspecting it, they pierced her to the heart with a reproach. So we lay there in the darkness.

The countryside breathed in the window. There was the acid odour of cut grass, the sweet metallic dankness of wet gravel on the river-banks, the secret mousy smell of the morepork that humped in the willow beyond the sill. I saw his shadow pass across the floor, but there was no sound from his down-edged wing feathers.

Ailie said, 'Next week it's your mother's birthday.'

What could this be? An introduction perhaps to a scolding which had as a theme my mother's disappointment in a daughter who lied, put curses on people, and gave little gentlemen bloody noses?

I said sullenly, 'How old would my mum be?'

'Twenty-eight.'

The little silence emboldened me. 'Who did she look like?'

'She had fair hair like me, but she looked like Auntie Barbara, I think.'

'Don't you know?'

'I was only eleven when she took you to Australia.'

'Was I nice?' I was overcome to hear myself say this, and rapidly amended it. 'Was he nice, my father?'

'He had brown hair and a soft silk shirt and dark-blue eyes.'

'Like the best china teapo?'

'Yes.'

I had long had a photograph of my distant father. Now with a deep satisfaction I fitted it out with brown hair and eyes like the teapo. I had never thought to ask questions about him, and the Radiant Aunts had not volunteered any information because, as I was perfectly aware, they disliked him. Now I asked timorously, 'Shouldn't my mum have married him?'

'Yes, because she loved him.'

'Would you marry a man you l-liked, if Grandpa and Auntie Barbie and Auntie Olga and the Hen and Chickens and Father FitzPeter and everyone were against him?'

'Yes.'

Auntie Ailie's voice gave the word the precise and unequivocal sound of a stroke on a bell. I became aware that beneath her chaste delicacy was a will made of solid ivory.

It made me so uncomfortable that I thumped over on to my side and tried to sleep. But I couldn't. Already the ghosts of my schoolmates and Miss Carroll were gibbering at me. I had remembered I had to go back to school and face their jeering laughter, her hard little icicle eyes.

My sorrow for the lost airmen, my intense remorse for my sins vanished instantly. These emotions became no more than discomforts in my stomach. The ordeal of going back to school loomed up as a horrifying prospect. Dread made me sweat coldly.

'I can't go, I can't go!' I gasped.

Auntie Ailie put her arms round me and hugged me. 'And you shan't, either,' she said. 'Not even if I have to catch chickenpox and give it to you.'

The aunties did not ask me to get up the next morning, or the next. I lay as quiet as a mouse, languid with reaction to shock, listening to the small pleasant sounds of the household. From without came the sisterly conversations of the ducks in the vegetable beds, and the steady swish-swash of Mrs Cuskelly's scrubbing-brush.

'Come on there, get up off yer hind shoulders,' she chided her husband. 'Chop me some stove-wood, or yer likely to get the floor-cloth across the moosh.'

'Saints and patience, aren't you the awful woman?' said his fading voice.

Sometimes I collapsed into weak tears, for my receding guilt and my approaching shame.

'She hasn't had a good hot nourishing meal for three days,' whispered Louisa like a mourning dove. Light feet moved gently beside my bed, where I lay apparently fast asleep.

'Poor little motherless child,' sighed Barbara.

'Oh, Thora, Thora, I hope we haven't failed you,' said Louisa sadly. I knew they were looking down on me contemplatively, and I made my top pyjama button rise and fall in skilful imitation of exhausted slumber.

'Well, she can't stay home from school for ever, good heavens' said Francey sharply. A testy resentment clenched my toes. Trust Auntie Francey to be there busy-bodying instead of grieving, like the others.

'Well, perhaps we could get her up tomorrow.'

As their voices were stilled by the gentle shutting of the door I rolled over on my face and chewed the pillow in an agony of terror. I wouldn't go. I just wouldn't. I couldn't face Miss Carroll without dropping dead. But what could I do?

'I could just sit down in the kitchen and refuse to move,' I thought, remembering that dramatic scene under the bed. I had a vivid daydream of the aunts brutally beating me over the head with the short-handled coal-shovel, and myself, bleeding and half unconscious, still indomitably refusing to move an inch. Finally my dead body thumped on the floor, and I gave a great croak of sympathy and sorrow. It was terrible, terrible.

But the next morning when Barbara told me to get up, I did so, unable to think of suitable first steps in my sit-down strike. I tottered wanly out to the kitchen, gave my breakfast a sickly look, and sat down in the big chair beside General Smuts, crying.

'Oh, Jenny, do stop it!' commanded Barbara.

Ailie was finishing her dressing in the kitchen. There she stood in a scoop-necked petticoat of apricot cambric, threaded round the hem with orange ribbon which exactly matched her ruched and frilled satin garters. In one hand she held a tiny vial of perfume, in the other a shoe. She was using a heel to batter the glass stopper out of the bottle.

'It's perfectly silly,' she said calmly, between blows. 'After all, Barbie, it's only a month until the new convent school opens...ooh, smell, Francey!'

Francey stopped scrambling eggs and took a lingering breath.

'Love's Dream,' she said. 'I must say it's stronger than Velvet Sin. But we can't keep Jenny home until it *does* open, Ailie dear.'

'I think it's a bit cabbagey,' said Louisa critically.

'Oh, Louie, really! Nowhere near as cabbagey as Flaming Youth. And, anyway, I don't see why not, when she'd be leaving school at the end of the month to go to the convent, wouldn't she, Barbie?'

'Desmond loves Flaming Youth,' said Louisa, a little resentfully.

'Well, yes, she would,' admitted Barbara. 'And she does look pale and peaky.'

'Of course he does,' agreed Francey with a gurgle. Louisa began to flicker round the table with plates and a hurt expression.

Ailie wriggled into her tussore frock, which was perfectly oblong and belted round the hips with a broad sash of dark-green marocain. She looped round her neck a tremendous string of amber beads as large as pigeons' eggs. They came right down to the jazz garters, and threw a scatter of dark-golden lights over the sash.

'Personally,' she said, 'I think we should send Jenny away to Auntie Fedora for a holiday, until the new school opens.'

Three of the aunts looked at each other with those intense looks every child out of the cradle can so fluently read. Louisa went on huffily laying plates.

I humped myself up like a cockroach and closed my eyes, sick with relief. I was praying.

'Oh, St Anthony, thank you,' I was saying. 'I'll make it up to you somehow, I truly will.'

Something more seemed to be needed, and I searched round in my memory for that splendid expression of ultimate praise which the films had recently brought to Te Kano.

But the words 'cats pyjamas' escaped me.

'Oh, St Anthony!' I sent the prayer up to heaven like choicest incense. 'You're the pussy's pants.'

'But *Pa*'s there,' quavered Francey.

'Fedora will love Jenny. She'll look after her like a chook with a chick,' answered Barbara firmly.

'I would like to know, Frances,' said Louisa in stately tones, 'what you *meant* when you said that about Desmond.'

'And she'll miss us so,' said Francey.

Ailie swooped on me, and pressed my face into that soft spot delicious with Love's Dream. 'Of course she will, but she's a big brave girl and she knows a holiday is going to make her well and strong again for her aunties.'

I became a big brave girl instantly.

'Did you or did you not, Frances, mean that Desmond liked Flaming Youth because it is cabbagey, not that it is?' said Louisa in loud clear tones.

'Don't you take that tone of voice with me, Louisa Admiral,' retorted Francey spiritedly. 'I merely meant that Desmond is flaming with love for you—'

'Francey, not before the child!' said Barbara faintly.

'And if you're going to twist every compliment I make, and it was a sincere compliment too, Louisa Admiral, into an unpleasant remark, then I shan't speak to you at all. So there,' concluded Francey, throwing down her spoon and leaving the eggs to scramble by themselves.

It took all Barbara's wit and wisdom and Louisa's offer of a loan of her gold-chain evening purse before Francey would even think of speaking to her again. Meanwhile Ailie and I had eaten our breakfast, and Ailie was saying, 'And think how adventurous it will be to go to Kawhia all by yourself!'

'What in?'

'A coach!'

A coach! Oh, the magic rumble of big gold wheels, and a coachman sitting high and conceited, with a cold red nose sticking out over his topmost cape collar! And myself within, like Cinderella, travelling to Kawhia and Auntie Fedora!

No need to see Miss Carroll ever again! If I met her in the street I could slide into a shop, or screw up my face and pretend to be someone else. And as for the children, well, I would outlive their jeers in time.

I was drunk with relief and happiness.

Proud and important, and still scared, I kept to my own backyard. Whenever I saw Pola's shadow sneaking along on the other side of the fence I scuttled inside. But one day she caught me. Her lovely soot-rimmed blue eyes and her wild pony's forelock appeared over the fence.

'Is it right that you're going away to live in Kawhia?' she asked with a sullen, uninterested expression.

'I'm going to have a holiday because I've been sick,' I answered, humbly waiting for her accusation or disbelief. But Pola had forgotten all my evil doings.

'Is it catching?' she asked excitedly.

'I think so,' I said.

'Is it a mysterious disease?' she asked.

'I think so,' I said cautiously. Pola tossed her head triumphantly.

'I *knew* you had somepin awful,' she said, out of the depths of her loyal friendship. I dawdled inside, feeling something strange and wonderful inside me. It was the first recognition of true friendship, the sort of thing felt by Betty Barton and Polly Linton, and all the other remarkable girls in *The Schoolgirls' Own*.

The catchingness of my disease was swiftly spread round Te Kano, and no one came to play with me except Huriana Hana, whose parents, wise and sober, understood very well the complaint from which I suffered.

Huriana never mentioned school, or the other children. Her soft placidity was as soothing as oil; even the look of her was enough to make me feel all was well. Though with Pola my games were all noisy, turbulent, and reckless, when I was with Huriana I played statues, and dressing up, and pretending, and house – all games which the aunts described as ladylike. Huriana rarely spoke, and when she did the thrilling violin-string quality of a Maori voice made each word worth saying. Against that sound my shrill chirp was like a kingfisher chick's.

'Sing to us, Huriana,' my Auntie Ailie would say, and

sometimes Huriana would just stand there, mute, flushing, her thick pale-amber eyelids drooping to hide those eyes where the lamplight made small golden speckles as though in water. Other times she sang, and'in her singing was the melancholy sound of voices mourning in distant islands, echoing across lagoons long forgotten. Though we were so far inland, the sea spoke in Huriana's voice, as it spoke in the shell I had brought with me from Australia.

Every night Huriana's big brother Donald called in on his way from work to escort her home. Her parents did not allow her to be out alone in the dusk.

Donald would stand in the shadow of the porch, asking in his deep shy voice for his sister, and would never come in.

He was perhaps twenty, and his hair was like tui feathers for blackness and softness.

I think I remember the very moment Donald Hana and Ailie fell in love.

Supposing the pagans were right, and love is indeed an exterior force – a random shot from a bow, a shake of the branch by some unknown Hand – would it not explain such phenomena as love at first sight?

Huriana and I were hiding in the dark parlour, peeping out of the bow-window as Donald came up the steps. Giggling, we watched him knock and the door open.

'We'll pretend you've disappeared,' I suggested, 'and then you can stay here all night.'

Huriana assented gravely. We saw Donald and Auntie Ailie walk to the edge of the porch and peer out into the dusk. She was on the step below him, her silvery hair level with his chin.

The night wind rose from the river; crickets scraped sharply in the grass.

They were not unlike in their stillness and silent modesty, this fair girl and the dark, strange boy.

The beautiful delicacy of their response to each other

109

was in their faces. They neither moved nor spoke. It was a chaste, infinitely gentle obedience to circumstance.

I felt awkward and afraid, observing and not recognizing, feeling myself on the outer edge of a spell.

I gave Huriana a rough, angry push. 'Go on, don't you see him waiting for you?'

Huriana went without a word, and I saw her join her brother. They said good-bye soberly, and disappeared into the thickening dusk, a prince and a princess, walking with deerlike quietness.

When I awoke in the morning I had forgotten what I had seen. There was nothing there but the memory of something uncomfortable, soon lost in the tremendous excitement of going away.

The aunts had made me two new frocks and turned and re-trimmed all the old ones. The gem of the collection was my travelling ensemble, a sailor outfit in dark-blue Indian Head, with a square collar outlined with white bias-binding, and a snappy pleated skirt about four inches long. I was enravished with this. The moment I put it on I felt strong and bold and boyish, able to face whatever perils Kawhia and Grandpa could offer.

The coach left very early, for in those days the road to Kawhia was clay a good deal of the way, and vehicles were always getting stuck for hours. At seven in the morning I was ready, tossing my sailor collar, prancing about in an ecstasy of excitement, saying yes to all the anxious advice I was getting, and thinking, in odd moments, of those four lovely white horses which would pull the coach.

What was my fury and disappointment when we reached the depot to find that the coach was really a colossal tin Lizzie with a frightful figure. She looked exactly as though someone had placed a careless hand on her silly little radiator and pushed, thus shoving the whole body back on the rear axle. She was hung all over with luggage, kitbags, hamper, swags, coops of chickens, and a meat-safe, inside were four Dalmatian boys with red embroidered waistcoats and bashful smiles, two pink farmer women who had come down to Te Kano to find babies and had found them, and a very small bit of seat reserved for me.

I was too ashamed of my Cinderella dreams to confess that the coach was such a sodden disappointment to me. Dismally I wedged myself into the small seat. A wet piece of baby overlapped onto my knees, and I looked away in horrid foreboding.

'She looks sick already,' I heard Louisa mutter. A handful of paper bags was thrust into my lap.

'And suck this.' Half a lemon magically appeared from Francey's bag.

Crimson and ashamed, I was kissed by them all. The Dalmatian boys eyed the aunts and muttered melodiously into one another's long foreign haircuts. The tin Lizzie shook like a bee-stung horse as the driver cranked her madly. Sweat poured off his forehead.

'Gawd, she's a proper cow!' he gasped, giving the crank handle one more terrific jerk. The motor started with a terrifying bark, the driver leapt in, and we were ready.'

The aunts presented me with four brave smiles.

'Hooray!' I yelled.

As we swept past the smiles I saw Henryorpus standing by the water-tank, cap arranged mathematically upon his freckled forehead, schoolbag in hand. Something soft and tender swelled in my heart. His nose looked as normal as it ever did, but I could not forget it puffy and hurt and dripping with blood. Remorse swamped me, and I longed to say something memorable that would wipe out the memory of the injury I had done him. But all I did was to hang over the edge of the coach and scream, 'Hullo, polecat!'

He must have thought I said something else, for he waved his cap and grinned, and I nudged my way back in the very small seat, seeking comfort for my long journey.

I was frightfully sick the whole way, and it must have

been with joy and gratitude that the driver finally roared into the main street in Kawhia, and I was decanted into the arms of the thinnest aunt in the world.

Aunt Fedora was perfectly aware of the fact that I had been sent to Kawhia in disgrace. This should have meant on her part a certain chill reserve, the occasional moist eye and sadly shaken head, as though I were a parlourmaid seduced by the Bad Lord Byron. But she was only too eager to forget my shady past. She was, in a mild way, in disgrace herself. I had an imaginary father, and she had f-a-i-r-i-e-s.

I can still see her, standing there in the dust beside the darkening road, the sunset putting a charm of gold on her foolish hat, and changing her hueless hair and skin to metallic silver. Her arms and legs were so long, her form so narrowly angular that she seemed, in her stillness, like some magical robot aunt. And there was, just behind her, the harbour like a pewter plate, a coal-black wharf paddling with spindly legs, and the liquid flutter of the evening tide.

Thus, whenever I think of Auntie Fedora, the gentle sound of water comes too, and the salt-sodden smell of seagrass, lying all one way, like combed hair.

She advanced doubtfully, and I stood frozen with shyness, and smelling awfully of my long, misadventurous journey.

'I yust know it is little Yenny!'

The next moment she had clapped me in an intricate knot of arms and legs to her bosom, and I was sniffing into that iron collar-bone, 'I want my Auntie Barbie, I want my Auntie Louie!'

'Vy don't you vant Auntie Fedora?'

Now, whilst Uncle Olga spoke normal English, and Grandpa a coarse and broken mixture which would have fallen aptly from the beak of a Swedish seagull, Auntie Fedora came pleasantly between the two. She had re-

mained in their homeland longer than her sister Olga, and
her tongue still had trouble with J's and W's. Yet she was
anxious to speak only the best English. She was, in fact, so
refined, that I was later to hear her refer to a statue as the
burst of a Greek god.

Ashamed of my tears, I looked hastily for my luggage.
It was a canvas kitbag. There it sat on its circular leather
backside in the dust. The coach and the Dalmatians had
vanished like magic, doubtless terrified lest I should climb
back and be sick just once more for luck.

I was swamped with homesickness. I wanted either to
die or be back in the kitchen at home, with Francey pes-
tering me about washing my disgusting filthy hands for
tea. In this indecisive agony I followed Auntie Fedora docilely along the wharf. If she had walked off the end I
would have followed, splashing to my doom in a daze of
hypnotized obedience. I was actually in the little rusty
launch before I woke up.

'Where are we going? Where are we going?'

'Home, dolling.'

I was not so much horrified as shocked and disapproving of the sight of a lady standing there in a silly little hat
driving a launch. I knew very well Barbara wouldn't like
it.

We bounded out on the deep water, the little lights of
Kawhia ran together in a blur, the sea breathed vastly,
and the cold fresh airs of the outer ocean funnelled in over
the bar. Against the southern saffron I saw a high jetty
shoreline like a castle wall.

Fedora pointed. 'You see, Yenny?'

On the cliff was a little house as square as a book.
Coldly I looked at it. A fat lot I cared about their old
house. They said it was at Kawhia and it *wasn't*. Starved,
chilled, every inch an orphan, I turned away and glared
over the side, to see the pallid ghost of a big stingaree flap
away like a bat under the keel.

That finished it. I didn't stop bawling until Fedora had me landed, fed, washed, and in bed. Protestingly I fell asleep, to the dim, haunted strains of Al Jolson, wailing somwhere in the house.

In the morning things were quite different. Already, during the night, the new environment had crept in, patted my various monitors on the head, and made itself at home. True, I thought of the Radiant Aunts with boundless love, but they had already receded considerably. They were like lovely books I had once read, and was quite content to know they were there on the shelf, waiting for me to pick them up again.

I approached breakfast with mingled desire and terror. Would Grandpa be there? But he never came to breakfast. Like many old people he needed very little sleep, spending most of the night mooching round playing the Pig Man's phonograph, fighting the mosquitoes, and brooding over the past. Consequently his idea of breakfast was a chew of tobacco and a cursing fit.

'Now, dolling,' said Fedora lovingly, 'the girls say I must build you up,' and she handed me a tumbler of some thick creamy fluid. In my new role as docile, eager-to-be-rehabilitated criminal, I drank it down, regardless of the outraged commotion from my taste-buds. A few moments afterwards a strange sensation filled me. My astral body dislocated itself from the physical, a faintly pink, dreamy haze enveloped everything, and the world was all of a sudden filled with springtime. I was a shade shickered.

'Oook!' I remarked. Auntie Fedora beamed.

'You can't beat old man's milk,' she commented.

Old man's milk, compounded of honey, brandy, raw egg, and fresh cream, would have built up Tutankhamen's mummy. I was squeezing out of my clothes in a fortnight.

Alone of all the tribe, Fedora had retained the family name of Albrechtsen, and until people learnt differently, some pretty scandalous rumours about Miss Albrechtsen and old Mr Admiral went about Kawhia. Sodom and Gomorrah, it seemed, were in full fling at Te Maika, which was the name of the remote headland across the bar where Grandpa had perversely decided to live. Naturally, it was locally known as The Mike. But although Grandpa could have been Gomorrah personified, no one who had really looked at Auntie Fedora believed scandal of her. She had that pure, gentle, snubby type of Scandinavian face, its beauty ruined in her case by two enormous rabbity front teeth. I think Grandpa had the same before some friend banged them with a bottle during a conversation in Pernambuco in '97. Still, this didn't stop him from giving her hell about them.

She was ardent, sensitive, and idealistic, and in her the Viking spirit had taken a form peculiar to females. It did not wear a horned helmet, but it got there in the end.

Her presence in Grandpa's house proved this. Long ago he had sworn no broddy vimmin would share his roof, but there she was, whipping up old man's milk-shakes and building people up in all directions.

She was like one of those humble dogs who apologize for their existence every time you look at them, gladly heap ashes on their heads at a glance from your Napoleonic self ... and then, the next time you look round, are curled up on your rug in front of your fire.

Fighting Auntie Fedora must have been like fighting a blancmange. She gave, she receded, she surrendered, and then one day you suddenly woke up to realize you were blancmange from crown to toes.

By the time I arrived at Kawhia Grandpa already had a pitiful feeling that he was sunk. You could see it in his desperate glance, his anxious tempestuousness, his intuitive terror that one day this awful woman would have him completely in her power, probably feeding him good nourishing broth from a baby's bottle, and talking to him soothingly about the lovely tombstone he was going to have.

But oh, there was nothing malicious about Auntie Fedora. She was only a good sweet woman who needed a dolling of her own. As Grandpa plainly could never be this, she chose me instead, at least for the duration of my visit.

Grandpa's dwelling at The Mike was a small, paintless Early Edwardian villa, like a bashed-in hat, with a cat-walk veranda running all the way round. On top of that cliff the healthful sea-breeze reached such velocity it was a wonder we didn't take off for Melbourne, house and all. A thin thread of path sneaked timorously down the cliff to the beach. Auntie Fedora didn't like it because one misty morning she had seen a sea-elemental crawling up it, inching along like a colossal slug. Grandpa didn't care. He said any broody nonsense that came crawling up his path would cop it, if he met it.

Every morning he stumped down to the beach to do his fishing. I would wait until the broad bowed figure, on its knobbly bare feet, had arrived on the sand. Then I would skitter down after him. This was not because we wanted to be together, but because I wasn't allowed to play on the beach unless 'someone was there.'

I spent the morning in a timeless daze of delight, no thoughts in my head, nothing but physical sensations to mark my existence. I was identified with the wheeling blackcaps, the pink-flashing snappers, and the surf which crashed in vaporous ruin upon the bar. So nothing concrete remains in my memory of that rapturous dissolution but the humped figure of my Grandpa, in his little old canvas hat, hurling an invisible line with graceful centrifugal movements of his strong arm.

When Fedora waved from the veranda it was an interruption and a resentment, until my stomach gave a growl of joy at the thought of food. Then I would wait, meekly, until Grandpa had scrunched upwards with his fish, before I, too, ascended, my sandshoes crisping on the snow-white pipi-shells.

It was a week before I could sit at that table and raise my eyes. For whenever I glanced up Grandpa would be staring at me. He had a horrid habit of throwing one arm protectingly round his plate, as though he expected people to snatch it from him. Over his defensive arm he would glare, meanwhile majestically grinding away with those broken teeth.

Fear stiffened my tongue, and once I discovered him looking at me it became a mechanical impossibility to swallow. I would simply sit, my mouth full of something unchewed, praying.

'Vimmin,' he grunted. 'I hate 'em. Look at Fedora dere. Buck toots. Ugerly vimmin.'

Tears would start instantly to Aunt Fedora's milky-blue eyes.

'And vot you tink, Yannie? he would resume. 'Her...she sees tings.'

This was true, Fedora saw lots of tings, and she was teaching me to see them too. An advanced and romantic Theosophist, the world was full of manikins to her. She couldn't throw the tea-leaves away in the scrub without seeing flocks of Little Folk doing something whimsical.

Having but newly vowed always to adhere to the truth, my first impression of Auntie Fedora was that she was an even more frightful liar than myself. I treated her first shy revelations about etheric substances and astral bodies with a shocked chilliness. Then I flamed with indignation. Here was I, banished to Kawhia merely because I had spread it round that the wrong man was my father, and here was Auntie Fedora, probably with a tongue as black as a nigger's ear, unpunished and uncondemned. It all went to show, as my friend Pola said, that grown-ups could get away with anything.

But she was so matter-of-fact about it that gradually, in spite of my embarrassment, I was convinced. There is something fascinating about a person who, on the way home from the store with a basket of groceries, can dart into the tea-tree to see the brownies, *and means what she says*.

These tiny creatures did not float about aimlessly. On the contrary they were tiresomely busy, vibrating round trees and plants of all kinds, and even Grandpa's canvas hat. After Auntie Fedora had told me of the crowds of diminutive elf-forms, green and gelatinous, which crowded the brim of that hat, 'venerating and tending,' I could never look at it again without a shudder.

She was patient with my lack of clairvoyance. She herself had tried for thirty years before she finally found vision. So I was encouraged, and spent much of my time squinting passionately at leaves and stems, finding praying mantises, spider-eggs, and fungus forests of all kinds, but no manikins.

Dearly I wanted to see a fairy. I would never be able to tell the Radiant Aunts about it, and if I told Pola she would be sure to blurt it out and cause me great sorrow, but I wanted to have the secret experience for myself.

'Oh, St Anthony,' I prayed, 'please let me see a fairy, and not one of those other awful things.'

For Auntie Fedora had told me, with a tight, nervous drawing of lips over the buck toots, that once the vision came, one was quite likely to see those greater nature-spirits, the mild and magnificent devas, who poised amidst the feathers of the clouds; super-human forms twenty feet high, with brilliant tilted eyes, and auras like peacock wings.

That was alarming enough, but what about those others, the elementals, evil sub-things, such as the one that crawled like a slug up the beach path?

'You would never see such a thing, Yenny,' she comforted me. 'A child is good and innocent, and does not understand evil.'

I wasn't so sure.

118

Only once did something inexplicable happen to me. Often, when we went into Kawhia, we saw from afar the crooked crouching grove of ancient tea-tree which sheltered the buried Tainui. Nobody in Kawhia doubted that the old Maoris had buried their canoe there, after its adventurous voyage from its lost and legendary homeland. You could plainly see the long canoe-shaped subsidence in the ground. Usually, somewhere amongst the manuka lurked the very old, malevolent guardian of the grove, ready to shoo any Kodak-bearing white tourist away. I whole-heartedly believed the tale I had heard round Kawhia that many years before this same old Maori had let a tardy tourist have a tomahawk where it wasn't appreciated.

This day he was nowhere to be seen. Auntie Fedora and I had been mushrooming. We had a basketful as we came over the hills towards the grove. It was an eminently un-eerie day, blue, gay, the hoary manuka leaves turning green-bronze and silver in the shore wind. The sound of the sea was a happy sigh.

'Let's go down to the Tainui!' Auntie Fedora was alarmed and excited at her own daring. I plodded down the track after her, a little reluctant, because I thought the old man might be hiding somewhere in the tree-shadows, and I didn't like tomahawks.

In a moment we were within the grove. We saw the sunken outline of the canoe which had not wed the water for six hundred years.

'Concentrate, dear,' said Aunt Fedora. 'You might see a dear little brown Maori fairy!'

So I concentrated.

I shut down my ears until the sea-sound was no more than a rustle, and shut up my nose to the strong native smell of sand and unploughed earth, for to the nimble nose of a young child a scent can be more disturbing than sight to her eyes. Then I was ready to stare and stare at what

119

was before me. Nothing it was, except the little javelin shapes of blue sky seen through the tea-tree, the coppery light that ran round the edges of the bristly leaves, the clotted, tissue-thin bark, the polished quartered berries.

All these things took on a flat and depthless dazzle: they were a hypnotic pattern imprinted on the air. They had no reality, and yet were the full content of my mind.

And suddenly I was drowning. One moment the sky and the tea-tree were there, and then, all at once I was in the water, and my last breath was gulping past my eyes in misshapen silvery bubbles. The bellowing of the blood in my ears was like gunfire. Then the thick glassy green above me broke, and I was tossed high into the air, spilling water like a broken bottle and suffocated by the rush of oxygen into my lungs. There was the blaze of daylight, gulls blowing like bits of paper, surf smoking on basaltic ledges, and then the green cat's-paws of the sea reached me down again to the bottom, where I settled, sunken and dead, against the blackened elbow-bend of the Tainui's bow.

I stood in the sun shuddering uncontrollably, with sweat pouring down my face and back, and Auntie Fedora squawking, 'Here he comes! Oh, God, oh, Yenny! Run, run!'

The recurrence of the real world was so great a shock to me I could not move a finger. I saw the old Maori coming down the hillside waving his stick and mouthing sinister things. Panic-stricken, Fedora dragged me along behind her, whimpering in Swedish. I fell and hurt my knees, and the small sticky heat of the blood was welcome because it was real. The old man's voice grew suddenly louder as a voice does on the radio when you turn up the volume. His old, blue-scribbled face, and the hair white as tow, came keenly into focus. My muscles loosened, and I galloped after Auntie Fedora, mushrooms bouncing from the basket at every step. The poor woman was trying to undo the wire loop on the gate which separated the sacred ground from the profane, safe roadway. She failed, clambered over it, and fell on the other side, screeching all the time: 'Yump, Yenny, yump!'

I jumped like a steeplechaser, and we scuttered away down the road, a haggard pair of trespassers, frightened out of our wits. Yet, the moment Auntie Fedora was in the launch, she asked avidly, 'Did you ... did you see one of the Little People, Yenny?'

I wouldn't have told her of my experience for the world. The very memory of it made me ill in the stomach. She must have seen the greasy shine on my forehead, for she kept silence. Before we reached home I had come out all over in hives, great white welts that itched abominably. Uncommonly grave, and I think filled with an overwhelming guilt, Aunt Fedora painted me with baking soda and put me to bed before Grandpa could see me. She never referred again to our escapade, and neither did I.

That night I was afraid to go to sleep, fearing that I would be drowned again. From the first time since I had left Te Kano I recalled the Radiant Aunts in minutest detail, and yearned for them grievously. I went to sleep reluctantly, dreaming of Donald Hana, drowned and dead like myself, his black hair like seaweed amidst the tumbling tons of grass-green sea.

The next day someone rowing past The Mike called in with a letter from the Radiant Aunts.

I was eager to hear what was in it, especially that they missed me, but I was too shy to ask. I went away and sat on the veranda, feigning carelessness about the whole thing. But I made sure I could see Fedora's face from where I sat, so that I could perhaps read upon that guileless page what the Radiant Aunts were thinking of me.

I read there dismay.

She had so little colour in her face that I could not say she had gone pale. But there were all the accompanying signs of pallor, the faintly suffused eyelids, the moving lips, the nervous flutter of the hand. Whatever was in the letter was not good. I forgot my shyness, and rushing in I cried, 'Is Auntie Barbie sick?'

She was startled, looking up and muttering, 'Nothing, dolling, nothing is the matter with Barbie.'

At The Mike there was no peach-tree to climb. But there was an overgrown bean-vine behind the house. I crawled beneath it into a dry and rustling cave. Not Auntie Barbie. Louisa, then? Had she fallen out with the Pig Man? Had she committed a crime, or been stricken with the nameless diseases adults were so subject to. ('She had a bad turn. She had one of her spells. She just withered away.') Or was it Francey? I didn't care so much for Francey, who understood me only too well. But though I tried to pass quickly on to Ailie I kept remembering Francey, flushed and healthy, standing beside General Smuts and stirring up something delicious... I suddenly loved Auntie Francey dreadfully. And surely, surely, it couldn't be Ailie? Not my darling little Auntie Ailie?

At lunch-time Fedora was pink-eyed and husky, abstracted, too, though she tried hard to hide it from Grandpa. Once when she was dishing out the pudding I heard her say to herself, 'Poor, poor child!'

My nervous forebodings crystallized. The only child in the family I knew was myself. Something had happened that concerned me deeply. I longed to ask her, but I could not in front of Grandpa's needly, intelligent eyes. He, too, knew something was wrong.

'Vot, vot?' he shouted. 'Something is bad, eh? Eh, Fedora?'

'Why, Syver!' she quavered. 'Have some more rhubarb.'

'Bee-yahhhh!' he said, with an expression unutterably anti-rhubarb. Fedora tremulously raised her spoon to her lips, but her emotion was too much for her and she gave a choked snort.

'Pigs! Pigs! Pigs!' shouted Grandpa. At first I thought he was referring to Auntie Fedora's table manners, but he was actually using the method common in our family of getting information obliquely.

'I go down to Te Kano and I tchuck him to his own pigs!' yelled Grandpa. Terrified, I went on posting bread and butter into my mouth until I almost foundered.

'It isn't Louisa and Desmond,' retorted Auntie Fedora. 'You know very well, Syver...'

'Vot, vot, vot? Barbara, den?'

'Not, not Barbara, and you know very well you broke off Louisa's friendship with—'

Francey vas always sly like fox!'

Bewildered by this sudden turn I gaped at them both. Fedora took the bait like a trout.

'It isn't Francey, it's...'

Frightened, she closed her lips, and I could almost see in the air about her Barbara's neat precise writing, 'Don't whatever you do, Auntie Fedora, let Pa find out.'

A slow, cruel, triumphant smile slid out of the wrinkles on Grandpa's face. His yellow teeth showed as he saw the weak tears gush down his sister's cheeks.

'So, it is Ailie. You tink to lie to me. Vot is the matter, eh? You tink I cannot guess. Young girl, no mudder, no fader, big ideas, and now she is ruined, eh?'

Auntie Fedora cast a desperate look at me, and an even more desperate one at Grandpa. 'Oh, no, no, Syver! Oh, how can you say such a thing about darling little...oh, you are a beast, a cruel unyust beast, yust like they say!'

Ah, the coarse and devilish face of the old man as he broke into raucous Swedish! It was downright vulgar stuff, I could see by the sensitive wincings of that romantic ineffectual woman. I crept away, and they did not see me go.

It is a common fallacy that because a child does not understand it does not suffer. The mystery adds to the suffering. And the world of childhood is full of mysteries, often foolish, often fantastic, nearly always overlooked by the grown-ups.

As for the mystery of Being Ruined, I did not know what it meant, but I knew what it *was*. I knew that people were socially punished for certain things; just why, no one would explain to me. But the fact remained, and it was a terrible, irrevocable fact like going to hell, or getting murdered if you talked to strange men. Going bankrupt was Being Ruined, and having your mother or father commit suicide was Being Ruined, and there was that other thing that happened to girls alone. I didn't know what it was, or whether it happened because of their own fault or the will of Heaven, but the fact was that you rarely heard of them again after it happened. They vanished into the limbo of 'helping mother'.

And now this had happened to Auntie Ailie, whatever it was.

With photographic clarity I saw her slender, pale, self-contained little face, and the silky fair hair, I heard again the crisp voice, so definite and clear, that I had heard that night I was repenting my sins so bitterly.

Perhaps they would magic her away, as the other girls were magicked, and I would never see her any more.

I mourned her tearlessly and bitterly, avoiding Grandpa and Fedora, finding in the curdled skies and the cold confusing winds the echo of my own sadness. By sunset the storm was upon us, driving before it across the sandhills tall and twisted pillars of sand. These flying disintegrating genii, their motes faintly luminous, were the last thing we saw as night fell.

All through the dark hours the sea hammered at the coast, and the air was full of sound and uneasiness. When I looked through the pane I saw that the wind was almost visible, like tossing black plumes. It flowed in channels of darkness, so that the lights on the hill were obscured by its passing.

124

I thought of the ships, tossed like feathers in the turmoil, each bathed in the feeble yellow mist of its lights, and I was comforted as I felt the house digging in its toes against the gale.

When morning came the storm had blown away, and I went down on the beach to gather driftwood. The ebbing tide had left the sands like vast sheets of mica, dazzling and blinding.

I was almost at the bottom of the pipi-shell path when I saw it, the gigantic thing, its humped back shining like wet leather, its tail flapping from side to side with a slapping sound and a geyser of spray. It was stranded in the shallows on the southern side of the bar.

My first thought was Auntie Fedora's elemental. Shrieking with excitement I tore back up the path, but Fedora and Grandpa were already hurrying down.

'What is it, what is it?' I yelled.

'Poor thing, poor poor thing,' whispered Auntie Fedora, her pale eyes moist.

I have never seen such a look as was on my Grandpa's weatherbeaten face. Irony, and humour, and a savage pleasure.

'The domn broddy hwal!' he said.

We hurried down to the beach and along the glittering sand. Already a crowd had gathered there to gape, Maoris, dogs, fishermen. And on the Kawhia side we could see a clot of frustrated sightseers, prevented from crossing over because of the still rough harbour.

Auntie Fedora let go my hand. I cowered close to the ground, and looked up at the monstrous and incomprehensible beast the gale had brought over the bar.

It was alive. The fact was as awesome as if a house had got up and walked.

It breathed. I looked upwards at the curved wet side, as high as a wall, and it swelled outwards. The water in the hollow it had made for itself during its struggles shuddered into irregular rings. In this wet and shining wall a dark-blue eye, as big as a cow's, gleamed with a fierce and desperate gleam. A double spout of vapour hissed upwards, umbrella'd, and disappeared like smoke.

I looked at the people, who were tall to me, and then upwards to the whale, which made them into dwarfs. And they were silent, awed, astonished, the Maoris with their thick dark lips trembling on the verge of shy smiles, the white people greedily taking in all the details of this strange castaway.

All except Grandpa. He crept forward beside the head of the creature, staring at it all the time as though to fix it immobile with his gaze. He squatted down on his heels, and slowly, composedly filled his cheek with tobacco.

But the whale threw itself into a frenzy, shaking and shuddering in a convulsion which cast up showers of water milky with sand. The great tail thrashed a criss-cross of grooves and ditches in the ground, and the gravel rattled amongst the spectators like shot. The crowd scattered and ran, all but Grandpa, who went on squatting and staring, his yellow teeth bared in a grin of pleasure.

The incoming wave curled and spread about the whale, and at the touch of the smooth cold water the beast again burst into a titanic fury of movement. Mute, it seemed to fill the air with the agony of its silent screaming. The air that hung above the long mealy curve of sand vibrated with its horror and despair. The noise of the quietening sea, the distant yo-hoing of the gulls upon the bar was lost. There was nothing left but the confusion and the alarm of this alien who had no business on the beach.

Aunt Fedora's hand closed harshly upon mine. Tears ran down her face.

'She's going to do it!' yelled someone.

'There she goes!'

The whale slewed over on its flank. Its jaw fell open, and we could see the unfolded lip, thick with barnacles

126

like insects in the bark of a tree. Plainly I could see the creamy hairy baleen standing in parallel ridges on the inner side of the mouth, which looked as though it were lined with felt. On the lower jaw lay the tongue, an immense white satin cushion, so soft and delicate it was.

'Oh, Yenny, Yenny...poor creature, poor creature!' sobbed Auntie Fedora.

Grandpa spat. The wind caught the brown splash of tobacco juice and blew it back upon the sand, but I knew what he had meant.

All that day and the next the whale lay stranded. Tide after tide welled round its body and aroused in its flagging heart the urge to be away. Up and down the coast the news had gone, and clouds of petrels, gannets, blackcaps, and mollymawks spiralled above – chattering, gloating, and quarrelling like a host of aerial shrews. The fish had come, too, flickering and flashing on the sea side of the mountainous body which lay almost within their kingdom. And at night, I knew, the crabs were on the move, the stony-eyed, hungry, sidewise walkers, scrabbling with a stealthy sound over the gravel towards the feast.

I lay in my bed and listened to the drumming on the sand, the silence, and then the steady flush of the tide. Now the furious splashing, and the cannon-cracks of the flukes upon the water, then once again the exhaustion and the stillness.

And Grandpa was down there, crouched in the chill and the wet, a sleepless gloating goblinesque form, staring at the struggle of his ancient enemy, and soaking in every moment of agony as though it were choicest music. The icy ropes, the chafed and bleeding hands, the frostbitten feet, the storm and the terror...all the bitter hardships of his long whaling life he personified in this struggling dying creature. He offered it up like a sacrifice to his ruined youth.

Auntie Fedora in her acute sensitive sympathy had put

her soul into the body of the whale. She suffered its torments with vicarious intensity, and out of her ceaseless tearful babble came enough to make me understand those torments.

By day its darkening eye stared into the blinding blue: by night into the moonlight which flowed over the dunes and through the jetty trees: that moonlight which it had known only as an uninterrupted spangling of the stainless ocean. To its hidden ear came the sounds of the land, untranslatable, terrible, like the noises of another dimension, the harsh chatter of the watchers, the barking of their dogs, the distant mill whistles, the screeching of the birds – all these things besieged the brain that lay beneath the ton-weight helmet of bone.

So the whale lay, while the hot sun dried out the skin like thin black silk, and the beating flukes cracked and frayed.

Now Grandpa had stirred from his walking stick, contemptuously and hatefully. I stared at him with icy loathing, longing to pray that the beast would roll over and crush him, but still remembering my promise to Auntie Barbara never to curse anyone again. So I phrased it differently.

'Oh, God, if the whale rolls over, don't let Grandpa get away.'

But it was twelve hours since it had stirred.

'Why don't they send someone from Kawhia to shoot it?' implored Auntie Fedora tearfully.

The Maoris shrugged and smiled gently. They were patient. Very soon the whale would die, and then was the time to get busy. They had already made their crude preparations.

Many of them had spades, which they had sharpened to keen edges. Some had slash-hooks and cleavers: others ropes. Out in the waves a little boat bobbed about.

The birds descended in a whirling pillar, to strut and

shriek and tear with their wild beaks at the black skin which stretched over the hairy undercoat.

'Chase them away, chase them away!' I yelled, rushing towards the whale. Grandpa held me back with his stick.

'Broddy fool, go avay!'

I saw the whale die and did not understand it. It is only now, looking back, that I can comprehend the desolation of the death of that greatest, gentlest sea beast.

It had gone too far to feel the assault of the birds. Far, far away it must have heard the forlorn and mysterious call of the turning tide.

The blood roared through the two-foot tunnel of its aorta, and deep within the flesh the atrophied bones of what had been legs in its land-dwelling ancestors stirred and quaked. In one gigantic effort it thrashed and splattered and the scavengers flew upwards in a screaming cloud. The shallow water boiled like a pot and the wet sand trembled and darkened at each impact. For five minutes the whale battled with its own immobility, greater and more implacable enemy than orca or swordfish. Then a column of red spouted from its blowholes, condensed darkly, and ran down upon the sand.

Somebody raised a half-hearted cheer, and my Grandpa broke into a raucous laugh. Harsh and malicious, it seemed to me the laugh of a devil. All my sorrow about Ailie, which had been for the past few days submerged, my homesickness and distress, centred on this cruel pagan old man. His hand dangled beside me, a gnarly block of wood. I dug my teeth into it so far I almost felt them meet.

Grandpa gave a roar of pain. He shook his hand as though a young dingo were attached to it, and like a young dingo I remained attached. He tasted of tobacco and sweat, and then of blood. It welled into my mouth and nearly choked me. This was the only reason I let go.

I knew very well how much it hurt to be bitten. On rare

occasions Pola and I bit each other ceremonially, and the wounds ached for weeks afterwards. A barbarous exaltation filled me as I saw Grandpa's face contorted with pain. I hated him as much as he now hated me.

He hit me across the side of the head with his knuckles, and his fingers felt as cold and hard as a bunch of candles. I reeled across the sand and fell into a pool. Auntie Fedora, making agitated bird-sounds, was beside me in a moment. I rose dizzily to my feet, and stared again at Grandpa. Even as she dragged me away I was still staring, not frightened, not angry, but cold and triumphant, knowing I would never be scared of him any more.

All the way up the cliff I was in this state of exaltation; the whale had died and I had avenged it. I had even avenged Ailie. I had made him yell, and the sound was sweet music to my ears. Thus did I duplicate Grandpa's feelings over the stranding of the whale, and did not recognize them.

Under her shock and distress Fedora was delighted too. I suppose there were dozens of people who wanted to bite Grandpa, and she venerated me secretly as the one who had done so.

'He's an old beast!' I yelled. 'He's an old swine, a *broddy* swine!'

'Dolling child!'

'He said awful things about Auntie Ailie!'

She went pale and faltered. 'You didn't understand?'

'I saw the way he looked,' I answered sullenly. Suddenly the moment had come. I blurted out, 'What's the matter with Auntie Ailie?'

Fedora kissed me. 'Oh, Yenny, Yenny, vill you promise never to tell the girls I told you?'

I promised, dreading and yet excitedly anticipating her answer.

'You know a Maori boy called Donald Hana?' she asked.

130

Donald Hana! Impatiently I stared at her. It was about Auntie Ailie I wanted to know. I was about to remind her of this when she said with a sigh, 'Ailie and he have fallen in love. Poor child, poor child!'

For a moment I was completely at a loss. Then I knew. Of course, Grandpa had got it all wrong. Ailie wasn't Ruined at all. And this was a secret, this wonderful glorious news, so Grandpa mustn't know. I completely ignored Auntie Fedora's sad tearful look. Grown-ups cried about all kinds of stupid things, anyway. I was so delighted I could hardly speak.

'Oh, Auntie Fedora, isn't it lovely! Do you think she'll let me be flower-girl? Oh, Auntie Fedora, Donald is just like a . . .' I was going to say a prince in a fairytale, but I felt embarrassed, so I substituted 'actor in the pictures. Can I go home to Te Kano soon, because I want to help with the wedding?'

I raced outside to see how they were getting on with the whale. All sadness connected with the incident had mysteriously vanished. I looked with brisk interest at the little dark figures of men legging each other up on the whale's back. Others were cutting off long strips of blubber. Down on the sand the spider-like figure of my Grandpa was gesticulating and stamping, directing operations.

But even this couldn't hold my interest. My joy and excitement over the news was too much. I rushed inside again.

'He's so handsome, Auntie! And Huriana, his sister, she's my friend, Auntie, and she's a real lady. You ought to hear her sing. Auntie Francey says she ought to be trained. And her great-grandfather is as old as the hills, and he doesn't wear pants, and he can make real spells, because he's a sorcerer.'

'Oh, Gott!' said Auntie Fedora in anguish. She disappeared into her room for a long time. I peeped through the keyhole and she was sitting on the bed with her face in her hands, probably communing with the spirits. Yet when she came out to cook dinner she was cheerful again. The momentary emotion had passed, she had resigned herself, and was drawing strength from her resilient sentimentality. Even the prospect of a trouserless Maori magician in a family already saturated with potential scandal did not more than set her back momentarily. She trembled, she yearned for the Radiant Aunts in their shame and anguish, but for herself the first shock was over, and she was prepared to hope for the best.

When we heard Grandpa boiling up the cliff path she sent me flying out the back door, lest he should beat me to a pulp with his walking-stick.

Happily I lurked amongst the bean-vines, making up pretends about Auntie Ailie and the wedding, floating on a romantic sea of dreams until Auntie Fedora came to tell me she had induced Grandpa to go to Kawhia to have his hand cauterized.

She had done this simply by telling him the wound was nothing but a flea-bite, and then bursting into tears during the resultant storm and saying she didn't mean anything, and he was most likely perfectly right.

We sat peacefully before our fire, Fedora occasionally pressing me passionately to her bosomless bosom and getting in a 'Poor dear! Poor dear!' before I struggled away.

I have said that after I bit my Grandpa I was never afraid of him again. Prudently, though, I did all in my power to avoid him. For a nippy child, backed by a psychic aunt, this was not difficult. When he came in, I flew out, and when he went down to the beach I emerged from my hidey-hole and strutted round boasting of how scared I wasn't. It was all very exciting and adventurous, and I barely noticed how wanly my Auntie Fedora co-operated. It must have been nerve-wracking for her, having a nasty old man and an irresponsible child playing Robinson Crusoe and the Savages in her house. There was not a great deal of her to wither away, but her skeleton became more emphatic daily.

The letters which frequently came from Te Kano did not help, either. These letters threw me into an agony of impatience. I was terrified in case the wedding was all over by the time I got home. Every day I asked Fedora when I was leaving, but she always put me off with mysterious sighs and grievous looks.

The frustration was great. I begged her to tell me why I couldn't go home. Perhaps, I thought, the Radiant Aunts considered I had not yet sufficiently purged my soul. But Auntie Fedora only said that I wouldn't understand. I used to go off and sit by myself in the tea-tree for hours, brooding.

In all the uproar about Donald Hana and Ailie, I suppose no one except myself looked at the affair completely impersonally.

Most people forget, in the anaesthesia of the years, the intense chaste romanticism of a little child. Already, at the age of eight, I longed for someone to love me. I could look at the clouds and the sea, and the movement of dancing air on a hilltop on a summer day, and long fiercely and wordlessly for that someone. He was not a boy, like Henryorpus, or a man, like the Pig Man. He was a faceless, bodiless conception of the beloved. I did not care where or when I should meet him: it was enough to know that somewhere he was existent, growing up, like myself, until he reached the moment where I was. Thus to me the loving of Ailie and Donald was a beautiful miracle. They *had* grown up, and they *had* met. It was right.

I turned shyly from the memory of his tui-dark head bent close to her silvery one, as though he were listening – and yet returned to that picture again and again, silent, wondering, and bashful.

In this innocent yet complete comprehension of the hypnosis of love, I wandered the gleaming beach where the salt lay like the most airy feathers, and the triangular foot-prints of the sea-birds had written messages in cuneiform.

I went to the skeleton of the whale, which stood like a half-built boat, the waves splashing through the bones with a melodious carefree sound. On the broken, flesh-tattered spine a sea-shag stood, its oily head serpentined sideways, observing me without a blink.

The whale offended me. It was no longer the castaway that had tormented me with its own agony. It was the source of a hideous smell, and that was all. I turned away and went into the scrub that was stiff with dry froth, its gnarly trunks encrusted and webbed with this sea-stuff from the last storm. And who should be there, at ease on his broad dungareed seat, but my Grandpa, his knobbly brown feet sunk in the warm sand, the sun pulling a little rusty colour out of his thatchy grey hair. For a moment we glared at one another, I poised on my toes like a bird, and quite capable of flitting out of his sight in an instant.

'Beee-yahhh!' remarked Grandpa. I suppose his wound ached at the sight of me.

There was a certain dignity in our hatred. I had no wish to poke my tongue out at him, which in other circum-stances would have been the natural answer to 'Beee-yahhh!'

He had something in his hands. It was a piece of wood, which he had been whittling as he sat at his ease upon the sand. With the greatest of deliberation he snapped shut his big clasp-knife and put it away in his pocket. Then, still ignoring me, he put the wooden thing to his lips. It was a whistle, almost lost in those immense, crabby, cramped hands, all puckered and scarred and misshapen. So it seemed as though Grandpa were coaxing music out of his cupped hands.

I stole forward as the notes came out, first of all little creaky whispers, like a bellbird warming up, and then a double note, split and mellow, and then a succession of four notes which ended in a question-mark. Grandpa's music was not adept, or even smooth. It came out awkwardly, as though it and its author had not got together for thirty years.

This is why it sounded natural, as though the chipped wooden whistle were a bird's beak.

Grandpa shot a scowl at me. 'Get away to hell,' he growled.

I retreated a little and sat down upon the sand, still tensed in every sinew like a puppet about to spring off the stage.

Grandpa went 'Pee-eww, pee-eww, pee-eww!' on the whistle. Like two wary dogs we kept our eyes on each other. Then he looked away, contemptuously, and went on with his practising.

He kept it up for an hour, and for an hour I crouched in the sand while the sun stopped warming one shoulder and started on the other, and the shadows that found themselves in the lower boughs of the manuka bloomed up towards the crowns.

Finally I said, 'You're being a bird, aren't you?'

'Shoot der mout!' he replied. 'Biting dawg.'

This amused me, and I gave a loud hoot of laughter. Grandpa took no notice. Now the bird-call was taking shape. But it belonged to none of the birds I knew.

'It vos nightingale,' said Grandpa, spitting out a shaving.

'Oh, I've read about nightingales,' I said loftily.

'Ven I var dirteen,' said Grandpa, 'I go woyage to Danmark. I am cabin-boy. Captain take me big house var is trees, flowers. People werry rich at dat place. Is called Rolighed, nigh unto Copenhagen.'

It was the longest speech he had ever made to me. I gaped in amazement, wondering what he meant by it.

'Was lady mit silken dress, pearlen on neck. Was Madame Melchior. She give me cake, senden me to sit in

135

garden. Dar vas old man, old fonny sick man, said, 'Listen, is nightingale in dat tree!' Is first time I hear nightingale, dat is vy I remember.'

What with trying to make sense out of his coarse jumbled accent, I could get no point out of this story. I suppose he saw the bewilderment on my face, for he added angrily, 'Dat old sick man is Hans Christian Andersen.'

'You mean the man that wrote my fairy-story book?' I asked.

He waited for my response, but there was none. Hans Christian Andersen meant nothing to me. I liked the Brothers Grimm much better because they weren't so gabby. Besides, I did not know Andersen had lived and died long ago.

But now it seems to me a wonderful thing that my very own grandfather saw Hans Andersen when he was dying of cancer at the home of the kindhearted Melchior family, and that together they listened to a bird that might have inspired *The Chinese Nightingale*.

Grandpa was very disappointed at my lack of reaction. I think that he had, in some dim reluctant way, tried to bring about conciliation proceedings with his small enemy.

He took his revenge in a typical way. Out of his pocket he brought a fistful of letters that had Auntie Barbara's writing on them. I knew at once they were the letters that had come for Fedora, and that he had pinched them from whatever naive hiding place she had chosen.

He opened one, and the dying sun shone on pages that were, no doubt, tear-stained and blotted, and began to read.

Certainly one of the valiant girls in *The Schoolgirl's Own* would have sprung on Grandpa and wrenched the letters from his iron clasp. But all I could think of was to tell Fedora. I fled like the wind along the beach and up the cliff path, and if I had met the elemental on the way I would have vaulted over it as though it were a butter-box.

Auntie Fedora had already discovered her loss. She sat face in hands, communing with the spirits, but the spirits weren't on the line. She was pale and sweaty. The fact that Grandpa knew the real details of the case was grave. His belief that Ailie was Ruined was bad enough, but it could be proved wrong. But his knowledge that his youngest girl was bent on marrying a Maori boy was calamitous.

'He'll kill her, Yenny,' said Fedora with despairing calmness. 'He used to beat your poor Grandma...a vicked, vicked man!'

Doubtless a different aunt would have contrived a different ripost for Grandpa's impending attack, but Fedora naturally thought of something dramatic.

She decided that the only thing to do was to flee The Mike as soon as possible, to get into the shelter of the family so that they could convert themselves into a sort of spiritual blockhouse and leave Grandpa to snipe round on the outside.

The poor woman had spread round the place a few of her little personal belongings, a funny brass clock with glass sides, a little red rocking-chair, a photograph album, and a painted wooden box full of clothes. Most of these things had come from Sweden and were very precious. But she left nearly all of them, in the full knowledge that Grandpa would gather them up and fling them over the cliff as soon as she left. Ailie's predicament came first.

We waited trembling until Grandpa had stumped in, ripped through his hermit's tea in the sitting-room, as was his wont since the biting incident, and then banged off to bed. Auntie Fedora was ashen. She was almost hysterical with fear lest he should come in and tax her about the information he had found in the letters. But he didn't. He was probably working out his offensive.

Then, carrying only my kitbag and Auntie Fedora's suitcase, we made the perilous descent to the beach in the dark, and rowed out to the little rusty launch.

'How will you ever find Kawhia?' I asked in trepidation. The town was a blob of lightness on the dark of the inner harbour. I could hardly distinguish it from the faint pricklings of the stars. But Fedora knew. She brought the launch to the wharf steps with hardly a hesitation. When she had me and the baggage safely on those slimy steps she faltered a moment, hearing the wheeze of the outgoing tide on the distant bar, then with sudden decision she kicked the launch away from the steps.

It slowly lolloped out into the dark water, a frightful danger to shipping, had there been any.

I was charmed. I pictured Grandpa starving to death on his cliff-top, or having an apoplectic fit when he discovered he had been marooned.

But actually the launch came ashore on the sand a mile or so down the harbour, and was returned to The Mike in good order not many days later.

We spent the night in some household I cannot recall, except that early the next morning the good woman of the house insisted on wrapping me in stout brown paper beneath my underwear, 'to keep off the car-sickness'. She also referred to me as 'poor little buntucky'. I was so enamoured of this sobriquet that I was a buntucky all the way home, sitting demurely on my little scut, and crackling loudly every time I moved, for my paper corset was secured at one side with seven or eight safety pins.

Fedora was ill with suppressed importance and anxious remorse, for she couldn't help wondering what Syver would say when he got up and found the kitchen fire unlit and the broddy vimmen gone off to take a message to Garcia.

Brown paper or not, I wasn't car-sick.

Late that night we staggered, enfeebled with weariness and lack of food, but still palpitant with importance, into the vast enveloping shadows of the walnut-tree, where the little house stood with all its blinds pulled down as though to keep its secrets to itself.

As the years have gone by, I have pieced together all those things which happened when I was at Kawhia, and knowing the aunts and Te Kano so well, I can make from these fragments of conversation and latter-day confidences a complete story.

As was characteristic of Ailie, she first made sure that she was in love with Donald Hana, and then she broke the news to the Radiant Aunts. If, as I think, I saw the enchantment fall on those two children, for they were hardly more, she must have taken about three days to make sure.

'We were sitting at breakfast,' Barbara said. 'Ailie wasn't saying a word, but that's usual with her, when all at once she looked up with a smile like an angel and said, "I love Donald Hana." Just like that.'

'Why, I love him, too,' said Louisa readily. 'He's just the nicest Maori boy round Te Kano, if you ask *me*.'

The most beautiful look went over Ailie's little face. For once the self-contained composure seemed to vanish, and for those other sisters it was like looking into a room they had never seen before. Even Louisa, who was deeply in love with her worthy Pig Man, had never, I am sure, experienced the tremulous, indescribable mystery that lay in Ailie's soul. Barbara, Louisa, and Frances recognized at once what Ailie had meant. Dumbly they stared at her, the little creature who had fixed her whole life on one who was as unattainable as a star.

And just as if she had, by some queer perversion, fallen in love with a planet, they could not understand what had made her do it.

Gentle Louisa was the first to speak. 'Oh, Ailie, oh, Ailie, *no*!'

'Why, you silly little thing!' cried Francey robustly. 'I never heard such rubbish in all my born days.'

Aileen looked at Barbara. There was a powerful bond between the eldest sister and the youngest.

'We love each other, Barbie,' she said gently and inflexibly.

Barbara saw that other sister, the dead one, my mother, looking out of Ailie's eyes.

'You know the way Thora would put her head on one side a little, like Jenny does sometimes? Well, Ailie did that. And she looked me straight in the eye and never wavered for a moment.'

It says much for Ailie's personality that from the first they took her seriously, and her words as anything but the sentimental fancies of a schoolgirl.

'Aileen,' said Barbara soberly, 'I forbid you to see Donald Hana ever again.'

'No, Barbara,' said Ailie softly.

'Why, you little monkey, you need a sound smacking!' cried Francey.

'Ailie, darling,' said Barbara, 'since Mother isn't here with us, I have to do my best to guide you. I only want to —'

'I know, Barbie,' said Ailie, 'but this is different.'

And nothing they could say had the slightest effect. At last, in despair, Barbara said with unsteady lips, 'Then I'll see Mr Hana. He's a good sensible man. He'll make Donald see how foolish, how impossible, it all is.'

'Very well,' said Ailie, and she closed up in her own particular way, which was as exquisite and acceptable and unprovoking as the closing of a flower.

Looking back, the things that 'weren't done' even in our immediate past seem quaint and humorous and unnecessary, like old battles. But our modern reaction does not in any way alter the validity of those happenings. We see the Charge of the Light Brigade as a criminal piece of mismanagement, but that does not restore to life the men who died there; we see the branding of the adultress's breast as an inhuman severity, but that does not subtract from the agony and humiliation she suffered. To me, grown up, the fuss that was created by Ailie's loving Donald Hana is almost incredible, but it existed, and it changed all our lives.

Well, Barbara went to see Mr. Hana, and it took her an hour to decide on her hat. She didn't know how to treat the problem at all. Francey thought she should be flippant about the whole thing, putting it down to a moonlight madness between two youngsters who didn't know what they were doing. Louisa thought she shouldn't go at all. She should ignore the whole thing. Barbara could only remember (which she didn't often) that she was only twenty-three.

'Oh, Louie,' she said, 'if only Mother were here. Or if I could only ask Uncle Ray to do it . . . but he's not the right kind of person. Oh, Louie, what shall I say to Mr Hana?'

In the end she wore her navy-blue sailor, which she thought made her look grim and twenty-eight.

She approached the Hana house with a tremulous footstep, and a characteristic determination to do her duty even if she died for it. She clung a moment to the gate as she opened it, then she said to herself, 'Well, I've faced up to Pa, so I can face up to this.'

Huriana opened the door. Barbara gave her a pitifully bright smile, and Huriana inclined her head silently as though Barbara were some supplicating commoner. With her infinite grace she ushered Barbara into a little sitting room that you would never guess belonged in the home of a Maori.

'The lace curtains were got up *exquisitely*,' said Barbara afterwards, reluctantly but honestly.

She had expected that Mr Hana would be excusatory, certainly embarrassed. But he was incredibly, amazingly angry.

Certainly he did not demonstrate it. His decorous ambassadorial manner did not alter. But Barbara sensed it at once.

'You could have knocked me over with a feather,' she said; and then, with an astonished resentment, 'The idea of him being like that!'

Perhaps this attitude of Mr Hana's completely destroyed any soft-hearted waverings towards the lovers' cause – which the three Radiant Aunts, being what they were, must occasionally have had. For, far from being a little flattered that a white girl had looked with favour upon his son, Mr Hana was shocked to the core. He came to the point at once.

'Miss Admiral,' and I can imagine that rich Maori voice making a melodic phrase of her name, 'I am as concerned as you are about this unfortunate happening.'

Barbara struggled desperately to retain her dignity; she succeeded only in sitting there like a little girl, her hands in her lap, being told what she must do.

'You are a young woman, Miss Admiral, but an intelligent one. You know as well as I do the consequence of a marriage between Maori and pakeha.'

For a second Barbara thought he was speaking of half-castes, and blushed liked a strawberry. But the man's heavy brown face was downcast, his sombre eyes veiled.

'Your sister would be outcast by her own people, and not accepted by mine without hurtful comment. My son, for whom I have planned so much, would be ruined.'

'Ruined!' For all her sweet nature, her Christian charity, Barbara could hardly keep the offended surprise from her voice.

'A man needs a wife,' said Mr Hana. 'A white woman could not be the kind of wife he needs, and still be happy.'

Barbara hardly knew what to say. The arguments she had prepared with such soul-searching were worthless, the attitude she had rehearsed was condescending where she would be better fitted with one that was supplicatory.

'Won't you,' she asked faintly, 'won't you do what you

can to stop it before it is too late? My sister is only seventeen.'

'Would you like to speak to Donald yourself?' asked Mr Hana. Before Barbara could flutter a denial he strode to the door and called, 'Donald! Kei te hiahia ahau ki te korero atu ki a koe!' ('I wish to speak to you.')

Barbara felt that he had used the Maori words deliberately to emphasize to both the brown boy and the white woman their difference in colour.

The boy came through the doorway with the gravity and presence common to him. His hand touched Barbara's for a fleeting second.

She looked at his striking and noble face and thought yearningly, 'Oh, Ailie, if only he were a white boy how happy I should be for you, darling!'

She could read nothing on his face, neither sullenness nor resentment nor embarrassment. There was candour there, and great dignity, and unselfconsciousness, and in face of that Barbara felt all of a sudden a little gauche.

'Donald,' she said hesitantly, and then looked imploringly at Mr Hana. She said to her sisters afterwards, 'Honestly, girls, I just couldn't remember that he was a – a – a native. I could only think that he was older and might handle things better.'

'Donald,' said the older man, 'we have discussed the reasons why your association with Miss Aileen Admiral must cease. In the presence of her older sister, I forbid you to see the young lady again.'

'I'm sorry, Dad,' said the boy. 'No!'

The thick smooth voluptuous face of the father, drawn in broad curves, could have been the face of a Spaniard, oblique and diplomatic. No expression altered it. But the boy's black eyes glimmered a little, as though it cost him a great deal to defy his father. But he said steadily enough, 'Dad, in any case I shall be twenty-one in a year's time, and then I shall do as I think best in this matter.'

'Until then you are under my authority!'

'You ask too much,' answered Donald.

'Donald,' pleaded Barbara, forgetting all her dignity, and becoming a flushed tearful elder sister not much older than himself, 'Ailie is only a little girl. Please don't see her any more. Be kind, Donald. She's too young for all this trouble.'

She saw in his face a deeper maturer shadow of the beautiful thing she had seen in Ailie's. It took her breath away with its apocalyptic quality. She groped after a word for it, and failed. It was a glimpse of something for which she herself had no comparison. Only a glimpse, for the tears welled uncontrollably into Barbara'e eyes, and with a stifled word to Mr Hana she stumbled from that house, knowing that no matter what any of them did it would be no use.

Of course Te Kano took the matter to its heart, took it between its teeth and mumbled it like a sweetmeat. Te Kano was accustomed to irregular unions between whites and Maoris. It accepted the fact that any pretty Maori girl should be remorselessly pursued by debauched white men, providing it was done 'decently', which meant without publicity. But the idea of two young and respectable people from well-established families actually *marrying* was disgraceful beyond words.

Barbara, Louisa, and Francey were placed in the difficult position of carrying on their business in a town seething with rumours about their sister. Completely loyal to her personally, they were forced to ignore her conduct from their professional viewpoint. All their customers wanted to cluck over the scandal with the Misses Admiral, and the Misses Admiral, through family pride, were unable to accept sympathy, or agree or condemn. All the time Ailie sat peacefully in the back room, embroidering vestees and making buttonholes and doing up other people's hems, and not making any comment at all.

'Oh, I could shake you, Ailie, honestly I could!' Francey would say furiously.

And Ailie went on seeing Donald.

This might have gone on for months, and eventually fizzled out of its own accord, if it hadn't been for Fedora.

Into this strung-up atmosphere of cups of tea, whispers, and tear-stained faces she came, worn to a frazzle, hysterical with self-importance and exaggeration.

'He'll be down here as fast as his pony can bring him, you yust see!' prophesied Auntie Fedora, cheeks chalk-pink transparent hands wildly gesticulating. 'His aura vas...vas...' she clutched helplessly in the air for the word, then hooked it down from the electric-light shade, 'murderous!'

The Radiant Aunts tried their best to be normal, welcoming me with kisses and cuddles, exclaiming over my mighty thighs and sausagey arms, which had been built up so bonnily by auld man's milk. They congratulated each other on the way my Indian Head ensemble had stood up to car-sickness, and went into genuine shrieks of laughter as they unpinned my brown-paper corset. But there was a certain hepped-up feeling about them all. My intuition thrust out little snail horns and sensed this, so that I retreated into a defensive camouflage of perfect behaviour. One thing was certain, I flattered myself: They had forgotten all my funny business about the airmen.

Yet, as I hoed into my dinner, looking lovingly meanwhile at all the familiar things, the clock, the pictures, the patch on the curtains where I had idly gnawed them one rainy day at the window, the ebon gleam of General Smuts... I was aware that things were far from well. Louisa, for instance, was jumpier than usual, given to pushing away her dinner and looking abstracted. (I suppose she was longing to send out an urgent message for the Pig Man to come and protect them all from a ravening Pa.) And Barbie was a little curt and short with us all,

145

and Francey's heels banged into the floor more emphatically than was common with them. And Ailie – paler, more pensive, and, to my discerning eyes, what I called 'upset'.

Oh, if she would only confide in me, I thought, tell me of the things Donald said to her in the moonlight! I knew darned well she wouldn't, but I went on hoping that a little of the stardust these two created would rub off on me.

After dinner Barbara said, 'You may run in and play with Violet if you like, Jenny, but you must promise on your honour not to say anything about Grandpa or Auntie Ailie.'

So I promised, then skipped outside. The crickets were stridulating in the dusky grass, and the willow, fully plumaged, came down to the ground all round like a crinoline. I slipped inside that magical circle and with passionate love rubbed my cheek against the warm bark. Erk! Something squashed and caterpillary prickled my cheek and fell murdered to the ground. A little chilled, I toed up the fence and saw the Cuskelly house winking yellow eyes like a cheerful cat. It gave me the greatest of pleasure just to see that house and hear all the rumpus, Mrs Cuskelly screaming out a hymn, Mr Cuskelly whining, the children all fighting, and two boarders doing weight-lifting exercises on the veranda.

I wanted to yell for Pola and see her limber little form come bouncing across the grass. But it was not yet time. Instead I crept round outside the window and listened to the conversation within.

'He'll forbid it, Aileen,' said Barbara definitely. 'And goodness knows what else he'll do, too. Maybe take you back to Kawhia with him.'

'I wouldn't go!' cried Ailie. But her composure was shaken. Tenseness was in her voice. Her age had suddenly crept up on her, that and the deeply bred fear of their father that characterized them all.

'Oh, dolling, he vill beat you blue and black!' cried Auntie Fedora. 'I tell you, Syver is a bad wiolent man, and he is so angry, you vould not beleaf!'

'He wouldn't dare,' said Ailie.

But she knew very well he would dare, and nothing much would be done to stop him. He still had jurisdiction over Louisa and herself, and the law would not interfere with that. I knew Ailie's face would be proud and undaunted, and perhaps her little hands would be tightly clenched together.

'I saw him punch mother once,' said Barbara in a low ashamed voice.

'The beast!' burst out Francey.

Then Ailie spoke. 'He won't stop me from marrying Donald, no matter what he does. I'm not like you, Louisa.'

'Don't you throw off at me, Aileen Admiral,' quavered Louisa.

'You won't go ahead and marry Desmond until you're twenty-one, just because Pa forbids it, and you know very well he forbids it only because he can't bear to see anyone happy. Well, he's not going to mess up *my* life, you just see.'

'No, dolling, *you* are!' wept Auntie Fedora.

Then there was a terrible commotion inside with people running for the smelling-salts, and Auntie Fedora sobbing hacking Swedish sobs, and agitated cries of 'Pull the windows down!' and 'The Cuskellys will hear!' and then the window thumped down and I couldn't hear a thing. Disconsolate but mightily excited I skittered round to the front veranda, just in time to meet Ailie, as she emerged from the front door in order to get away from the hysteria within.

She put her slender arms round me and pressed me to her childish bosom.

'Well, you horrid little eavesdropper, have you been listening?' she whispered. I felt dampness on her face.

'Oh, Auntie Ailie,' I burst out, 'no one will tell me if I can be your flower-girl.'

Did she know that in my heart there was some small

comprehension of what was in hers? She whispered, 'Jenny, when you grow up, you'll know that I was right. Remember that, Jenny.'

Oh, if one could only look back and see the expression on her little face as she said that! I have tried and tried, but there are only shadows, and the voice, and a feeling I had of sad astonishment.

Then she was gone, running across the wet grass that was just beginning to shine under the moon. When I got to the gate I saw her just beyond, and the tall dark figure that stepped out from the shadow of the trees to welcome her. Did she know I had followed her? She turned, and he turned, and I saw the moonlight on those faces for a moment, changing them to two profiles on a coin. As she asked me, I have remembered, for that was the last time I saw my Auntie Ailie.

In the morning, when the Radiant Aunts got up, she was gone.

I was first made aware of this by a voice which pierced even my drunken-deep sleep, a voice which cried, 'Oh, my little sister, my little sister!'

I went alarmed and silently to the door, to see my Auntie Barbara there, in her nightie, weeping as I had never seen her weep.

'Oh, is it my fault, is it my fault?' she was saying, and Louisa was stroking her hair and trying to say things which wouldn't come out. And while I stood gaping at this amazing tableau, Francey in her hat and coat came in from the back door.

'Oh, Francey,' said Louisa, 'is he . . .?'

Francey nodded. Then she took off her coat and hung it up tidily, and a moment later I heard General Smuts's damper being bashed back and forth till his teeth rattled.

'Don't wake poor Fedora,' faltered Louisa. 'She's had enough upsets already.'

I got back into bed and pulled the blanket up over my

head. What could be the matter? So many amazing things had happened that I was baffled. A feeling more of resentment than anxiety surged over me. But even that didn't help solve the mystery. I shot out of bed with sudden energy, dressed, and hopped through the window. I had remembered that I hadn't yet seen Pola.

I tallyhoed at the fence, impatience filling me. There she was, a little more tousled of hair, a little taller. The first thing she said was, 'Has your auntie really run off?'

'Which auntie?'

'I dunno. But Mum saw someone getting away at two in the morning when she was up to the baby.'

'You're barmy,' I said. Pola's blue eyes flamed. Her fingers shot out and I got my nose back just in time. From behind the shelter of the fence I said plaintively, 'And I brought you back some shells from Kawhia, too.'

The blue eye came down and gleamed through a crack in the fence.

'Who was it went off in the night, Jen?'

I knew at last. But I couldn't say it. I stared dumbly at the eye, and then I wandered inside, leaving it there, shining after me with a kindly but insatiable curiosity.

'Why, there you are, Jenny! Aren't you hungry?' Francey was trying her best to be ordinary.

I went straight up and leant against her skirt. Usually I kept well away from Auntie Francey, for her strong work-hardened fingers had a nasty way with an ear that was in her road. Now her hand came down and smoothed my hair.

'Won't she ever come back?' I mumbled.

She did not express surprise. 'Why, dear, Auntie Ailie's just gone on a holiday.'

This was one of the cruellest fictions of my childhood. Some children, even, whose parents had died were told that they had gone on a holiday, and those children were left wondering for years why they didn't come back. I suppose the kind and misguided relatives thought that 'the kiddies would forget.' But they don't, and the mystery is worse than the fact.

Well, I pretended I had forgotten. I who had found so many tears for the lost airmen, found none at all for Ailie. There was only a deep dumb grieving, the first real sorrow of my life. It stayed there, forgotten sometimes but never destroyed.

Her bed disappeared from Louisa's room, and the clothes which she had left in the wardrobe went into Grandma's old trunk in the linen press. What the Radiant Aunts did to explain her absence from home and the town I do not know. Perhaps people were kind and didn't speak about Ailie, except amongst themselves. And as for Donald's family, I don't know either, for Huriana never came to play with me any more. It was like that great riddle, when the girls who had been Ruined were whisked away and sometimes never seen again.

Ailie hadn't been gone a week before Grandpa arrived in town, breathing fire and brimstone and after Fedora's scalp as well as the collective hides of the Radiant Aunts. Louisa dearly wanted to summon the Pig Man, but she dared not, seeing that her engagement with him was still secret. So the only other male who could interpose his might between this mass of terrorized women and the formidable Pa was poor Uncle Ray.

Did I tell you what Uncle Ray did for a living? He conducted people through the Waitomo Caves, and restrained them from bumping pieces off stalactites with their great vulgar head-bones.

He came up from Waitomo reluctantly and with considerable foreboding. He collected a heap of newspapers on the way, and, darting into the railway lavatory as he passed, he came out with one *Humour* and a torn

Aussie. This cheered him up a little, so that by the time he entered the battlefield he was feeling at least half a man.

I don't know why, but nowadays there simply isn't the family spirit there used to be. All my relations believed that Blood is Thicker Than Water in exactly the same unquestioning way that they accepted God and the Royal Family. I often heard people say, with simple earnestness, how much they had enjoyed a funeral.

So there was a certain sad pride about Uncle Olga. She knew that Grandpa would massacre Uncle Ray, but it was nice to know she was the prospective corpse's next-of-kin.

And the Hen and Chickens came belting down from the Awakino, in new blacks that were even more grief-stricken than the old ones, and settled in with thrilled rustlings, determined not to miss a thing.

The first and briefest discussion point on the agenda was:

Shall the Child be Present?

The veto was not unanimous by any means. There was a small, vociferous party which declared I should be regarded as an adult, not to be excluded from this vital caucus.

After all, they cried, who except this gallant child has actually bitten Pa? Let her stay if she wants to, the little dear, they said, looking fondly at my formidable teeth.

But they were solidly outvoted. I didn't care. The deep discomfort of Ailie's disappearance was like an aching bone. I didn't want to touch it, or hear references to it. I just wanted it to lie quietly and get better by itself. Besides, I had just started at the new convent school, and it was wonderfully engrossing. Pola was one of the foundation pupils, too, and she and I threw stones at our old schoolmates all the way home, screaming 'Proddyhopper!'

However, I was delighted to see my dear Uncle Ray, who looked more like a sozzled bantam than ever. His emergence from the dank atmosphere of the Waitomo Caves into the fresh, healthful air of the open countryside had given him a shocking cold. He carried on like a lawn-sprinkler.

'Crumbs, your nose is all rubbed up the wrong way,' I remarked penetratingly, and he gave me a feeble smile and exploded lushly into a handkerchief.

'It's simply disgusting,' moaned Uncle Olga. 'Keep away from him, love. He's spraying disease everywhere.'

Uncle Ray sprayed again. He raised a pair of inflamed and beseeching eyes to his wife, but she turned away in exasperation.

'It's exactly like Ray to get a cold right now,' she boomed.

Uncle Ray was hurt. He came and sneezed moodily at me for a while, gratefully accepted a few old *Stars* I had saved for him, and said he had a jolly good mind to go home. Uncle Ray was not afraid of Grandpa; he just didn't like him.

I was cheated on every side. It was Pola who was up the peach-tree and spied Grandpa from afar, lashing along his neurasthenic pony. It was Pola who treacherously slithered down and tore inside with the news which set the household all a-shake.

By the time I got there Auntie Francey was already standing at the back door, two large slices of daffodil-yellow shop-cake in her hands, and a firm, kind look.

'Now, dears, run along to school. We have things to speak about.'

Pola took hers delightedly, I reluctantly. I tried to see inside, hoping dimly that by some miracle Ailie had come home along with Grandpa. But although I could hear him ranting and roaring I couldn't hear her. With angry disappointment I turned away. I couldn't eat my cake, and although I knew very well Pola wanted it, I crumbled it up in front of her eyes and stood on it. Pola said in a stifled voice, 'I couldn't help seein' your ole grandpa.' She understood me so well. I walked off, and she trotted along behind for a little way, falling back all the time, until at last in the distance I heard an almost inaudible lament, 'And I couldn't help *smellin'* your ole grandpa, either.'

I was so upset over Grandpa's arrival that I wanted to do something forbidden. But all I could think of was to play a game, possibly peculiar to our town, called Ridin' Tyres. In this incomprehensible pastime one got inside the tyre, arched the body like a hoopworm, and bowled away down a hill like an animated swastika. After the crash one got out feeling like death and did the same thing all over again. After I had come down the hill half a dozen times I didn't feel any too well, and when I saw a large crowd surging about on the Domain my first feeling was of resentment that they had thus cluttered up a place I intended to be sick in.

Then, all at once, I saw that half a dozen of them had their faces painted *bright yellow*. They looked like lunatic Chinese. The star of our local musical society, a Miss Olive Urgent, was there, looking remarkably embarrassed in a long dress and a poke-bonnet. There was also a complete stranger with a little narrow squeaky face under a motor-cyclist's cap with great big check eaves sticking out all round. He was grinding savagely away at a movie camera. And, best of all, my old Maori friend Blackleaf Forty was standing nearby, smoking torori and sending out blasts of oily smoke that no doubt gave an arty halated effect to the finished film.

I was so excited I forgot everything – Grandpa, my aunts, Ailie, and my dear friend Pola, who was now a disconsolate little speck on the other side of the railway line. Somebody making a picture! Not in Te Kano! I clutched my large lunch-packet of pickle sandwiches to my bosom and got there as fast as I could.

I had not seen Blackleaf Forty since the flood, except for

that time when I had observed from afar the local sergeant arresting her and red-facedly hoying her off to the police-station. He was red-faced because she insisted on walking with her arm round his waist.

Now I stood close to her and felt all the old friendship and respect well up beneath the pickle sandwiches. I loved the way she looked, her withered face eroded by the storms of sixty years of turbulent life, her bulging lower lip an intricate scroll of tattoo, her ear-lobes stretched like rubber with decades of supporting shark's-tooth ear-drops. She was still dressed in her long dirty serge skirt and bottle-green blouse, but she had a Maori mat over her shoulders, and someone had removed the man's hat from her great mass of springy coarse black hair. She looked spectacular.

Looking back, I can see how the mystery came about. Some enterprising man with a film camera decided to make a quick sixpence by barnstorming through the Auckland Province, making one-reel films of each hamlet as he whizzed through. He would cook up some appalling little story, call upon the free services of the eager native talent, shoot off a few hundred feet of film, and the result would be *The Hero of Kopaki*, or *One Dark Night in Otorohanga*. Later the picture would be screened in the local theatre, the latter packed to the doors, with resultant largesse for the canny camera-man.

Imagine then my joy when I found that Blackleaf Forty had been impressed for service in the film! She was a superb actress. Far from blushing and throwing her feet round like our Miss Urgent, she strode about making dramatic gestures with her face, and gleaming her sunken black eyes in a truly fearful manner. She was supposed to be some sort of native sorceress, threatening Miss Urgent, who was Alice, a pioneer's daughter. She was something Jesse M. Lasky would have given a lot to get his hands on, I can tell you.

154

Suddenly Blackleaf Forty caught sight of me, her little friend, her very own little ginger biscuit, and instantly an imperious command issued from her perverse lips. I had to be in the film, too.

'No!' I cried. 'I've got to go to school! I'm on me way now! Naow! Naow! I can't!'

But she wanted me. She wanted to see me up there on the screen in the People's Palace, along with herself. Either I was in the picture, or she was out. Her lip bulged sullenly. She grabbed up her pipe, wich was chugging away quietly to itself on a nearby fence-post, and thrust more sausagey black slices of torori upon the red embers. She blew a blast of smoke at the director, and even the checks on his cap turned pale.

'Give the kid a part,' he gasped at his lieutenant, and the script was hastily revised. Trembling, I was led to one side and draped with a Maori mat from a stock he evidently carried about with him.

'I'll be late for school,' I whispered, being by then almost paralysed by the thought of all those people staring at me. But the lieutenant wasn't listening. He was too busy worrying whether my hair would photograph black.

My part was then explained to me. I was a little messenger from the tribe. I had to run in and interrupt the sorceress's threatening conversation with the pure pioneer maiden, registering alarm and pointing in the direction of the football goal-posts. I then had to run away, not falling over the tussocks which were heaped round for the purpose of throwing at the referee on Saturday afternoon. A half-wit could do it, explained the director.

To the accompaniment of jeering shouts from the spectators – 'Aw, look at old Hoodie pretending she's Norma Talmadge!' – and other vulgarisms, I staggered into the scene, moved my lips as directed, pointed to the goal-posts and staggered out of camera range once more. This lip-moving was important. Though actors in silent films recited no dialogue they had to appear as though they did say words which eventually appeared as a title or caption on the bottom of the film when screened. Naturally enough, there was great discrepancy between what they said and what they were supposed to say. The scene between Miss Olive Urgent and Blackleaf Forty, a pungent speaker at any time, went somewhat as follows:

BLACKLEAF FORTY: ....!.......!

TITLE: Me foretell many bad things happen to pakeha maiden.

MISS URGENT: What the dickens is the old sod saying?

TITLE: Oh, please, please, tell me where my papa is held prisoner!

BLACKLEAF FORTY: ....!

TITLE: Pakeha maiden too must die!

MISS URGENT: Now look here, I didn't come here to be insulted.

TITLE: Spare me, spare me, I have done no wrong.

BLACKLEAF FORTY: ....!....!.......!

Once I had acted my little scene I became aware of how easy it all was. I wanted badly to do it again, this time flashing my eyes and poking my lips out, and perhaps even gesturing in a graceful, Mary Pickford way, instead of merely raising my arm like a railway signal. I was deaf to the ribaldries of my friends in the crowd. The magic of show business had caught me. I just stood there breathing heavily through my adenoids, hypnotized, until the ringing of the school bell made me tear off the Maori mat in a hurry and rush away on my lawful business.

All day long I sat in a dream, incurring heavy penalties from the teacher and scornful remarks such as, 'She tinks she's Rin-tin-tin,' from those who had watched me act. Pola gazed wistfully at me, too proud to ask questions. I didn't care about any of them. I had made my mark.

It was only when I was let out at lunch-time, and was

hurriedly leafing through my sandwiches looking for bits of gherkin, that a sudden coldness seized me. That lunch...had I been clutching it all the time under my Maori mat? Would the little native messenger eventually be seen on the silver screen bearing a highly anomalous packet of pickle sandwiches? My artistic soul agonized. What would the critics say? Probably something like: 'Miss Jenny Hood appeared briefly, hanging on like grim death to a large lunch evidently cut by Te Kooti himself.'

I can feel the mortification of that moment to this very day.

It was nothing, however, to what the Radiant Aunts were going through that afternoon. It was so bad I didn't hear about it in detail for years. I had it on good authority that Grandpa looked like a devil, and used language. He'd been getting into the schnapps all the way down from Kawhia, and he was in a fearful mood. The first thing he said was that he was going to get the police after Ailie and Donald.

'Ay'll showem up,' he kept saying, 'Ay'll makem hide dere broddy heads, by gar.'

'But Pa,' faltered Barbara, 'they've been married a week now. Ailie sent us a wire from —' She stopped herself just in time.

'Ha!' snorted Grandpa. 'Dey are under age. Is no real marriage.'

'Oh, Got,' whispered poor Fedora.

It was bad enough to think Ailie was married to a Maori boy, but worse to think that Pa might get her unmarried. Then she would be as good as Ruined.

'And that's what the old beast wants to do to her!' whispered Francey vehemently to Louisa. Louisa blushed hotly.

Meanwhile Uncle Ray, in a torpor broken only by his volcanic nose-blowings, sat silently on his chair, red-eyed, red-nosed, sniffling to himself in what his wife described as an utterly selfish way.

Grandpa despised him, of course. He thought anyone mad enough to marry Uncle Olga deserved all he got. In a lull of brow-beating the Radiant Aunts he turned suddenly to Uncle Ray and demanded, 'Vot you do here, eh?'

Uncle Ray gave him a sour look. 'Vot you?' he retorted.

'Vot?'

'Vot you do here yourself?' asked Ray. Grandpa nearly fell over. His eyes looked like death-rays. 'Vot, vot, vot?' he roared.

'You said that before,' commented Uncle Ray. He coughed contemptuously at Grandpa, and Grandpa tried to pierce him through and through with those awful eyes. But Uncle Ray only drew out a clean hanky and blew in it.

'You are beeg slob,' said Grandpa.

'Set a slob to catch a slob,' retorted Uncle Ray. The Hen and Chickens caught one another's eyes and went into agonies of silent giggles. The slightly hysterical Chicken got stabbed in the midriff with a corset bone and had to withdraw. As for the other ladies, they all looked at dear Uncle Ray as though he had gone off his head. Standing up to Grandpa was a perilous thing, but giving him lip was tantamount to suicide. But Ray didn't care. He was too busy looking for a clean corner on his hanky.

Barbara hastily drew Uncle Olga aside. 'Oh, Auntie,' she implored, 'Uncle Ray isn't taking the right attitude ... this will only make Grandpa go to market all the more. Do stop him somehow.'

Uncle Olga couldn't imagine how. Every time she began to speak to her husband he said, 'just a moment, dear,' and made a noise like a semi-submerged clarinet. And by the time he had finished someone else had started speaking.

'Efer Ay tell you about Olga here, fallen in love mit nightman?' began Grandpa.

'Oh, Syver, *please*!' groaned my great-aunt like a feeble foghorn.

'Disgraceful, poor dear Olga,' said the Hen and the surviving Chickens, enravished by the prospect.

That was the end. The sight of Uncle Olga, shrinking piteously at the detestable prospect, sent Uncle Ray's temperature up to a hundred and five degrees. His nice mild face was bright pink. His eyes glittered, foggily, it is true, but still dangerously. With a stupendous sneeze that showered Grandpa and the Hen impartially he barked, 'Ah, shut your big trap, you silly old coot!'

At first Grandpa couldn't believe it, then he sprang to his feet and, to quote Barbara, 'he carried on like a beast in a den.'

'You're nothing but a barmy old squarehead!' yelled Uncle Ray. 'Squarehead, squarehead, you've got corners on your square head!'

'Ray, Ray!' moaned Uncle Olga, looking up at this coruscant husband with the dazed adoration of a Stone Age bride who has just been beaned with a lump of lime-stone.

There were feminine shrieks and squawks in all directions, and in the midst of it all Mrs Cuskelly flung up her window and shouted, 'For the love of heaven will yous be quiet in there, the shame of it, and me trying to put the baby to sleep this last hour!'

She was so overwrought that she picked up a pie-melon ripening on the sill and hurled it against the wall of our house.

The sound of that exploding vegetable shocked the Radiant Aunts as they had never been shocked before. No one had ever had to speak to the Admiral girls about making a commotion. Even during Grandpa's previous rages they had always managed to keep the windows down and the noise in. But this was different. They looked at each other, scarlet with humiliation, and Francey, the strong-willed bossy Francey, began to cry like a child.

As for poor Auntie Fedora, she had such a bad turn that the Hen and Chickens gloatingly took her away to the Awakino with them, no doubt hoping that she would find a few pixies in their runner-beans.

Grandpa behaved very curiously. He was so shaken by Uncle Ray's change of form that he went to bed at once. He lay on the sitting-room sofa staring stonily at the ceiling and sucking at a hollow tooth.

But the Radiant Aunts were so upset that Grandpa and even the original cause of the family discussion were thrust into the background.

'Oh, girls,' whispered poor Barbie, 'I shall never hold up my head again. To think that *neighbours* had to throw things ... oh, girls!'

Then someone put the kettle on, and what with their youth, and the nice hot cup of tea, and the current belief that one didn't Give Way, they all pulled themselves together and agitatedly spoke about something else.

Meantime I was coming home. I was bursting with all the marvellous things I had to tell the aunts.

'I've been in a picshua!' I was going to cry. (I learnt elocution, threepence a week and cheap at the price.) And then my eldest Radiant Aunt would breathe, 'Oh, girls, just imagine! Our own little Jenny a film star', and they would all three flock round and gaze adoringly with ravishing blue eyes while I told them every single detail.

But it happened differently. I burst into the middle of afternoon tea and there they were eating ginger-snaps and to an *obbligato* of sharp reports, discussing the amazing thing which had happened that morning in Te Kano.

'Oh, Auntie Barbie,' I gulped, 'I been in a—'

'Hush, dear,' said my Auntie Barbie. '... and then

Mrs Bedding told me there was that silly article Olive Urgent, twenty-six if she's a day, in a dress so tight the back seams of her stockings showed like ridges.'

'I don't know how she could bring herself to make such an exhibition of herself,' shuddered my Uncle Olga.

'And the camera-man...*ohhhhh*!' Auntie Francey rolled up her eyes. 'Those clothes...and that face...and the girl at the hotel says that the porter had to carry his socks out with the tongs.'

'And that ghastly old Maori lady,' squeaked Louisa. She turned upon me as grim an eye as she could produce.

'Jenny, don't you ever *ever* speak to that awful woman. Barbie, just look, she's leaving her mouth open again!'

Of course I was, because the clammy feeling which was creeping up from my toes called for no other expression. They didn't think much of film-making, that was plain. Obviously, also, there was something peculiarly low-down about it in a way only grown-ups could know. I listened in horror and dread to their strictures. I gathered that this was the beginning of the end, that the older residents would all turn over in their graves, Te Kano would shortly be a sink of iniquity, and as for Miss Olive Urgent, the star of *The Daughter of Te Kano*, she would irrevocably end up a dopefiend or married to Fatty Arbuckle. Of course I should have spoken up stoutly right there, admitting that I too had played a part in this iniquitous production. But I was too filled with dread, not of punishment, but of that awful reproach, 'Oh, Jenny, not again?'

Besides, there was no opportunity to speak up, for Francey suddenly put down her cup and said despairingly, 'Oh, Barbie, I don't care about Olive. What about *him*?'

And she rolled her eyes tragically at the hall door, behind which, presumably, Grandpa was gathering his sinister forces.

But I was too distressed even to ask the meaning of it all. Choking on the ginger-snap with which they had muzzled me, I ran away into the yard, crawled under the passionfruit vine behind the washhouse and frantically prayed, 'Oh, St Anthony, don't let them find out!'

I helped him a bit by making my peace with Pola.

'I'm sorry I stood on my cake,' I mumbled. She forgave me at once, and listened enthralled to my story.

'You told before,' I said accusingly. 'Now I s'pose you will run off and pimp again!'

Pola turned dark red, sank beneath the level of the fence, and wouldn't come up again for ages. But I knew she wouldn't tell. I think she found in me the faint glamour that always hangs round the sinner.

After a few days I believed that the skilful saint had come across with the goods. *The Daughter of Te Kano* was never mentioned. I came to the conclusion that either I had been invisible or none of my aunts' acquaintances had been amongst the spectators. But what about when the picture was shown on the screen? So great was my happy optimism that I did not consider the possibility.

Poor aunts! They had more to think of than films. After Uncles Ray and Olga went back to Waitomo they had to face things all alone.

Uncle Ray had done his work better than anyone knew. In the morning after the battle Grandpa had a frightful cold. He sounded like an egg-beater. Pompously I went for the doctor, calling in on the way to inform Pola that my grandfather would probably die, and she could come to the funeral.

'God's holy will be done,' said Mrs Cuskelly hopefully.

Grandpa was sinisterly meek with the doctor, who came out with the news that the old gentleman must be shifted at once to a bedroom, and plied with all comforts, for at his age his chest couldn't be expected to be the best. The same chest was to be rubbed with hot oil once every three hours, and the diet was to be kept light and nourishing.

The Radiant Aunts looked half killed at the thought of rubbing Grandpa's chest.

'Barbie,' trembled Louisa, 'I just...just couldn't!'

'I could *murder* Ailie!' burst out Francey.

'Oh, Barbie,' Louisa faltered, 'I'm just awful, I know, but if you will rub Pa's chest he can have my room.'

And this was heroic, for everyone knew that Grandpa's own personal perfume would hang round the room for months afterwards.

It was only about twenty feet from the sitting-room sofa to Louisa's bed, but getting Grandpa that distance was like transporting Napoleon's army from Paris to Moscow. Finally they had him in bed, all humped up at one end with his feet sticking out like two tree-roots. He persisted in wearing the blankets like a scarf, and glared over the resultant woolly chaos with his death-ray eyes.

'I vant to go home,' said Grandpa.

'Now, Pa,' said Barbara, tremulous but firm, 'you can't possibly go back to Kawhia with that cough. Why, you might get pneumonia and die all alone away from your family!'

Grandpa snorted. 'I vill not die until I break Ailie's broddy neck,' he croaked. Barbara shivered. She produced the saucerful of hot camphorated oil and advanced to the bedside.

'It will be all over in a moment,' she wheedled.

'Vot, vot, vot?'

The resultant commotion brought Francey and me flying. Louisa was down town looking after the shop. There was Barbara with camphorated oil all down her front and Grandpa calling her everything in Swedish. Barbara's eyes were flashing, and I said, 'Go on, Auntie Barbie, throw the saucer at him!'

Grandpa stopped cursing and waited expectantly. I am sure that if Barbara had thrown the saucer she would have won his fatherly admiration. But she didn't. He began to curse again, choked, turned mauve and fell

163

into such a hideous paroxysm of coughing that Francey cried, 'Oh, he's dying, run for Mrs Cuskelly!'

Mrs Cuskelly had a grand way with her. She had faced so many crises in her time that upsets were the breath of life to her nostrils.

She marched in and looked at Grandpa, flanked by the frightened aunts. Grandpa stopped coughing and began to turn even more purple.

'Ah, yer smell like a sackful of ould hens,' was her greeting.

A stupefied expression stole over Grandpa's face. Mrs Cuskelly stood over him like a lighthouse, rippling her muscles. On the back of her rugged skull a few strands of ropey black hair were carelessly skewered, and she had little peepy eyes of frightening blue.

'The poor man,' she said, arranging his pillow. She did this by dragging it from under him, so that his head thudded like a pumpkin on the mattress.

And what with her brogue and her looks, Grandpa got her all wrong from the start.

'It's a Rooshian,' he said, and fell into such a fit of coughing he ended up crowing like a rooster.

'Ah, will yer listen to thee ojus old cow?' said Mrs Cuskelly caressingly. 'He's nearly stufficated.'

'Vot, vot, vot?' croaked Grandpa.

But he had met his match at last. Within half an hour he had camphorated oil on one side of him and a mighty, steaming bread-poultice on the other. His medicine was within, and a hot-water bottle without. He kept staring at Mrs Cuskelly fascinatedly, muttering, 'The Rooshians have come.'

Perhaps he did have a very bad cold. Perhaps he had truly been worried about Ailie. But from then on he seemed to weaken. When Cocky Cuskelly, who was at home just then, wandered over looking for his mother, and stuck his immense head inside the door, Grandpa pulled the blankets up over his face. Not that I blamed him, for if ever anyone looked like a demented mushroom it was Cocky.

'Oh, Mrs Cuskelly, how shall I ever thank you?' said Barbara. 'You've taken all the spirit out of him in the most astonishing way.'

'Ah, he's a hidjust old baste,' said Mrs Cuskelly complacently. 'But I've got the measure of him. If he wasn't behaving like a Christian, I said, I'd take the head off him with a rapin' hook.'

Now all this time I heard no mention of Ailie, except that one of the kids at school told me that she was in the South Island. The kid had heard it from her mother, and had a ferrety curiosity to see how I would react. But I too was half Admiral. I said loftily, 'I know. And I'm going to visit her next holidays. See?'

But inwardly I was dismayed, because to me the South Island was very far away. And I longed terribly to ask Auntie Barbie about it all, and why they had never had any letters except that first one. Also I prayed passionately to my dear St Anthony that some day I might receive a secret little note from Auntie Ailie, perhaps hidden under my pillow, or in my nightdress case, telling me she missed me and was soon coming back.

But I said nothing to any of them, and they said nothing to me, and life went on in its usual way, with even Grandpa becoming part of the scene, as a thorn in the flesh has a habit of doing, if you stick with it long enough. Then one day my Auntie Barbie let out a shrill scream and pointed to a large advertisement in the Te Kano paper.

SEE YOUR FRIENDS
Te Kano's Own Masterpiece
Starring Musical Comedy Celebrity OLIVE URGENT
With a Cast of Hundreds
See it! See it! See it! ...

'Barbie, you're not going!' exclaimed Francey.

'Not after what you said,' I croaked.

'How can I tell how bad it is until I see it?' asked my Aunt Barbie with simple dignity, and with squeals of glee her sisters seized on me with the intention of whittling me into shape for the world *premiere*.

'We can't leave Grandpa,' I cried.

'Mrs Cuskelly is going to sit with him and read him her prayer-book,' answered Francey with malicious glee.

Barbara put the finishing stitches in my new tussore dress, Louisa shampooed me, and Francey mowed my toenails. But it takes more than aunts to beat a child of nine. I had one weapon in reserve. I could always have a catastrophic bilious attack and keep the whole lot of them at home.

I commenced my campaign by crawling under the passionfruit vine and devouring ten worm-eaten apples, a piece of mouldy bread, and the dregs from a tomato-sauce bottle. But my stomach was of iron. Tense with mental agony, but otherwise outstandingly well, I produced a bottle of castor oil and lingeringly sniffed it.

Oh, that glutinous, sweetish, incomparably oily smell! Usually it was enough to make me take to my bed for days, but this time not a thing happened.

'Oh, I can't let them find out,' I moaned. 'I wish I was dead.'

After all my promises, my resolutions that I would do no more wrong!

'I didn't know it wasn't a nice thing to do,' I could protest.

But I knew how they'd answer that, with the unanswerably adult sentence, 'We thought a well-brought-up little girl wouldn't have to be told.'

But there seemed no help for it. Throwing looks of disgust at St Anthony I emptied the castor-oil bottle into the dog's dinner-plate and gave myself up to the Radiant Aunts. Any other time I would have been delighted to go out at night wearing a new dress with a waistline so fashionably low that every time I sat down I was wounded by my belt-buckle, which Messrs Butterick had unreasonably designed to go at the back. Pallid and grim I set out with my aunts and shortly found myself in the dazzling lobby of that aged theatre the People's Palace.

The People's Palace had long spells of being bankrupt, during which time grateful tramps would come in and camp in the dress-circle, some even going so far as to boil up their billies on kerosene stoves, with the result that many a marble Venus suffered from heavily sooted buttocks. The seats were bald red plush which did not so much sink beneath one as slowly submerged. The asbestos fire-curtain was covered with placards from the theatre's vaudeville and legitimate history... Harry Lauder, Frances Alda, Galli-Curci, Adeline Genee, Allan Wilkie, and Ladies Please Remove Hats.

There was a tremendous smell of crayfish from somewhere, and an agitated usher yelling, 'Put out that pipe!' so that I knew my forbidden friend Blackleaf Forty had arrived. She had brought most of the Pa with her, and they swept down to the front stalls as though they were going to cut down the flagstaff. Blackleaf Forty didn't see me, because I was down between the seats, cravenly searching for a non-existent Mintie.

I can tell you the whole of Te Kano was there, barefoot Maoris, mill-boys, rosy farmers' wives, and the haughty Upper Crust with haughtier Upper Crustesses in printed marocain, Ciro pearls, and teddy-bear coats. It was a tense, giggling audience, a keg of powder due to explode.

'Oh, look, there's a new pianist!' cried Louisa.

Suddenly this pianist gave a terrible roll on the bass, the curtain shot up with a clang, and there was revealed in the cavernous depth of that vast stage a weeny screen which came galloping towards us with the manager's frantic legs beneath it.

Two long rays of light stabbed down from the operator's box, and the Epic Film commenced.

From the very first scene, when our Mr Minogue, the grocer, was revealed lying on his stomach scanning the horizon for attacking Maoris, the audience went into hysterics. Even mild cracks like, 'He's looking for the chook that laid that last bad egg!' made us fall off our seats. And when Mr Portwine, the baker, waveringly advanced and jerkily moved his jaws up and down in some silent but heroic words, the audience yelled, 'He's trying to eat one of his own rock cakes!' and nearly went into a fit. When our musical-comedy-society star Miss Olive Urgent appeared as Alice the heroine the roars of laughter drowned even the frantic clapping of her family *claque*, and her father stood up and offered to fight anyone, one at a time or all together.

'Oh, I never enjoyed myself so much before!' exclaimed my aunt Louisa, the tears rolling down her cheeks.

But Blackleaf Forty was the one. Her own sinister personality came across all the crudities of photography, and a deathly silence fell, broken only by the deep voice of Blackleaf Forty herself, booming, 'How dat, eh? Pretty bruddy good, eh?'

But by now I was bathed in a chill sweat, for this was the part in the picture when I appeared. What would they say? Would they be angry with me? I was paralysed with fear. Yet with a fascinated recognition I saw the silent antics between Alice and Blackleaf Forty, and the very cue where, as the little Maori messenger, I ran in to do my bit.

Here I came! The camera-man had thoughtfully given me a shot all to myself. A queer, dim little pyramid in a Maori mat, its head cut off at eyebrow-level like a boiled egg, it bobbed across the screen, waved a nebulous arm, and bobbed off again. No one could have told whether it was Jenny Hood or a wandering piece of ectoplasm. My relief and joy were suddenly submerged by bitterest disappointment. I began to sob loudly.

'Whatever's the matter?' cried Auntie Barbara.

'I'm going to have a bilious attack,' I gasped, and it was true.

Pale and exhausted, half asleep, heartbroken and relieved all in one, I was led home, and as we were nearing our moonlit gate I heard these words, 'I was *so annoyed*,' said my Auntie Barbie. 'Why, you couldn't even recognize the child!'

'All her pretty curls cut off by that fool photographer,' said Louisa.

'I only went to see her scene,' said Barbara. 'Poor little thing!'

'I'm so disappointed I could cry,' whispered Louisa the tender-hearted.

'Oh, my!' breathed Auntie Francey, mysteriously, 'did you see the new pianist!'

That was the first time I discovered the perfidy of grown-ups. Paralysed with this new knowledge I was borne into the front porch. In fact, I was so shocked that I could hardly spare time to be pleased that castor oil made dogs bilious, too.

Mrs Cuskelly had read the whole prayer-book to Grandpa, right through to the Burial Service and the Churching of Women. When Barbara tiptoed in to have a look at him he was moodily sitting up taking pot-shots at the bedpost with his whittling knife.

'H-how do you feel, Pa?' she asked timidly.

He did not answer, but, as she breathlessly reported to her sisters, he looked as if he were going to cry.

The next day he got up, threw his gear into his buggy, and harnessed up the nerve-wracked pony, which had grown so fat in our back paddock that it needed a corset.

Fedora had been summoned down from the Awakino, and she came, obedient but quaking.

Grandpa looked at no one but her. He was magnificent.

'Ay forgif you,' he announced. 'You can come back and look after me.'

'Oh, Syver, really!' squealed Auntie Fedora rapturously. She peered at him intently. 'And your aura's gone quite pink. That is goot sign, dear dear brudder.'

Honestly, that woman could have loved a wart-hog, had she put her mind to it. She cast a radiant look at the three aunts, who stood in an anxious row.

'Go on, Barbie!' hissed Francey.

Barbara said bravely, 'And Pa...'

'Vot, vot, vot?'

'You won't...interfere...with Ailie?' she faltered.

'Broddy vimmin!' said Grandpa. 'Ay vant no more talk of anything. Nodding. You hear? Is finished. Nefer I come back. Bah!'

He looked at Fedora and coughed beautifully.

She started forward, hand out in sympathy. 'Syver...'

He felt his chest. 'Is sore,' he commented in a sick little old man's voice.

'Pa,' squeaked Louisa imploringly.

He added a brief phrase in Swedish, gave the pony a whang on the middle-aged spread, and drove off. I thought he threw me a sideways glance as he left, but he might have been spitting or something. I always did think he liked me a little.

Auntie Fedora was standing there pink as a picotee.

'What *did* he say?' asked Francey cautiously.

'Oh, my dollings, how can I say it? Oh, he is naughty old man. Oh, dollings, he say you can all go to hell!'

There was a stupefied silence, and then the Radiant Aunts burst spontaneously into squeals and little cries of joy such as I had not heard since Ailie went. Louisa went round kicking up her heels in the Charleston, crying, 'That means I can get married! That means I can get married!'

'No it doesn't, Auntie Louie,' I corrected her. 'It means——'

But no one listened to me.

'He's cut us off without a shilling,' cried the aunts with relief and pleasure.

Auntie Fedora was just a little bit shocked. She was already starting to look on Grandpa as a poor old man whom nobody loved but herself. She wouldn't even stay for Louisa's wedding. Her brudder needed her she said; and next day, weeping happy tears, she took the coach to Kawhia.

'Well,' said Francey in her keen, capable way, 'now for Stanley.'

Stanley was the new cinema pianist, fresh from Auckland, with exuberant trousers (which he called bags), a rosy face, and sparkling brown eyes. He had a new kind of hair-do, parted in the middle with a bird's nest of curls on each side, and he played the piano in a way we had not heard it played in Te Kano. Well I recalled the melancholy and masterly ripplings of the departed Mr Fantocini, and of course I often heard demure tinklings from the new convent of a Saturday afternoon. But Stanley treated a tune like an enemy. He beat it over the head, twisted its arm, throttled it until at last it gave in and was thrown panting into a corner.

He was, in short, a jazz pianist.

Francey resolved to knock all that nonsense out of him after they were married.

She set about promoting their romance with the same brisk unsentimental spirit with which she would have looked at a nice piece of steak and decided whether to crumb it or do it with chutney in the pie-dish. Her clear blue eyes sized him up and saw all his disadvantages, but these, she considered, were easily to be removed by adroit engineering.

Francey, like the other aunts, was very pretty, with

chestnut hair which fell forward in cat's whiskers on the cheeks. In no time at all love had done its deadly work, and Stanley was a constant visitor. He had a very lofty black tin Lizzie with a distressing complaint in the exhaust, so that it burped sooty smoke over everyone's legs. I don't suppose I ever had a pair of clean socks after Stanley entered our lives. But I had lots of rides, and so did Pola, for he was a generous enthusiastic creature, fully prepared to love Francey's friends and relations along with Francey.

They did most of their wooing in the vast empty theatre after the *matinee*, and I was taken along as chaperone. Sometimes Pola came too, and we played hide-and-seek amongst the seats.

We thought the statues rude and embarrassing and never looked at them if we could help it.

Most of the time I was a very dutiful chaperone and wouldn't leave Stanley and Francey alone for an instant. If he kissed her I stared fascinated, thinking how much better he did it than the Pig Man kissed my Auntie Louisa. I meant to tell Louisa about it, but something always stopped me, mostly Francey.

So with Francey newly in love, and Louisa gloating over her trousseau and Ailie lost and doomed with her Maori boy, Barbara was in a way quite alone. She was sad and a little silent, though she entered with pleasure and gusto into her sisters' excited plans; she was too sweet a girl to spoil their romances with her own grief. But I don't think Barbie would have allowed herself to fall in love while the shadow of Ailie's disappearance lay over the household.

The banns were called, and, though the aunts had half feared it, no Grandpa appeared to forbid them. So the date of Louisa's wedding was fixed, and the Pig Man went to the tailor to be measured for a gigantic navy suit, with extra pair of trousers entirely free.

He, too, had not been idle during the betrothal months.

He had piped-in water to the kitchen and washhouse of his little dwelling, and also built on a new bedroom calsomined a lettuce-green which Francey said looked like a sick Chinaman. It cost her her second-best camisole, but Louisa started speaking to her again after a while.

Normally, the wedding of one of the Admiral girls would have been a grandly festive occasion, but in Ailie's scandalous absence the Radiant Aunts thought that this would be bad taste.

'People are going to talk, anyway,' said wistful Louisa, eyes filled with dreams of white satin and a lace veil and a bandeau of itchy little organdie rosebuds about her lovely eyebrows. 'But I know you're right, Barbie, and I don't mind, really.'

So it was decided that they would have a very quiet wedding, just with Relations present, and a very small breakfast afterwards.

'Stanley has promised a ham,' said Francey briskly, 'and Desmond a sucking pig, and Uncle Ray will manage some game...wild duck, I hope...and Mr. Cuskelly is sure to pot a few rabbits.'

'Must we have the Cuskellys?' moaned Louisa, 'I won't have Cocky. I warn you girls, if Cocky comes I'll screech.'

'We'll all screech,' said Francey practically. 'But we've just got to ask them in to look at the presents and have some cake. Don't forget we owe simply everything to Mrs Cuskelly and her prayer-book, Louisa love.'

The house was full of little bits of wedding dress, a baby-blue *crêpe de Chine* with the very latest hemline dipping 'way down towards the heels at the back. It worried Barbara very much, because she was most conscientious about getting hems even, and she kept peering at Louisa and saying that she could see the back from the front and it looked as though Louisa were losing some of her underwear.

So Francey, who was by then on the verge of a nervous

breakdown with Stanley's city-styled ardour and all the preliminary cooking, christened Louisa 'Droopy Drawers', and Louisa had hysterics and said she wouldn't get married at all, and the Pig Man came in from Waitomo and swore that if Louisa didn't marry him he'd damn well vote Labour at the next election.

"And I don't care if the country *does* go to rack and ruin,' he said.

It was thrilling. I enjoyed every moment of it, and one day said unguardedly, 'Wouldn't Auntie Ailie just love all this?'

Only Barbara was there at the time. She looked up over the gold-scrolled top of the old Singer they kept at home and said, 'Do you ever think of her, Jenny?'

I blurted out, 'All the time.'

Then I thought she would be angry, but instead she got up and put her arms round me. 'Oh, Jenny! Oh, I am so glad. Oh, Jenny!'

Then she said hurriedly, 'Run away and play with Violet, there's a good girl.'

For a moment I had almost entered the adult world. I had felt her tremble and it was a confidence. The break in her voice had brought me closer than I had ever been to understanding.

I wanted to say something, but I did not know what to say. All I could do was to be obedient, and to offer the obedience up like a sacrifice to my love for Auntie Barbara.

So I went out, like a good girl, and played with Violet. But my heart wasn't in it. I wanted to talk to Auntie Barbara again, to be admitted to her confidence entirely, to be on her level of understanding, to say the right things . . . to offer, as it were, my own contribution of privy knowledge. Only I had none.

'Do you ever see Huriana Hana?' I asked Pola shyly.

'Nope,' answered Pola. 'Haven't seen her since we started at the convent.'

I looked away dismally, wanting to ask her to go with me and look at the Hana house, but not daring to. I did not even know why I wanted to look at it, except to be able to report to Auntie Barbara that it seemed empty, or uncared for, or different in some way since the happening that had apparently been as tragic to them as it had been to us.

'Let's go and visit old Pou,' I said. I had hardly suggested it before all the potentialities of such a visit came brightly before me.

It seemed to be years since I had seen him. He belonged to that carefree time before Auntie Ailie, before Kawhia, before the crossing of the Tasman Sea. All at once I wanted to see him badly. Besides, the dog's puppies would be grown up.

Pola wouldn't come in. She was afraid of Pou, though she did not admit that. Hanging her head, and dragging a stubby toe through the dust, she said she'd wait in the tea-tree and play with the dog.

The little shanty was as solitary as ever. Only the faint glaze of smoke above the roof showed that it was inhabited. The tank bled a rusty dribble, and the dog jumped beneath it, snapping at the drops. She had the currish, furtive-eyed look of a Maori dog, but she came wriggling to Pola and me, eager for caresses.

Pola was very proud of my bravery. So I swaggered to the door, shouting, 'Pou! You home?'

The door flapped to behind me, and I was once more in the malodorous dusk I knew so well. But I was older now, and a little trepidation I had never experienced since my first visit crept slowly up my back.

At first the old man was just a shapeless hummock, and the holes in the roof were stars which sent down patches of light to lie upon him. Then I saw the dim flicker of his eyes. There was life there, but life seen down a long tunnel.

175

In the soft swathes of ash on the fireplace a few embers gasped. I had hardly got inside before I wanted to go out again, but I was too vain to face Pola's inquiring look. So I sat down on the other side of the fire. The big head dipped falteringly towards me.

He did not look surprised. The capacity for feeling surprise seems to be lost to the extremely old. The sun rises, the wind blows, faces appear and vanish, but these things are all part of a pattern which has ceased to have novelty.

'I've got a loose tooth,' I informed him.

He mumbled awhile, then began to sing. It was a tuneless quavering whine, half a chant. He often did this, so I took no notice.

'When will your dog have more puppies?' I asked.

But he went on singing. Then I saw that he had something in his hands. At first I thought it was a doll, but it was a wooden marionette, long, skinny-limbed, carved intricately, painted in dim blots of red ochre and black spiderings like the coaly patterns in punga wood. As I watched, it feebly raised an arm and stamped a foot.

I squawked with delight. The old man was manipulating it with flaxen cords, and it was doing a haka. Ai-ai, the waggling hand, and the thigh-slap, the sound simulated by the old man by a tongue-click! The wooden feet made prints in the ash, like those of a tiny animal. The flaxen piupiu swayed and my head swayed with it.

The old man's chant, its rhythm betrayed by his tremulous vocal cords, was no more than a whisper, but it had pleasure for me. I was half hypnotized. The thing, like all puppets, had taken on a delicious miniature life, and when the singing stopped, and the doll clapped all its limbs together and tumbled face downwards into the ash as though unconscious, I gave a cry of concern and leaned forward to help it.

Pou said abruptly, 'Do not touch!' and I remembered his presence and looked at him amazed.

The fire was dimmer, the house was darker, his withered flesh was invisible. I could see only cheekbone and jawline, and thick hair that was a shape and not a colour, and these things seemed to belong not to him but to Donald Hana. He was Donald's great-great-grandfather. Their blood was the same.

I said shyly and humbly, 'I'm a kind of relation of yours now.'

But he did not respond, and I felt that perhaps I had been impudent and, very greatly abashed, turned aside and pretended to be interested in the dying fire. The image of Auntie Ailie came very clearly before me, a static image like a photograph, her head turned a little to one side, her eyes downcast, and a strand of linty hair blowing against one cheek. I wanted her so much. Oh, where was she, and what was she doing, and when was she coming home to talk to me and be as she had been?

The feeling of personal affront, that she had preferred Donald's company to mine, was deep and real. Yet I had no grudge against Ailie. I just wanted her. Why could she not stay in Te Kano with Donald, so that I could see her sometimes?

The feeling of her presence was so strong I could almost smell her perfume. With joy I looked up to see her but there was no one there. No one but Pou.

'How long will my Auntie stay away?' I whispered.

And he said, 'I nga wa katoa,' which I think means 'Ever', or 'Always'.

I did not know what to say. The words really had little meaning for me. If he had said 'Five years', it would have been much more hurtful, for that was a comprehensible period, and in my opinion, one of appalling length.

All I could think of saying was 'Why?'

Maybe in some peculiar way old Pou had taken a fancy to me. I think what followed happened that way because he wanted to please me. Or perhaps he wanted to demonstrate, probably for the last time, the powers that had once made him feared throughout the King Country.

You are thinking that I am going to tell you Pou raised up an apparition of Auntie Ailie, or that in some way I was able to see her in the distant town to which she and Donald Hana had fled. Well, he didn't do those things, but looking back, I am convinced that *he tried*.

No one can deny that the real Maori sorcerer could do some inexplicable things. We have, for instance, the evidence of that thoroughly matter-of-fact and honourable man, Bishop Selwyn, that he was shamefully bested in a contest with Unuaho the Arawa wizard, some time in the late eighteen forties. The Established Church could scarcely be expected to run to magic, but the heathen did, blasting a cabbage-tree to a dead skeleton before the bishop's eyes, and then restoring it.

The three-fingered gods lived in the fern-hills then. For all I know they still do.

When I first heard the wind blowing, not outside, but *inside* the house, I was not frightened, but astounded. I sat there and listened to the whistlings and whisperings, the croonings and the tiny squeaks and whimpers of air which could not be felt. For the embers still glowed steadily, and there was no movement against my cheek. The old man was muttering to himself short, sharp, indistinguishable sentences with a pronounced rhythm. It did not sound like Maori, and indeed there is no reason to suppose it was. And the wind rose more strongly all the time.

He had begun to play again with the puppet. It lifted its long arms, brought them together, walked a step or two, turned its head ... and all these things were so characteristic of Ailie that I recognized them at once. Then it collapsed.

'Do it again, do it again!' I cried, overjoyed. So you see, I wasn't scared. Fear didn't hypnotize me into believing these things happened. The old man picked up the puppet once more. Again it moved in Ailie's blithe girlish manner, smoothed the back of its head, as she was wont to do, turned and looked over its shoulder as I had seen her look. . . .

Its shape was so attenuated it was inhuman, and yet for a moment or two it was something like her in shape as well as manner. Then it tumbled over once more, all of a heap.

He did this over and over again. But he did not seem to be able to sustain the impersonation. He threw the marionette to one side, angrily, as though it had failed him. I longed to pick it up and comfort it.

I could see the wind now, fluttering the edges of the broken tin round the holes in the roof. It seemed to be captive, and just beneath the roof itself. But there was yet stillness round the fireplace.

Then Pou began to speak in Ailie's voice. It was a dreadful shock. The voice was not hers – it was just an imitation of her voice. The inflexions were exact, the tone perfect, yet there was a phony, tinny ring about it, as though it were a record on a cheap phonograph.

She said, 'But honestly, girls . . .,' and 'Nobody would ever persuade *me* *to* do the Charleston,' and then, 'When you grow up you'll know that I was right.'

Only with that last sentence Pou's throat-muscles failed, and he . . . or she . . . went on repeating 'Know I was right, know I was right, know I was right', and growing more distant with each repetition until the sound was that of a budgie shut up in a tin.

Even then I wasn't afraid. I was surprised, yes, and faintly angry, because I didn't for a moment think it was anything but Pou imitating my Auntie Ailie. And I thought he had a cheek to do it.

The old man's face was incredibly sunken, a little wee face like that of a sick baby. And the colour had changed to a greyish hue plainly visible in the half light. His lips moved ceaselessly. I thought he had gone to sleep, and I was pleased, because then I could go away and have a game with Pola and the dog.

Then he began to speak again. All kinds of voices poured between those livid lips, in English and Maori, and what I thought was Dalmatian, the only foreign tongue I had heard. Women's voices, clear and treble, grumbling men's voices, and once that of a giggling child. He was like a wireless set, pouring out sounds that belonged to other people.

I sat in enraptured amazement. Everyone likes to eavesdrop, and now I was certainly eavesdropping. It was as though Pou, having failed to contact Ailie, except in some false, long-distance way, had sent his entranced mind roaming round Te Kano, past and present. For I was beginning to recognize the voices. The enormous rolling laughter surely belonged to Mr Georgie Wi, the Maori farmer who brought round the vegetables, and the mean whine of Mr Minogue, the grocer. I heard my ex-teacher, Miss Carroll, and then a dozen voices involved in an argument, which ended in blows and curses, and a solitary woman crying.

I thought it was like the magic pipkin in Hans Andersen, which enabled one to know what everyone else was eating for supper that night. And I wanted urgently to call Pola in, so that she could hear this delightful thing too.

And then... then there was a single, plangent sound like a harp-string plucked, and silence.

I heard the wind again, crying and whimpering in the roof.

A woman spoke, a thick and treacly voice that said wicked and insulting things. I had heard it before. I knew it at once.

A man answered her, sobbing, weeping, 'You did it on purpose! You destroyed it on purpose! My manuscript! My work!'

It was then that I began to feel queer. I backed away

from the fire on my hands and knees, until I came against the heap of kindling and could go no farther. The harp-string sound came again out of Pou's withered mouth. Oh, it was strange to hear that rich reverberant sound issue from a chest that was nothing but bones!

Then a flood of a foreign language poured out, half whispered, half screamed . . . it palpitated with grief and a passionate fury. The woman's laugh answered it, cut off short with a gurgling hoot that made me break out all over in a sweat. There were gasps, loud in the silence, and then the man weeping harshly.

I didn't even look at Pou. I flew out of that hut as though the Devil were after me, and ran full pelt into my friend Pola, who had been listening at the door. Perhaps everything would have been all right if she had only cut and run with me. But she caught me by the arm and said, 'How did the Fantocinis get in there?'

'There's no one in there but old Pou,' I retorted.

Pola's beautiful eyes blazed. 'I heard Mr and Mrs Fantocini fighting,' she insisted.

Even then I didn't realize that this was the end of the Fantocini story, which had commenced when Pola and I had gone into that silent, empty house down the street.

It is only since, remembering the indolent, fleshly wickedness, the sadistic look of that half-crazy woman, and the sad anxiety of that poor little man, that I have felt pleased that Pola and I happened to be the two interfering kids who removed from that sinister house enough evidence to hang Mr Fantocini.

I pushed past her and ran for my life through the tea-tree. Pola panted an arm's length behind, yelling breathlessly, 'I did so hear Mr Fantocini, and he was talking Italian like he did sometimes . . . I did *so*, and you're a liar, Jenny Hood!'

We fought all the way home, scratching and punching and breaking away and running, and then turning to pounce on the pursuer. And somehow by the time we had reached our own street we had worked off the excitement and unnaturalness of it all, and were walking along quite quietly, snarling sideways at each other, and each waiting for her companion to make the first overture of friendship.

Then, all at once Pola was crying. I felt no pity for her, but much shock and embarrassment.

'What's the matter with you, *boob*?' I inquired brutally.

'I just . . . I just didn't like it,' she jerked out between her sobs.

'Didn't like what?'

'Them voices and everything.'

Pola's Celtic perception had seized without reason or understanding on the truth. What had happened at Pou's shanty hadn't been normal. But neither of us knew how to say this.

'I feel funny about it, Jen,' whispered Pola pleadingly.

'Well, go on, pimp!' I retorted, angrily and fearfully. Pola shook her head and dawdled away, and I was left wanting to run after her, and not knowing what to say if I did.

We entered into a tacit avoidance of each other. We embarrassed ourselves unbearably by our very determination not to mention the Pou incident again. Pola made into a temporary alliance with those horny-kneed Kirbys whose idea of a game was a ding-dong battle with horse manure. I struck up a friendship with Nora Bedding, a feeble-minded snob who could keep her Christmas dolls' tea-set for a whole year without breaking a saucer. Her conception of fun was to pour out make-believe tea from her dolls' teapot and address me as Mrs Pom, in an unintelligibly refined accent. At first I thought this was nice, and answered 'rayther', and 'Oh, fawncy,' to her remarks, but after a while it palled, and I jumped up hurriedly and stood on her cream jug, and was never allowed to come again.

So, my dear friend Pola battered and soiled, and myself an exiled Mrs Pom, we remained apart yet longed to be together.

And the wedding day drew nearer and nearer until it was tomorrow. Louisa's bits of furniture had been moved into the Pig Man's house, and the Radiant Aunts had made curtains and bedspreads and table-runners, and every little thing in every room had a frilly doily under it, except the Pig Man. The Pig Man had had his wedding haircut, straight up the back like a wall, and his scalp shone confidingly through the maize-yellow stubble. Mr Bonnet had given Louisa something known as a marcel wave, and her hair was ridged in circular bands from ear to ear. It was considered pretty snazzy, I can tell you, especially when worn with long, skinny pearl eardrops, like fishbones.

Our bridesmaid's dresses were ready, sheaths of pale-mauve *crêpe de Chine* for the aunts, trimmed with long slanting bands of silk fringe, and for me pale pink with no fringe. We all had picture hats of crinoline with floating streamers and wore our gold bangles which were a present from the Pig Man.

That tense, giggly, weepy atmosphere which marks a house preparing for a wedding rose to a climax. The weather grew suddenly hot and the jellies all unjelled. The Hen and Chickens arrived and went into an instant orgy of what might have been. One kept finding Chickens crying into sodden little hankies, and then looking up bravely and saying: 'Oh, aren't I awful?'

Louisa was pale and nerve-wracked and inclined to back out, and Barbara was sweet and firm, and Francey was desperately involved with a blowfly.

Regarding the common housefly, the Te Kano world had but recently emerged from the era of swat. The idea of the vaporized insecticide was there, but only just. Most people preferred flypaper, and were a little alarmed at the thought of injecting all that poison into the domestic atmosphere.

'Suppose it hangs around,' they mused, 'and we all wake up dead?'

But the Radiant Aunts were all for innovation, and puffed enthusiastically. I use the verb correctly. We did not have sprays. With the bottle of Flit the manufacturer supplied a thin metal tube with a little flat mouthpiece. You put the end of the tube in the Flit bottle, puffed frenziedly into the mouthpiece, and were usually rewarded by a feeble cloud of vapour.

This was known as Flitting.

Auntie Francey was a great Flitter. She detested flies and would chase an isolated specimen round until she was purple in the face and the fly set off through the valley of the shadow.

On the wedding morning she rose at five and went through the house puffing like a steamship. She was quite winded, I think, for she kept feeling her solar plexus with a pained expression and sitting down for little rests.

When the sitting-room atmosphere was deemed safe for human consumption we went in and laid the table with the best linen and silver. It looked a whizz, I thought, with little cocked-up serviettes and the wedding cake white as snow in the centre, and bowls of flowers here and there. There were also a couple of bottles of cider 'for the men'. The Admiral girls, having sprung from a long line of schnapps-sodden ancestors, were blue-ribbon.

Auntie Francey was irritable in a suppressed, patient kind of way when I kept putting the forks upside down. I thought maybe she wanted to be in the bedroom helping Louisa. I was itching to get in there myself, but not to look at Louisa, but to climb into my own pale-pink array.

Barbara was having a difficult time with Louisa, who was as white as wax, and consequently looked prettier

184

than ever, like a fairy bride. She kept whimpering, 'Oh, Barbie, I'll faint, I know I will!'

And then Barbara would say soothingly, 'Oh, Louie darling, of course you won't. Besides, think of Desmond! He's thinking of *you*, right at this moment.'

'No, he isn't,' replied Louisa crankily. 'He's feeding the mother pigs.'

Wonderful girl, she had adapted herself to the pigs, but she still thought 'sows' was a rude word.

At last we were all ready, and we looked beautiful. Mrs Cuskelly came in for a peep, burst into tears, and threw her apron over her head. I was baffled to know why, but the Radiant Aunts seemed to understand.

Stanley drew up outside on his bucking steed, and anxiously unscrewed the radiator cap. A geyser of steam shot out, and he shook his head and said, 'She's heating, for some reason, heating like a lunatic.'

Louisa and Francey were to go with Stanley, and Barbara and myself in the taxi. The Hen and Chickens, who were staying with Uncles Olga and Ray at Waitomo, were coming up with them.

Well, just as we were dashing round shutting the windows and having a final look to see that all was in readiness for the breakfast, Francey discovered a blowfly on the ceiling of the sitting-room. An insect of iron constitution, it had survived the Flit.

All her tenseness of the morning came to a head. She threw down her bridesmaid's bouquet and looked with anguish at the sullen, steel-blue blob on the ceiling.

'I can't possibly go with that up here,' she cried despairingly.

'But we'll cover the table up,' said Barbara firmly, taking a surreptitious peep at her watch.

'No good,' wailed poor Francey. 'It might get into the safe.'

'Oh, darling, it *won't*,' said Louisa.

'But it *might*. We might come home to find the sucking pig all thinged.'

'Francey,' said Barbara tenderly, 'you're just all upset and overworked. That's a perfect meat-safe and we've never had any of our meat thinged before. Now come along, like a good girl.'

Then to our horror Francey burst into tears. Not stormy great boo-hoos but little shuffles and dabbings and nose-blowings, and cries of, 'Oh, I am so sorry...don't let Louie get upset...it's nothing really...great big blue-bottomed beast of a blowfly...I suppose I *am* a bit out-of-sorts...it's just that I thought with all the wedding atmosphere and everything Stanley might propose, and he didn't...and oh, Barbie, it doesn't seem natural to have one of us married without darling little Ailie here!'

Barbara patted Francey's back, making womanly noises.

'How could we ask her, when we don't know where she is?' said Louisa in a stifled voice.

Then they caught sight of me standing there with my mouth open, and Francey blew her nose and tried to smile, and said, 'My, aren't I a big booby, Jenny, and all because I'm a bit tired!'

At this moment Stanley poked his head into the kitchen and cried, 'She'll explode if you don't come soon!'

So, with little screams and squeaks, the Radiant Aunts pushed me out, locked the door, waved to the Cuskellys on the fence, and tore up the path, rubbing their noses with their powder 'shammies' as they went.

Stanley drove with grave decorum which well befitted the occasion. As he explained afterwards, it wasn't so much that he wanted to give Te Kano a good look at the bride, but that he was afraid the tin Liz would go to kingdom come in a shower of boiling water.

As for Barbara and me, we had hardly reached the corner of our street before she began to have frightful misgivings about that blowfly.

186

'Oh, Jenny...imagine if it *did* do something awful. Imagine if we did come home to find everything thinged. And did I shut that safe properly? Jenny! *Did I?*'

Within ten seconds she had convinced herself that in the flurry she had left it wide open.

'I've got to go back,' she cried in agony. 'I couldn't enjoy the wedding a bit. I'm sure we've got time, Stanley's going so slow.'

The taxi-driver reckoned he could go back to the house and catch up to Stanley again before the latter could change gears, so we turned round and scorched back to the house.

I heard the hullaballoo in Cuskellys' even before Auntie Barbara and I tore infuriatedly inside, to find naturally that the meat-safe was tightly closed, and the blowfly had gone to its eternal rest on the sitting-room window-sill. Then in dashed Pola with her mother after her, holding a shaving strop. Pola's face was blubbered beyond recognition, and her mother was scarlet with anger. Formidable, she was.

'Tell her it wasn't my fault, Jenny,' Pola screamed. 'Tell her I never went inside!'

My Auntie Barbara was very shocked. 'Whatever is the matter, Mrs Cuskelly?'

'The little devil's been down in the scrub with the Maoris, getting up to God knows what hobblegobblins!'

And she gave Pola a crack round the legs with the strop, which nearly knocked the feet from under her.

'I didn't go inside!' screeched Pola. 'I just listened. Didn't I, Jen? Don't hit me, don't hit me!'

Now meantime my poor aunt was ducking this way and that, trying to get past Mrs Cuskelly, and endeavouring to get in a word about he wedding and how late we already were for it, but Mrs Cuskelly stood there like a policeman. As for me, a guilty and chilly premonition was pricking my skin into goose-pimples.

Suddenly Mrs Cuskelly turned on me. 'And she knows more than her prayers, too, the same one! Sarsery, and spells, and haythen superstitions. Bringing back the dead, no doubt. Oh, blessed hour! What am I to do with yez both at all, at all!'

My poor friend, led by goodness knows what simple honesty in her nature, had confessed about Pou.

Meanwhile my aunt had drawn herself up and said crisply, 'We'll speak about it when I return, Mrs Cuskelly. Now, if you'll excuse us, we have a wedding to attend.'

'Tell her I on'y listened, Jen,' beseeched Pola.

'Yes, she only listened,' I croaked. 'I was the one that went inside.'

'I'm not surprised, yer little munx,' said Mrs Cuskelly. Like an enraged elephant she turned and lumbered away, driving Pola before her, a crumpled, hysterical figure. In deathly silence Barbara locked up, and we returned to the taxi. I was shocked to the core. I shrank into my corner, hardly daring to look at her. Then she said:

'What Maoris?'

'The...the old man. Pou,' I said in a whisper.

'Who's he?'

The breath would hardly come round the lump in my throat. I choked, 'He's Huriana's great-grandfather. He lives...down in the scrub past Kirbys'.'

'What did she mean, sorcery?'

I didn't know what to say. I looked at her imploringly.

'He made voices come. Pola was listening outside and she heard them. And I was frightened so I ran away.'

Heaven knows what sort of a tale it must have sounded to my Auntie Barbara. Only one thing was sure. She believed in the supernatural as firmly as did Mrs Cuskelly, though she did not have the same superstitious horror of it. Her lips came together firmly. She said in a low voice, 'How many times have we told you not to play with the Maoris?'

'You only said Blackleaf Forty,' I protested. 'You never said anything about Pou.'

The taxi-driver was suffering extremely trying to catch the conversation above the rattle of his engine. Barbara lapsed into silence.

'There's Stanley ahead,' she observed in a tight conversational voice.

And indeed the tin Liz was standing out very boldly on the skyline, like a pitch-black covered wagon.

'You *didn't* say I wasn't to see Pou!' I burst out, injured to the soul. 'And I only went to see if his dog had more puppies.'

'Sssssh, dear,' said Auntie Barbara. The driver's ears slowly swivelled forwards again. We drew close behind the tin Liz, and pulled up beside the church. There was a little knot of people by the steps, the Hen and Chickens all blowing their noses, and Uncle Olga smiling happily, and Father FitzPeter just about to bustle off and get into his surplice.

'Where on earth did you get to?' breathed Francey as we grouped ourselves.

'I went back to see about the blowie and it's dead,' answered Barbara.

'No things?'

'Not a thing,' Barbara assured her.

Francey and Louisa bloomed. They cast each other congratulatory looks as we formed ourselves into a little procession in the church porch. The church was a small amber cavern, with the big round rose-window shining at one end, and the altar shining beneath it, and the Pig Man's yellow head shining in front of the altar.

'*Uncle* Pig Man,' I said tremulously to myself. A terrible sentimentality swept over me.

'Oh, wish me luck, girls!' came Louisa's whisper, and then we went slowly down the aisle to the thin sweet wheeze of the old harmonium.

All through the ceremony a green linnet sat on a beam near the windows and watched with a silver-ringed eye.

And when the wind blew I could hear the sea-sound of the bush on the Awakino Hill.

I still think Louisa's was the nicest wedding I ever saw.

In a romantic haze I floated out of the church after my aunts, and lifted up my face to have the confetti fall on it like rain. Only it was rice. The Hen was old-fashioned.

'You're quite certain you can see all right, Jenny dear?' Auntie Barbie was asking me a moment or so later, in the car.

'Simply absurd,' one of the Chickens snapped. 'A bit of rice in the eye. Why, I've been to weddings in my time when the bride and bridegroom were positively *wounded*. And no fuss about it, either.'

I loved leaning against Auntie Barbie's slight bosom, with her arms round me. I reclined there all the way home, one eye shut, the other surveying all the adult wonders with interest and surmise. I had forgotten all about the Cuskelly incident, and it wasn't recalled until we reached home, and the Relations spread rustling and laughing and diffusing little waves of lavender water and violet and carnation all over the house. The house had lost Grandpa's imprint. It was easy to see it was inhabited only by women. Big hats lay on beds, a sunshade hung from the hallstand, there was the birdlike murmuration of feminine voices everywhere.

The Pig Man and Uncle Ray hardly knew what to do with themselves. They sat politely on the back porch, keeping out of the way of the women. Stanley was in the kitchen, under Francey's feet, where he was destined to be for the rest of his life.

'Come along, dear, and get your pinny on,' said Barbara, and she led me unresisting but chilly with alarm into the bedroom.

I waited for an accusation, but she was silent, tying my pinny strings and giving an occasional happy little sigh. It seemed as though she had forgotten.

'You *didn't* tell me not to go to Pou's place, you know!' I burst out.

'Umm? Oh. Well, never mind that now, dear.'

'*Nobody* told me not to go there but Mr Hana.'

Barbara looked at me sharply. Her face paled a little. 'Mr Hana? Why?'

'He said Pou was a magician.'

Now I was sorry I had said anything at all, for Barbara went over and shut the door. 'What did Mrs Cuskelly mean, when she said raising the dead?'

'He didn't raise the dead,' I said scornfully. 'Pou just sort of went to sleep, and then all the voices spoke.'

'Whose voices?' said Barbara, dread coming into her own again.

'Oh, Georgie Wi's. He was saying D-words and B-words.' I saw the look on her face and added primly, 'Of course *I* didn't listen to *that*. And then there was Mrs Fantocini saying things to Mr Fantocini. I never did like her. And ... um ... well, Miss Carroll and Mr Minogue, and lots and lots of people I didn't know.'

There was a shriek of laughter outside, and someone banged on the bedroom door. 'Come on, Barbara, the photographer's here, dear!'

Barbara cast a desperate look at the door. 'Already, Auntie Olga?' She had stopped being alarmed and was eaten up with a slightly incredulous curiosity.

'And then there was Auntie Ailie. She said ...'

Barbara's cheek was white as milk. She removed her hat with trembling fingers.

'Ailie?' she asked, with touching casualness.

Just then the door flew open and the Chicken fluttered

in, still red-nosed and pink-eyed, but very excited and wedding-happy.

'Quick, Barbie darling, everyone's ready...oh, she's taken her hat off. Put it on again, you silly article. Oh, you should see the photographer, Barbie, he's a bobby-dazzler. Hurry up, take that silly pinny off Jenny. And her nose needs wiping. Blow *hard*, dear. Hurry up, mustn't keep him waiting. Oh, he's a *dream*, Barbie. You'll *die!*'

In a moment or two we were all lined up, with Louisa and the Pig Man in the centre. The Pig Man was taking a cautious suck or two at his fingers which Uncle Ray had by mischance jammed in the kitchen door. The brides-maids pulled their hats dashingly down over their fore-heads, so that they would look completely *a la mode*, quite forgetting that thirty years later they would look at that very picture and shriek, 'Oh, those hats! Girls, just *look* at those hats!'

The picture is faded and brown, stuck on an old-fashioned fox-marked mount. It gives nothing of the beauty of that first family wedding group...Stanley's dancing brown eyes, and his tie of Eastern splendour, the yellow hair of the new husband, the glitter of our bangles, Uncle Ray's moustache like a blond bow-tie, the girlish pink faces of the Radiant Aunts, the long, long necklace that Uncle Olga wore, full of sea-blue, grass-green, and lemony lights.

It is, frankly, a funny picture. Louisa is holding her bouquet like a fireman's hose, Francey as though she is going to whip up a cake. The Hen is just about to cry again. She has the expression of one who has bitten on a bad peanut. As for me, my features are screwed up in agony.

I was, however, only waiting for the photographer, who I thought was called Bobby Dazzler, to emerge from his shroud. He took hours to arrange his demurely tweeded tail under the black cloth. First it would go up then it would hunch down. Sometimes it would be tucked under so far that I thought he had vanished altogether, like a pigeon into a magician's handkerchief.

Finally it began to swing almost imperceptibly from side to side, as a cat's does when it is about to pounce.

'Smale, please!' cried a vibrant voice, and we smaled, and there was a click, and we had been immortalized.

Instantly everyone began to talk. The Pig Man and Auntie Louisa beamed at each other, a lovely beam compact of shyness and relief and love and that simple indivisibility that was going to be a characteristic of their married life. Stanley whipped a mouth-organ out of his pocket and began to jazz through the Wedding March. Uncle Ray threw his head back suddenly and hit the Hen on the beak. Francey rushed at General Smuts and with joyful tears gave his damper such a kick it nearly came out the back of the chimney. But the Chickens and I were all standing round staring at Mr Bobby Dazzler.

'Oh, what an interesting life you must lead!' smarmed the youngest Chicken.

'May I peep-o inside the camera and see my picture?' beseeched the second Chicken. 'I do *so* want to see if I look nice.'

'Won't you stay and have a teeny slice of wedding cake, oh, *doooo!*' cried the third.

They fluttered their black wings and gave forth waves of perfume. Mr B. Dazzler said, 'Owww, you are so keend. Ay don't meend if I do.' Although the fourth Chicken had treacherously stolen away to the wedding-breakfast table and kept a vacant seat beside her for the photographer, he came and sat beside me. I was overcome by shyness, but managed to answer his kind chirpings, 'Yes, Mr Dazzler, no, Mr Dazzler.'

Finally he said. 'And tell me, gellie, wee do you call me Mr Dazzler?'

'Don't you want me to?' I stammered.

'Oooooo, nooo, how could I?'

So after that I called him Bobby, and he was even more mystified.

It was a lovely breakfast. I enjoyed it tremendously. Everyone was so busy talking that I could eat what I liked. For the first time I had pork, ham, quail, custard, and trifle all on the same plate.

Happiness reigned until the toasts were being given, when the Hen and Chickens found the habit of years too much for them and burst into spontaneous weeping. ('Oh, darling little Louie, won't we miss her? I can't help thinking of what-might-have-been. Oh, aren't I *awful*? Dear, dear Louisa!')

The Chickens cried neatly and attractively, but the Hen dropped her cake into her ginger-ale with a shocking splash.

'Oh, really, mother darling!' carped the Chickens.

But Mr Dazzler tenderly took his flawless handkerchief and with exquisite propriety removed a sodden crumb from the fourth tuck on the right of the Hen's black satin bosom.

'Pooor leedy,' he commented.

The Hen was bowled over like a one-legged skater. In a moment or two one could hear, amidst the clink of china and the babble of happy voices, such phrases as, 'But I'm old enough to be your mother, you naughty boy!' and, 'You have known greet grief, ooooh, yes, you have! Tell me about it, dear, dear leedy.'

The Chickens were infuriated, and Uncle Ray, the Pig Man and Stanley, knowing that no New Zealander could possibly talk that way, kept mumbling things about blasted foreigners.

But the Chickens didn't get their mother away home until Mr Dazzler had extorted from her a promise to come along for a free sitting.

'Sitting's the word, the silly old chook,' muttered Uncle Ray.

Then the photographer, after many graceful compliments all round, clapped on a large furry cycling cap shaped like a bicycle-seat, and roared away.

'Most embarrassed...at her age...getting childish ...do forgive, Barbie dear,' said the departing Chickens. I was so engrossed with my eavesdropping that it was ages before I woke up to the fact that Uncle Pig Man had gone too.

I had thought I would be sad, but I was too full to feel anything. I just sat on the sofa looking bloated, and ruminating quietly on the mysteries of life.

Now, several times during the festivities my Auntie Barbara had looked yearningly at me, as though longing to ask a question forbidden by the press of company. I knew very well what it was. I realized now that she would attach no criminal intent to my visit to the old man Pou. I just hadn't known any better. So I didn't mind in the least telling her what had happened there. Except about the Fantocinis, perhaps.

Nevertheless, when I heard the voice of Mrs Cuskelly in the kitchen my instinct was to get behind the sofa. But I was too sluggish and overfed.

Mrs Cuskelly was protesting that she had come only to help wash the dishes, there being such a cruel lot of them, and the two Radiant Aunts such frail slips av girls, Barbie in particular not being the width of a ha-penny herring.

And the aunts were hospitably pressing cake and cider on her, and urging her to come and see Louisa's presents before they were packed.

The next moment the sitting-room was full in all directions of Mrs Cuskelly. Behind her, a fox-footed shadow, was my friend Pola. I knew at once she had been forgiven her transgressions. She had about her that ceremonial humility a dog displays when it has been justly chastised and admitted once more to its master's favour.

Francey, of course, did not know of Pola's crime and

punishment. But Barbara, who did not approve of child-beating, was a little distant and delicately acid.

Mrs Cuskelly hadn't forgiven me, either. Her frosty blue eyes sliced through me, and she gave a ponderous huff of the shoulder in my direction, like an offended parrot. This so disturbed the precarious balance of my stomach that I didn't know whether to feel sick or hungry. I reached out and took a piece of pork-crackling from the littered table and chewed on it languidly.

'Green eyes greedy,' commented Mrs Cuskelly.

Barbara chilled. 'I do hope your family can help us out by eating up some of these left-overs, Mrs Cuskelly,' she said. 'Francey and I couldn't possibly dispose of a quarter of them.'

Her princessy air was designed to warn Mrs Cuskelly away from making any more rude remarks about me, but Mrs Cuskelly didn't notice.

'How many pigs did you say Louisa's man is owning?' she asked.

'Several hundred, I think,' said Francey with restraint.

The aunts still thought it would have been nicer if the Pig Man had been a Chook Man.

'Several hundred it is,' marvelled Mrs Cuskelly, 'and he a fine lump of a lad into the bargain. Well, that's the way av it, some have the luck and some have the sorra.'

'Just look at all the linen Louisa has had given her!' cried Francey hastily. 'These worked tablecloths came from our cousins at Napier.'

'Now, take my man,' continued Mrs Cuskelly, rolling over Francey like a locomotive, 'it'd be asier to crack an egg indways than to get him to work.'

'And Auntie Olga and Uncle Ray gave Louie this lovely set of spoons,' said Francey desperately. 'See the wreath roses on the handles?'

'A pernicious little miscreant if ever there was one, always sitting down and takin' a blast av his pipe, and me drowned with the washing and the cooking and the ironing, till I have the feel of ivery bone in my body.'

'And look at this lovely pair of pictures!' roared **Francey**. 'And these lovely saucepans from Auntie Fedora, a whole set. See this frying pan? It's got a lovely double bottom.'

'Ay, ye never spoke a truer word,' said Mrs Cuskelly in deep dejection. 'If he only got up off his lovely double bottom I'd be the happy woman.'

'And Barbara and I gave her the chiming clock,' whispered Francey pathetically.

'I'd be the one to pick an ould gazabo like that one,' mused Mrs Cuskelly, 'instead of a young fella with lashin's av pigs and the grand blue eyes you could play mubbles wit'.'

The bitterness of it all seemed to swamp her, and she turned to me and said I should be ashamed of myself, leading a God-fearing bit av a child like Violet astray with me antics.

'Oh, for goodness' sake, Mrs Cuskelly,' said Barbara crisply, 'it wasn't as bad as all that. And if you don't want Violet to play with Jenny, then it's quite easy to keep them apart.'

Pola's eyes and mine briefly met in furtive alarm.

'Now, darlin',' back-tracked Mrs Cuskelly, 'I wasn't meaning. . . .'

Francey gazed from one to the other of us in exhausted despair. From the kitchen came the merry sound of dishes being washed, and Uncles Olga and Ray harmonizing with Stanley's mouth-organ. Needless to say Uncle Olga was doing the bass.

Barbara went on firmly, 'After all, nobody *told* them not to speak to the old Maori, and I'm sure that neither of the girls will go there again now that they know, will you, dears?'

I still had my mouth full of unwanted crackling, so I shook my head mutely.

'V'ices of people that aren't there,' said Mrs Cuskelly. 'What kinds of fanteagues are *them*?' But I could detect her growing doubt.

Barbara laughed lightly. 'Oh, Mrs Cuskelly. It was nothing more or less than ventriloquism. Goodness me, fancy your taking it seriously!'

'You mean throwing the v'ice and that, like the man on Fuller's?' asked Mrs Cuskelly in deep dismay.

'Of course!'

'I never thought of it, it never came in to me blessed head,' moaned Mrs Cuskelly. 'Light of grace! And here I've been ballyraggin' the poor child, and leathering the legs off her into the bargain, the creature!'

She flung open her arms and Pola disappeared into them like a rabbit into a hedge. Doubtless all was made well in a moment.

'Oh, what a gom I am,' wailed Mrs Cuskelly. 'What a cruel baste of a woman. I must be light in the head to be taken in so asy.'

'Goodness, it's a mistake anyone might have made,' soothed Barbie. 'Now, we'll just wrap up some of this nice pork in a clean tea-towel, and look, there's lots of trifle left, I do wish the kiddies could finish it up...'

But nothing would content Mrs Cuskelly but to do penance for her sin, and out she went to bully Stanley into helping her clean up a bit av the mess round the blessed house.

'Now, Barbie,' said Francey, 'what *is* this all about?'

'Oh, just some Irish fancy of Mrs Cuskelly's,' said Barbara tolerantly. 'The kids were playing with the Maoris, and she got cross about it, the silly article. Now, Francey dear, are you going to take that ride with Stanley?'

Francey blushed. She seemed to hesitate, then she stuck out her soft little chin and said,'I certainly will!'

The moment she had gone I burst out: 'But Auntie

Barbie, it wasn't like the man at the Fuller show! Lots of the voices spoke at once.'

She said agitatedly, 'I didn't want any fuss...Mrs Cuskelly...besides, Francey wouldn't believe. Oh, Jenny, what did he say about Ailie?'

'Won't you tell Auntie Francey, or anybody?' I asked in astonishment.

'No, not if you don't want me to. Oh, Jenny, I worry about her so much...Jenny, what did he say?'

It was our secret, to be kept in the deep places of the heart and the memory, something that would link Barbara and me together all our lives. Something of the comprehension of love that had come to me at Kawhia when I first heard of Ailie and Donald came to me, and I knew that nothing mattered but to answer Barbara the right way and make her happy and at peace. So I said, 'He didn't say anything about her, but her voice came, and she said, "Tell them all that I was right."'

Barbara closed her eyes tightly, but I could see the tears beneath the lower lashes. I said timidly, 'What did she mean, auntie?'

'Everything I need to know, Jenny,' she answered. We were silent for so long that I prayed for Uncle Olga or someone to burst into the room, then she said in a low voice, 'I don't care, I don't care about anyone as long as Ailie's happy and contented.'

I stood beside her, leaning on her shoulder, knowing that she too was happy at last. I was so exalted I did not think for a moment of the fact that I had given the wrong version of Auntie Ailie's words, or that I hadn't even believed in the authenticity of her voice.

Then Francey, in her nicest afternoon frock, white georgette with no sleeves and a baggy neck, and a scarlet belt round her hips, romped in.

'Well, Barbie, I'm off for a ride with Stanley.'

Their eyes met in a long impassioned stare, then Barbara nodded confidently.

'And I've put on some of Louie's Flaming Youth,' giggled Francey. 'Look what it did for *her*!'

And she was gone, to a *diminuendo* of explosions.

'I hope the darned thing doesn't blow up,' mused Barbara. She heaved a great sigh and began to strip the table. I hovered for a moment, the pale and feeble intention of giving her the correct version disappearing with the rapidity of a shooting star. Besides, I understood that the subject was closed.

Contentment settled over me in a flood of lethargy. I could hardly put one foot in front of the other.

'Off you go and play with Violet, Jenny. And take this cake for her.'

I kept my eyes averted from the cake. Somehow the thickness of the icing, and the multiple sticky black eyes of the currants, made me feel unwell. But Pola received it with glad cries.

'Let's go up the peach-tree and eat it, eh, Jen?'

Eventually I got up the peach-tree, and flopped on a branch like a gorged pigeon. Pola talked between bites, of school, and the new basketball team, and a fancy-dress ball at the end of the year. All our little differences had vanished. I doubt whether she even remembered them.

Even on a weekday afternoon Te Kano seemed to drowse in its bowl of hills. There was a faint and amber sea of heat and haze, and from it rose a hundred islands, the curdly green of willows, the bottle-black pines, the church spires drawn into fragile euclidean patterns against the air.

Not far away, an irregular darkness upon the irregular perimeter of the hills, was the bush, the brilliant green of the pasture lands rising phoenix-like out of the forest ash.

And the sound of water dominated the land. The little

voice of Te Kano was no more than a bird-chirp against the authoritative mutter of the Koropungapunga, and the fluent flutter of the rapids half a mile below the township. One could imagine that a stammer as of shaken water rose from the flax swamps as the wind blew, or that there was a vast and formless rain-sound in the clouds.

I wanted the warmth and the contentment and the shut-in-ness to be with me for good. I wanted to be nowhere else, ever.

It was hard to pray with Pola right there at my elbow, but I stared very hard at the grey-bearded bough and said inwardly, 'Oh, St Anthony, thank you for helping me to tell the right lie to Auntie Barbara.'

A faint wonder at the anomaly of this crossed my mind, but I was too full of wedding breakfast to pursue it.

Mrs Cuskelly came out in our yard seeking the cat. 'Push, push, push!' she cried, and the word filled me with infinite pleasure. But I did not remark on it, and for a long time Pola and I sat there in a companionable silence.

Then all at once there was a sound like an old sewing-machine in the distance, and Stanley's tin Liz bucked to a stop beside the gate.

'I must say he didn't take Auntie Francey for a very long drive,' I observed disapprovingly.

He didn't even turn the engine off. He and Auntie Francey climbed down very fast, and hand-in-hand ran inside the house.

The tin Liz said: 'Buddha-buddha-buddha-buddha!' with great emphasis, and the radiator cap flew off and up shot a little white umbrella of steam like a whale's spout. Then there was a great reverberant boop in the exhaust, and the tin Liz gave several convulsive hiccups and died.

But, you know, Stanley didn't tear out to see what had happened. Instead all kinds of shrieks of joy and hilarity came from the house under the walnut-tree.

'I just bet your Auntie Francey and that old honkus are going to be married,' said Pola contemptuously.

'I don't know what's got into them all,' I said.

'Love and getting married and all that stuff,' said Pola, warmly.

'That's all grown-ups ever think of, I bet.'

'It just makes me *sick* to think of it,' said Pola. 'Catch *me* getting married.'

'I bet I never even go out with a boy, not ever!'

'Me either,' said Pola.

We congratulated each other generously on our complete immunity to those evils which seemed to beset the world of adults. Complacently, we fell silent once more.

But strange and melancholy misgiving stole into my heart, a sad loneliness I had never felt before. I glanced quickly at Pola, and found that she was staring at me with wistful doubt.

We were growing up. The pink flannel petticoat was already becoming too short.

Also by Ruth Park

The Harp in the South

A nostalgic and moving portrait of the eventful family life of the Darcys, of Number Twelve-and-a-Half Plymouth Street, in Sydney's Surry Hills. There grow the bittersweet first and last loves of Roie Darcy, who becomes a woman too quickly amid the brothels and the razor gangs, the tenements and the fish and chip shops.

Poor Man's Orange

She knew the poor man's orange was hers, with its bitter rind, its paler flesh, and its stinging, exultant, unforgettable tang. So she would have it that way, and wish it no other way. She knew that she was strong enough to bear whatever might come in her life as long as she had love.

In this poignant sequel to *The Harp in the South* Ruth Park tells of the Darcy family, and their vitality and humour in the midst of acute poverty.

A Power of Roses

Roses were rarely seen at the old Jerusalem hotel. For its assortment of wretched tenants, a luxury might be warm feet, cat's meat stew or a five-bob coat from a jumble sale.

In *A Power of Roses*, Ruth Park draws vivid portraits of Miriam, the tough adolescent heroine; her Uncle Puss, a canny old Irishman, and a colourful assortment of inhabitants who live in the hotel's damp rat-infested rooms.

Serpent's Delight

When Geraldine, youngest of the good-looking Pond
sisters, announces that she has had a vision of the Blessed
Virgin, her family is shot from its mundane middle-class
existence into the glare of publicity. The once peaceful,
closely knit family is suddenly full of mistrust and tensions.

Serpent's Delight, a story of five women, each determined to
get her own way, is a tender and perceptive study that
highlights the irony of the human condition.

The Witch's Thorn

Johnny Gow is the witch's thorn, whose influence poisons
the lives of everyone he touches in the sleepy New Zealand
township of Te Kano. His illegitimate daughter, Bethell
Jury, suffers perhaps most of all.

After the death of her grandmother, Bethell moves from
one family to another. But it was not until she came to
know the kind-hearted and fun-loving Maori family living
on the outskirts of the town that she had any chance of
escaping her father's curse.

The Frost and the Fire

In the 1860s Australian miners flocked to New Zealand,
feverishly pursuing rich new discoveries of gold. With them
went hangers-on, adventurers, girls-on-the-make,
washerwomen, orphans, doctors and the rest. Crowding
the pages of this masterly adventure novel, loving, hating,
giving birth, dying, are a host of these rugged characters –
wonderfully brought to life by Ruth Park.

PRAISE FOR THE WIND SINGER

Winner of the Blue Peter Book Award
and the Smarties Prize Gold Award

'In terms of imagination and sheer scale, it's as ambitious
as books get . . . think Star Wars and then some'
Daily Telegraph

'Positively surreal imagery, a fast-moving adventure and
a cutting satire all in one. An original and striking read'
Melvin Burgess

'An accessible, rebellious and fast-paced adventure,
and, as you would expect from the author of
Shadowlands, a heart-wringing celebration of love'
Sunday Times

'. . . a gripping read . . . A beautifully narrated, warm thriller
of a book, full of inventiveness, action and passion'
Guardian

'A lyrical, evocative and powerful story'
Kate Agnew

'. . . a story that delves deeper into
human nature and relationships'
The Bookseller

Books by William Nicholson

The Wind on Fire Trilogy
The Wind Singer
Slaves of the Mastery
Firesong

The Noble Warriors Trilogy
Seeker
Jango
Noman

For older readers
Rich and Mad

THE WIND SINGER

WILLIAM NICHOLSON

MODERN
CLASSICS

**MODERN
CLASSICS**

First published in Great Britain 2000
This edition published 2017 by Egmont UK Limited
The Yellow Building, 1 Nicholas Road, London W11 4AN

Text Copyright © 2000 William Nicholson
Cover illustration copyright © 2017 Jack Gerard

The moral rights of the author and cover illustrator have been asserted

ISBN 978 1 4052 8531 5

www.egmont.co.uk
www.williamnicholson.com

A CIP catalogue record for this title is available from the British Library

Typeset by Avon DataSet Ltd, Bidford on Avon, Warwickshire
Printed and bound in Great Britain by the CPI Group

66469/1

Flame: Fourleaflover/Shutterstock
Houses pp343: Tiwat Kongwichianwat/Shutterstock
Older houses pp343: RYGER/Shutterstock
Egyptian Sistrum: pp348 wikipedia
Orpheus's lyre pp349 Aleks Melnik/Shutterstock
Conch shell pp350 MSSA/Shutterstock
Harp pp350 Khabarushka/Shutterstock
Piper's pipe pp351 GR70/Shutterstock

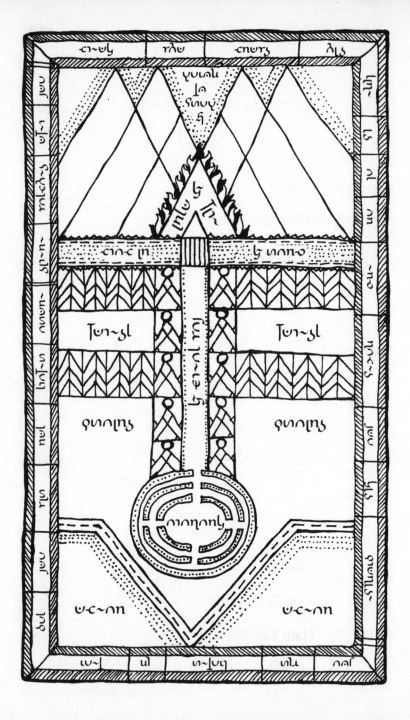

CONTENTS

LONG AGO

At the time the strangers came, the Manth people were still living in the low mat-walled shelters that they had carried with them in their hunting days. The domed huts were clustered around the salt mine that was to become the source of their wealth. This was long before they had built the great city that stands above the salt caverns today. One high summer afternoon, a band of travellers came striding out of the desert plains, and made camp nearby. They wore their hair long and loose, men and women alike, and moved slowly and spoke quietly, when they spoke at all. They traded a little with the Manth, buying bread and meat and salt, paying with small silver ornaments that they themselves had made. They caused no trouble, but their near presence was somehow uncomfortable. Who were they? Where had they come from? Where were they going? Direct questions produced no answers: only a smile, a shrug, a shake of the head.

Then the strangers were seen to be at work, building a tower. Slowly a wooden structure took shape, a platform higher than a man, on which they constructed a second narrower tower, out of timber beams and metal pipes. These pipes were all of different sizes, and bundled together, like the pipes of an organ. At their base, they opened out into a ring of metal horns. At their upper end, they funnelled together to form a single cylinder, like a neck, and then fanned out again to end in a ring of large leather scoops. When the wind blew, the scoops caught it and the entire upper structure rotated, swinging round to face the strongest gusts. The swirling air was funnelled through the neck to the ranked pipes, to emerge from the horns as a series of meaningless sounds.

The tower had no obvious purpose of any kind. For a while it was a curiosity, and the people would stare at it as it creaked this way and that. When the wind blew hard, it made a mournful moaning that was comical at first, but soon became tiresome.

The silent travellers offered no explanation. It seemed they had come to the settlement with the sole purpose of building this odd structure, because when it was done, they rolled up their tents and prepared to move on.

Before leaving, their leader took out a small silver object, and climbed the tower, and inserted it into a slot in the structure's neck. It was a tranquil summer dawn, the day the travellers departed, and the air was still. The metal pipes and horns were silent as they strode away across the desert plains. The Manth people were left as baffled as when they had arrived, staring at the overgrown scarecrow they had left behind.

That night, as they slept, the wind began to blow, and a new sound entered their lives. They heard it in their sleep, and woke smiling, without knowing why. They gathered in the warm night air, and listened in joy and wonder.

The wind singer was singing.

1

Baby Pinpin Makes her Mark

'Sagahog! Pompaprune! Saga-saga-HOG!'

Bowman Hath lay in bed listening to the muffled sounds of his mother oathing in the bathroom next door. From far away across the roofs of the city floated the golden boom of the bell in the tower of the Imperial Palace: *mmnang! mmnang!* It was sounding the sixth hour, the time when all Aramanth awoke. Bowman opened his eyes and lay gazing at the daylight glowing in the tangerine curtains. He realised that he was feeling sad. What is it this time? he thought to himself. He looked ahead to the coming day in school, and his stomach tightened, the way it always did; but this was a different feeling. A kind of sorrowing, as if for something lost. But what?

His twin sister Kestrel was still asleep in the bed next to him, within reach of his outstretched arm. He listened to her snuffly sleep-breathing for a few moments, then sent her a wake-up thought. He waited till he heard her grumpy answering groan. Then he counted silently to five, and rolled out of bed.

Crossing the hall on the way to the bathroom, he stopped to greet his baby sister Pinpin. She was standing up in her cot in her fuzzy night-suit, sucking her thumb. Pinpin slept in the hall because there was no room for a cot in either of the two bedrooms. The apartments in Orange District were really too small for a family of five.

'Hallo, Pinpin,' he said.

Pinpin took her thumb out of her mouth and her round face lit up with a happy smile.

'Kiss,' she said.

Bowman kissed her.

'Hug,' she said.

Bowman hugged her. As he cuddled her soft round body, he remembered. Today was the day of Pinpin's first test. She was only two years old, too little to mind how well or badly she did, but from now till the day she died she would have a rating. That was what was making him sad.

Tears started to push into Bowman's eyes. He cried too easily, everyone told him so, but what was he to do? He felt everything too much. He didn't mean to, but when he looked at somebody else, anybody else, he found he knew what they were feeling, and all too often it was a fear or a sadness. And then he would understand what it was they were afraid of or sad about, and he would feel it too, and he would start to cry. It was all very awkward.

This morning what made him sad wasn't what Pinpin was feeling now, but what he knew she would feel one day. Now there were no worries in her sunny little heart. Yet from today, she would begin, at first only dimly, but later with sharp anxiety, to fear the future. For in Aramanth, life was measured out in tests. Every test brought with it the possibility of failure, and every test successfully passed led to the next, with its renewed possibility of failure. There was no escape from it, and no end. Just thinking about it made his heart almost burst with love for his little sister. He hugged her tight as tight, and kissed and kissed her merry cheeks.

'Love Pinpin,' he said.

'Love Bo,' said Pinpin.

A sharp rending sound came from the bathroom, followed by yet another explosion of oaths.

'Sagahog! Bangaplop!'

And then the familiar wailing lament:

'O, unhappy people!'

This had been the cry of the great prophet Ira Manth, from whom his mother was directly, though distantly, descended. The name had been passed down the family ever since, and his mother too was called Ira. When she flew into one of her rages, his father would wink at the children and say, 'Here comes the prophetess.'

The bathroom door now burst open, and Ira Hath herself appeared, looking flustered. Unable to find the sleeve-holes of her dressing-gown, she had fought her way into the garment by sheer fury. The sleeves hung empty on either side, and her arms stuck out through burst seams.

'It's Pinpin's test today,' said Bo.

'It's what?'

Ira Hath stared for a moment. Then she took Pinpin from Bowman and in her turn held her close in her arms, as if someone was trying to take her away.

'My baby,' she said. 'My baby.'

At breakfast there was no reference to the test until near the end. Then their father put away his book and got up from the table a little earlier than usual and said, as if to no one in particular:

'I suppose we'd better get ready.'

Kestrel looked up, her eyes bright with determination.

'I'm not coming,' she said.

Hanno Hath sighed, and rubbed his wrinkly cheeks with one hand.

'I know, darling. I know.'

'It's not fair,' said Kestrel, as if her father was making her go. And so in a way he was. Hanno Hath was so kind to his children, and understood so exactly what they felt, that they found it almost impossible to go against his wishes.

A familiar smoky smell rose from the stove.

'Oh, sagahog!' exclaimed his wife. She had burned the toast again.

The morning sun was low in the sky, and the high city walls cast a shadow over all Orange District, as the Hath family walked down the street to the Community Hall. Mr and Mrs Hath went in front, and Bowman and Kestrel came behind, with Pinpin between them holding a hand each. Other families with two-year-olds were making their way in the same direction, past the neat terraces of orange-painted houses. The Blesh family was ahead of them, and could be heard coaching their little boy as they went along.

'One, two, three, four, who's that at the door? Five, six, seven, eight, who's that at the gate?'

As they came into the main square, Mrs Blesh turned and saw them. She gave the little wave she always gave, as if she was their special friend, and waited for Mrs Hath to catch her up.

'Can you keep a secret?' she said in a whisper. 'If our little one does well enough today, we'll move up to Scarlet.'

Mrs Hath thought for a moment.

'Very bright, scarlet,' she said.

'And did you hear? Our Rufy was second in his class yesterday afternoon.'

Mr Blesh called back,

'Second? Second? Why not first? That's what I want to know.'

'Oh, you men!' said Mrs Blesh. And to Mrs Hath, in her special-friend voice, 'They can't help it, can they? They have to win.'

As she spoke these words, her slightly poppy-out eyes rested for a moment on Hanno Hath. Everyone knew that poor Hanno Hath hadn't been promoted for three years now, though of course his wife never admitted how disappointed she must feel. Kestrel caught her pitying look, and it made her want to stick knives into Mrs Blesh's body. But more than that, it made her want to hug her father, and cover his wrinkly-sad face with kisses. To relieve her feelings, she bombarded Mrs Blesh's broad back with rude thoughts.

Pocksicker! Pompaprune! Sagahog!

At the entrance to the Community Hall, a lady Assistant Examiner sat checking names against a list. The Bleshes went first.

'Is the little one clean?' asked the Assistant Examiner. 'Has he learned to control his bladder?'

'Oh, yes,' said Mrs Blesh. 'He's unusually advanced for his age.'

When it was Pinpin's turn, the Assistant Examiner asked the same question.

'Is she clean? Has she learned to control her bladder?'

Mr Hath looked at Mrs Hath. Bowman looked at Kestrel. Through their minds floated pictures of Pinpin's puddles on the kitchen floor. But this was followed by a kind of convulsion of family pride, which they all felt at the same time.

'Control her bladder, madam?' said Mrs Hath with a bright smile. 'My daughter can widdle in time to the National Anthem.'

The Assistant Examiner looked surprised, then checked the box marked CLEAN on her list.

'Desk twenty-three,' she said.

The Community Hall was buzzing with activity. A great chalkboard at one end listed the names of the examinees, all ninety-seven of them, in alphabetical order. There was Pinpin's name, looking unfamiliar in its full form: PINTO HATH. The Hath family formed a protective huddle round desk twenty-three while Mrs Hath removed Pinpin's nappy. Now that she was down as clean it would be counted as cheating to leave her in a nappy. Pinpin herself was delighted. She liked to feel cool air on her bottom.

A bell rang, and the big room fell quiet for the entrance of the Examiners. Ninety-seven desks, at each of which sat a two-year-old; behind each one, on benches, their parents and siblings. The sudden silence awed the little ones, and there wasn't so much as a cry.

The Examiners swept in, their scarlet gowns billowing, and stood on the podium in a single line of terrible magnificence. There were ten of them. At the centre was the tall figure of the Chief Examiner, Maslo Inch, the only one in the hall to wear the simple shining white garments of the highest rating.

'Stand for the Oath of Dedication!'

Everyone stood, parents lifting little ones to their feet. Together they chanted the words all knew by heart.

'I vow to strive harder, to reach higher, and in every way to seek to make tomorrow better than today. For love of my Emperor and for the glory of Aramanth!'

Then they all sat down again, and the Chief Examiner made a short speech. Maslo Inch, still only in his mid-forties, had been recently elevated to the highest level: but so tall and powerful was his appearance, and so deep his voice, that he looked and acted as if he had been wearing white all his life. Hanno Hath, who had known Maslo Inch a long time, saw this with quiet amusement.

'My friends,' intoned the Chief Examiner, 'what a special day this is, the first test day of your beloved child. How proud you must be to know that from today, your little son or daughter will have his or her own personal rating. How proud they will be, as they come to understand that by their own efforts they can contribute to your family rating.' Here he raised a hand in friendly warning, and gave them all a grave look. 'But never forget that the rating itself means nothing. All that matters is how you improve your rating. Better today than yesterday. Better tomorrow than today. That is the spirit that has made our city great.'

The scarlet-gowned Examiners then fanned out across

the front row of desks and began working their way down the lines. Maslo Inch, as Chief Examiner, remained on the podium like a tower, overseeing all. Inevitably his scanning gaze fell in time on Hanno Hath. A twinkle of recognition glowed for a moment in the corner of one eye, and then faded again as his gaze moved on. Hanno Hath shrugged to himself. He and Maslo Inch were exact contemporaries. They had been in the same class at school. But that was all long ago now.

The tests were marked as they were completed, and the marks conveyed to the big chalkboard at the front. Quite soon, a ranking began to emerge among the infants. The Blesh child was close to the top, with 23 points out of a possible 30, a rating of 7.6. Because B came earlier than H, the Blesh family were finished before the Haths had begun, and Mrs Blesh came down the aisle with her triumphant infant in her arms to pass on the benefit of their experience.

'The silly fellow left out number five,' she explained. 'One, two, three, four, six.' She wagged a mock-angry finger at the child. 'Four, *five*, six, you silly! You know that! I'm sure Pinto does.'

'Actually, Pinpin can count to a million,' said Kestrel.

'I think we're telling tiny stories,' said Mrs Blesh, patting Kestrel on the head. 'He got cow, and book, and cup,' she went on. 'He didn't get banana. But 7.6 is a good start. Rufy's first rating was 7.8, I remember, and look at him now. Never below 9. Not that I care for ratings as such, of course.'

The Examiner was now ready for Pinpin. He approached the desk, his eyes on his papers.

'Pinto Hath,' he said. And then raising his eyes, his face took on an all-embracing smile. Pinpin met this look with instinctive suspicion.

'And what are we to call you, my little fellow?'

'By her name,' said Mrs Hath.

'Well then, Pinto,' said the Examiner, still beaming. 'I've got some pretty pictures here. Let's see if you can tell me what they are.'

He presented Pinpin with a sheet of coloured images. Pinpin looked, but said nothing. The Examiner pointed with his finger to a dog.

'What's this?'

Not a sound from Pinpin.

'What's this, then?'

Silence.

'Does he have a hearing problem?'

'No,' said Mrs Hath. 'She can hear you.'

'But he doesn't speak.'

'I suppose there's nothing much she wants to say.'

Bowman and Kestrel held their breath. The Examiner frowned and looked grave, and made a note on his papers. Then he returned to the pictures.

'Well now, Pinto. Show me a doggy. Where's a doggy?'

Pinpin gazed back at him, and neither spoke nor pointed.

'A house, then. Show me a little house.'

Nothing. And so it went on, until at last the Examiner put his pictures away, looking graver still.

'Let's try some counting, shall we, little chap?'

He started counting, meaning Pinpin to follow him, but all she would do was stare. He made another note.

'The last part of the test,' he said to Mrs Hath, 'is designed to assess the child's level of communication skills. Listening, understanding, and responding. We find the child is usually more at his ease when held in the arms.'

'You want her in your arms?'

'If you have no objection.'

'Are you sure?'

'I have done this before, Mrs Hath. The little fellow will be quite safe with me.'

Ira Hath looked down at the ground, and her nose twitched just a little. Bowman saw this, and sent an instant thought to Kestrel.

Mama's going to crack.

But all she did was lift Pinpin from her seat and give her into the Examiner's waiting arms. Bowman and Kestrel watched with keen interest. Their father sat with his eyes closed, knowing it was all going as wrong as it possibly could, and there was nothing he could do about it.

'Well, Pinto, you're a fine fellow, aren't you?' The Examiner tickled Pinpin under the chin, and pressed her nose. 'What's this, then? Is this your nosey?'

Pinpin remained silent. The Examiner pulled out the

large gold medal which hung round his neck on a chain, and dangled it in front of Pinpin's eyes. It shone in the morning light.

'Pretty, pretty. Do you want to hold it?'

Pinpin said nothing. The Examiner looked up at Mrs Hath in exasperation.

'I'm not sure you realise,' he said. 'As matters stand at this moment, I shall have to give your child a zero rating.'

'Is it as bad as that?' said Mrs Hath, her eyes glittering.

'I can get nothing out of him, you see.'

'Nothing at all?'

'Is there some rhyme or word game he likes to play?'

'Let me think.' Mrs Hath proceeded, rather ostentatiously, to mime the act of thinking, lips pursed, finger stroking brow.

Bowman sent a thought to Kestrel.

She's cracking.

'Yes,' said Mrs Hath. 'There is a game she likes to play. Try saying to her, wiss wiss wiss.'

'Wiss wiss wiss?'

'She'll like that.'

Bowman and Kestrel sent the same thought at the same time.

She's cracked!

'Wiss wiss wiss,' said the Examiner to Pinpin. 'Wiss wiss wiss, little fellow.'

Pinpin looked at the Examiner in surprise, and wriggled a little in his arms, as if to settle herself more comfortably.

Mrs Hath watched, her nose now twitching uncontrollably. Bowman and Kestrel watched, their hearts thumping.

Any minute now, they thought to each other.

'Wiss wiss wiss,' said the Examiner.

'Any minute now,' said Mrs Hath.

Now, Pinpin, now, willed Bowman and Kestrel. *Do it now*.

Mr Hath opened his eyes and saw the looks on their faces. Suddenly realising what was going on, he rose from the bench and reached out his arms.

'Let me take her – '

Too late.

Hubba hubba Pinpin! exulted Bo and Kess in the joyous silence of their thoughts. *Hubba hubba hubba Pinpin!*

A faraway look of contentment on her round face, Pinpin was emptying her bladder in a long and steady stream down the Examiner's arms. The Examiner felt the spread of the gentle warmth without at first understanding what was happening. Then seeing the look of rapt attention on the faces of Mrs Hath and her children, he dropped his gaze downward. The stain was seeping into his scarlet cloak. In utter silence, he held Pinpin out for Mr Hath to take, and turned and walked gravely back up the aisle.

Mrs Hath took Pinpin from her husband, and smothered her with kisses. Bowman and Kestrel dropped to the floor and rolled about there, quaking with silent laughter. Hanno Hath watched the Examiner report the incident to Maslo Inch, and he gave a small private sigh. He knew what his wife and children did not, which was that they had needed a good rating this morning. Now, with no points at all, they would probably have to leave their house in Orange District and make do in humbler quarters. Two rooms if they were lucky; more likely one room, with the use of a kitchen and bathroom on a communal landing. Hanno Hath was not a vain man. He cared very little what others thought of him. But he loved his family dearly, and the thought of failing them hurt him deep inside.

Ira Hath cuddled Pinpin tight and refused to think about the future.

'Wiss wiss wiss,' murmured Pinpin happily.

2

KESTREL MAKES A HORRIBLE FRIEND

On getting to school, Bowman and Kestrel found they had forgotten to bring their homework.

'Forgot?' roared Dr Batch. 'You forgot?'

The twins stood side by side at the front of the long classroom, facing their teacher. Dr Batch smoothed his hands over his substantial stomach, and ran the tip of his tongue over his substantial lips, and proceeded to make an example of them. Dr Batch liked making an example of his pupils. He considered it part of his job as a teacher.

'Let's begin at the beginning. Why did you forget?'

'Our little sister had her first test this morning,' said Bowman. 'We left the house early, and we just forgot.'

'You just forgot? Well, well, well.'

Dr Batch liked lame excuses.

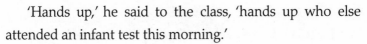

'Hands up,' he said to the class, 'hands up who else attended an infant test this morning.'

A dozen hands went up among the serried ranks of desks, including the hand of Rufy Blesh.

'And hands up who else forgot their homework.'

All the hands went down again. Dr Batch turned to Bowman, his eyes popping out with friendly attention.

'It seems you are the only ones.'

'Yes, sir.'

Throughout this proceeding, Kestrel remained silent. But Bowman could hear the seething of her angry thoughts, and knew she was in one of her wild moods. Dr Batch, unaware of this, began to waddle up and down in front of them, conducting a ritual exchange with the class.

'Class! What happens if you don't work?'

Back came the familiar response from fifty-one young mouths.

'No work, no progress.'

'And what happens if you make no progress?'

'No progress, no points.'

'And what happens if you get no points?'

'No points ends up last.'

'Last.' Dr Batch relished the word. 'Last! La-a-ast!'

The whole class shivered. Last! Like Mumpo, the stupidest boy in the school. Some eyes turned furtively to look at him, as he sat glowering and shivering right at the back, in the seat of shame. Mad Mumpo, whose upper lip was always shiny with nose-dribble, because he had no mother to tell him to wipe it. Smelly Mumpo, who stank so badly that no one would ever go near him, because he had no father to tell him to wash.

Dr Batch waddled over to the class ratings board, on which every pupil's name was written in class order. Every day, at the end of the day, the new points were calculated, and the new class order written up.

'I shall deduct five points each,' said Dr Batch. And there and then, he recalculated the class order. Bowman and Kestrel dropped two places, to twenty-fifth and twenty-sixth respectively, while the class watched.

'Slipping, slipping, slipping,' said Dr Batch as he made the changes. 'What do we do when we find ourselves slipping down?'

The class chanted the response.

'We strive harder, and reach higher, to make tomorrow better than today.'

'Harder. Higher. Better.' He turned back to Bowman and Kestrel. 'You will not, I trust, forget your homework again. Take up your places.'

As they walked back down the rows of desks, Bowman could feel Kestrel seething with hatred, for Dr Batch, and the big ratings board, and the school, and all Aramanth.

It doesn't matter, he thought to her. *We'll catch up.*

I don't want to, she replied. *I don't care.*

Bowman came to a stop at the desk where they were

now to sit, two places behind their old desks. But Kestrel went on, all the way to the back, where Mumpo sat. Beside Mumpo there was an empty place, because he was always bottom of the class. Here Kestrel sat down.

Dr Batch stared in astonishment. So did Mumpo.

'Hallo-o,' he said, breathing his stinky breath all over her.

Kestrel turned away, covering her face.

'Do you like me?' said Mumpo, leaning closer.

'Get away from me,' said Kestrel. 'You stink.'

Dr Batch called sharply from the other end of the room.

'Kestrel Hath! Go to your correct place at once!'

'No,' said Kestrel.

The whole class froze.

'No?' said Dr Batch. 'Did you say no?'

'Yes,' said Kestrel.

'Do you wish me to deduct five more points for disobedience?'

'You can if you want,' said Kestrel. 'I don't care.'

'You don't care?' Dr Batch went a bright red. 'Then I shall teach you to care. You'll do as you're told, or – '

'Or what?' said Kestrel.

Dr Batch stared back, lost for words.

'I'm already at the bottom of the class,' said Kestrel. 'What more can you do to me?'

For a moment longer, Dr Batch struggled with himself in silence, searching for the best way to respond. During this moment, in which the whole class held its breath, Mumpo shuffled closer still to Kestrel, and Kestrel twisted further away from him, screwing up her face in disgust. Dr Batch saw this, and the look of bewilderment on his face was replaced by a vindictive smile. He set off at a slow pace down the room.

'Class,' he said, his voice smoothly under control once more. 'Class, turn and look at Kestrel Hath.'

All eyes turned.

'Kestrel has found a new friend. As you see, Kestrel's new friend is our very own Mumpo. Kestrel and Mumpo, side by side. What do you think of your new friend, Mumpo?'

Mumpo nodded and smiled. 'I like Kess,' he said.

'He likes you, Kestrel,' said Dr Batch. 'Why don't you sit closer? You could put your arm round him. You could hug him. He's your new friend. Who knows, maybe in later years you'll marry each other, and you can be Mrs Mumpo, and have lots of little Mumpo babies. Would you like that? Three or four little Mumpo babies to wash and wipe?'

The class tittered at that. Dr Batch was pleased. He felt he had regained the upper hand. Kestrel sat stiff as a rod and burned with shame and anger, and said nothing.

'But perhaps I'm making a mistake. Perhaps Kestrel is making a mistake. Perhaps she simply sat down in the wrong seat, by mistake.'

He was close to Kestrel now, standing gazing at her in silence. Kestrel knew that he was offering her a deal: her obedience in exchange for her pride.

'Perhaps Kestrel is going to get up, and go back to her correct place.'

Kestrel trembled, but she didn't move. Dr Batch waited a moment longer, then hissed at her:

'Well, well. Kestrel and Mumpo. What a sweet couple.'

All that morning, he kept up the attack. In the grammar lesson, he wrote up on the board:

NAME THE TENSES
Kestrel loves Mumpo
Kestrel is loved by Mumpo
Kestrel will love Mumpo
Kestrel has loved Mumpo
Kestrel shall have loved Mumpo

In the arithmetic lesson, he wrote on the board:

If Kestrel gives Mumpo 392 kisses and
98 hugs, and half the hugs are
accompanied by kisses, and one-eighth
of the kisses are slobbery, how many
slobbery kisses with hugs could
Kestrel give Mumpo?

And so it went on, and the class snickered away, as Dr Batch intended. Bowman looked back at Kestrel many times, but she just sat there, doing her work, not saying a word.

When time came for the lunch-break, he joined her as she walked quietly out of the room. To his annoyance, he found the dribbling Mumpo was coming with Kestrel, sticking close to her side.

'Get lost, Mumpo,' said Kestrel.

But Mumpo wouldn't get lost. He simply trotted along beside Kestrel, his eyes never leaving her face. From time to time, unprompted, he would murmur, 'I like Kess', and then wipe his nose-dribble on to his shirt sleeve.

Kestrel was heading for the way out. 'Where are you going, Kess?'

'Out,' said Kestrel. 'I hate school.'

'Yes, but Kess – ' Bowman didn't know what to say. Of course she hated school. Everyone hated school. But you had to go.

'What about the family rating?'

'I don't know,' said Kestrel. And walking faster now, she began to cry. Mumpo saw this, and was devastated. He skipped around her, reaching out his grubby hands to paw her, and uttered small cries designed to give her comfort.

'Don't cry, Kess. I'll be your friend, Kess. Don't cry.'

Kestrel brushed him away angrily.

'Get lost, Mumpo. You stink.'

'Yes, I know,' said Mumpo humbly.

'Kess,' said Bowman, 'come back to school, sit in

your proper place, and Batch will leave you alone.'

'I'm never going back,' said Kestrel.

'But you must.'

'I'm going to tell pa. He'll understand.'

'And I will,' said Mumpo.

'Go away, Mumpo!' shouted Kestrel, right in his face. 'Go away or I'll bash you!'

She raised a threatening fist. Mumpo dropped whimpering to his knees.

'Hurt me if you want. I don't mind.'

Kestrel's fist remained suspended in mid-air. She stared at Mumpo. Bowman too was watching Mumpo. Suddenly he was caught unawares by the feeling of what it was like to be Mumpo. A dull cold terror rolled over him, and a penetrating loneliness. He almost cried out loud, so intense was the hunger for kindness.

'She doesn't mean it,' he said. 'She won't hit you.'

'She can if she wants.'

His face gazed adoringly up at her, his eyes now as shiny as his upper lip.

'Tell him you won't hit him, Kess.'

'I won't hit you,' said Kestrel, dropping her fist. 'You're too stinky to touch.'

She turned and walked fast down the street, Bowman at her side. Mumpo followed a few paces behind. So that he wouldn't hear, Kestrel talked to Bowman in her head.

I can't go on like this, I can't.

What else can we do?

I don't know, she said. *Something. Something soon, or I'll explode.*

3

BAD WORDS SAID LOUD

As she left Orange District with Bowman and Mumpo following her, Kestrel had no plan in her head, other than to get away from the hated school: but in fact she was making her way down one of the city's four main streets to the central arena, where the wind singer stood.

The city of Aramanth was built in the shape of a circle, a drum even, since it was enclosed by high walls, raised long ago to protect the people from the warrior tribes of the plains. No one had dared attack mighty Aramanth for many generations now, but the great walls remained, and few people ventured out of the city. What was there in the world beyond that anybody could possibly want? Only the rock-strewn seashore to the south, where the great grey ocean thundered and rolled; and the barren desert wastes to the north, stretching all the way to the distant mountains.

No food out there; no comfort, no safety. Whereas within the walls there was all that was necessary for life, more, for a good life. Every citizen of Aramanth knew how fortunate they were, to live in this rare haven of peace, plenty, and equal opportunity for all.

The city was arranged in its districts in concentric rings. The outermost ring, in the shadow of the walls, was formed by the great cube-shaped apartment blocks of Grey District. Next came the low-rise apartments that made up Maroon District, and the crescents of small terraced houses of Orange District, where the Hath family lived. Nearest the central sector of the city lay the broad ring of Scarlet District, a region of roomy detached houses, each with its own garden, laid out in a pleasing maze of twisting lanes, so that each house felt special and different, though of course all were painted red. And finally and most gloriously, at the heart of the city, there was White District. Here was the Imperial Palace, where the Emperor, Creoth the Sixth, the father of Aramanth, looked out over his citizen-children. Here were the great houses of the city leaders, built in marble or polished limestone, beautiful and austere. Here was the huge pillared Hall of Achievement, where the family ratings were displayed; and facing it, across the plaza where the statue of Emperor Creoth the First stood, the many-windowed College of Examiners, home of the Board of Examiners, the supreme governing body of Aramanth.

Next to the plaza, beneath the towering walls of the

Imperial Palace, at the meeting point of the four main streets, lay the city arena. This great circular amphitheatre had originally been designed to bring together the entire population of Aramanth, for the debates and elections that had been necessary before the introduction of the ratings system. Today there were far too many citizens to cram into the arena's nine descending marble tiers, but it had its uses, for concerts and recitals. And of course this was the venue for the annual High Examination, when the heads of all the households were tested, and their family ratings adjusted for the following year.

In the centre of the arena, in the circle paved with white marble that formed the stage, there stood the curious wooden tower known as the wind singer. Everything about the wind singer was wrong. It was not white. It was not symmetrical. It lacked the simplicity and calm that characterised the whole of White District. It creaked this way and that with every passing breeze, and when the wind blew stronger, it let out a dismal moaning sound. Every year a proposal would come up at the meeting of the Board of Examiners to dismantle it, and replace it with a more dignified emblem of the city, but every year the proposal was vetoed; by the Emperor himself, it was whispered. And it was true to say that the people regarded the wind singer with affection, because it was so very old, and had always been there, and because there was a legend that one day it would sing again.

Kestrel Hath had loved the wind singer all her life.

She loved it because it was unpredictable, and served no purpose, and seemed, by its sad cry, not to like the orderly world of Aramanth. Sometimes, when the frustrations of her existence grew too hard to bear, she would run down the nine tiers of the arena and sit on the white flagstones at the bottom and talk to the wind singer, for an hour or more. Of course, it didn't understand her, and the creaky groany noises it made back weren't words, but she found that rather restful. She didn't particularly want to be understood. She just wanted to vent her feelings of fury and powerlessness, and not feel entirely alone.

On this day, the worst so far, Kestrel headed instinctively for the arena. Her father would not be home from the library yet, and her mother would be at the clinic, where Pinpin had to have her two-year-old physical assessment. Where else was there to go? Later she was accused of plotting her disgraceful actions in advance, but Kestrel was not a schemer. She acted on impulse, rarely knowing herself what she would do next. It would be more true to say that Bowman, following her, sensed that she would get herself into trouble. As for Mumpo, he just followed her because he loved her.

The main street to the centre led past the courtyard of the Weavers' Company, where, because it was lunch-time, all the weavers were out in the yard doing their exercises.

'Touch the ground! Touch the sky!' called out their trainer. 'You can do it! If you try!'

The weavers bent and stretched, bent and stretched, in time with each other.

A little further on they came upon a street-cleaner sitting by his barrow eating his midday meal.

'I don't suppose you've got any litter you'd care to drop?' he asked them.

The children searched their pockets. Bowman found a piece of charred toast that he'd put there so as not to hurt his mother's feelings.

'Just drop it in the street,' said the street-cleaner, his eyes brightening.

'I'll put it in your barrow,' said Bowman.

'That's right, do my job for me,' said the street-cleaner bitterly. 'Don't you worry about how I'm to meet my target, let alone exceed it, if nobody ever drops any litter in the street. Don't ask yourself how I'm supposed to get along, you're from Orange, you're all right. It doesn't occur to you that I want to better myself, same as everyone else. You try living in Grey District. My wife has set her heart on one of those apartments in Maroon, with the little balconies.'

Bowman dropped his piece of toast on to the street.

'Well, there you are,' said the street-cleaner. 'I may just look at it for a while, before I sweep it up.'

Kestrel was already far ahead, with Mumpo trailing after her. Bowman ran to catch them up.

'When are we going to have lunch?' said Mumpo.

'Shut up,' said Kestrel.

As they crossed the plaza the bell in the high palace tower struck two. *Mnang! Mnang!* Now their classmates would all be trooping back to their desks, and Dr Batch would be marking the three truants down as absent without leave. That meant more lost points.

They passed through the double row of marble columns that ringed the highest tier of the arena, and made their way down the steps to the bottom.

Mumpo came to a sudden stop on the fifth tier, and sat down on the white marble step.

'I'm hungry,' he announced.

Kestrel paid no attention. She went on down to the bottom, and Bowman followed her. Mumpo wanted to follow her, but now that he had become aware of his hunger he could think of nothing else. He sat on the step and hugged his knees and yearned for food with all his heart.

Kestrel came to a stop at last, at the foot of the wind singer. Her rage at Pinpin's test, and Dr Batch's taunts, and the whole suffocating order of Aramanth, had formed within her into a wild desire to upset, to confuse, to shock – she hardly knew who or what or how – just to fracture the smooth and seamless running of the world, if only for a moment. She had come to the wind singer because it was her friend and ally, but it was only when she stood at its foot that she knew what she was going to do.

She started to climb.

Come down, Bowman called in alarm. *They'll punish you. You'll fall. You'll hurt yourself.*

I don't care.

She hauled herself up on to the platform, and then she started climbing the tower. This wasn't easy, because it swung in the wind, and the footholds were slippery among the pipes. But she was wiry and agile, and held on tight as she ascended.

A sharp cry sounded from the top tier of the arena.

'Hey! You! Get down at once!'

A scarlet-robed official had seen her, and came hurrying down the steps. Finding Mumpo sitting hunched on the fifth tier, he stopped to question him.

'What do you think you're doing? Why aren't you in school?'

'I'm hungry,' said Mumpo.

'Hungry? You've just had lunch.'

'No, I haven't.'

'All children eat school lunch at one o'clock. If you didn't eat your lunch, then you have only yourself to blame.'

'Yes, I know,' said the unhappy Mumpo. 'But I'm still hungry.'

By now Kestrel had reached the wind singer's neck, and was making an interesting discovery. There was a slot cut into the broad metal pipe, and an arrow etched above it, pointing to the slot, and a design above the arrow. It looked like the letter S, with the tail of the S curling round and right over its top.

The scarlet-robed official arrived at the base of the wind singer.

'You, boy,' he said sharply to Bowman. 'What's she doing? Who is she?'

'She's my sister,' said Bowman.

'And who are you?'

'I'm her brother.'

The fierce official made him nervous, and when nervous, Bowman became very logical. Momentarily baffled, the official looked up and called to Kestrel:

'Get down, girl! Get down at once! What do you think you're doing up there?'

'Pongo!' Kestrel called back, climbing ever higher up the structure.

'What?' said the official. 'What did she say?'

'Pongo,' said Bowman.

'She said pongo to me?'

'I'm not sure,' said Bowman. 'She might have been saying it to me.'

'But it was I who spoke to her. I ordered her to come down, and she replied, pongo.'

'Perhaps she thinks it's your name.'

'It's not my name. No one is called Pongo.'

'I didn't know that. I expect she doesn't know that.'

The official, confused by Bowman's tremulous but

reasonable manner, turned his face back up to Kestrel, who was now almost at the very top, and called out:

'Did you say pongo to me?'

'Pongo pooa-pooa pompaprune!' Kestrel called back.

The official turned to Bowman, his face rigid with righteousness.

'There! You heard her! It's a disgrace!' He called back up to Kestrel, 'If you don't come down, I'll report you!'

'You'll report her even if she does come down,' said Bowman.

'I certainly shall,' said the official, 'but I shall report her more if she doesn't.' He shouted up at Kestrel, 'I shall recommend that points be deducted from your family rating!'

'Bangaplop!' called Kestrel. She was on a level with one of the wide leather scoops as she called out this rude word, and the sound travelled down the pipes of the wind singer and emerged from the horns, a second or so later, in a fuzzy distorted form.

'Bang-ang-anga-plop-op-p!'

Kestrel then put her head right into the leather scoop, and shouted:

'Sagahog!'

Her voice came booming out of the horns:

'SAG-AG-AG-A-HOG-G-G!'

The official heard this aghast.

'She's disturbing the afternoon work session,' he said. 'They'll hear her in the College.'

'Pompa-pompa-pompaprune!' called Kestrel.

'POMP-P-PA POMP-P-PA POMP-P-PA-PRU-U-UNE!' boomed the wind singer across the arena.

Out of the College of Examiners, in a flurry of white robes, poured the high officials of the city to see what was intruding on their afternoon.

'I HA-A-ATE SCHOO-OO-OOL!' cried Kestrel's amplified voice. 'I HA-A-ATE RA-A-ATINGS!'

The examiners heard this in shock.

'She's having a fit,' they said. 'She's lost her wits.'

'Get her down! Send for the marshals!'

'I won't strive ha-a-arder!' cried Kestrel. 'I won't rea-ea-each hi-i-igher! I won't make tomorr-orr-ow better than today-ay-ay!'

More and more people were gathering now, drawn by the noise. A long crocodile of children from Maroon District, who had been on a visit to the Hall of Achievement, appeared between the double row of columns to listen to Kestrel's voice.

'I don't love my Emperor-or-or!' Kestrel was now crying. 'There's no glor-or-ory in Aramanth-anth-anth!'

The children gasped. Their teacher was too shocked to speak. A band of grey-coated marshals came running down the steps, their batons in their hands.

'Get her down!' cried the scarlet-robed official.

The marshals formed a ring round the wind singer, and their captain called up to Kestrel:

'You're surrounded! You can't get away!'

'I don't want to get away,' Kestrel replied, and putting her head back into the leather scoop, she called out:

'PONGO-O-O TO EXAM-AM-AMS!'

The Maroon children started to titter.

'Oh, the evil child!' exclaimed their teacher, and herded her class back to the Hall of Achievement. 'Come along, children. Don't listen to her. She's a wild thing.'

'Come down!' roared the captain of the marshals. 'Come down or you'll be sorry!'

'I'm sorry now,' Kestrel called back. 'I'm sorry for me, and I'm sorry for you, and I'm sorry for this whole sorry city!'

She put her head into the scoop and called out over the wide arena:

'WON'T STRIVE HAR-AR-ARDER! WON'T REACH HI-I-IGHER! WON'T MAKE TOMORROW-OW-OW BETTER THAN TODAY-AY-AY!'

Bowman made no more attempts to control his sister. He knew her too well. When she got into one of her rages, there was no reasoning with her until her passions were exhausted. The schoolteacher was right: Kestrel had become a wild thing. The wildness coursed through her, glorious and liberating, as she swung from side to side on the top of the wind singer, and shouted all the terrible unthinkable thoughts that had been buried within her for so long. She had gone so far now, she had broken so many rules and said such wicked things, that she knew she would suffer the most severe punishment; and since what was done could not be undone, she was free to be as bad as she wanted to be.

'Pongo to the Emperor!' she cried. 'Where is he anyway? I've never seen him! There isn't any Emperor!'

The marshals started to climb the wind singer to bring her down by force. Bowman, afraid they would hurt her, slipped away to fetch their father from the sub-library in Orange District where he worked. As he left the arena on one side, the Chief Examiner himself entered from the other, and stood gazing down on the chaotic scene in grim silence.

'POMP-PA   POMP-PA-PRU-U-UNE   TO   THE EMPEROR-OR-OR!' rang out Kestrel's amplified voice.

Maslo Inch drew a long breath and strode steadily down the steps. By the fifth tier he felt a small hand clutch at the hem of his clean white robe.

'Please, sir,' said a small voice. 'Do you have any food?'

The Chief Examiner looked down and saw Mumpo, his nose dribbling, his face grimy, his moist stupid eyes gazing up at him, and he snatched his robe away in sudden fury.

'Don't you touch me, you poxy little brat!' he hissed.

Mumpo was used to being brushed off, or laughed at, but the pure hatred he heard in the Chief Examiner's voice astounded him.

'I only wanted – '

Maslo Inch did not wait to hear. He strode on down to the stage of the arena.

His arrival caused panic among the officials and marshals.

'We've ordered her down – we're doing all we can – she must be drunk – have you heard her? – she won't listen to us – '

'Be quiet,' said the Chief Examiner. 'Someone remove the filthy child back there, and wash him.' He made a gesture over his shoulder towards Mumpo.

One of the marshals hurried up the steps and took Mumpo by the wrist. Mumpo went slowly, looking back many times at Kestrel high in the wind singer. He didn't complain, because he was used to being dragged here and there by people in authority. The marshal took him to the fountain by the statue of Creoth the First, and held his head under the stream of cold water. Mumpo screamed, and struggled violently.

'You better watch out,' the marshal said, cross at being splashed. 'We don't want your sort in Aramanth.'

He released his hold, and washed his hands in the fountain bowl.

'I don't want to be in Aramanth,' said Mumpo, shivering. 'But I don't know where else to go.'

In the arena, Maslo Inch watched the efforts of the marshals clambering over the wind singer, trying to catch hold of the lighter and more agile child.

'Come down,' he ordered the marshals.

'They'll get her in the end, sir,' said the captain of the marshals.

'I said, come down.'

'Yes, sir.'

The marshals descended, panting and red in the face. Maslo Inch looked with his steady and contemptuous gaze at the assembled crowd.

'Has nobody here got any work to do this afternoon?'

'We couldn't let her say those wicked things – '

'You are her audience. Go away, and she will become silent. Captain, clear the arena.'

So the officials and the marshals trickled away, looking back over their shoulders as they went to see what the Chief Examiner would do next.

Kestrel did not become silent. She made a kind of song out of all the bad words she knew, and sang it through the wind singer.

'Pocksicker pocksicker pompaprune!

Banga-banga-banga plop!

Sagahog sagahog pompaprune!

Udderbug pongo plop!'

Maslo Inch gazed up at her for a few moments, as if to familiarise himself with her face. He said nothing more. The girl had mocked and insulted everything that Aramanth most respected. She would be punished, of course; but the case called for more than punishment. She must be broken. Maslo Inch was not a man to shrink from hard decisions. Young as she was, it must be done, and it must be done once and for all. He gave a single brisk nod of his head, and turned and strode calmly away.

4

PRACTISING FOR MAROON

By the time Bowman returned with his father, the arena was empty and the wind singer was silent. The marshals guarding the perimeter refused to let them enter. Hanno Hath told them he was the wild child's father, and had come to take her home. The marshals sent for their captain, and their captain sent for instructions to the College of Examiners. Back came a simple order:

'Send her home. She'll be dealt with later.'

As father and son made their way down the arena steps, Bowman asked in a low voice:

'What will they do to her?'

'I don't know,' said Hanno.

'They said we'd lose points from our family rating.'

'Yes, I expect they'll do that.'

'She said pompaprune to the Emperor. She said the

Emperor doesn't exist.'

'Did she now?' said her father, smiling to himself.

'Does the Emperor exist, pa?'

'Who knows? I've never seen him, and I've never met anyone else who's seen him. Perhaps he's just one of those useful ideas.'

'Will you be cross with Kess?'

'No, of course not. But it would have been better if she hadn't done it.'

They reached the wind singer, and Hanno Hath called up to the top, where they could see Kestrel curled up among the leather scoops.

'Kestrel! Come down now, darling.'

Kestrel looked over the edge, and saw her father below.

'Are you angry with me?' she said in a small voice.

'No,' he replied gently. 'I love you.'

So Kestrel climbed down, and as she reached the ground her courage suddenly forsook her, and she started to tremble and cry. Hanno Hath took her in his arms, and sat down on the bottom step of the arena, and held her close. He hugged her, and let her sob out all her tears of anger and humiliation.

'I know, I know,' he said over and over again.

Bowman sat beside them, waiting for his sister to calm down, and shivered, and wanted to cuddle close to his father too. He moved nearer, and leaned his head against a wool-rough arm. Pa can't help us, he thought. He wants to, but he can't. It was the first time he had ever thought this thought, clear and simple like that. He said it to Kestrel in his head.

Pa can't help us.

Kestrel thought back, *I know. But he does love us.*

Then they both felt it at the same time, how much they loved their father, and they both started kissing him at once, all over his ears and eyes and scratchy cheeks.

'That's better,' he said. 'That's my bright birds.'

They walked home quietly, the three of them arm in arm, and nobody troubled them. Ira Hath was waiting for them, with Pinpin in her arms, and they told her briefly what had happened.

'Oh, I wish I'd heard you!' she exclaimed.

Neither of Kestrel's parents blamed her, or said she'd done wrong. But they all knew there would be a price to pay.

'It'll be bad for us, won't it?' said Kestrel, watching her father's eyes as she spoke.

'Well, yes, I expect they'll want to make an example of us somehow,' said Hanno, sighing.

'Will we have to go to Maroon District?'

'Yes, I think so. Unless I astonish the world with my brilliance at the next High Examination.'

'You are brilliant, pa.'

'Thank you, darling. Unfortunately whatever brilliance I have remains undetected in exams.'

He pulled a funny face. They all knew how he hated exams.

There was no visit from the marshals that evening, so they had supper together, and Pinpin was given her bath, just as if nothing had happened. Then before Pinpin's bedtime, as the setting sun turned the sky a soft dusty pink, they made their family wish huddle, as they always did. Hanno Hath knelt down on the floor and reached up his arms. Bowman nestled under one, and Kestrel under the other. Pinpin stood with her face pressed to his chest, and her short arms round his body. Ira Hath knelt behind Pinpin, and wrapped her arms over Bowman on one side and Kestrel on the other, making a tight ring. Then they all leaned their heads inwards until they were touching, and took turns to say their night wish. Often they wished for comical things, especially their mother, who had once wished five nights running for the Blesh family to get ulcerated boils. But tonight the mood was serious.

'I wish there were no more exams ever,' said Kestrel.

'I wish nothing bad happens to Kess,' said Bowman.

'I wish my darling children to be safe and happy for ever,' said their mother. She always wished like that when she was worried.

'I wish the wind singer would sing again,' said their father.

Bowman nudged Pinpin, and she said, 'Wish wish.' Then they all kissed each other, bumping noses like they always did, because there wasn't an agreed order. Then Pinpin was put to bed.

'Do you think it'll ever happen, pa?' said Bowman. 'Will the wind singer ever sing again?'

'It's only an old story,' said Hanno Hath. 'Nobody believes it any more.'

'I do,' said Kestrel.

'You can't,' objected her brother. 'You don't know any more about it than anyone else.'

'I believe it because nobody else believes it,' she retorted.

Her father smiled at that.

'That's more or less how I feel,' he said.

He had told them the old story many times before, but Kestrel wanted to hear it again. So to calm her down, he told them once more about the time long ago when the wind singer sang. Its song was so sweet that everyone who heard it was happy. The happiness of the people of Aramanth angered the spirit-lord called the Morah –

'But the Morah's not real,' put in Bowman.

'No, nobody believes in the Morah any more,' said his father.

'I do,' said Kestrel.

The Morah was angry, went the old story, and sent a terrible army, the army of the Zars, to destroy Aramanth. Then the people were afraid, and took the voice out of the wind singer, and gave it to the Morah. The Morah accepted the offering, and the Zars turned back without destroying Aramanth, and the wind singer never sang again.

Kestrel became very excited as she heard this.

'It's true!' she cried. 'There's a place in the wind singer's neck for the voice to go. I've seen it!'

'Yes,' said Hanno. 'So have I.'

'So the story must be true.'

'Who knows?' said Hanno quietly. 'Who knows?'

Kestrel's words reminded them all of her defiance that afternoon, and they fell silent.

'Maybe they'll just forget about it,' said Ira Hath hopefully.

'No,' said Hanno. 'They won't forget.'

'We'll have to go down to Maroon District,' said Bowman. 'I don't see what's so bad about that.'

'The apartments are quite small. We'd all have to sleep together in the one room.'

'I'd like that,' said Bowman. 'I've always wanted us to sleep in one room.'

Kestrel thanked him with her eyes, and his mother kissed him and said, 'You're a dear boy. But your father snores, you know.'

'Do I?' said Hanno, surprised.

'I'm quite used to it,' said his wife, 'but the children may be kept awake for a while.'

'Why don't we try it?' said Bowman. 'Why don't we practise for Maroon District tonight?'

They took the mattresses from the twins' beds, and carried them into their parents' room. There stood the big bed, with its bedspread in stripes of many colours: pink and yellow, blue and green, colours rarely seen in Aramanth. Ira Hath

46

had made it herself, as a small act of rebellion, and the children loved it.

By pushing the big bed against the far wall they could fit both mattresses side by side on the floor, but there was no room left to walk on, and certainly no space for Pinpin's cot. So they decided Pinpin would sleep between Bowman and Kestrel, on the crack of their mattresses.

When they were all ready for bed, the twins lay down, and their father lifted the sleeping Pinpin out of her cot in the hall, and laid her between them. She half woke, and finding her brother on one side and her sister on the other, her small round face broke into a sleepy smile. She wriggled in her space, turned first one way and then the other, murmured, 'Love Bo, love Kess,' and went back to sleep.

Their parents then went to bed. For a little while they all lay there, squeezed together in the dark, and listened to each other's snuffles. Then Ira Hath said, in her prophetess voice:

'O, unhappy people! Tomorrow comes the sorrow!'

They laughed softly, as they always did at their mother's prophetess voice; but they knew what she said was true. Shivering, they wriggled deeper into the bedclothes. It felt so friendly and safe and family-ish to be sleeping together in the same room that they wondered why they had never done it before, and when, if ever, they would be able to do it again.

5

A WARNING FROM THE CHIEF EXAMINER

The summons came early, while they were still at breakfast. The doorbell rang, and there outside was a messenger from the College of Examiners. The Chief Examiner wished to see Hanno Hath at once, together with his daughter Kestrel.

Hanno rose to his feet.

'Come on, Kess. Let's get it over with.'

Kestrel stayed at the table, her expression showing stubborn resistance.

'We don't have to go.'

'If we don't, they'll send marshals to fetch us.'

Kestrel stood up slowly, staring with extreme hostility at the messenger.

'Do what you like to me,' she said. 'I don't care.'

'Me?' said the messenger, aggrieved. 'What's it got to do with me? All I do is carry messages. You think anyone ever explains them to me?'

'You don't have to do it.'

'Oh, don't I? We live in Grey District, we do. You try sharing a toilet with six families. You try living with a sick wife and two thumping great lads in one room. Oh no, I'll do my job all right, and more, and one fine day, they'll move us up to Maroon, and that'll do me nicely, thank you very much.'

Maslo Inch was waiting in his spacious office, sitting at his broad desk. He rose to his full imposing height as Hanno and Kestrel entered, and to their surprise, greeted them with a smile, in his high grand way. Coming out from behind the fortress desk, he shook their hands, and invited them to sit down with him in the circle of high grand chairs.

'Your father and I used to play together when we were your age,' he told Kestrel. 'We sat together in class, too, for a while. Remember, Hanno?'

'Yes,' said Hanno. 'I remember.'

He remembered how Maslo Inch had been so much bigger than the rest of them, and had made them kneel before him. But he said nothing about that. He just wanted to get the interview over with as soon as possible. Maslo Inch's white clothes were so very white that it was hard to look at him for long; that, and his smile.

'I'm going to tell you something that may surprise you,' the Chief Examiner said to Kestrel. 'Your father used to be cleverer than me at school.'

'That doesn't surprise me,' said Kestrel.

'Doesn't it?' said Maslo Inch evenly. 'Then why am I Chief Examiner of Aramanth, while your father is a sub-district librarian?'

'Because he doesn't like exams,' said Kestrel. 'He likes books.'

Hanno Hath saw a shadow of irritation pass across the Chief Examiner's face.

'We know this is about what happened yesterday,' he said quietly. 'Say what you have to say.'

'Ah, yes. Yesterday.' The smile turned to hold Hanno in its steady shine. 'Your daughter gave us quite a performance. We'll come to that in due course.'

Hanno Hath looked back at the smooth face of the Chief Examiner, and saw there in those gleaming eyes a deep well of hatred. Why? he thought. This powerful man has nothing to fear from me. Why does he hate me so?

Maslo Inch rose to his feet.

'Follow me, please. Both of you.'

He set off without a backward glance, and Hanno Hath and Kestrel followed behind, hand in hand. The Chief Examiner led them down a long empty corridor, lined on both sides with columns of gold-painted names. This was such a commonplace sight in Aramanth that neither father nor daughter looked twice at them. Anyone who achieved anything noteworthy was named on some wall somewhere, and this practice had been going on for so long that virtually no public wall was spared.

The corridor linked the College of Examiners to the Imperial Palace, and emerged into a courtyard at the heart of the palace, where a grey-clothed warden was sweeping the pathways. Maslo Inch began what was clearly a rehearsed speech.

'Kestrel,' he said, 'I want you to listen to what I say to you today, and look at what I show you today, and remember it for the rest of your life.'

Kestrel said nothing. She watched the warden's broom: swish, swish, swish.

'I've been making enquiries about you,' said the Chief Examiner. 'I'm told that at school yesterday morning you placed yourself at the bottom of the class.'

'What if I did?' She was watching the warden. His eyes looked down as he worked, and his face looked vacant.

What is he thinking? Bo would know.

'And that you said to your class teacher, What more can you do to me?'

'What if I did?'

Why does he go on sweeping? There's nothing to sweep.

'You then went on to indulge in a childish tantrum in a public place.'

'What if I did?'

'You know of course that your own rating affects your family rating.'

'What if it does?'

Swish, swish, swish, goes the broom.

'That is what we are about to find out.'

He came to a stop before a door in a stone wall. The door was heavy, and closed with a big iron latch. He put his hand on the latch, and turned to Kestrel once more.

'What more can you do to me? An interesting question, but the wrong one. You should ask, What more can I do to myself, and to those I love?'

He heaved on the iron latch, and pushed the heavy door open. Inside, a dank stone tunnel sloped downwards into the gloom.

'I am taking you to see the salt caves. This is a privilege, of a kind. Very few of our citizens see the salt caves, for a reason that will soon become evident.'

They followed him down the tunnel, their footsteps echoing from the arched roof. The sides of the tunnel, Kestrel now saw, were cut out of a white rock that glistened in the dim light: salt. She knew from her history that Aramanth had been built on salt. The Manth people, a wandering tribe in search of a homeland, had found traces of the mineral, and had settled there to mine it. The traces became seams, the seams became caverns, as they tunnelled into a huge subterranean treasure-house. Salt had made the Manth people rich, and with their wealth they had built their city.

'Have you ever asked yourself what became of the salt caves?' said Maslo Inch, as they descended the long curving tunnel. 'When all the salt had been extracted, there was left only a great space. A great nothingness. A void. What use, do you think, is a void?'

Now they could hear the sound of slow-moving water, a low deep gurgle. And on the dank air they could smell an acrid gassy smell.

'For a hundred years we took from the ground what we wanted most. And for another hundred years, we have poured back into the ground what we want least.'

The sloping tunnel suddenly opened into a wide underground chamber, an indistinct and shadowy space loud with the sounds of moving water, as if a thousand streams here disgorged into a subterranean sea. The smell was unmistakable now: pungent and nauseating.

Maslo Inch led them to a long railing. Beyond the railing, some way below, lay a vast slow-swirling lake of dark mud, which here and there bubbled up in ponderous burps, like a gigantic simmering cauldron. The walls of the chamber above this lake glistened and shone, as if with sweat. They were pierced at intervals by great iron pipes, and out of these pipes issued grey water, sometimes at a trickle, sometimes at a gush.

'Drains,' said the Chief Examiner. 'Sewers. Not beautiful, but necessary.'

Instinctively, both Kestrel and her father raised their

hands to cover their noses against the stench.

'You think, young lady, that if you do as you please, and make no effort at school, you and your family will go down from Orange to Maroon. You think you don't mind that. Perhaps you will go down again, from Maroon to Grey. You think you don't mind that, either. Grey District isn't pretty, or comfortable, but it's the bottom, and at least they'll leave you alone there. That's what you think, isn't it? The worst that can happen is we'll go all the way down to Grey.'

'No,' said Kestrel, though this was exactly what she thought.

'No? You think it could be worse?'

Kestrel said nothing.

'You're quite right. It could be far, far worse. After all, Grey District, poor as it is, is still part of Aramanth. But there is a world below Aramanth.'

Kestrel stared out over the murky surface of the lake. It stretched far into the distance, further than she could see. And far, far away she seemed to glimpse a glow, a pool of light, like the light that sometimes breaks through clouds on to distant hills. She fixed her gaze on this distant glow, and the stinking lake appeared to her to be almost beautiful.

'You're looking at the Underlake, a lake of decomposing matter that's bigger than all Aramanth. There are islands in the lake, islands of mud. Do you see?'

They followed his pointing finger, and could just make out, far away across the slithering grey-brown surface of the lake, a group of low mounds. As they watched, they caught a movement near the mounds, and staring, half-incredulous, saw what looked like a distant figure pass over the mud, and sink abruptly out of sight. Now, their eyes attuned to the gloom, they began to spot other figures, all as uniformly dark as the mud over which they crept, slipping silently in and out of the shadows.

'Do people live down here?' asked Hanno.

'They do. Many thousands. Men, women, children. Primitive, degraded people, little better than animals.'

He invited them to step closer to the railing. Directly ahead, through a gate in the rails, there projected a narrow jetty. Tethered to its timbers some twenty feet below were several long flat-bottomed barges, half-filled with refuse of every kind.

'They live on what we throw away. They live in rubbish, and they live on rubbish.' He turned to Kestrel. 'You asked, What more can you do to me? Here's your answer. Why do we strive harder? Why do we reach higher? Because we don't want to live like this.'

Kestrel shrugged. 'I don't care,' she said.

The Chief Examiner watched her closely.

'You don't care?' he said slowly.

'No.'

'I don't believe you.'

'Then don't.'

'Prove you don't care.'

He opened the gate in the railing and held it wide, inviting her to pass through. Kestrel looked out along the slick boards.

'Go on. Walk right to the end. If you really don't care.'

Kestrel took one step on to the narrow jetty, and stopped. In truth, she was frightened of the Underlake, but she was bursting inside with angry pride, and would have done anything to wipe that smooth smile from the Chief Examiner's face. So she took another step.

'That's enough, Kess,' said her father. And to the Chief Examiner, 'You've made your point, Maslo. Leave her to me.'

'We've left your children to you for too long, Hanno.' He spoke evenly as always, but now there was an undertone of sharp displeasure. 'Children follow the example given by their parents. There's something broken inside you, my friend. There's no fight in you any more. No will to succeed.'

Kestrel heard this, and went cold inside with fury. At once, she started to walk briskly down the jetty. She looked straight ahead, fixing her gaze on the place where the far-off light streamed down on to the dark surface of the lake, and put one foot in front of the other, and walked.

'Kess! Come back!' called her father.

He started after her, but Maslo Inch seized his arm with one hand, and held him in a grip of iron.

'Let her go,' he said. 'She has to learn.'

With his other hand, he operated a long lever by the jetty

gate, and there came a hissing gurgling sound, as the posts supporting the far end of the jetty began to sink into the lake. The jetty sloped downwards, becoming a ramp tilting ever more steeply down into the mud. Kestrel gave a cry of alarm, and turned and tried to run back up the boards, but they were coated with slime, and she couldn't get a grip. She started to slither backwards.

'Papa!' she cried. 'Help me!'

Hanno lunged towards her, pulling furiously in the Chief Examiner's hold, but he could not free himself.

'Let me go! What are you doing to her? Are you insane?'

Maslo Inch's eyes were locked on to Kestrel, as she tried in vain to stop her downward slide.

'Slipping, slipping, slipping,' he cried. 'Well, Kestrel, do you care now?'

'Papa! Help me!'

'Get her out! She'll drown!'

'Do you care now? Will you try harder now? Tell me! I want to hear!'

'Papa!' Kestrel screamed as she slithered off the end of the sloping jetty, and into the lake. Her feet hit the brown water, and with an awful sucking sound they disappeared into liquid mud.

'I'm sinking!'

'Tell me you care!' called out Maslo Inch, his hand gripping Hanno's arm so tight his fingers had gone white. 'I want to hear!'

'You're mad!' said Hanno. 'You've gone mad!'

In desperation, he swung his free arm, and struck the Chief Examiner hard across the face.

Maslo Inch turned on him, and suddenly he lost all his self-control. He shook Hanno like a doll.

'Don't you dare touch me!' he screamed. 'You worm! You dribble! You maggot! You failure! You fail your exams, you fail your family, you fail your country!'

At the same time, Kestrel realised she wasn't sinking any more. Somewhere beneath the surface there was hard ground, and she had only sunk to her knees. So she took hold of the sides of the narrow jetty with both hands, and began to claw her way back up. She didn't call out any more. She just fixed her eyes on the Chief Examiner and willed herself up the slope.

Maslo Inch was too absorbed in screaming at her father to notice.

'What use are you? You're a nothing! You do nothing, you make no effort, you expect others to do it all for you, all you do is read your useless books! You're a parasite! You're a germ! You infect everyone round you with your sick lazy failure! You disgust me!'

Kestrel reached the top of the jetty, took a deep breath, and with a yell of blood-curdling fury, threw herself on the Chief Examiner's back.

'Pocksicker!'

She locked her arms round his neck and her legs round

his waist and squeezed with all her might, to make him let go of her father.

'Sagahog! Pooa-pooa-pooa-banga-pompaprune! Pock-sicking udderbug!'

The Chief Examiner, taken by surprise, released Hanno Hath's arm and turned about to pull Kestrel off him. But whichever way he swung, she was always behind him, her wiry little arms throttling him, her muddy feet kicking at his ribs.

The tussle was short but intense. During it, much of the mud on Kestrel's legs was wiped on to the Chief Examiner's clothing. When at last he got a grip on her and tore her off, she let go, and he threw her further than he intended. At once she sprang to her feet and ran.

He made no attempt to chase her. He was too shocked at the sight of his muddy clothes.

'My whites!' he said. 'The little witch!'

Kestrel was gone, streaking away as fast as she could, up the tunnel towards the distant door.

Maslo Inch brushed himself down, and pulled back the lever that raised the jetty to its former position. Then he turned to Hanno Hath.

'Well, old friend,' he said, icily calm. 'What do you have to say to that?'

'You shouldn't have done that to her.'

'Is that all?'

Hanno Hath was silent. He would not apologise for his

daughter's behaviour, but nor was it wise to say what he really felt, which was that he was intensely proud of her. So he kept a neutral expression on his face, and looked with inner satisfaction at the mudstains on the Chief Examiner's once-pure robes.

'I now see,' said Maslo Inch quietly, 'that we have a far more serious problem with the girl than I had realised.'

6

SPECIAL TEACHING

Kestrel ran out of the tunnel, and straight into the grey-clothed warden. He must have heard her coming, since he had dropped his broom and was waiting for her, arms spread wide. As soon as he had her tight, he picked her up and dangled her in the air, where she kicked as hard as she could, and screamed at the top of her voice. But he was a big man, bigger than he'd looked bent over his broom, and he was strong, and her screams didn't seem to trouble him in the least.

Maslo Inch came out into the courtyard, followed by her father, just as two more wardens came running, drawn by the noise she was making.

'Papa!' she screamed. 'Papa-a-a!'

'Put her down,' said Hanno Hath.

'Be silent!' cried the Chief Examiner, with such terrible

authority that even Kestrel stopped screaming.

'Get this man out of here,' he said more quietly, and the two wardens started to hustle Hanno Hath away. 'Take the girl to Special Teaching.'

'No!' cried Hanno Hath. 'I beg you, no!'

'Papa!' screamed Kestrel, kicking and struggling. 'Papa-a-a!'

But she was already being carried off in the opposite direction. The Chief Examiner watched them both go with a grim and unmoving look on his face.

'What more can you do to me, eh?' he said softly to himself. And he strode away to change into clean white robes.

The separate building set aside for Special Teaching was inside the old palace compound, on one side of a small deserted square. It was a solid stone structure, much like any other in this grandest of the city's districts, with a high handsome door at the top of three steps. This door was opened from the inside, as the warden approached with Kestrel in his arms. It was closed after them, by a doorman dressed in grey.

'Referred by the Chief Examiner,' said the warden.

The doorman nodded, and opened an inner door. Kestrel was pushed through into a long narrow room, and left there without a word. The door closed with a click behind her.

She was alone.

She realised for the first time that she was shaking violently, out of a combination of fear, rage and exhaustion. She took several deep breaths to steady herself, and looked round the room. It was empty and windowless.

She turned her attention to the door, hoping to find a way of opening it. The door had no handle. She felt all over it, and round its edges, but it was close-fitting, and there seemed to be no way to open it from the inside. So she turned back to examining the room.

All along one wall hung a plain grey floor-length curtain. She drew the curtain back, and found there was a window behind it, looking through to a much larger inner room. Cautiously, she drew the curtain all the way back, and stared at the strange scene beyond. It was a classroom. Sitting at the rows of desks, with their backs to her, were a large number of children, perhaps as many as a hundred. They were all bent studiously over their books, working away in silence; or so she supposed, for no sound of any kind came through the glass. There was a teacher's desk at the far end, and a blackboard, but no teacher.

The children at the back of the class were quite close to the window. Perhaps they would help her. She tapped on the glass softly, just in case a teacher was nearby. The children didn't move. She tapped more loudly, and then as loudly as she could, but they seemed to hear nothing. It began to strike her that there was something strange about them. They kept their heads so low to their books that she couldn't see their faces, but their hands were unusually wrinkly. And their hair was grey, or white, or – she saw it now – some of them were bald. Now that she looked properly, she asked herself why she had thought they were children at all. And yet, they were the size of children, and the shape of children. And surely –

The door opened behind her. Kestrel turned round, her heart hammering. A scarlet-robed examiner entered, a middle-aged lady, and closed the door behind her. She held a file open in her hands, and she looked from the papers in it to Kestrel and back again. She had a friendly face.

'Kestrel Hath?' she said.

'Yes,' said Kestrel. 'Ma'am.'

She spoke quietly, clasping her hands before her and lowering her gaze to the floor. She had decided, on the spur of the moment, to be a good girl.

The examiner looked at her in some perplexity. 'What have you done, child?'

'I was frightened,' said Kestrel in a tiny voice. 'I think I must have panicked.'

'The Chief Examiner has referred you for Special Teaching.' As she spoke, she glanced through the window at the silent class working in the room beyond, and shook her head. 'It does seem a little extreme.'

Kestrel said nothing, but tried very hard to look sad and good.

'Special Teaching, you know,' said the lady examiner, 'is

for the most disruptive children. The ones that are entirely out of control. And it is so very, well, permanent.'

Kestrel went up to the lady examiner, and took her hand and held it trustingly, gazing up at her with big innocent eyes.

'Do you have a little girl of your own, ma'am?' she asked.

'Yes, child. Yes, I do.'

'Then I know you'll do what's best for me, ma'am. Just as you would for your own little girl.'

The lady examiner looked down at Kestrel, and gave a little sigh, and patted her hand.

'Well, well,' she said. 'I think we should go and see the Chief Examiner, don't you? Maybe there's been a mistake.'

She turned to the handleless door and called:

'Open, please!'

The door was opened by a warden on the far side, and the lady examiner and Kestrel, hand in hand, went out into the square.

Now that she wasn't being carried, Kestrel could see that one side of the square was formed by the back wall of the Great Tower, which was the building at the centre of the Imperial Palace. This tower, the highest building in Aramanth, could be seen even from Orange District. This close, it seemed immensely tall, reaching up and up even higher than the city's encircling walls.

As they crossed the square, a small door at the foot of the tower opened, and two white-robed men came sweeping out. Seeing the lady examiner holding Kestrel's hand, the older of the two frowned and called out to them.

'What is a child from Orange District doing here?'

The lady examiner explained. The man in white studied the file.

'So the Chief Examiner ordered Special Teaching for the girl,' he said sharply. 'And you have taken it upon yourself to question his judgment.'

'I think there may have been a mistake.'

'Do you know anything about this case?'

'Well, no,' said the lady examiner, going rather pink. 'It's more a kind of feeling, really.'

'A kind of feeling?' The man's voice was cutting with contempt. 'You propose to make a decision that affects the rest of this child's life on a kind of feeling?'

The rest of this child's life! A chill ran through Kestrel. She looked round for a way of escape. Behind her stood the Special Teaching building from which they had come. Ahead, the men in white.

'I meant only to speak to the Chief Examiner, to make sure I understood his wishes.'

'His wishes are written here. They are perfectly clear, are they not?'

'Yes.'

Kestrel saw that the door into the tower had not closed all the way.

'Do you suggest that when he made this order, and

signed it, he didn't know what he was doing?'

'No.'

'Then why do you not carry it out?'

'Yes, of course. I'm sorry.'

Kestrel knew then that she had lost her one source of protection. The lady examiner turned distressed eyes on her, and said once again, this time to Kestrel:

'I'm sorry.'

'That's all right,' said Kestrel, and gave the lady's hand a little squeeze. 'Thank you for trying.'

Then she released the hand, and she ran.

She was through the tower door and pushing it shut behind her before they realised what was happening. There was a bolt on the inside, which she drew shut. Only then, heart beating fast, did she look to see where she was.

She was in a small lobby, with two doors, and a narrow curving flight of stairs. Both doors were locked. She heard voices shouting outside, and the outer door rattling as they tried to open it. Then she heard louder bangs, as they tried to break the bolt. Then she heard a voice call out:

'You stay here. I'll go round the other way.'

She had no choice: so she set off up the stairs.

Up and up she climbed, and the stairwell grew darker and darker. She thought she could hear doors opening and closing below, so she kept climbing as fast as she could. Up and up, round and round, and now there was light above. She came to a small barred window, set deep in the stonework of the tower. Through the window she could see the roofs of the palace, and a brief glimpse of the square where the statue of Emperor Creoth stood.

Still the stairs rose above her, so breathing hard now, her legs aching, she climbed on and on, and the light from the little window dwindled away below her. Strange distorted sounds came floating up from below, the clatter of running feet, the boom of voices. Up and up she climbed, slower now, wondering where the staircase led, and whether, when at last she reached the top, there would be another locked door.

A second window appeared. Exhausted, trembling, she allowed herself to rest a moment here, and looked out over the city. She could make out people passing in the streets, and the elegant shops and houses of Scarlet District. Then she heard a sound which was very like boots climbing the winding stairs below her, and fear gave her strength to get up and go on. Up and up, forcing her legs to push, half giddy with exhaustion, she followed the tightly winding staircase that seemed to have no end. *Clop, clop, clop*, went the noise of the boots below, carried up to her by the stone walls. *Not far now*, she said to herself, in time with her steps. *Not far now, not far now*. Though in truth she had no way of knowing how much further she must climb.

And then, just when she knew she could go no further, she came out on to a tiny landing, and there before her was a door. Her hand shook as she reached out to try the handle.

Please, she said inside her head. *Please don't be locked*. She turned the handle, and felt the latch open. She pushed: but the door didn't move. At once her fear, held at bay by this last hope, broke through and overwhelmed her. Bursting into bitter tears, she crumpled up in a ball at the foot of the door. There she hugged her knees and sobbed her heart out.

Clop, clop, clop. The boots were coming up the stairs, getting nearer all the time. Kestrel rocked and sobbed, and wished she was dead.

Then she heard a new sound. Shuffling footsteps, close by. The slither of a bolt.

The door opened.

'Come in,' said an impatient voice. 'Come in quickly.'

Kestrel looked up and saw a blotchy red face staring down at her: watery, protruding eyes, and a grizzly grey beard.

'You've certainly taken your time,' he said. 'Come in, now you're here.'

7

The Emperor Weeps

The bearded man closed the door and bolted it after Kestrel, and then made a sign to her to stay quiet. On the far side they could hear quite clearly now the sound of the climbing boots. Then whoever it was reached the landing at the top, and came to a stop.

'Well, boggle me!' said a surprised voice. 'She's not here!'

They saw the door handle turn as he tried to open it. Then the sound of his voice shouting down the stairs.

'She's not here, you stupid pocksickers! I've climbed all these hogging stairs and she's not hogging here!'

With that, he set off back down the long winding staircase, muttering as he went. The bearded man gave a soft chortle of pleasure.

'Pocksicker!' he said. 'I haven't heard that for years. How reassuring to know that the old oaths are still in use.'

Taking Kestrel's hand, he led her into the light of one of the windows, so that he could see her better. She in her turn stared at him. His robes were blue, which astonished her. No one wore blue in Aramanth.

'Well,' he said. 'You're not what I expected, I must say. But you'll have to do.'

He then went to a table in the middle of the room, where there stood a glass bowl full of chocolate buttons, and ate three, one after the other. While he did this, Kestrel was gazing in wonder out of the window. The room must have been near the top of the tower, if not at the top itself, for it was higher than the city walls. In one direction, she could see over the land to the ocean; in the other, the desert plains lay before her, reaching all the way to the misty line of the northern mountains.

'But it's so big!' she said.

'Oh, it's big all right. Bigger than you can see from here, even.'

Kestrel looked down at the city below, laid out in its districts, the scarlet and the white, her own orange streets, the maroon and the grey, all circled by the massive city walls. For the first time, it struck her that this was an odd arrangement.

'Why do we have to have walls?'

'Why indeed?' said the bearded man. 'Why do we have to have districts in different colours? Why do we have to have examinations, and ratings? Why do we have to strive harder,

71

and reach higher, and make tomorrow better than today?'

Kestrel stared at him. He was speaking thoughts she supposed only she had ever had.

'For love of my Emperor,' she said in the words of the Oath of Dedication. 'And for the glory of Aramanth.'

The bearded man gave a soft chuckle.

'Ha!' he said. 'I'm your Emperor.'

And he ate three more chocolate buttons.

'You?'

'Yes, I know, it must seem implausible. But I am Creoth the Sixth, Emperor of Aramanth. And you are the person I've been waiting for all these years.'

'Me?'

'Well, I didn't know it would be you. To be honest, I had assumed it would be a strapping young man. Someone brave and strong, you know, given what has to be done. But it turns out to be you.'

'Oh, no,' said Kestrel. 'I wasn't looking for you. I didn't even know you existed. I was running away.'

'Don't be foolish. It must be you. No one else has ever found me. They keep me shut away here so no one will ever find me.'

'You're not shut away. You opened the door yourself.'

'That's another matter entirely. The point is, here you are.'

He was clearly put out at being contradicted, so Kestrel said nothing more, and he went on eating chocolate buttons.

He seemed to be unaware that he was eating them, and altogether unaware that it would have been polite to offer her some. She wasn't sure if she believed that he was the Emperor, but as she looked about her she saw that the room was furnished in a very grand manner indeed. On one side was an ornate bed with curtains round it, like a tent. On the other was a beautifully carved writing desk, flanked by bookcases filled with handsome volumes. There was the round table, where the glass bowl stood, and some deep leather armchairs, and a great high-sided bath; and soft rugs on the floor, and embroidered drapes at the windows. The windows that ran all round the room were deeply recessed, and between each set was a door. Eight windows, eight doors. One was the door she had entered by. Two others stood open, and she could see that they led into cupboards. That left five. Surely one out of five would lead her out of the tower again.

The bearded man now moved away from the bowl of chocolate buttons, and went to his writing desk. Here he started opening the little drawers, one by one, clearly searching for something.

'Please, sir,' said Kestrel. 'Can I go home now?'

'Go home? What are you talking about? Of course you can't go home. You have to go to the Halls of the Morah, and fetch it back.'

'Fetch what back?'

'I have the directions here somewhere. Yes, here it is.'

He drew out a paper scroll, dusty and yellow with age, and unrolled it.

'It should have been me, of course.'

He sighed as he looked at it.

'There, now. All perfectly clear, I think.'

Kestrel looked at the scroll he held out before her. The paper was cracked and faded, but it was recognisably a map. She could make out the line of the ocean, and a little drawing that was clearly meant to be Aramanth itself. There was a marked trail, that led from Aramanth across plains to a line of pictured mountains. Here and there on the map, and most of all where the trail ended, there were scribbled markings, clusters of symbols that seemed to be words written in letters that were unfamiliar to her.

She looked up, bewildered.

'Don't gape at me, girl,' said the Emperor. 'If you don't understand, just ask.'

'I don't understand anything.'

'Nonsense! It's all perfectly simple. Here we are, you see.'

He pointed to Aramanth on the map.

'This is the way you must go. You see?'

His finger traced the track north from Aramanth. 'You have to follow the road, or you'll miss the bridge. It's the only way, do you see?'

His finger was pointing to a jagged line that crossed the map from side to side. It had a name, in spidery lettering, but like the rest of the writing, it meant nothing to her.

'But why must I do this?'

'Beard of my ancestors!' he exclaimed. 'Have they sent me an infant with no brain? To fetch back the voice, so the wind singer sings again.'

'The voice of the wind singer!'

A shiver went through Kestrel.

It's real, she said inside herself. *It's real*.

The Emperor turned the map over, and there on the other side was more writing, in the strange letters, beside a faded drawing of a shape that Kestrel recognised. It was the curled-over letter S she had seen etched into the wind singer.

'Here it is.'

Kestrel stared at the drawing, and was filled with a confused mixture of excitement and fear.

'What will happen when the wind singer sings again?'

'We'll be free of the Morah, of course.'

'Free of the Morah?'

'Free – of – the – Morah,' he repeated, slowly and loudly.

'But the Morah's just a story.'

'Just a story! Beard of my ancestors! Just a story! The city worse than a prison, the people scratching their lives away in envy and hatred, and you say it's just a story! The Morah rules Aramanth, child! Everybody knows that.'

'No,' said Kestrel, 'they don't. Nobody knows it. They all think the Morah is a story from long ago.'

'Do they?' The Emperor peered at her suspiciously.

'Well then, that just goes to show how clever the Morah is, doesn't it?'

'Yes, I suppose it does,' said Kestrel.

'So you believe me now?'

'I don't know. All I know is I hate school, and I hate tests, and I hate examiners, and I hate Aramanth.'

'Of course you do. That's all the work of the Morah. They call Aramanth the perfect society. Ha! Have they done away with fear and hatred? Of course not. The Morah sees to that.'

The strange thing was, as Kestrel listened to him, it all made a kind of sense. She looked again at the drawing on the back of the map.

'Where did you get this?'

'From my father. He had it from his father, who had it from his, and so on back to Creoth the First. He was the one who took the voice out of the wind singer.'

'To save the city from the Zars.'

'Oh, so you do know something, after all.'

'Why did the Morah want the voice?'

'To stop the wind singer from singing, of course. The wind singer was there to protect Aramanth from the Morah.'

'Then why did the first Emperor give the voice away?'

'Why? Ah, why indeed!' He sighed, and shook his head. 'But who are we to blame him? He had seen the army of the Zars, and we have not. Fear, child. That is the answer to your question. He knew the wind singer had power, but could it stop the Zars? Dared he take the risk? No, it's not for us

76

to blame him for what he did so long ago. As you see –' he pointed one finger at the strange lettering that ran round the frame of the map – 'he lived to regret what he had done.'

Kestrel stared at the incomprehensible writing.

'So does the wind singer have the power to stop the Morah?'

'Who knows? My grandfather, who was a wise man, said that there must be power in the voice, or why did the Morah want it so much? And as you see, it says on the back of the map, *The song of the wind singer will set you free.*'

'Free of the Morah?'

'Of course free of the Morah. What else would it be, free of flying fish? And don't gape at me, child!' The Emperor was becoming impatient again. 'I thought we'd been over this already.'

'Then why hasn't anyone gone to get it back before now?'

'Why? Do you think it's easy? Mind you,' he interrupted himself hastily, 'I'm not necessarily saying it's all that difficult. And it must be done, of course. But you see, for a long time, it seemed like it was all for the best. The Zars had gone away, and the changes came so slowly that nobody really noticed what was happening. It wasn't till my grandfather's time that it was clear it had all been a terrible mistake. And he was very old by then. So he gave the map to my father. But my father became ill. My father gave me the map before he died, but I was only a very small child. So now you've come, and I'm giving the map to you. What could be simpler than that?'

He went back to his desk and started closing all the little drawers he had opened: click, click, click.

'You're not little now,' said Kestrel.

'Of course I'm not little now.'

'So why can't you go?'

'Because I can't, that's all. It has to be you.'

'I'm sorry,' said Kestrel. 'There's been some kind of mistake. I'm nobody special.'

The Emperor looked at her accusingly.

'If you're nobody special, how come you're the only person who's ever found their way here?'

'I was running away.'

'Who from?'

'The examiners.'

'Ha! There you are! That's a very unusual thing to be doing in Aramanth. Nobody else runs away from the examiners. So you must be someone special.'

'I just hate examiners and I hate school and I hate tests.'

She was close to tears.

'Well, now,' said the Emperor. 'That shows you're precisely the right person. Once you've got the voice, and put it back in the wind singer, there'll be no more tests.'

'No more tests?'

'So you have to go, you see.'

'You should go, if you're the Emperor.'

He gazed at her sadly.

'I would,' he said. 'Truly, I would. Only, there's a difficulty.'

He went from door to door, opening them all. Three doors led on to landings, from which stairs could be seen descending.

'I sometimes think of going,' he said. 'For example, I might like the look of that door. So I might set off.'

He took a few steps towards the doorway, and then stopped.

'Just one more chocolate button before I go.'

He returned to the bowl in the middle of the room. 'Take a handful,' said Kestrel. 'Then you won't need to come back.'

'It sounds so easy,' said the Emperor with a sigh. But he did as she said, and scooped up a handful of chocolate buttons. Then eating as he went, he headed back to the door. On the threshold, he stopped once again.

'What about when these run out?' He started to count the chocolate buttons in his hand. 'One, two, three – '

'Take the bowl,' said Kestrel.

So he went back to the table and picked up the glass bowl. But just before the doorway, he stopped again.

'It looks like a lot,' he said, 'but eventually they'll run out.'

'They'll run out anyway.'

'Ah, that's just it, you see. The bowl is filled up again every day. But if I've taken the bowl away, how can they fill it up?'

He returned to the table and put the glass bowl back.

'Probably best to leave it here.'

Kestrel stared at him.

'Why do you like chocolate buttons so much?'

'Well, I don't know that I like them particularly. They just seem necessary.'

'Necessary?'

'Do we have to talk about this? It's very hard to explain. I must have them there, even if I don't eat them. To tell the truth, sometimes days go by and I don't have any at all.'

'You've been eating them without stopping.'

'That's because I'm feeling nervous. I don't get many visitors. In fact, I don't get any at all.'

'How long have you been like this?'

'Oh, all my life.'

'All your life? You've lived all your life in this room?'

'Yes.'

'But that's stupid!'

'I know.'

He raised one hand, and suddenly smacked himself in the face.

'I am stupid. I'm good for nothing.'

He smacked himself again, harder.

'I'm a disgrace to my ancestors.'

He started to beat himself all over, on his face and chest and stomach.

'I do nothing but eat and sleep, I'm fat and tired, and so, so dull! I never go anywhere, I never see anyone! No conversation, no fun! I'd be better off dead, but I don't even have the strength of mind to die!'

He sobbed as he beat himself.

'I'm sorry,' said Kestrel. 'I don't know what I can do.'

'Oh, it doesn't matter,' said the Emperor, weeping copiously. 'It always ends like this. I get overtired very easily, you see. I'd better have a rest.'

And without further ado, he climbed fully clothed into his grand canopied bed, pulled the covers over himself, and went to sleep.

Kestrel waited, expecting something more. After a few moments, he began to snore. So she tiptoed softly to one of the doors that opened on to a staircase, and trod cautiously down the stairs, still carrying the rolled-up map.

8

THE HATH FAMILY SHAMED

When Kestrel reached the tower door through which she had entered, she stopped, and peeped through the keyhole into the courtyard beyond. There she saw two marshals striding up and down, in a cross but aimless fashion. She pushed the map out of sight in one pocket, drew a deep breath, opened the door, and shouted:

'Help! The Emperor! Help!'

'What!' cried the nearest marshal. 'Where?'

'Up in his room! The Emperor! Help him quickly!'

She sounded so distressed that the marshals didn't stop to ask any more, but set off up the spiral staircase as fast as they could go. Kestrel at once ran helter-skelter across the courtyard, down the long corridor, out of the door at the end, and found herself in the main plaza, by the statue of Creoth the First.

She made her way back to Orange District by alleys and back ways, taking care not to be seen by anyone in authority. But as she turned into her home street, she saw at once that there was no hope of slipping into her house unnoticed. A small crowd was gathered in front of the house, and most of the neighbours were leaning out of their windows to watch. On the doorstep, on either side of the closed door, stood two district marshals, fingering their medallions of office and looking grave. Everyone seemed to be waiting for something to happen.

As Kestrel drew near, her footsteps dragging ever more slowly, Rufy Blesh saw her, and came running to her side.

'Kestrel,' he cried excitedly. 'You're in big trouble. So's your father.'

'What's happened?'

'He's being taken away on a Residential Study Course.' He lowered his voice. 'Really it's a kind of prison, my father says, whatever they call it. My mother says it's awfully shaming, and thank goodness we're going up to Scarlet, because after this we won't be able to talk to you any more.'

'Then why are you talking to me?'

'Well, he hasn't actually been taken away yet,' said Rufy.

Kestrel went as close to the house as she dared, and then slipped down the side. She ran swiftly along the alley where the rubbish bins stood, and so came to the back of her home. She could see her mother through the kitchen window, moving back and forth, carrying Pinpin in her arms, but no sign of Bowman. She sent him a silent call.

Bo! I'm here!

She felt him at once, and his wave of relief that she was safe.

Kess! You're all right!

He appeared at their bedroom window, looking out. She showed herself.

Don't let them see you, Kess. They've come to take you away. They're taking pa away.

I'm coming in, said Kestrel. *I have to talk to pa.*

Bowman left the window and went downstairs to the front room, where his father was standing in the middle of the floor, packing an open suitcase. The twins' class teacher, Dr Batch, sat on the sofa, beside a senior member of the Board of Examiners, Dr Minish. Both men wore expressions of grim seriousness. Dr Batch took out a watch and looked at it.

'We're already half an hour behind schedule,' he announced. 'We have no way of knowing when the girl will return. I suggest we proceed.'

'You are to notify the district marshals as soon as she comes home,' said Dr Minish.

'But I won't be here,' said Hanno Hath mildly.

'Come along, sir, come along.'

It irritated Dr Batch to see how the fellow stood looking

so distractedly at the muddle of clothing and books on the floor.

'Don't forget your wash things, pa,' said Bowman.

'My wash things?'

Hanno Hath looked at his son. Bowman himself had brought down his toothbrush and his razor, half an hour ago.

'In the bathroom,' said Bowman.

'In the bathroom?' He understood. 'Ah, yes.'

Dr Minish followed this exchange with exasperation.

'Well, get on with it, man.'

'Yes, very well.'

Hanno Hath went away up the stairs to the bathroom. Ira Hath came into the front room, carrying Pinpin, who could feel the anxiety in the house and was crying in a low whining way.

'Would you like a drink while you're waiting?' Mrs Hath asked the two teachers.

'Perhaps a glass of lemonade, if you have it,' said Dr Minish.

'Do you like lemonade, Dr Batch?'

'Yes, ma'am. Lemonade would do very well.'

Mrs Hath went back into the kitchen.

Up in the bathroom, Hanno Hath found his daughter waiting for him. He took her silently in his arms and kissed her, deeply relieved.

'My darling darling Kess. I had feared the worst.'

'I don't want a second chance. I hate them.'

'But I couldn't bear it if you – '

He cut himself off with a shrug.

'I'd do anything for you, my darling one. I'd die for you. But it seems the trial I have to endure is knowing I can do nothing.'

He fell silent, gazing at the map. From the foot of the stairs they heard Dr Minish's cross voice calling up.

'Come along, sir! We're waiting!'

'The Emperor said if I brought the voice back, and the wind singer sang, there'd be no more tests.'

'Ah, did he say that?'

For a moment the sadness left his eyes.

'But, my darling one, you can't go, you're only a child. And anyway, they'll never let you leave the city. They're watching out for you. No, this must wait until I come home again.'

In the front room downstairs, the waiting teachers were growing more impatient and thirstier by the minute. When Mrs Hath returned from the kitchen, she was carrying Pinpin, now fast asleep in her arms. Dr Batch, eagerly awaiting his lemonade, stared at her in a pointed way. Dr Minish frowned and looked at his watch again.

'You said something about lemonade,' said Dr Batch.

'Lemonade?' said Mrs Hath.

'You offered us a drink,' said Dr Batch, a little more sharply.

'Did I?' She sounded surprised.

'You did, ma'am. You asked if we would like some lemonade.'

'Yes. I remember that.'

'And we replied in the affirmative.'

'Yes. I remember that too.'

'But you don't bring it.'

'Bring it, Dr Batch? I don't understand.'

'You asked us if we would like some lemonade,' said the teacher slowly, as if to a particularly stupid pupil, 'and we said yes. Now it is for you to fetch it.'

'Why?'

'Because – because – because we want it.'

'But Dr Batch, there must be some misunderstanding. I have no lemonade.'

'No lemonade? Madam, you offered us lemonade. How can you deny it?'

'How could I offer you lemonade, when I have none in the house? No, sir. I asked you if you liked lemonade. That is not the same thing at all.'

'Good grief, woman! Why ask a man if he likes something if you don't mean to give it to him?'

'This is very odd, Dr Batch. Am I to give you everything you say you like? No doubt you like long summer evenings, but I hope you don't expect me to fetch you one.'

Dr Minish stood up.

'Call the marshals,' he said. 'Enough is enough.'

Dr Batch stood up.

'Your daughter will be found, and she will be dealt with. You can be sure of that.'

Dr Minish called up the stairs.

'Are you coming, sir? Or must you be fetched?'

The bathroom door opened and Hanno came out. As he came down the stairs, Dr Batch opened the street door.

'Mr Hath is leaving now,' he said to the marshals.

The crowd outside pressed closer.

Hanno Hath came into the front room, and made his farewells. He kissed baby Pinpin, still sleeping in Mrs Hath's arms. He kissed his wife, who for all her defiance couldn't keep the tears from her eyes. Then he kissed Bowman, whispering to him as he did so:

'Look after Kess for me.'

He swung his suitcase into one hand and strode out of the door. The marshals fell into step, one on each side, and the two scarlet-gowned teachers waddled along behind. The crowd fell back to gaze in silence at the little procession as it passed. The Hath family stood together on their front step, watching him go. They held their heads high, and waved after him, as if he was going on a holiday. But the onlookers shook their heads and murmured, 'Poor man,' at the shame of it all.

As the procession reached the corner of the street, Hanno Hath stopped for a brief moment, and looked back. He gave a last wave, a wide sweep of his arm above his head, and smiled. Bowman never forgot that wave, or that smile, because as he watched from the steps he caught his father's feelings in a sudden very clear moment. He felt the immensity of his father's love for them all, warm and strong and inexhaustible, and he felt too a silent cry of desolation, which if it had words would be saying, Must I leave you for ever?

At the same time Rufy Blesh's father, who was standing close by, saw that smile and that defiant wave, and Bowman heard him say to his wife, 'He can smile as much as he wants, they'll never let him see his family again.'

That was when Bowman decided, deep inside himself, that there was nothing he would not do to bring his father back, that he would destroy all Aramanth if he had to, for what did he care for a lifetime of this neat and orderly world compared to one moment of his father's brave loving smile?

9

ESCAPE FROM ARAMANTH

That night, wardens took up positions in front of the house and behind, so that they could catch Kestrel when she came home; which they believed she would do once it was dark. Kestrel, of course, was already inside the house, keeping out of sight of the windows. Once night fell, and they could draw the curtains without arousing suspicion, she moved about more freely.

Ira Hath refused to panic or cry. She repeated so many times, so steadfastly, 'Your father will come back to us,' that the twins began to believe it. She fed Pinpin, and bathed her, just as always. She made the wish huddle with her three children, just as always, though it felt wrong without their father. But they all wished for him to come home, which somehow made it feel as if he was there after all. Then she tucked Pinpin up in her cot, just as always. And only after

Pinpin was asleep did she sit down with the twins and fold her hands in her lap and say:

'Tell me everything.'

Kestrel told all that had happened to her, and also what her father had said. Then she took out the map and, before she forgot them, wrote beside each set of squiggly letters the words her father had told her: *The Great Way, Crack-in-the-land, The Halls of Morah, Into the Fire*.

On the back she copied out the translation of the writing, also from memory:

The song of the wind singer will set you free. Then seek the homeland.

'Ah, the homeland,' said Ira Hath with a sigh. 'This place was never meant to be our true home.'

'Where is the homeland?'

'Who knows? But we'll know it when we find it.'

'How?'

'Because it'll feel like home, of course.'

She looked a little longer at the map, and rolled it up again.

'Whatever it is, it had better wait till your father comes back,' she said. 'Right now, we have to decide what to do about you.'

'Can't I hide here, in the house?'

'My darling, I don't think we'll be allowed to stay in this house very much longer.'

'I won't let them take me away. I won't.'

'No, no. We must hide you. I'll think of something.'

The emotions of the long day had exhausted them, Kestrel most of all, so Ira Hath decided to leave further discussion until the morning. But they had not reckoned how speedily they were to be punished.

The sun had barely risen when they were woken by a loud banging on the front door.

'Up! Get up! Time to go!'

Mrs Hath opened her bedroom window and leaned out to see what was going on. A squad of marshals was outside in the street.

'Pack up your things!' cried one of the marshals. 'You're moving out!'

They had been reallocated: not to Maroon, as they had expected, but to Grey District. Their new home was to be a single room in a ten-storey-high block, shared by three hundred families. Their house in Orange was to be handed over by noon at the latest to a new family.

Ira Hath was undaunted.

'All the less cleaning to do,' she said, as she roused Pinpin from sleep.

The immediate problem was Kestrel. The marshals were still on the lookout for her, and they had now taken up positions at the back as well as the front of the house. How could the family leave without Kestrel being discovered?

In a little while, two wardens came down the street

wheeling an empty cart to move the Hath family's possessions to Grey District. The neighbours were now up, and many of them had come out of their houses to watch the interesting spectacle that would soon unfold.

'There'll be tears. The mother'll come out weeping. They always do when it's a demotion. But the new ones, oh, they'll be smiling.'

'What about the baby? Isn't there a baby? She'll have no idea what's happening to her.'

'Those twins though, they're sharp as knives, the two of them.'

'Did you hear what the girl did? I knew she'd come to no good.'

'Well, she'll be sorry now.'

Inside the house they were discussing whether Kestrel could be smuggled out inside the big blanket trunk. Bowman looked out of the window at the marshals, and the wardens, and the neighbours, and shook his head.

'It's too risky.'

As he looked, his eyes fell on a small figure at the back of the crowd. It was Mumpo. He was skulking about, his eyes fixed hopefully on the front door, evidently waiting for Kestrel.

'Mumpo's out there,' he said.

'Not stinky old Mumpo,' said Kestrel.

'I've had an idea.'

Bowman went to the cupboard in their bedroom and

took out Kestrel's winter cloak, a long orange garment with a hood for the cold weather. He bundled it up tight and pushed it down the front of his tunic.

'I'm going out to talk to Mumpo,' he said. 'Don't do anything till I come back.'

'But Bo – '

He was gone.

'You ready, then?' called one of the grey wardens, as he came out of the front door.

'Not yet,' said Bowman, trotting past him on to the street. 'My mother's a fussy packer.'

He ran all the way down the street, to avoid having to talk to the curious neighbours, and only came to a stop when he was out of sight round the corner. As he had expected, Mumpo shortly came into view, puffing and dribbling.

'Bo!' he cried. 'What's happening? Where's Kess?'

'Do you want to help her?'

'Yes. I'll help her. Where is she?'

Bowman pulled the orange cloak out from under his tunic and shook it open.

'Here's what you have to do.'

Bowman had been back in the house a good hour when at last his mother opened the door and told the wardens they could carry out the trunks. To the wardens' surprise, the trunks had been packed in the top back bedroom, the furthest point in the house from the front door.

'Why couldn't you pack in the hall? These hogging stairs are no joke, you know.'

To add to the confusion, the family who were to move into the house, who were called Warmish, arrived early, trailed by two heavily-laden carts. They were naturally eager to come in and look round, but Ira Hath planted herself in the doorway so that they couldn't get past, and smiled at them implacably.

'How much room is there in the kitchen?' asked Mrs Warmish. 'Would you call it a kitchen-breakfast room, or more like a kitchen-dinette?'

'Oh, it's very roomy,' said Mrs Hath. 'The kitchen table seats thirty-six, at a pinch.'

'Thirty-six? Good heavens! Are you sure?'

'And just you wait till you see the bathroom! We've had eight fully-grown adults bathing at once, and every one of them with room to lie and soak.'

'Well, my word!' Mrs Warmish was so bewildered by this information that she didn't know what to say, and fell back on the little she could see beyond Mrs Hath's broad body.

'So is the flooring polished, or is it varnished?'

'Varnish?' said Mrs Hath witheringly. 'Pure beeswax, I assure you, as in all the best homes.'

One by one the trunks were hauled out into the cart. The furniture was all to stay behind, since their new apartment would be so much smaller. When the last trunk had been carried out of the house, Mrs Hath, still guarding the doorway against the eagerness of the Warmishes, hoisted Pinpin up into her arms, and turned to catch Bowman's eye. He gave her a brief nod, and slipped past her on to the front step. From here, he set off as if to the laden cart, but then suddenly pointed to the back of the crowd, and called:

'Kess!'

Everybody turned, and saw the figure of a child, hooded and cloaked, standing at the far end of the street.

'Run, Kess, run!' shouted Bowman.

The child turned and ran.

At once, the marshals and the wardens set off at a gallop after the child, and the crowd of neighbours hurried down the street in the hope of witnessing the moment of capture.

Kestrel slipped out of the front door, and would have got away entirely unnoticed, had Pinpin not seen her, and cried in delight, 'Kess!' The slowest of the wardens, who had been tying the trunks on to the cart when the chase began, heard this cry and turned to see Kestrel bolting down the side alley, with Bowman close after her.

'She's here! I seen her!' he yelled, and lumbered off down the alley after them.

The children were faster on their feet than the warden, and had soon put some distance between them, but the truth was, they did not know where they were going. The plan had been to get Kestrel out of the house. After that, they had trusted to instinct and luck.

They stopped running, to get their breath back. Nearby there was a small alcove, where rubbish bins were standing waiting to be emptied. They ducked down behind the bins, for safety.

'We have to get out of the city,' said Kestrel.

'How? We haven't got passes. They don't open the gates without a pass.'

'There's a way out through the salt caves. I've seen it. Only I don't know how to get into the salt caves.'

'You said the caves are used for sewage, didn't you?' said Bowman.

'Yes.'

'Then it must be where all the sewers go.'

'Bo, you're brilliant!'

Their eyes searched the street, and there, not far away, was a manhole cover. At the same time, they heard the distant sounds of their pursuers, shouting to each other as they searched the streets.

'They're getting closer.'

'You're sure we can get out of the salt caves?'

'No.'

A warden came into view at the far end of the street. They had no choice. They ran for the manhole.

The cover was round, and made of iron, and very heavy. There was a ring set into it which lifted up, to pull it open. Just raising the ring wasn't easy, it had rusted into its socket: but at last they got it up enough to fit their fingers round it.

The warden had spotted them now, and set up a cry.

'Here they are! Hey, everybody! I've found them!'

Fear gave them strength, and they pulled together, and succeeded at last in getting the manhole cover to move. Inch by inch they dragged it clear of the hole, until there was enough space for them to pass through. There were iron rungs in the brick-lined shaft beneath, and below that, the sound of water.

Kestrel went first, and Bowman followed. Once he was below the level of the cover, he tried to push it back into place above them, but it was impossible.

'Leave it,' said Kestrel. 'Let's go.'

So Bowman followed her down the ladder, and stepped into the dark water at the bottom. He was too anxious about where he was going to look back, but had he done so, he would have seen a shadow fall over the open manhole above.

'It's all right,' said Kestrel. 'It's not deep. Follow the water.'

They made their way along the dark tunnel, up to their ankles in water, and slowly the light from the open shaft down which they had come faded into darkness. They walked steadily on, for what seemed like a very long time. Bowman said nothing, but he was afraid of the dark. They could hear many strange sounds around them, of water gurgling and dripping, and the echo of their own steps. They passed other channels flowing into their tunnel, and they could sense that the tunnel was becoming bigger the further they went.

Then for the first time they heard a sound that was watery, but not made by water. It was some way behind them, and it was unmistakable: *splosh, splosh, splosh*. Someone was following them.

They hurried on faster. The water was deeper now, and pulled at their legs. There was a glow of faint light ahead, and a thundery sound. Behind them they could still hear the steady footfall of their pursuer.

All at once the tunnel emerged into a long cave, through the middle of which ran a fast-flowing river. The light which faintly illuminated the glistening cave walls came from a low wide hole at the far end, through which the river plunged out of sight. The tunnel water now drained away to join the river, and they found themselves on a smooth bank of dry rock.

Almost at once, Bowman felt something terrible, very close by.

'We can't stop here,' he said. 'We must go, quickly.'

'Home,' said a deep voice. 'Go home.'

Kestrel jumped, and looked into the darkness.

'Bo? Was that you?'

'No,' said Bowman, trembling violently. 'There's someone else here.'

'Just a friend,' said the deep voice. 'A friend in need.'

'Where are you?' said Kestrel. 'I can't see you.'

In answer, there came the hiss of a match being struck, and then a bright arc of flame as a burning torch curved through the air to land on the ground a few feet away from them. It lay there, hissing and crackling, throwing out a circle of amber light. Out of the darkness beyond, into the soft fringe of its glow, stepped a small figure with white hair. He walked with the slow steps of a little old man, but as he came closer to the flickering light they saw that he was a boy of about their own age: only his hair was completely white, and his skin was dry and wrinkly. He stood there gazing steadily at them, and then he spoke.

'You can see me now.'

It was the deep voice they had heard before, the voice of an old man. The effect of this worn and husky voice coming from the child's body was peculiarly frightening.

'The old children,' said Kestrel. 'The ones I saw before.'

'We were so looking forward to having you join our class,' said the white-haired child. 'But all's well that ends well, as they say. Follow me, and I'll lead you back.'

'We're not going back,' said Kestrel.

'Not going back?' The soothing voice made her defiance sound childish. 'Don't you understand? Without my help, you'll never find the way out of here. You will die here.'

There was a sound of laughter in the darkness. The white-haired child smiled.

'My friends find that amusing.'

And into the pool of light, one by one, stepped other children, some white-haired like himself, some bald, all prematurely aged. At first it seemed there were only a few, but more and more came shuffling out of the shadows, first ten, then twenty, then thirty and more. Bowman stared at them, and shivered.

'We're your little helpers,' said the white-haired child. And all the old children laughed again, with the deep rumbling laughter of grown-ups. 'You help us, and we'll help you. That's fair, isn't it?'

He took a step closer, and reached out one hand.

'Come with me.'

Behind him all the other old children were moving closer, with little shuffling steps. As they came, they too reached out their hands. They didn't seem aggressive, so much as curious.

'My friends want to stroke you,' said their leader, his voice sounding deep and soft and far away.

Bowman was so frightened that the only thought in his head was how to get away. He stepped back, out of reach of the fluttering arms. But behind him now was the river, flowing rapidly towards its underground hole. The old children shuffled closer, and he felt a hand brush his arm. As it did so, an unfamiliar sensation swept through him: it was as if some of his strength had been sucked out of him, leaving him tired and sleepy.

Kess! he called silently, desperately. *Help me!*

'Get away from him!' cried Kestrel.

She stepped boldly forward and swung one arm at the

white-haired child, meaning to knock him to the ground. But as her fist touched his body, the blow weakened, and she felt her arm go limp. She swung at him again, and she felt herself grow weaker still. The air round her seemed to become thick and squashy, and sounds grew far away, and blurred.

Bo! she called to him. *Something's happening to me.*

Bowman could see her falling to her knees, and could feel the overwhelming weariness that was taking possession of her body. He knew he should go to her help, but he was frozen: immobilised by terror.

Come away, Kess, he pleaded. *Come away.*

I can't.

He knew it, he could feel it. She was growing faint, as if already the old children were carrying her away.

I can't move, Bo. Help me.

He watched them gather round her, but he was sick with fear, and he did nothing; and knowing he was doing nothing, he wept for shame.

Suddenly there came a crash and a splash, and something came charging out of the tunnel behind them. It roared like a wild animal, and struck out on all sides with windmilling arms.

'Kakka-kakka-kak!' it cried. 'Bubba-bubba-bubba-kak!'

The old children jumped back in alarm. The whirlwind passed Bowman, pushing him off the bank and into the fast-moving river. The splash doused the flaming torch. In the sudden darkness, Kestrel felt herself being dragged to the river's edge, and toppled into the water. There came a third splash, and there were three of them tumbling round and round in the current, being swept towards the roaring hole.

The cold water revived Kestrel, and she began to kick. Forcing herself to the surface, she gulped air. Then she saw the low roof of rock approaching, and ducked back down underwater, and was sucked through the hole. A few moments of raging water, and suddenly she was flying through air and spray, and falling, falling with the streams of water, down and down, fighting for breath, thinking, *This is the end, this is the smash,* when all at once, with a plop and a long yielding hiss, she found she had landed in soft deep mud.

10

IN THE SALT CAVES

Once she had recovered from the shock of her fall, Kestrel smelled the sick-making air and realised that she had landed in a part of the Underlake. Up above was the great arching roof of salt rock she had seen before, and not far off was one of the several holes in the cave's roof, through which fell such light as there was in this shadowy land. Before her stretched a dark gleaming region of water and stinking mud. Behind, the gushing waterfall down which they had fallen. She searched for the platform with the jetty, and the moored barges, but they must have been in some other part of the great salt caves, lost in the gloom.

She heard a low whimper and, turning, saw Bowman, floundering in the mud.

'Are you all right, Bo?'

'Yes,' he said, and then started to cry; a little out of relief that they had survived, but mostly from shame.

'Don't cry, Bo,' said Kestrel. 'We don't have the time.'

'Yes, I know. I'm sorry.'

Silently he begged her forgiveness.

I should have helped you. I was so afraid.

'This is the Underlake,' said Kestrel aloud, to turn his thoughts to practical matters. 'There's a way out on to the plains, I'm sure.'

She turned to look across the watery mud, and as she did so a half-familiar form rose up, spluttering and grunting. It got itself upright, and wiped the mud from its face, and beamed at her.

'Mumpo!'

'Hallo, Kess,' said Mumpo happily.

'It was you!'

'I saw you go down the hole,' he said. 'I followed you. I'm your friend.'

'Mumpo, you saved me!'

'They were going to hurt you. I won't let anyone hurt you, Kess.'

She gazed at him, covered from head to toe in mud, and marvelled that he could look so pleased with himself. But then, they were all just as muddy, and all stank as much as each other now.

'Mumpo,' she said, 'you were brave and strong, and I'll always thank you for saving me. But you must go back.'

Mumpo's face fell.

'I want to be with you, Kess.'

'No, Mumpo.' She spoke kindly but firmly, as if to a small child. 'It's me they're looking for, not you. You have to go home.'

'I can't, Kess,' said Mumpo simply. 'My legs are stuck.'

That was when Kestrel and Bowman realised that they were sinking. Not fast, but steadily.

'It's all right,' said Kestrel. 'I've been here before. We'll only sink as far as our knees.'

She tried to pull her leg out, and found she couldn't.

Kess, said her brother silently. *What if they come after us*?

She looked round, in all directions, but there was no sign of the old children.

If they do, Kestrel replied, *they'll get stuck too*.

So there they stood, their drenched clothing clinging to their shivering bodies, breathing the fetid air, feeling themselves sinking. When they had sunk past their knees, Bowman said:

'We're still sinking.'

'There has to be a bottom somewhere,' said Kestrel.

'Why?'

'We can't just sink all the way.'

'Why not?'

For a while, nobody said anything, and they went on sinking. Then Mumpo broke the silence.

'I like you, Kess. You're my friend.'

'Oh, shut up, Mumpo. I'm sorry. I know you saved me, but honestly . . .'

Another silence fell. By now they had sunk to their waists.

'Do you like me, Kess?' said Mumpo.

'A bit,' said Kestrel.

'We're friends,' said Mumpo happily. 'We like each other.'

His idiotic cheerfulness at last goaded Kestrel into saying aloud what she'd been afraid even to think.

'You stupid pongo! Don't you get it? We're going to be sucked under the mud!'

Mumpo stared at her in utter astonishment.

'Are you sure, Kess?'

'Take a look round. Who's going to pull us out?'

He looked round, and saw nobody. His face crumpled with fear, and he started to scream.

'Help! I'm sinking! Help! I'll go under! Help!'

'Oh, shut up. There's nobody to help.'

But Mumpo only screamed louder; which was just as well, because Kestrel was wrong. There was somebody to help.

Not so far off, a small round mudman named Willum was stooped over the lake surface hunting for tixa leaves. Tixa grew wild in unexpected places, and the only way to find it was to wander about half looking for it in a slow dreamy sort of way for several hours. If you looked too hard at the murky grey surface of the lake you could never see the tixa plants, which were murky-coloured too. You had to not look, and that way, you caught sight of them out of the corner of your eye. Then if you found some, you picked the leaves and put them in your bag, keeping one to chew as you went on. Chewing tixa leaves made you feel slow and dreamy, and that made you even better at finding them.

When Willum heard the faraway screams, he straightened up and peered through the gloom, and tried for once to look.

'My, oh my,' he murmured to himself, smiling. He didn't know he was smiling. He'd been out most of the day, chewing tixa most of the time, and really he should be thinking about going home. The nut-socks strung round his neck were full, and his wife would have expected him back long ago.

But the shrill shrieks didn't stop, so Willum decided to set off towards them, following the network of trails that all the mudpeople learned as soon as they could walk. These trails ran beneath the surface of the mud, sometimes just below, sometimes down to the knees. There was a way of walking the trails which all the mudpeople had, a slow steady stride, easing one foot in, easing the other out, in a swinging even pace. You couldn't go fast, you just swung along, particularly after a day of tixa hunting.

All this time, the children went on sinking. The mud was up to their necks now, and still their desperately wriggling toes could feel no hard ground. Kestrel was frightened, and would have started to cry, if it wasn't that Mumpo was crying enough for all of them.

'Yaa-aa waa-aaa!' shrieked Mumpo, exactly like a baby. 'Yaa-aaa waa-aaa!'

None of them heard Willum approaching behind them until he spoke.

'Oh my sweet earth!' he exclaimed, coming to a stop on the nearest part of the trail.

'Yaa-aaa waa – Glup!'

Mumpo suddenly went quiet: not because help was at hand, but because his mouth had filled with mud. All three children tried to twist their heads round, but they couldn't.

'Help us!' said Bowman, choking on mud.

'I should think so,' said Willum.

Like every mudman out on the lake, he carried a rope, wound several times round his plump waist. He unwound it now, and threw it neatly over the surface of the lake so that it lay within reach of the three children.

'Take ahold,' he said. 'Slow, mind.'

As the children worked their hands up out of the mud, and towards the rope, Willum noticed a bunch of tixa growing right by them. It was a big bunch, with broad mature leaves, the very best sort.

'They leaves,' he said. 'Just you bring they along too, eh?'

The children's efforts to reach the rope were making

them sink faster, and now the mud was half suffocating them. Willum was so excited by the sight of the tixa leaves he forgot this.

'They leaves,' he said again, pointing. 'Take ahold of they, eh?'

Bowman had the rope now, and pulled hard on it, very nearly jerking Willum off the trail. With his other hand, Bowman reached for his sister, and held her while she too took the rope. Kestrel in turn reached for Mumpo, who was the one nearest to the tixa plants.

'Pull!' cried Bowman, feeling them start to sink again. 'Pull!'

'I should think so,' said Willum, not pulling. 'Just you fetch me they leaves.'

It was pure chance that Mumpo's hand, scrabbling for the rope, closed over the tixa plant. And as soon as Willum saw that he had it, he proceeded to pull. Leaning forward to get all his weight on the rope, he set off along the trail hauling like a pack mule. His short sturdy legs were immensely strong, like all the mudpeople's, and soon the children felt themselves rising up out of the clinging mud.

With a spluttering gasp, Kestrel freed her face, and drew a huge gulping breath. Mumpo spat the mud out of his mouth and started howling again. And Bowman, panting, heart hammering, tried hard not to think what would have happened to them if the mudman hadn't found them.

When they felt the solid land of the trail beneath them,

they collapsed and lay there in a mud-coated heap, made weak by the shock of it all. Willum bent over Mumpo and took the tixa leaves from his hand.

'That'll do. Thanky kindly.'

He was very pleased. He broke off the tip of one leaf, brushed the mud off, and popped it in his mouth. The rest went in his little bag.

He turned then to studying the children he had pulled out of the lake. Who were they? Not mudpeople, certainly. They were far too thin, and no mudpeople wandered off the trails into the deeps, not without being roped. They must have come from up yonder.

'I know who you'm are,' he said to them. 'You'm skinnies.'

They followed the small round mudman down winding trails that only he could see, across the dark surface of the Underlake. Too exhausted to ask questions, they tramped along behind him in single file, still holding the rope. Their legs ached from the effort of pulling them in and out of the mud, but on and on they went, until dusk started to gather in the great sky-holes above. Willum sung softly as he went along, and occasionally chuckled to himself. What a stroke of luck it was finding the skinnies! he was thinking. Won't Jum be surprised! And he laughed aloud just thinking about it.

Willum had wandered far in his day's hunting, and by the time they were back again by his home it was almost night. The shadows were so deep that the children could no longer see where they were going, and kept to the trail by feeling the tug of the rope. But now at last, Willum had come to a stop, and with a sigh of satisfaction announced to them:

'No place like home, eh?'

No place indeed: there were no signs of any house or shelter of any kind, but for a thin wisp of smoke rising from a small hole in the ground. The children stood and shivered, fearful and exhausted, and looked round.

'Follow me, little skinnies. Mind the steps.'

With these words, he walked straight down into the ground. Kestrel, following behind, found that her feet went through the mud into a sudden hole, where there seemed to be a descending staircase.

'Mouth shut,' said Willum. 'Eyes shut.'

One moment Kestrel felt the mud round her neck, the next moment her mouth and nose and eyes were clogged and smothered, and the next moment she had stepped down into a smoky firelit underground room. Bowman followed, and then Mumpo, both spitting and pushing mud from their eyes. Above them, at the top of the staircase, the mud had resealed itself like a lid.

'Well, Willum,' said a cross voice. 'A pretty time you've been.'

'Ah, but looky, Jum!'

Willum stood aside, to display the children. A round mud-coated woman sat on a stool by the fire, stirring a pot and scowling.

'What's this, then?' she said.

'Skinnies, my love.'

'Skinnies, is it?'

She lumbered up from her seat and came over to them. She patted them with her muddy hand and stroked their trembling cheeks.

'Poor little mites.'

Then she turned to Willum and said sharply:

'Teeth!'

Obediently, Willum bared his teeth. They were stained a yellowy-brown.

'Tixy. I knew it.'

'Only the smallest leaf, my dearest.'

'And harvest tomorrow. For shame, Willum! You should lie down and die.'

'Mudnuts, Jum,' he said placatingly. Untying the long nut-socks, he fingered out a surprisingly large number of brown lumps.

Jum stumped off back to the fire, refusing to acknowledge the fruit of his labours.

'But my love! My sweet bun! My sugar plum!'

'Don't you sugar me! You and your tixy!'

The children, forgotten for the moment, stared at the room in which they now found themselves. It was a big round burrow, with a dome-shaped roof, at the top of which the smoke of the fire escaped through a hole. The fire was built in the middle of the room, on a platform of stone that raised it up to table height; and round it was a kind of wide-barred cage of iron rods. This arrangement allowed pots and kettles to be suspended over the fire on all sides, at various levels. A large kettle hung high up, steaming softly; a stew-pot lower down, popping and spitting.

Beside the fire there was a wooden bench, on which sat the members of Willum's immediate family, all as round and mud-covered as each other, so that apart from the differences in size there wasn't much to distinguish them. They were in fact a child, an aunt, and a grandfather. All were staring curiously at the newcomers except for the grandfather, who kept looking at Willum and winking.

The floor of the burrow was covered with a litter of soft rugs, mud-stained and rumpled, thrown one on top of the other like a huge unmade bed.

'Pollum!' said Jum, stirring the stew. 'More bowls!'

The mudchild jumped up and ran to a wall cupboard.

'Good day, then, Willum?' said the old man, winking.

'Good enough,' said Willum, winking back.

'You'll not be wanting your supper, then,' said Jum, banging the stew-pot. 'You'll be in the land of tixy.'

Willum went right up close behind her and put both his arms round her and hugged her tight.

'Who loves his Jum?' he said. 'Who's come home to his sweet Jum?'

'Who stayed out all day?' grumbled Jum.

'Jum, Jum, my heart does hum!'

'All right, all right!' She put down her ladle and let him kiss her neck. 'So what are we going to do with these skinnies of yours?'

The silent aunt now spoke up.

'Fill'um poor skinny little bellies,' she declared.

'That's the way,' said Willum. And he went and sat down by the old man, and fell to whispering with him.

Pollum put bowls on a table, and Jum filled the bowls with thick hot stew from the stew-pot.

'Sit'ee down, skinnies,' she said, her voice more kindly now.

So Bowman and Kestrel and Mumpo sat down at the table and looked at the stew. They were very hungry, but the stew looked so exactly like lumpy mud that they hesitated to eat it.

'Nut stew,' said Jum encouragingly. She popped a spoonful into her own mouth, as if to show them the way.

'Please, ma'am,' said Bowman. 'What sort of nut?'

'Why,' said Jum, 'mudnut, of course.'

Mumpo started to eat. He seemed not to mind it, so Kestrel tried it. It was surprisingly good, like smoky potato. Soon all three were spooning it up. Jum watched with pleasure. Pollum twined herself round her mother's stout legs and whispered to her.

'What are they, mum?'

'They'm skinnies. They live up yonder. Poor little things.'

'Why are they here?'

'They'm escaped. They'm run away.'

As they ate, the children's spirits revived, and they began to be curious about where exactly they were.

'Are we in the Underlake?' asked Kestrel.

'I don't know about that,' said Jum. 'We'm under, that's for sure. We'm all under.'

'Is the mud – ? I mean, does it come from – ?' There didn't seem to be a polite way to ask the question, so she changed tack. 'The mud doesn't seem to smell so much down here.'

'Smell?' said Jum. 'I should hope it does smell. The smell of the sweet sweet earth.'

'Is that all?'

'All? Why, little skinny, that's all and everything.'

There came a sudden chuckle from the aunt by the fire.

'Squotch!' she exclaimed. 'They'm thinking our mud is squotch!'

'No-o,' said Jum. 'They'm not daft.'

'Ask'ee,' said the aunt. 'You do ask'ee.'

'You'm not thinking our mud is squotch, little skinnies?'

'What's squotch?' said Bowman.

'What's squotch?' Jum was baffled. Pollum started to giggle. 'Why, it's – squotch.'

Willum now entered the discussion.

'Why, so it is squotch,' he said. 'And why not? Everything goes into the sweet earth, and makes for the flavour. One great big stew-pot, that's what it is.'

He dipped the ladle into the stew-pot and drew out a spoonful of thick stew.

'One day I shall lay my body down, and the sweet earth will take it, and make it good again, and give it back. Don't you mind about squotch, little skinnies. We'm all squotch, if you only see it aright. We'm all part of the sweet earth.'

He consumed the stew straight from the ladle. Jum watched him, nodding with approval.

'Sometimes you do surprise me, Willum,' she said.

Mumpo finished his stew first. As soon as he was done, he lay down on the rug-covered floor, curled himself up into a tight ball, and went to sleep.

'That's the way, little skinny,' said Jum, pulling a rug over the top of him.

Bowman and Kestrel wanted to go to sleep too, but first they wanted to remove the mud that was caked hard all over them.

'Please, ma'am,' said Bowman. 'Where can I wash?'

'A bath is it you're wanting?'

'Yes, ma'am.'

'Pollum! Get the bath ready!'

Pollum went to the fire and unhooked the steaming kettle. She heaved it over to one side of the burrow, where there was a saucer-shaped depression in the earth floor. There she poured the hot water from the kettle in a swirling stream straight on to the ground. It slicked the sides of the hollow, and gathered in a shallow steaming puddle at the bottom.

'Who's go first?' said Jum.

Bowman and Kestrel stared.

'Show'ee, Pollum,' called out the aunt. 'No baths up yonder. Poor little things.'

It wasn't often Pollum was allowed first roll in the bath, when the water was new, so she jumped in without waiting to be told twice. Down on to her back, splayed out like a crab, and then over and over, wriggling and turning, covering herself with a fresh coat of warm slime. She giggled as she writhed about, obviously loving it.

'That's enough, Pollum. Leave some for the skinnies.' Bowman and Kestrel said it was very kind of them, but they were too tired to have a bath after all. So Jum made them up nests on the floor among the piles of rugs, and they curled up as Mumpo had done. Bowman, worn out by the terrors of the day, was soon deeply asleep, but Kestrel's eyes stayed open a little longer, and she lay there watching the mudpeople and listening to what they were saying. Willum had taken something out of his bag and was giving it to the old man, and they were chuckling together softly in the corner. Jum was cooking by the fire, making what seemed to be an enormous amount of stew. Pollum was asking questions.

'Why are they so thin, mum?'

'Not enough to eat. No mudnuts up yonder, see.'

'No mudnuts!'

'They don't have the mud for it.'

'No mud!'

'Don't'ee forget, Pollum. You'm a lucky girl.'

Kestrel tried to listen, but the voices seemed to be getting softer and fuzzier all the time, and the flame-shadows flickering on the domed ceiling softened into a warm blur. She snuggled deeper into her cosy nest, and thought how much her legs ached, and how good it was to be in bed, and her eyes felt so heavy she closed them properly, and a moment later she was fast asleep.

11

THE MUDNUT HARVEST

When they awoke, soft grey daylight was filtering into the burrow through the smoke-hole above the fire. Everybody had gone except for Pollum, who was sitting quietly by the fire waiting for them to wake. Mumpo was nowhere to be seen.

'Your friend's out on the lake,' said Pollum. 'Helping with the harvest.'

She had breakfast waiting for them: a plate of what looked like biscuits, but turned out to be fried sliced mudnuts.

'Don't you ever eat anything but mudnuts?' asked Kestrel. But Pollum seemed not to understand the question.

While they ate, the twins talked over what they should do. They were lost, and frightened. They knew their mother would be sick with worry over them. But Kestrel also knew, beyond a shadow of a doubt, that she could not go back to Aramanth as it was.

'They'll send us to join the old children,' she said. 'I'd rather die.'

'Then you know what we have to do.'

'Yes.'

She took out the map the Emperor had given her, and they both studied it. Bowman traced the line called the Great Way.

'We have to find this road.'

'First we have to find the way out of here.'

They asked Pollum if there was a way to go 'up yonder', but she said no, she'd never heard of one. Again, the question itself seemed to puzzle her.

'There must be a way,' said Kestrel. 'After all, the light gets in.'

'Well,' said Pollum, after some thought. 'You can fall down, but you can't fall up.'

'The grown-ups'll know. We'll ask them. When are they coming back?'

'Not till late. It's harvest today.'

'What kind of harvest?'

'Mudnuts,' said Pollum.

She got up and started to clear away the breakfast. Bowman and Kestrel talked in low voices.

'What are we going to do about Mumpo?' said Kestrel.

'He'd better come with us,' said Bowman. 'He's more use than I am.'

'Don't talk like that, Bo. You'll start crying again.'

And indeed he was on the point of tears.

'I'm sorry, Kess. I'm just not brave.'

'Being brave's not the only thing.'

'Pa told me to look after you.'

'We'll look after each other,' said Kestrel. 'You're the one who feels, and I'm the one who does.'

Bowman nodded slowly. It felt like that to him too, but he'd never put it to himself quite so clearly.

By now, Pollum had put all the dishes in a puddle of watery mud to soak. She said to them:

'Time to go out on the lake. Harvest time, see. Everyone helps with the harvest.'

They decided to go with her, and to look for Willum. Somehow they had to find their way out.

The scene that met their eyes as they climbed out of the burrow was very different from the bleak Underlake of the previous night. There was light gleaming and bouncing everywhere, shafting down through the holes in the great salt-silver cavern roof, creating pools of sunshine so bright they hurt the eyes. From these brilliant pools, the light spread outwards, as if in ripples, softening as it went, making the sheen of watery mud glisten all the way into the hazy distance. And moving back and forth over this sheet of light there were hundreds of busy little people. They were working in lines and in columns, and on great flat rafts. They were gathered round immense open bonfires and round large winch-like contraptions. And wherever they were gathered, they sang. The songs wove in and out of each other like sea shanties; and like sea shanties, they were work songs. For the mudpeople were working, and working hard.

'It doesn't smell stinky any more,' said Kestrel in surprise.

'It does,' said Bowman. 'We've just got used to it.'

They looked round for any sign of the old children, but there was none. They looked too for someone they recognised, but all the mudpeople seemed the same to them: all very round, and all very muddy. Following Pollum, they made their way, a little fearfully, along a ridge towards the nearest of the great bonfires. As they went, they watched the people at work, and began to understand what it was they were doing.

The mudnuts grew in shallow fields below the surface of the lake, down in the soft mud. The harvesters were picking them by walking slowly across these fields, and stooping down, and plunging their arms into the mud. Long lines of mudpeople were snaking across the lake in a methodical fashion, all taking a step forward at the same time, all bending and plunging in an arm together. The nuts they pulled up, each one the size of an apple, they dropped into shallow wooden buckets that they drew behind them. As they moved and picked, they sang their song, and so the whole line was kept in time.

It was a remarkable sight, to see those swaying strands of people all over the lake, all linked in one great ebb and flow of motion, their chanting voices climbing to the high cavern roof and bouncing back again in deep muffly echoes. Round the tall bonfires the people were singing too, though in a more ragged and disorganised way, picking up the thread of one song here, another there. The task of the people by the fire was far less active; indeed, several of them appeared to be doing nothing at all, though they did it with a great deal of laughter. Some were roasting mudnuts, rolling them into the embers and raking them out again with long sticks; and some were scouring mudnuts, chipping the mud off the skins; and a considerable number were coming and going with buckets.

Pollum picked up three empty buckets, gave one each to Bowman and Kestrel, and said:

'Follow me. I'll show you what to do.'

She took it for granted they would help with the harvest, and as there was no sign of Willum, and everyone else was so hard at work, it seemed ungrateful to refuse. So they followed Pollum into the mudfield and did as she told them.

The children of the mudpeople had the job of emptying the wooden buckets as they became full. The mudnut pickers worked away in their lines, and as the buckets filled up they would cry, 'Bucket up!' and a child would dash forward with an empty bucket and haul the full one away. The mudnuts were piled up in great mounds round the bonfires, which were built on the ridges alongside the fields, so the children didn't have all that far to go. Even so, as Bowman and Kestrel soon discovered, it was exhausting work. The full buckets were heavy, and had to be carried through squelchy mud that came halfway up their shins. By the time they reached the fire their arms and legs were aching, and they were sweating into their layer of mud. But in a while they found that there was a rhythm to it, and the singing of the lines of harvesters somehow lifted up their tired hearts. There was usually a moment of rest before the cry went out, 'Bucket up!' and the heaving struggle began again. As they approached the fire they felt its fierce exhilarating heat, and heard the laughter of the mudmen raking the nuts out of the embers. Then came the sweet moment when the bucket tipped and the load fell out, and suddenly their bodies felt light as air. The journey back over the lake was like flying, it was so effortless, like dancing among the sunbeams and the shadows that speckled the lake's surface.

After they had been working for what felt like all of a long day, and the sunlight had faded in the sky-holes, the twins saw that the harvesters were straightening up and rubbing their sore backs, and turning to head for the bonfires.

'Dinner,' said Pollum.

The people gathered in large crowds round the fires, where there were big basinfuls of fresh-roasted mudnuts waiting for them, and tubs of water. They drank first, straight from the long-handled scoops, scoop after scoop to quench the thirst of a day's labour. Then they sat down in little chattering clusters, and the basins were handed round, and they chewed away at the mudnuts as if they were apples.

The twins made no attempt to look for their friends. They were so hungry that they simply took themselves a big fat mudnut each and started to eat. They ate in silence for a few moments, and then their eyes met. They both knew they had never tasted anything so good in all their lives. Sweetly nutty, and yet somehow creamy at the same time; crisp towards the rind, tender in the middle; the skin singed by the embers to give it a smoky tang that crunched tastily in the mouth –

'Nothing like it, eh?'

This was Willum, wandering up to them, grinning from ear to ear.

'Fresh out of the mud, hot out of the fire. Life don't come sweeter than a harvest mudnut.'

He winked at them, and then burst into laughter for no apparent reason.

'Please, sir,' said Kestrel, seeing that he was about to wander away again. 'Could you help us?'

'Help you, little skinny? Help you how?'

He stood there, rolling gently from side to side and chuckling.

'We want to know the way out of the salt caves, and on to the plains.'

Willum blinked and frowned and then started to smile again.

'Out of the salt caves? On to the plains? No, no, no, you don't want any of that!'

And off he wobbled, laughing softly to himself.

The twins looked round and saw that several other mudpeople were acting like Willum, moving in a slow random sort of way and laughing. Here and there they were gathered in swaying groups, roaring with laughter.

'I think it's those leaves they chew,' said Bowman.

'So it is,' said a familiar voice with a sigh. 'All the menfolk'll be in tixyland tonight.'

It was Jum, taking round a full basin of roasted mudnuts.

'The womenfolk have too much sense, see. And too much to do.'

'Please, ma'am,' said Kestrel. 'Do you know the way out of here?'

'The way out? Well, now. That depends on where you want to go.'

'To the north. To the mountains.'

'The mountains?' Jum wrinkled up her brow. 'What would you be'm wanting with the mountains?'

'We're going to the Halls of the Morah.'

A sudden silence fell all round her. People began to get up and shuffle away, glancing nervously back at the twins as they went.

'We don't talk of such things here,' said Jum. 'Nor even give them a name.'

'Why not?'

Jum shook her round head.

'There's none of that here, and we don't want any, neither. There's enough of that up yonder.'

She turned her eyes up to the cave roof.

'In Aramanth?'

'Up yonder,' said Jum, 'live the people of the one we don't name. But you know that, little skinny. That's why you'm running away.'

'No – ' said Kestrel. But her brother cut her off.

'Yes,' he said. 'We know that.'

Kestrel stared at him.

'Do we?'

'Yes,' said her brother; though he hardly knew how to explain what it was he had just realised. Indistinctly, he was sensing that the world he knew so well, the only world he had ever known until now, was a sort of prison, and that its people, his people, were trapped within its high walls.

'Up yonder is the world of the one we don't name,' said Jum again. 'One way or t'other, they'm all belong to the one. Only here in the sweet earth, they do let us alone.'

'But when the wind singer sings again,' said Bowman, 'we won't belong to – to the one you don't name – not any more.'

'Ah, the wind singer, is it?'

'Do you know about it?'

'They'm be stories. Old stories. I should like to hear that wind singer, I should. We do take pleasure in song.'

'Then please help us find our way.'

'Well,' she said after a moment's thought. 'You'm best talk with the Old Queen. She'll know what to tell you.'

She pointed with a stubby finger to a mound that rose up out of the lake, some way off. On the top of the mound was a low timber stockade.

'You'll find her in the palace, over yonder.'

'Will they let us in to talk to her?'

Jum looked surprised.

'Why wouldn't they?' she said. 'Yes, you talk with the Old Queen.'

So the twins thanked her and set off along the ridge towards the palace. All round them the mudmen were in high spirits, laughing and singing, even dancing in a roly-poly fashion. The tixa leaves evidently filled them with affection for all mankind, for as the twins passed they were forever receiving waves and smiles, and even hugs.

In a little while they passed a region of mudfields where the mud was too deep to be harvested on foot, and the mudnuts were reached by rafts. These long wooden frames were designed to lie on the lake's surface, over which they were slowly pulled by ropes wound round great winches. During the harvest, the pickers lay prone all round the edges of the raft, reaching their arms into the mud below. Now that work had stopped for the day, the rafts had come to rest, and the winches were unmanned. This was the opportunity for the bolder young men to compete in the sport of mud-diving.

Bowman and Kestrel paused to watch them, amazed at the sight. At the corners of one of the rafts, tall slender poles had been fixed, rising up about twenty feet into the air. The mud-divers tied ropes round their waists and shinned up these poles like monkeys. They hung on at the top, swaying back and forth, throwing out first one hand, then the other, in a display of daring. Then, with a loud cry, they leaped from the pole into the mud, the rope snaking out behind them. The mud was so liquid here that they disappeared at once below the surface. For a few heart-stopping moments, nothing at all happened. Then the rope began to twitch and jerk, and there was a surge in the mud, and up would pop the mud-diver, to wild cheers. The ones who were cheered the loudest were those who stayed under the longest.

Kestrel was watching the mud-divers with admiration, when she saw a familiar figure shinning up one of the poles.

'That's Mumpo!'

And so it was. He looked thin and fragile alongside the others, but he was the most daring of them all. He swung himself about on top of the pole, and swooped and sprang back again, as if he hadn't a care in the world. And when he dived, he flung himself further than any of them, and stayed beneath the mud longer than any of them, and surfaced to the grandest cheer of all.

The twins were astounded.

'How did he learn to do that?'

'Mumpo!' cried Kestrel. 'Mumpo! We're over here!'

'Kess! Kess!'

As soon as he spotted them, he made another dive, just to show off. Then he unhitched his rope, and came bounding along the trail to join them.

'Did you see me?' he cried. 'Did you see me?'

He was tremendously pleased with himself, all grinning and bouncy like a puppy. It was Bowman who saw the yellowish stains on his teeth.

'He's been eating those leaves.'

'I love you, Kess,' said Mumpo, embracing her. 'I'm so happy, are you happy? I want you to be as happy as me.' And he gambolled around her, laughing and waving his mud-encrusted arms.

Bowman saw the look on Kestrel's face, and before she could speak he said quietly:

'Let him be, Kess.'

'He's gone mad.'

'We can't leave him here.'

He took hold of Mumpo's outstretched arm as he came swirling by.

'Come on, Mumpo. Let's go and see the Old Queen.'

'I'm so happy! Happy, happy, happy!' chortled Mumpo.

'Honestly,' complained Kestrel, 'I think I liked him better when he was crying.'

But Bowman was reflecting on the image of Mumpo diving from the top of the high pole. His body had been so surprisingly graceful. It gave him a different sense of Mumpo altogether. He was like a wild goose: ungainly on the ground, but beautiful in flight. Bowman liked this thought, because there was no pity in it. It struck him now that the pity he felt for Mumpo was a form of indifference. Why had he not been more curious about him? After all, Mumpo was in his way a mystery. Where did he come from? Why did he have no family? Everybody in Aramanth had a family.

'Mumpo – ' he began.

'Happy, happy, happy,' sang Mumpo.

This was not the time to ask questions. So they walked on, and Mumpo didn't stop laughing and singing all the way to the palace.

12

A QUEEN REMEMBERS

As they got near the palace, they realised there was a very odd noise coming from within. A babbling squeaking gurgling sort of noise. There also seemed to be an immense amount of pattering footsteps, and voices calling out, 'Stop that!' and 'Get down!' Whatever was going on was screened from their view by the timber stockade, in which there was a single door.

As they approached the door, even Mumpo became interested, and stopped his own carolling to listen. This came as a relief to Kestrel.

'Now try and behave yourself, Mumpo. We're going to see the Queen. She's the most important person here, so we have to be very respectful.'

She then knocked on the door. After a few moments, realising that no one inside could possibly hear her knock with such a cacophony going on, she opened it.

Inside there was a wide open space, completely full of muddy babies. There were tiny ones lying on mats, and crawling ones scurrying about like small dogs, and toddling ones toppling into each other, and walking ones, and ones that ran about yelling at the tops of their little voices. They were all completely naked, though of course also completely coated in mud. And they seemed to be having the time of their lives. They were forever colliding and trampling on each other in the most chaotic way, but somehow none of them came to any harm, or even made much complaint. They just bounced up again, and got on with their infant concerns.

In the midst of this writhing mass of babies there sat a number of very fat old ladies. Unlike the children, they remained motionless, like mountain islands in a seething sea. The babies clambered over and around them exactly as if they were land masses, and here and there the old ladies reached out a protective arm, or called out a warning. But mostly, they did nothing at all.

Faced by such confusion, the twins weren't sure what to do. They saw that there was a wide opening in the middle of the stockaded space, with steps leading down to what was presumably an underground room or rooms, and they guessed that the Queen was to be found down there. But clearly the thing to do was to ask.

Kestrel approached the nearest old lady.

'Please, ma'am,' she said. 'We've come to see the Queen.'

'Of course you have,' the old lady replied.

'Could you tell us where to go, please.'

'I shouldn't go anywhere, if I were you,' the old lady said.

'Then may we be taken to the Queen, please.'

'Why, I'm the Queen,' she replied. 'Leastways, I'm one of them.'

'Oh,' said Kestrel, going very red. 'Are there very many queens?'

'A good many, yes. All these ladies here, and plenty more besides.'

Seeing Kestrel's confusion, she shook her head and said:

'Don't you worry yourself about that, young skinny. You just tell me what it is you want.'

'We want to talk to the Old Queen.'

'Ah! The Old Queen, is it?'

At this point, three toddlers who had been mountaineering over her back all fell off at once, and set up a lamentation. The Queen put them on their feet again, and patted them, and said:

'It'll be bedtime soon enough. I'll take you to see the Old Queen after they've gone to bed. It'll be quieter then.'

At that moment, a bell rang, and all the old ladies lumbered to their feet and started shooing the babies down the broad steps. Bowman, Kestrel and Mumpo followed behind, more or less unnoticed. The effect of the tixa leaves was wearing off, and Mumpo had gone quiet.

At the bottom of the steps there was a burrow-like

room of the same kind they'd seen before, only this one was enormous. It was so wide that when it had been dug out pillars of hard earth had been left in place to support the roof. The effect of these rows of pillars was to make the room seem to go on forever, as alcove succeeded alcove far into the shadowy distance.

The tribe of babies was put to bed in the simplest possible way. As in Willum's burrow, the floor was deep in soft cloths, and the babies laid themselves down, crowded together in piles, all tangled up with each other, and mumbled and squeaked. The fat old ladies waddled among them, patting and stroking and rearranging, pinning on nappies where necessary, pulling rugs over the tops of them in places, but mostly leaving them to lie as they chose. Then they sat down round the edges and sang them a lullaby, in their creaky old voices, and the song filled the great burrow, lapping softly round the great nest, and the babies snuffled and yawned and slipped quickly into sleep.

Mumpo complained that his head felt funny. Then he looked at the sleeping babies, and gave an enormous yawn, and said he might sit down for a moment. Before they could stop him, he had curled up on the rugs among the babies, and he too was fast asleep.

Within a surprisingly short time, silence reigned; if silence it can be called when the air is rippled by hundreds of tiny breaths. Then the old lady who had first spoken to the twins turned to them and beckoned them, and they made their way to the further end of the colonnaded room.

As they went, she told them that her name was Queen Num, and they mustn't think that the babies usually spent the night at the palace. On ordinary days the queens looked after the babies during the day only, but tonight it was harvest night, and the people stayed up late feasting. Kestrel said it was strange to have queens looking after babies, and Queen Num laughed and said, 'Why, what else are queens good for? We'm too old to work in the fields, you know.'

At the far end of the great underground hall they found a little group of even older ladies, sitting in a circle of armchairs round a fire, staring vacantly into space. One of these was so very old that she really did seem to be almost dead. It was to this one that Queen Num led the children.

'Are you awake, dear?' she said, speaking very clearly. And to the children, 'This is the Old Queen. She doesn't hear very well.'

There was a moment of silence, then a cross little voice emerged from the withered face.

'Of course I'm awake. I haven't slept in years. I wish I could.'

'I know, dear. Very trying for you.'

'What would you know about it?'

'There's some young skinnies come to see you, dear. They want to ask you some questions.'

'Not riddles, is it?' said the peevish voice. She hadn't

shown any sign of seeing the children, though they stood directly before her. 'Riddles bore me.'

'I don't think it's riddles,' said Queen Num. 'I think it's memories.'

'Oh, memories.' The Old Queen sounded disgusted. 'Too many of them.' Suddenly her bird-like eyes fixed on Kestrel, who was the nearest. 'I'm a thousand years old. You believe that?'

'Well, not really,' said Kestrel.

'Quite right. It's a lie.' And she burst into a cackle of slow dry laughter. Then the laughter faded away, and her face set once more into disagreeable lines. 'You can go now,' she said.

'Please, dear, won't you talk to them just a little?' said Queen Num. 'They have come a long way.'

'More fools them. They should have stayed at home.'

She shut her eyes, screwing them up tight. Queen Num turned to the twins with a helpless shrug.

'I'm sorry. When she gets like this, there's nothing we can do.'

'Could I talk to her?' said Bowman.

'I don't think she'll answer you.'

'It doesn't matter.'

Bowman settled himself down on the ground beside her and closed his own eyes, and turned his mind towards the Old Queen. After a few moments, he began to feel the slow buzz of her thoughts, like winter flies. He felt her angry mutterings, and faraway regrets, and beneath it all, a dull bone-aching weariness. And then, waiting patiently, reaching deeper and deeper, he came upon a region of fear, that was dark and silent as night. And there – suddenly he felt it – was a hole, an emptiness, a nothingness, that opened into terror.

Without realising he was doing it, he cried out loud.

'Aah! Horrible!'

'What is it?' said Kestrel anxiously.

'She's going to die.' Bowman was whispering, his voice shaking. 'It's so close now, and so horrible! I never knew dying was like that.'

At this, the Old Queen spoke, more to herself than to Bowman.

'Too tired to live,' she said, her creaky voice breaking in what could have been amusement. 'Too afraid to die.'

And as she spoke, tears began to stream down her withered cheeks. She opened her eyes and gazed on Bowman.

'Ah, skinny, little skinny,' she said, 'how did you creep into my heart?'

Bowman wept too, not out of sadness, but because for the moment the two of them were joined. The Old Queen raised her thin trembling arms, and knowing what she wanted, Bowman climbed on to her chair and let her fold him in a fragile embrace. She pressed her wet cheeks to his face, and their tears mingled.

'You'm a little thief,' she murmured. 'You'm a little heart thief.'

Kestrel watched, proud and full of wonder. Even though she was Bowman's twin and sometimes felt as close to him as if they shared the same body, she didn't understand this trick he had of going into people's feelings. But she loved him for it.

'There, there,' said the Old Queen, soothing herself and Bowman together. 'No use crying over it.'

Queen Num looked on, awestruck.

'My dear,' she said. 'Oh, my dear.'

'Nothing to be done,' said the Old Queen, stroking Bowman's mud-encrusted hair. 'Nothing to be done.'

'Please,' said Bowman. 'Will you help us?'

'What use is an old lady like me, little skinny?'

'Tell us about – 'He hesitated, and caught Kestrel's silent warning. 'About the one you don't name.'

'Ah, so that's it.'

She stroked him some more in silence. Then she began to speak, in a faraway remembering kind of voice.

'They say the nameless one is sleeping, and must never be woken, because . . . There was a reason, but I forget. All long, long ago. Ah! Wait! I remember now . . .'

Her eyes widened in memory of a long-forgotten fear. 'They march, and they kill, and they march on. No pity. No escape. Oh, my dears, let me die before the Zars come again.'

She stared into the shadowy space before her, sitting up stiff with terror, as if she could see them coming even now.

'The Zars!'

'Oh, my little skinnies!' said the Old Queen, trembling. 'All these long years, and I had forgotten till now. My grandmother told me such tales of terror. It was her grandmother saw the last march of the Zars – oh pity, pity! Better we all die than the Zars march again.'

She began to breathe with difficulty, showing signs of distress. Queen Num stepped forward.

'That's enough, my dear. You rest now.'

'We know how to make the wind singer sing again,' said Kestrel.

'Ah . . .' The Old Queen seemed to become calmer when she heard this. 'The wind singer . . . If I could hear the song of the wind singer, I'd not be afraid . . .'

Kestrel took out the map and unrolled it for the Old Queen to see.

'This is where we have to go,' she said. 'Only we don't understand it.'

The Old Queen took the map and peered at it with watery eyes. Several times as she studied it, she sighed, as if for the lost days of long ago.

'Where did you get this, little one?'

'From the Emperor.'

'Emperor! Tchah! Emperor of what, I'd like to know.'

'Do you understand it?'

'Understand it? Yes, oh yes . . .'

She raised one trembling wrinkled finger, and traced

the path on the yellowed paper.

'This is what they called the Great Way . . . Ah, it was fine once! There were giants, to guide you. I saw them, when I was a little girl . . .'

The bony finger moved on.

'Just the one bridge over the ravine. Over the – the – what was it called? Oh, perish it, I hate growing old!'

'Crack-in-the-land,' said Kestrel.

'That's it! How did you know that?'

'My father can read old Manth.'

'Can he? There's not many left can do that. He must be even older than me. Crack-in-the-land, there, you see. You must follow the Great Way, because it leads to the only bridge . . .'

Her voice faded.

'You're getting tired, my dear,' said Queen Num. 'You should rest.'

'Time enough to rest, soon enough,' came the murmured reply.

'And what happens after that?' asked Bowman.

'After that, there's the mountain . . . There's fire . . . There's the one we don't name . . . There's going into the fire, but there's no coming out . . .'

'Why not? What would it do to us?'

'What does it do to all world, little skinnies? It steals your loving heart.'

'We have no choice,' said Kestrel in a low voice. 'We have

to make the wind singer sing again, or the unkindness will never end.'

The Old Queen opened her eyes and squinted at her.

'The unkindness will never end . . . You're right there. Well, well, maybe this is how it's to be . . . You'd best put the skinnies on the path to the uplands, Num. Help them in any way you can. Send our love after them. Do you hear me?'

'Yes, dear.'

The Old Queen's voice sank to an exhausted murmur.

'If it must come, it must come,' she said. And they were the last words she spoke, before falling into a shallow dream-tossed sleep.

Queen Num indicated to the visitors that they should leave, and took them to another part of the palace, where there was a late supper laid out.

'Nothing to be done till morning,' she said in her sensible way.

She showed them an empty space where they could lie down after they had eaten. She herself was proposing to pass the night in a chair, watching over the sleeping babies.

'I never sleep on harvest nights,' she said. 'I just sit and watch till morning. It does my heart good, watching the sleeping babies.'

The twins knelt down on the rug-strewn floor, and there, before settling down for the night, they made a small wish huddle. It felt all sad and wrong without the broad arms of their parents, and without their little sister's hot breath on their faces, but it was better than nothing, and it reminded them of home.

Kestrel laid her brow against her brother's brow and made her wish first, speaking very quietly in the sleepy soft-breathing room.

'I wish we might find the wind singer's voice and come quickly home.'

Bowman then made his wish.

'I wish ma and pa and Pinpin are safe and not sad that we're away and know that somehow we'll come back again.'

Then they curled up in each other's arms to go to sleep.

'Kess,' whispered Bowman. 'Are you afraid?'

'Yes,' whispered Kestrel back. 'But whatever happens, we'll be together.'

'I won't mind if you're with me.'

And so at last they slept.

13

THE HATH FAMILY PUNISHED

Ira Hath had not slept since the twins had vanished. That night, alone with Pinpin in their one room in Grey District, she had put her to bed as usual, and had then sat up late into the night, expecting to hear a soft tap at the door. They were hiding somewhere in the city, she knew, and would surely make their way to her under cover of darkness. But they did not come.

The next morning she had a visit from two stern-faced marshals, who asked her many questions about the twins, and warned her that she must report them as soon as they came home. This visit gave her new hope. Clearly they had not been caught. She now realised they would not have dared to approach their new apartment, in case it too was being watched. So she decided to go out into the district and show herself, in the hope that they might see her from

147

their hiding place, and send her a message.

As soon as she stepped out on to the street with Pinpin by her side, she found every passer-by stared at her in an angry sneering sort of way. None of them approached her, or spoke to her. They just stared, and sneered.

There was a bakery nearby, and she went into it to buy some corn-cakes for their breakfast. The baker's wife also stared, in the same insolent manner, and said as she handed over the cakes:

'I don't suppose they eat corn-cakes in Orange.'

'Why do you say that?' said Ira, surprised.

'Oh, they'll have fancy cakes in Orange,' said the baker's wife, tossing her fringe out of her eyes. 'Quite a come down for you, I'm sure.'

Out in the street she found a little crowd of grey-clothed neighbours had gathered, all hissing and clucking together like chickens. One of them, the mother from a family that lived on the same passage, suddenly dashed forward and said sharply:

'No use putting on airs round here. Grey's good enough for us, so it's good enough for you.'

Only then did Ira Hath realise that in all the bustle and stress of the removal she had forgotten to change her clothing. Both she and Pinpin were still wearing orange.

Another neighbour called out:

'We've reported you! You'll be in trouble now, and serve you right.'

'I forgot,' said Ira.

'Oh, she forgot! Thought she was still in Orange!'

'She's no better than us. Not with children running wild in the streets like rats.'

'Look at her poor little mite! It's wrong, that's what it is.'

Pinpin began to cry. Ira Hath looked from face to face and saw on them all the same expression of hatred.

'I don't think I'm better than you,' she said. 'I'm on my own for now, and it's not easy.'

This was in its way a plea for sympathy, but she spoke in such a calm voice that it only enraged her neighbours more.

'Whose fault is that?' said Mrs Mooth, the one from down the passage. 'Your husband should work harder, shouldn't he? You don't get anything for nothing in this world.'

O, unhappy people, thought Ira Hath within herself. But she said no more. She hoisted the crying Pinpin into her arms and made her way back up three flights of stairs, and along the gloomy passage to Number 318, Block 29, Grey District, the single room which was now their home.

She had not spoken back to her neighbours, but as she closed the door behind her, and put Pinpin down, her heart was blazing with anger. She missed her husband desperately, she was frantic with worry about the twins, and she hated the people of Grey District with a terrible burning hatred.

She sat down on the bed, which filled half the room, and stared out of the small window at Block 28 across the road. The buildings were made of grey concrete. The walls of her room were unpainted grey cement. The single curtain was grey. The door was grey. The only colour in the room came from the orange clothes she wore, and the striped bedspread she had brought with her from Orange District, on which she was now sitting.

'O, my dear ones,' she said aloud. 'Please come home . . .'

At about this time, Hanno Hath was sitting at his desk alongside the forty-two other candidates, as they were termed, in the main seminar room of the Residential Study Centre, listening to Principal Pillish telling them that he was only there to help them.

'You have all performed poorly in the High Examination in the past,' he intoned, in the kind of voice always used by people who have said the same thing in the same words many times before. 'You have all let yourselves down and let your families down, and you are all very sorry. Now you are here to put it all right again, and I am here to help you. But most of all, you are here to help yourselves, because the only way to better your unhappy condition is by hard work.'

He clapped his hands sharply together to emphasise this most important point, and repeated:

'Hard work!'

He took up four brown-backed books.

'The High Examination is not especially difficult. Its questions are wide-ranging. It does not favour only those with natural aptitude. It favours those who work hard.'

He held up the brown books one by one.

'Calculation. Grammar. General Science. General Art. Everything you need to know for the High Examination is in these four study books. Read. Remember. Repeat. That is all you have to do. Read. Remember. Repeat.'

Hanno Hath heard none of this. His mind was entirely occupied with fears for his family. During the mid-morning break, he walked round the high-walled yard, trying to calm himself, and think clearly. He had heard nothing since he left home. That would seem to suggest that Kestrel had not been caught, but was still in hiding somewhere in the city. If so, it was surely only a matter of time, for there was no way she could get out of Aramanth.

The tormenting thoughts went round and round in his brain, following the circular course of his walk, until the sound of low sobbing broke through to him, and brought him to a stop. One of the other candidates, a small man with thinning grey hair, was standing with his face to the wall, weeping.

Hanno approached him.

'What is it?'

'Oh, nothing,' said the man, and he dabbed at his eyes. 'Sometimes I just can't stop myself.'

'Is it because of the High Examination?'

The little man nodded.

'I do try. But as soon as I sit down at my desk, everything I've ever learned goes clean out of my head.'

His name was Miko Mimilith. He was a tailor, who lived with his family in Maroon District. He worked hard, he said, and he was good at his job, but the annual High Examination was a terror to him.

'I'll be forty-seven years old this year,' he said. 'I've sat the High Examination twenty-five times. It's always the same.'

'Can you answer any of the questions?'

'I can do the calculations, some of them, if I don't get too flustered. But that's all.'

'Then you're lucky.' This came from a youngish man with fair hair, who had overheard their conversation. 'I wish I could do calculations. Now, if they'd only ask me about butterflies, I could tell them a thing or two.'

'Or cloud formations,' put in a third man.

'I know every butterfly that's ever been seen in Aramanth,' said the fair young man earnestly. 'And one that's not been seen for thirty years and more.'

'Ask me a question about clouds,' said the third man, not to be outdone. 'Give me the wind strength, the wind direction, and the air temperature, and I'll tell you where the rain will fall, and when.'

'What I'd like,' said little Miko Mimilith, stroking the air with his delicate fingers, 'is questions about fabrics. Fine cotton, cool linen, warm wool tweeds. I know them all. You could blindfold me and touch the tip of my little finger to a swatch of cloth, and I could tell you what it is, and most likely where it was woven.'

Hanno Hath looked from one to the other, and saw how the dulled listless look had gone from their eyes, and how they held their heads high and butted in on each other in their eagerness to speak.

'Oh, but wouldn't it be grand,' said the cloud man with a long sigh, 'if we could be tested on what we really know.'

'Maybe we should be,' said Hanno Hath.

Before he could explain further, the voice of Principal Pillish came booming across the yard.

'Candidate Hath! Report to the Principal's office.'

Hanno entered the book-lined room to find Principal Pillish in conversation with the Chief Examiner himself, Maslo Inch.

'Ah, here he is,' said Principal Pillish. 'Should I absent myself?'

'No need,' said Maslo Inch. He turned his cold smile on to Hanno. 'Well, my old friend. I hate to break in on your studies. But no doubt you want to know what has become of your children.'

Hanno said nothing to this, but his heart began to beat hard.

'The news is not good. They were seen entering the Underlake, yesterday around noon. They have not emerged. I fear there can be very little hope that they are still alive.'

He was watching Hanno closely as he spoke, and Hanno kept his expression as blank as he could, but inside, hope had suddenly blossomed.

There was daylight down there, he told himself. *Kess saw it. They're on their way.*

He felt a surge of pride in his beloved children, that they had dared to set out on such a dangerous journey. But this was followed immediately by a chill of dread.

Keep them safe, he said, as if there was someone or something out there to whom he could appeal. *They're so young. Watch over them.*

'You have only yourself to blame, my friend.'

'Yes,' said Hanno. 'I see that now.'

The Chief Examiner had brought him this news in person because he wanted to punish him. Hanno understood that well enough. He let his head droop low, hoping he looked chastened. He didn't want to arouse any suspicions.

'You have one child remaining to you. As yet, she is too young to have been damaged by your poor example. My advice to you is to apply yourself from this moment on. Let this unfortunate business teach you the value of discipline, proper ambition, and plain hard work.'

'Hard work,' echoed Principal Pillish reverently.

'I will see to it that your wife is informed.'

'She'll be very distressed,' said Hanno in a low voice. 'Might I be allowed to tell her myself?'

The Chief Examiner looked to the Principal.

'I think a short interview might be permitted, under the circumstances,' he said.

*

Ira Hath was wearing sober grey when she was escorted into the visiting room of the Residential Study Centre. Hanno was waiting for her, also wearing grey. Principal Pillish watched the encounter, as it was his duty to do, through a closed window. He was gratified to see that there was much sobbing and embracing by the bereaved couple. What he did not hear were the words they said to each other, which struck a very different note. Now that they had reason to believe the twins had escaped, they were filled with new courage. Bowman and Kestrel were risking everything to break the grim power that was crushing their lives. They could do no less.

'I'm going to fight back,' said Hanno.

'So am I,' said his wife. 'And I know how.'

14

RETURN OF THE OLD CHILDREN

When Bowman and Kestrel woke, they found all the mudbabies were gone, and Mumpo was up and full of bounce, having eaten a large breakfast. An escort of mudmen arrived, to guide them out of the Underlake. Among them was Willum, looking very grey and sorry for himself.

'Hard work, harvest,' he mumbled to no one in particular. 'Leaves a body well wore out.'

'We're going on an adventure,' Mumpo announced. 'Kess is my friend.'

The sun was already beaming down through the roof-holes, so the twins ate quickly, and made their farewells. Queen Num patted them, and looked unexpectedly sad as she handed them the nut-socks she'd filled for their journey.

'There's two socks for each of you, which is all you'll want to carry. You'm be careful, little skinnies. 'Tis a cruel dry world up yonder.'

They tied the heavy nut-socks together in pairs and hung them round their necks, as the mudmen did. The dangling mudnuts bumped against their chests and stomachs as they walked, but they soon grew used to this, and found it comforting.

They departed from the palace accompanied by an escort about twenty strong. As they marched along the ever-lightening trail others joined them, and more and more, until in time there were over a hundred mudpeople swinging along behind.

'We're the three friends, we're the three friends,' sang Mumpo, until Kestrel told him to shut up.

The land rose almost imperceptibly, and the mud hardened underfoot, the nearer they approached to the mouth of the great salt cave that contained the Underlake. After a while they began to feel a cool breeze on their faces, and the silver stone of the cavern roof seemed to grow brighter as the light strengthened.

Their first sight of the cave mouth was no more than a strip of burning brightness, far ahead. But as they drew closer, walking now on moist but firm sand, they saw that the cave narrowed here to a span of barely half a mile, and arched downwards, to form an overhead lip no higher than the topmost branches of a tall tree. Beyond the cave, the brightness was now taking shape, revealing an expanse of sandy plain beneath a deep blue sky.

When the marching column at last reached the point where direct sunlight fell on to the hard earth, they came to a halt, keeping themselves well in the realm of shadows. The children understood that from this point onwards they were to proceed alone.

'Thank you,' they said. 'Thank you for looking after us.'

'We'll sing for you,' said Willum. 'To see you on your way.'

As they set off, the mudpeople raised their hands in a gesture of farewell, and then they started to sing. It was a sweet soft farewell song, no words, just wave upon wave of melody.

'It's their love,' said Kestrel, remembering what the Old Queen had said. 'They're sending it after us.'

As the children made their way out of the mouth of the salt cave and up on to the dusty plains, the song of the mudpeople followed them, warm and loving like the burrows in which they slept. And then it came fainter on the breeze, and fainter, until at last they could hear the song no more, and they knew they were alone.

After the protective shadows of the Underlake, the plains across which they now walked seemed to be without limits. Only to the north, far far away, could they make out the pale grey line of the mountains. Then as the sun climbed higher, the heat haze rising up from the baked earth melted the horizon into the sky, sealing them in a featureless shimmering world in which they were the only living creatures. For a little while they could see, if they turned their heads, the long dark mouth of the cave out of which they had come, but then that too was swallowed up by the dusty air and the distance, and they were without any sense of direction at all.

They tramped northward, in what they supposed was a straight line, hoping to come upon some signs of the high road called the Great Way. The wind was picking up, skittering the sand, making the land shiver. Bowman and Kestrel didn't speak, but they could sense each other's anxiety. Mumpo alone was without a care, as he followed behind Kestrel, planting his feet in her footsteps, calling out:

'I'm like you, Kess! We're the same!'

The wind grew stronger, lifting more sand into the air, dulling the brightness of the sky. Walking became difficult, because the sand stung their faces, and they had to twist their heads away from the wind. Then through the blurred air ahead of them there loomed a low square structure, like a hut without a roof, and they turned their steps towards it to take shelter.

Close up against it, they saw that it was some kind of wagon, lying on its side. Its axles were broken, and its wheels lay half-buried. Sand had piled up against the windward side, but on the lee there was a protected space where they could huddle out of the wind. Here they untied their nut-socks, and ate a much-needed lunch of roasted mudnuts.

The smoky taste brought back images of the harvest, and the cheery faces of the mudpeople, and made them wish they were back in the comfortable burrows of the Underlake. While the wind remained so strong there was no point in struggling on, so Kestrel took out the map and she and Bowman studied it.

There were no landmarks in the desert, only the position of the sun in the sky to tell them where north was, and perhaps a distant sight of the mountains; but somehow they must find the Great Way, or what was left of it.

'The Old Queen said it had giants.'

'That was long ago. There aren't any giants nowadays.'

'We'd better just keep going north. As soon as the storm passes.'

Kestrel looked up from the map, and saw Mumpo watching her and grinning.

'What are you so pleased about, Mumpo?'

'Nothing.'

Then she saw both his nut-socks lying empty before him.

'I don't believe it! Have you eaten all of them?'

'Most of them,' admitted Mumpo.

'You have! There's none left!'

Mumpo picked up the empty nut-socks and gazed at them in surprise.

'None left,' he said, as if someone else had taken them.

'You great pongo! That was supposed to last you for days and days.'

'Sorry, Kess,' said Mumpo. But his stomach was full and he felt very happy and didn't look sorry at all.

Bowman turned to studying the wagon against which they were sheltering, and the pieces of debris lying around. Apart from the wheels, which were surprisingly large and very slender, there were broken sections of long thick pole, and fragments of cloth and netting, and strands of rope: all very like the wreck of a sailing ship. He got up and walked round the wreck, squinting his eyes against the stinging sand, and saw where the masts had been fixed to the wagon's bed, and realised that it had been a land-sailer of some kind. Back in the shelter of the craft, he dug about in the wind-heaped sand and found a pulley-wheel, and then a leather drive-belt; and he almost cut open his hands unearthing two long iron blades. It was clear that the craft had carried machinery. But what had the machinery been designed to do?

Because for the moment he had no better way to occupy himself, and because his mind worked that way, Bowman began to reconstruct the craft in his mind out of the pieces he could see lying around. It had two masts, that was clear enough; and it must have ridden very high, on its four immense wheels. The prow looked as if it had once narrowed to a ram-like prong. On either side there had been arms, stout timber beams reaching outwards; and hanging from them, still visible in a fragmentary form, there were nets. The land-sailer must have been designed to sweep across the plains, arms outstretched, nets trailing, entangling and carrying away – what?

As if looking for an answer, he gazed out into the storm. And as he looked, he thought he saw something that hadn't been there before. He strained his eyes to make out the moving shape far off in the swirling haze of sand. Now he saw two shapes. Now there were three. Dim figures, slowly approaching. His heart began to beat fast.

'Kess,' he said. 'Someone's coming.'

Kestrel put away the map and looked out into the wind. They were quite easy to see now, a line of dark forms against the dull sky. She looked round, and saw others to the side of them. And behind.

'It's them,' said Bowman. 'I know it.'

'Who?' said Mumpo.

'The old children.'

Mumpo at once started to jig about from foot to foot, waving his arms.

'Then I'll give them another bashing!' he cried.

'Don't let them touch you, Mumpo!' Kestrel's warning rang sharp over the sound of the wind. 'Something happens when they touch you. Keep out of their reach.'

The dim figures kept coming closer, shuffle shuffle shuffle, through the sandstorm, all round the wrecked land-sailer against which the children huddled. A voice now came to them out of the wind, deep and soothing, like before.

'Remember us? We're your little helpers.'

And from all round came the low rumble of their laughter.

'You can't get away from us, you know that. So why don't you come home with us now?'

Mumpo danced about, punching the air.

'I'm Kess's friend,' he cried. 'You come any nearer and I'll bash you!'

Bowman looked round for some sort of weapon with which to fend them off. He pulled at a half-buried section of broken mast, but it wouldn't move. The old children were close enough now for their faces to be visible, those eerie wrinkled faces that were ancient and childlike at the same time. Their shrivelled hands started now to reach out towards them, ready for the touch.

'Or shall we stroke you to sleep?' said the deep voice. 'Stroke, stroke, stroke, and you wake up old, like us.'

The rest of them laughed at that, and their low cackling laughter was swept up by the wind and carried round and round in the roaring air.

We'll have to run for it, said Kestrel silently to Bowman. *Can you see a gap in the circle?*

No. They're all round us.

There's no other way. I'm sure we can run faster than them.

All the time, the old children were coming closer, shuffle shuffle shuffle, tightening the ring round them.

'Bubba-bubba-kak!' shouted Mumpo, punching the air. 'You want a squashed nose?'

If Mumpo hits one of them, we could run through the gap.

But what about Mumpo?

Even as Bowman sent this thought, Mumpo bounced forward and biffed one of the old children on the nose. At once he fell back, wailing miserably.

'Kess! Kess!'

Kestrel caught him as he collapsed, whimpering, in her arms.

'I've gone wrong, Kess. Help me.' The old children giggled, and their leader said:

'Time to come home now. You've missed too many lessons already. Think of your ratings.'

'No!' shouted Kestrel. 'I'd rather die right here!'

'Oh, you won't die', said the deep soothing voice, moving closer. 'You'll just grow old.'

There was no way out. Terrified, Bowman closed his eyes, and waited for the dry bony hands to touch him. He heard their footsteps as they shuffled ever closer. Then, over the moaning of the wind, he heard a new sound, the sound of a horn, rising and falling like a siren, approaching at great speed.

Suddenly the sound was on top of them, accompanied by a tremendous crashing and snapping and creaking, and out of the storm, driven by the wild wind, there swept a high-wheeled land-sailer, its outstretched arms trailing a skirt of flying nets. Kestrel saw it, and knew what she must do. In the instant before it passed, she seized Bowman's wrist in one hand, and Mumpo's in the other, and threw all three of them into its path. Almost at once, the nets struck them and swept them away. Entangled in the heavy mesh, they were hurled along in the storm, racing before the wind at heart-stopping speed, over the sand-blind plain.

As soon as she had regained her breath, Kestrel started to climb the net to the supporting arm. Clinging on here, in the rushing air, she was able to look about her. She could see Mumpo below, caught like a wild animal, both legs through the netting, hanging upside down and screaming. Bowman had righted himself, and was now following her lead and pulling himself up the net. It wasn't easy, because the land-sailer was travelling so fast that every rut and stone in the ground over which it passed made it buck and lurch; and all the time the stinging sand was whistling by. The horn on the mast-top wailed like a banshee, and at the outer ends of the projecting timber arms huge scythe-like blades rotated at speed, making a fearful hissing screeching sound.

Kestrel looked into the well of the craft and saw that it was unmanned. She looked for a tiller or steering mechanism, hoping to steer them out of the wind, but she could see none. The land-sailer was completely out of control: any large rocks or trees in its headlong path, and it would crash at full speed, smashing them along with itself. Somehow she had to slow the craft down.

'You all right?' she called to Bowman.

'Yes. I think so.'

'Get Mumpo into the ship. I'm going to cut the sails.'

He turned at once and climbed down to Mumpo. Chivvied by Bowman, Mumpo managed to right himself, and follow him up the net. Once inside the craft, the two of them held tight to the masts as the land-sailer thundered on its way.

Kestrel found the anchorage for the mainsail, and started to unwind the rope. A sudden savage lurch threw her clear of the craft, but she was holding tight to the rope, and swung crashing back against the timber side. Hand over hand, she pulled herself up again, and braced herself against the timbers once more, and loosed the mainsail. She meant the whole sail to fly free, to cut their frantic speed, but only one side came undone. The sail veered sharply, forcing the craft on to two wheels. For a few crazy moments, the land-sailer hurtled along with two wheels in the air, the blade on the lower side thrashing the sand. Then the blade locked, and the craft cartwheeled into the air, spun over itself and over again, tumbling and somersaulting, impelled by the sheer force with which it had been travelling. As it rolled, the great blades snapped and the masts broke and the wheels smashed, but the heavily-built chassis to which the children clung remained intact. When at last the battered craft came tumbling to a rest, the children found that although their bodies hurt all over, and they were struggling for breath, they were still alive, and none of their bones was broken.

They lay in silence, feeling their wildly beating hearts gradually settle into a more even rhythm. The storm still

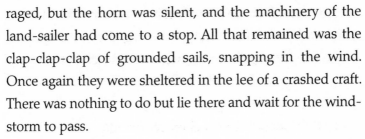

raged, but the horn was silent, and the machinery of the land-sailer had come to a stop. All that remained was the clap-clap-clap of grounded sails, snapping in the wind. Once again they were sheltered in the lee of a crashed craft. There was nothing to do but lie there and wait for the wind-storm to pass.

Worn out by the terror of the old children and the violence of their escape, all three of them fell into a fitful sleep, in which their bodies felt as if they were still careering wildly across the plains in the runaway land-sailer. Dream and memory mingled with the howling wind, and in sleep they were tumbled over and over, and awoke crying out loud and holding on to each other for dear life.

As the confusion of daytime sleep passed, they realised that a great silence had fallen all round them. The storm was over. The wind had dropped to a breeze. The air had cleared, and above them, when they crept out from under the crashed land-sailer, the sky was a brilliant blue. Now for the first time since they had left the salt caves they were able to see for a long way in every direction.

They were in the middle of a featureless sandy plain made up of low undulations as far as the eye could see. To the north, the line of mountains rose up on the horizon. Apart from that, there was nothing by which the traveller could orient himself. The mountains were nearer, but still many days' walk away. They had enough food left to last them for perhaps one more day, if they were careful. What after that?

'We go on,' said Kestrel. 'Something will happen.'

The sun was descending in the sky; no point in continuing their journey today. So she took out her supply of mudnuts.

Mumpo at once announced that he was hungry, as she had known he would.

'We all had the same amount, Mumpo.'

'But mine's all gone.'

'I'm sorry about that,' said Kestrel. 'But you're not having any of mine.'

'But I'm hungry.'

'You should have thought of that before.'

She was determined to make him learn the lesson; and so she ate her mudnuts in proud silence. Mumpo sat and watched her, like a sad faithful dog.

'It's no use looking like that, Mumpo. You've had yours and now I'm having mine.'

'But I'm hungry.'

'Too late now, isn't it?'

He started to weep, in a quiet dribbly sort of way. After a few moments, Bowman pulled out one of his mudnuts, and gave it to him.

'Thank you, Bo,' said Mumpo, cheering up at once.

Kestrel watched him eating it, and felt annoyed. Her brother's kindness made her feel cross with herself.

'You really are useless, Mumpo,' she said.

'Yes, Kess.'

'We've got a long way to go, you know.'

'No, I don't,' he said simply. 'I don't know where we're going.'

It was true: they had never taken the time to tell him. Bowman suddenly felt ashamed. 'Show him the map, Kess.'

Kestrel unrolled the map and explained their journey as best as she could. Mumpo listened quietly, watching Kestrel's eyes. When she was finished, he said:

'Are you afraid, Kess?'

'Yes.'

'I'll help you. I'm not afraid.'

'Why aren't you afraid, Mumpo?' asked Bowman.

'What is there to be afraid of? Here we are, the three friends. The storm's gone away. We've had our supper. Everything's all right.'

'But don't you worry about what might happen to us later?'

'How can I? I don't know what's going to happen until it happens.'

Bowman looked at Mumpo curiously. Maybe he wasn't so stupid after all. Maybe –

He froze. Kestrel sensed his fear at once.

'What is it, Bo?'

'Can't you hear it?'

She listened, and she heard: a far-off thunder. They all turned their eyes to the near horizon.

'Something's coming. Something big.'

15

PRISONERS OF OMBARAKA

Out of the dunes, a flag had appeared, and was moving towards the children. A red-and-white flag high on a flagpole, flapping in the breeze. Whatever supported the flagpole was out of sight, on the other side of a rise in the land, but they knew it was heading towards them, because the flagpole was rising higher all the time.

Soon they saw that it wasn't a flagpole at all, but a mast, because now a sail was coming into view. They crept into the hull of the crashed land-sailer, so as not to be seen by whoever was approaching; and from this hiding place, they went on watching.

The one sail became many, ranged in a long line of masts, smaller sails at the top, larger sails beneath. Now they could see the superstructure of the craft, an elaborate housing lined with windows and crossed with walkways.

There were people on the walkways, running about, though too far away to identify. Still the craft was rising, as it climbed slowly out of the hollow, and now they could hear its noise clearly: a huge low rumble. More sails were appearing, on lower masts, below the level of the walkways. And then a second level of superstructure loomed over the sand, far wider than the first, a higgledy-piggledy collection of shacks and shelters linked by rope bridges and wooden passages. Crowds of people were milling about here, and now that they were nearer they could be heard shouting instructions to each other. They wore long flowing robes, and moved about with agility, swinging themselves from level to level, their robes ballooning about them.

The low sun caught the flank of the giant craft as it creaked and clambered up the rise, its myriad sails puffing in the breeze. Now as the children watched in fearful wonder, a third level of wooden buildings loomed up into view. This level was far more elaborately constructed, a classical sequence of houses with beautifully carved windows and handsome porticoes, gathered round three pillared open-sided halls. The great masts rose up through these buildings, and up through the two further levels above, all the way to the highest sails, and the flags at the very top. And still the vast structure was growing in size, as it crested the rise towards the crashed land-sailer. Its noise was deafening now, a groaning and a rattling and a creaking that seemed to fill the whole world. Already it towered high above, filling the sky. Now the wheels on which it moved became visible, each one higher than a house. And between the wheels there was yet another level, of storerooms and manufactories and farmyards and smithies, all joined by winding gangplanks and internal roads. This was no land-ship, this was a town on wheels, a whole rolling wind-driven world.

For all its colossal size, the mountainous craft was being steered with great accuracy directly towards the crashed land-sailer. The children could do nothing but crouch inside, and hope they were not crushed by the passing of the juggernaut. But it did not pass. As its shadow fell over them, they heard a new series of cries ring out from level to level, and the hundred sails were reefed in, and the monster shuddered and rolled to a halt, its nearest wheels within a few yards of where the children lay.

More commands were issued. A long timber crane arm came swinging out from a level high above, and from its end there descended a pair of massive iron jaws. The men working the beam and tackle were skilled at their job. Before the children had realised what was going on, the jaws had closed about the land-sailer, and with a great jerk, they felt themselves being hoisted up into the sky.

As they rose up and up, they saw people on the mother craft pointing towards them and gesticulating. The crane arm now swung inwards, and the smashed land-sailer was lowered with shuddering jerks down a well in the upper decks, to a lower deck. Already the order to move on had been given, the sails had been unfurled, and the whole huge edifice was juddering on its way. As the land-sailer hit the deck, the children saw a ring of ferocious-looking men waiting on every side, their arms folded before them. They all looked alike: they were tall and bearded, they wore sand-coloured robes cinched by leather belts, and their long hair was tied in hundreds of narrow braids, each one of which had plaited into it a brightly-coloured thread.

'Out!' commanded one of the men.

The children climbed out. At once they were seized and held.

'Chaka spies!' said the commander, and spat contemptuously on to the deck. 'Saboteurs!'

'Please, sir –' began Kestrel.

'Silence!' screamed the commander. 'Chaka scum! You don't speak until I tell you to speak!'

He turned to the land-sailer. Some of his men were inspecting it to assess the damage.

'Is the corvette destroyed?'

'Yes, sir.'

'Lock them up! They'll hang for this!'

He strode away, followed by a gaggle of his subordinates. Bowman, Kestrel and Mumpo were pushed towards a cage on the side of the deck. Their guards came into the cage with them, and called out, 'Down! All the way!' The cage was then lowered, running between vertical timber rails, to the lowest level. As they descended, the guards glared at the children with hatred and open disgust.

The cage bumped to a stop, and the children were marched down a dark passage to a barred door. A rough push sent them tumbling into what was all too clearly a prison cell. The door closed behind them, and they could hear the sounds of a big key being turned in the lock.

The cell was empty, not even a bench to sit on. It had one window, which looked out on to an exercise yard. As the children stood up, and looked round them, and took stock of their new situation, they heard the sound of marching feet. Through the window they saw a troop of bearded robed men lining up in the yard. The men's leader barked out an order, and they all drew long swords and held them out before them.

'Kill the Chaka spies!' he cried.

'Kill the Chaka spies!' cried all his men.

There followed a sequence of violent cries and gestures, which seemed to be a war dance. The leader called out on a rising note, 'Baraka!' and the men struck the air with their swords and howled back, at the tops of their voices, 'Raka ka! ka! ka!' and 'Kill the Chaka spies!' This was repeated many times, louder and more violently each time, until the men were stamping and red-faced with passionate fury, ready to fight anything and everything.

Kestrel and Bowman watched this with mounting dismay, but Mumpo followed the war dance with admiration. Most of all, he was struck by their hair.

'Do you see how they do it?' he said, fingering his own lank locks. 'They wind red and blue string into each plait. And green and yellow. And every colour.'

'Shut up, Mumpo.'

The lock rattled, and the door opened to admit a man who looked just like all the others, except that he was older and somewhat stouter. He was breathing heavily, and carried a tray of food.

'Can't say I see the point,' he said, putting the tray down on the floor. 'Seeing as you're to be hanged. But it's as the Morah wills.'

'The Morah!' exclaimed Kestrel. 'You know about the Morah?'

'And why wouldn't I?' said the guard. 'The Morah watches over all of us. Even me.'

'To protect you?'

'Protect me!' He laughed at the idea. 'Oh, yes, the Morah protects me, all right. With storms and diseases, and good milk-cows dying for no reason. That's how the Morah protects me. Just you wait and see. Here you are, all bright and bonny, but tomorrow you'll be hanged. Oh, yes, the Morah watches over every one of us, all right.'

The food was corn-bread, cheese and milk. Mumpo sat down and started eating at once. After a moment's hesitation, the twins followed suit, eating more slowly. Their guard stayed by the door, watching them suspiciously.

'You're small for spies,' he observed.

'We're not spies,' said Kestrel.

'You're Chaka scum, aren't you?'

'No, we're not.'

'Are you telling me you're Barakas?'

'No – '

'Then if you're not Barakas, you're Chakas,' said the guard simply. 'That's what Chakas are.'

Kestrel didn't know what to say to this.

'And we kill Chakas,' added the guard.

'I like your hair,' said Mumpo, who had now finished his food.

'Do you?'

The guard was taken by surprise, but it was evident he was pleased. He reached up and tugged carelessly at his braids.

'I'm trying greens and blues this week.'

'Is it difficult to do?'

'I wouldn't say it's difficult. But getting the braids evenly spaced as well as tight, that takes a bit of practice.'

'I bet you're good at it.'

'I do have quite a deft hand,' said the guard. 'You're a bright young fellow, I must say. For a Chaka scum.'

The twins followed this with astonishment. All the hostility had left the guard's voice.

'The blue's the same as your eyes,' said Mumpo.

'Well, that was the idea,' the guard admitted. 'Most people like a touch of red, but I prefer the natural tones.'

'I don't suppose you could do mine,' said Mumpo wistfully. 'I'd love to look like you.'

The guard contemplated him thoughtfully.

'Well, I could,' he said at last. 'I mean, seeing as you're going to hang anyway, I don't see that it would make much difference. What colours would you like?'

'What colours have you got?'

'All of them. Any colour you please.'

'Then I'd like all of them,' said Mumpo.

'That's not very subtle, you know,' said the guard. 'But then, it is your first time.'

The guard left them, locking the door behind him.

'Honestly, Mumpo!' said Kestrel. 'How can you be thinking about your hair at a time like this?'

'What else is there to think about?' said Mumpo.

The guard reappeared, carrying a comb and a bag full of hanks of coloured string. He sat down cross-legged on the floor and set about braiding Mumpo's hair. As he worked away, he became almost friendly to them. His name was Salimba, and his normal job was being a cowman. He told them that Ombaraka, the huge rolling town in which they lived, carried a herd of over a thousand cows, as well as a herd of goats and a flock of long-horned sheep. Kestrel took advantage of the guard's friendliness to discover more essential information. Who, for a start, were the Chakas?

Salimba took this question to be a trick.

'Ah, you don't catch me like that. Now, here's a fine rich

purple. Your hair could do with a wash, you know.'

'Yes, I know,' said Mumpo.

'Are the Chakas the enemies of the Barakas?' pursued Kestrel.

'How can you ask me that? Enemies? You Chakas have butchered us without mercy for generations! You think we've forgotten the Massacre of the Crescent Moon? Or the murder of Raka the Fourth? Never! No Baraka will rest until every Chaka scum is dead!'

Salimba became so agitated that his hand slipped, and the braiding went wrong. Cursing, he undid the braid and started again.

Kestrel asked the same question, but in a more politic way.

'So Baraka will win in the end?'

'Of course,' said Salimba. Every Baraka male over the age of sixteen, he explained, was drafted into the army, and underwent daily military training. He gave a nod towards the yard outside, where the troop had just ended their round of exercises. They all had other jobs, he said, as sailmen or carpenters or fodder-gatherers, but their first duty was always the defence of Ombaraka. When the battle-horns sounded, every man would drop his work, gird on his sword, and report to his assigned station. They came eagerly, because more than anything else in the world, a true Baraka lived for the day when Omchaka would be destroyed. And that day would surely come, he said, as the Morah wills.

The braiding of Mumpo's hair took over an hour, but

when it was done it was a thing of glory. He still looked filthy, but from the eyebrows up, he was dazzling. His hair had been so matted with mud that when braided, it stuck out in stiff spikes. Salimba said that wasn't customary, but it did have a certain panache, and it was clear from the way he looked at Mumpo that he was rather proud of the result.

There was no mirror in the prison cell, and Mumpo was impatient to see his new look.

'What's it like? Do you like it, Kess? Do you?'

Kestrel truly didn't know what to say. It was mesmerising. He looked like a rainbow porcupine.

'You look completely different,' she said.

'Is that good?'

'It's just – different.'

Then Salimba remembered that the tray had a shiny underside. He held it up for Mumpo to get a blurry reflection of his new hair. Mumpo gazed at himself and sighed with pleasure.

'Thank you,' he said. 'I knew you'd be good at it.'

The tramp of many footsteps in the passage outside brought guard and prisoners down to earth. There came a loud hammering on the door. Salimba hastily assumed a stern expression, and unlocked the door.

'Prisoners, stand!' he yelled.

The children stood.

In came an elderly Baraka man with a long grey braided beard and long grey braided hair. Behind him, stiffly at attention, arms folded across their chests, stood a troop of a dozen soldiers. The grey-haired man looked in surprise at Mumpo, but chose not to comment on his colourful hair.

'I am Kemba, counsellor to Raka the Ninth, Warlord of the Barakas, Suzerain of Ombaraka, Commander-in-chief of the Wind Warriors, and Ruler of the Plains,' he announced. 'Guard, leave us!'

'Yes, Counsellor.'

Salimba retreated, drawing the door closed behind him. Kemba went to the window and looked out, fingering his belt of coloured beads. Then he sighed, and turned round to face the children.

'Your presence here is profoundly inconvenient,' he said. 'But I suppose you must be hanged.'

'We're not Chakas,' said Kestrel.

'Of course you're Chakas. If you're not Barakas, you're Chakas. And we are at war with all Chakas, to the death.'

'We're from Aramanth.'

'Nonsense! Don't be absurd. You're Chakas, and you must hang.'

'You can't hang us!' exclaimed Kestrel hotly.

'As it happens, you're quite right,' said the counsellor, more to himself than to her. 'We can't hang you, because of the treaty. But on the other hand, we can't possibly let you live. Oh, dear!' He sighed a long exasperated sigh. 'This really is most profoundly inconvenient. Still, I shall think of something. I always do.'

He clapped his hands to summon the troop outside.

'Door!'

And to the children, almost as an afterthought:

'I have to take you before Raka. It's purely a formality. But all sentences of death have to be passed by Raka himself.'

The door opened.

'Form escort!' commanded Kemba. 'The prisoners will proceed at once to the Court.'

Closely guarded all the way, the children were marched across the base deck of the huge rolling edifice that was Ombaraka, to a central lift shaft. Here the lift cage was far bigger than the one in which they had been taken down, and easily held the entire troop escorting them. Up it creaked, carrying them past ladders and walkways, to the court deck. From the lift, their route took them across a handsome avenue and into one of the broad pillared halls. As they went, passers-by stopped and stared, and hissed with hatred; but when they saw Mumpo, they just gaped. Kestrel could hear their escort discussing Mumpo's braids in low voices.

'Far too loud,' one was saying.

'All that orange! So vulgar.'

'I wonder how he makes it stick out straight like that,' said another. 'Not that I'd want that for myself.'

They marched right down the echoing open hall to the doors at the far end. The doors opened as they approached. Inside was a long room, dominated by a central table, the entire surface of which was a giant map. Round this table stood several important-looking men, scowling; among them the commander who had witnessed the children emerge from the crashed land-sailer, and Tanaka, chief of the armed forces, a man with a red face etched all over with deep angry lines. When he saw Mumpo's new braids, he too gaped with surprise.

'What did I tell you?' he cried. 'Now one of them's in Baraka disguise!'

The smallest of the men round the table came strutting forward, staring at the children with extreme hostility. Raka the Ninth, Warlord of the Barakas, Suzerain of Ombaraka, Commander-in-chief of the Wind Warriors, and Ruler of the Plains, had the misfortune to be short. He made up for his lack of stature by cultivating the most ferocious manner imaginable. His braids were the only ones in all Ombaraka to be threaded with tiny steel blades, which flashed in the light every time he moved his head. His robe was criss-crossed with belts and bandoleers, into which were stuck knives and swords of every size. He moved with a stocky aggression, as if bristling at the world; and his voice positively barked.

'Chaka spies!'

'No, sir – '

'You dare to contradict me? I am Raka!'

His rage was so violent that Kestrel didn't say another word.

'Commander!'

'Yes, my lord.' Tanaka stepped forward.

'They destroyed a battle corvette?'

'Yes, my lord.'

'The Chakas will pay for this!' He ground his teeth and stamped the deck. 'Is Omchaka within range?'

'No, my lord.' This came from one of the others, by the map-table. He made a rapid calculation. 'A day at the most, my lord.'

'Set course for interception!' cried Raka. 'They have provoked me. They have only themselves to blame.'

'You mean to give battle, my lord?' asked Kemba quietly.

'Yes, Counsellor! They must learn that if they strike at me, I strike back tenfold!'

'Quite so, my lord.'

Already the new orders were ringing out, and even the children could feel from the grinding and shuddering of the timbers round them that Ombaraka was changing course.

'Commander! Prepare the attack fleet for dawn!'

'Yes, my lord!'

'And the Chaka spies, my lord?'

'Hang them, of course.'

'I wonder if that is wise.'

This was Kemba's pensive voice.

'Wise? Wise?' shrieked the little warlord. 'What are you talking about? Of course it's wise! What else is there to do with spies?'

Kemba stepped closer, and whispered in his master's ear.

'Interrogate them. Learn the secrets of the Chaka fleet.'

'And then hang them?'

'Quite so, my lord.'

The little warlord nodded, and strode about the room, deep in meditation. Everyone remained still and silent.

Then he came to a stop, and announced his decision in a ringing voice.

'The spies will be interrogated first, and then hanged.'

Once more, Kemba murmured low in his ear.

'You must tell them they won't be hanged if they co-operate, my lord. Otherwise they won't tell us anything.'

'And then hang them?'

'Quite so, my lord.'

Raka nodded, and said again, in ringing tones, 'The spies will not be hanged, if they co-operate.' Tanaka choked with angry surprise.

'Not hanged, my lord?'

'This is an intelligence matter, Commander,' said Raka testily. 'You wouldn't understand.'

'I understand that the counsellor shrinks from doing his duty,' said Tanaka with grim pride.

Raka chose to ignore this.

'Take them away, Counsellor,' he said, making shooing gestures with his hands. 'Interrogate them.' He moved back to the map-table. 'You and I, Commander, have a battle to prepare.'

*

The children were marched back to their prison cell. Once there, the guards were dismissed, but Kemba himself remained.

'I have bought us a little time,' he said. 'And I need a little time, to think of a way out of our dilemma. I do not propose to waste any of that little time asking you for the secrets of the Chaka battle fleet.'

'We don't know the secrets of the Chaka battle fleet.'

'It's really not important. The dilemma is this. We can't hang you, without breaking the treaty. But we can't let you live, without dishonouring our ancestors and all Ombaraka. To a man, we are pledged to avenge our dead with Chaka blood. This hasn't caused a difficulty up till now, because we've never actually held any Chaka prisoners. And believe you me, I wish we didn't now.'

He proceeded to explain. It seemed that some time ago, to stem the bloodshed of the perpetual war between the Barakas and the Chakas, a treaty had come into being between the two warrior peoples. This treaty stated, very simply, that from that time forward no Chaka blood would be spilled by Baraka warriors, unless Baraka blood was spilled first; and vice versa.

'So the war ended?'

'Not at all,' said Kemba. 'That was and is unthinkable. The war can never end. The very existence of Ombaraka depends on war. We live on a moving island to protect ourselves from attack. We are a warrior people, all the ranks in our society are military ranks, and most importantly of all, our leader, Raka of Baraka, is a warlord. No, the war goes on. It is the killing that has stopped. No Baraka or Chaka warrior has died in battle for a generation now.'

'How can you have a battle where nobody gets killed?'

'With machines.'

Kemba pointed out of the window. On the far side of the exercise yard, the masts of land-sailers could just be seen.

'Our battle fleet attacks their battle fleet. Sometimes we come out the winners, sometimes they do. But no men are at risk on either side. The corvettes and the destroyers and the battle-cruisers go into battle all by themselves.'

'So it's all just a game.'

'No, no. It's war, and we fight with all the passions of war. It's not easy to explain to outsiders. Raka truly believes that one day his army will destroy Omchaka, and he will be the sole ruler of the plains. We all believe it; even I, in a way. You see, if we stopped believing it, we'd have to live quite differently, and then we wouldn't be Barakas any more.'

'But even so, you don't really need to hang us, do you? You're not as cruel and heartless as that.'

'Oh yes, we are,' said the counsellor absently, his mind revolving the problem. 'I don't care a button for you. But I do care about the treaty. If the Chakas learn that we've hanged some Chaka spies, they'll have to avenge you, and then all the killing will start again.'

'There you are, then. You can't hang us.'

'But all Ombaraka now knows you're here. Everyone's expecting a hanging. You've no idea how excited they are. We're all brought up to kill Chakas, and now here at last, after all these years, we have three Chaka spies, caught in the act of sabotage. Of course you have to be hanged.'

He was gazing out of the window once more, speaking more to himself than to them.

'I negotiated the treaty, you know. It was my finest hour.'

He sighed a long melancholy sigh.

'You could let us escape.'

'No, no. That would bring shame on us all.'

'You could pretend to hang us.'

'How would that help? If the pretence succeeded, the Chakas would say we'd broken the treaty, and the killing would start again. And if the pretence failed, the people of Ombaraka would tear you to pieces with their bare hands, and probably me as well. Please try to think clearly, and make sensible suggestions, or remain silent, and let me think for myself.'

So silence fell; but for the constant creaking and rumbling of the entire structure, as Ombaraka rolled on across the plains.

After a few minutes, the counsellor clapped a palm to his brow.

'Of course! What a fool I've been! There's the answer, staring me in the face!'

Bowman and Kestrel hurried to the window, to see what

it was he was gazing at. There was nobody out there in the yard. Nothing seemed to have changed.

'What?'

'The battle fleet! Let the punishment fit the crime!'

He turned to them, his aged face positively glowing with excitement.

'I knew I'd think of something! Oh, what a brain I have! Just listen to this.'

There was to be a battle the next day, he explained. The Baraka battle fleet would be launched, and the Chaka battle fleet would be sent out to meet them. The armed land-sailers would collide at enormous speeds in mid-plains, and would destroy each other with their spinning blades. What better death could there be for the Chaka saboteurs? Send them out in one of the battle corvettes, to be smashed to pulp by the Chaka battle fleet!

'Do you see the beauty of it? You would die, which would satisfy us, but you would be killed by the Chakas themselves, so the treaty would not be broken! Isn't that perfect?'

He strode about the cell, throwing out his arms like a man doing deep-breathing exercises.

'The symmetry of it! The purity, the elegance!'

'But we end up dead?'

'Exactly! And all Ombaraka can watch! Yes, truly, I believe this is one of the best ideas I've ever come up with in all my life!'

He swung round and headed for the door, no longer interested in the children.

'Guard! Open up! Let me out!'

'Please,' cried Kestrel, 'couldn't we – '

'Silence, Chaka scum!' said the counsellor, not unkindly, and strode out of the cell.

16

THE WIND BATTLE

Kemba's plan evidently met with the approval of the Raka of Baraka, because when Salimba next came into the prison cell he told the children that the people of Ombaraka could talk of nothing else.

'We've never had a battle with a real killing before,' said Salimba, his eyes glowing. 'At least, not that anyone can remember. Oh, I'll be out there to see, you can count on that.'

'How can you be so sure we'll be killed?' said Kestrel. 'The corvette may be blown off across the plains without hitting anything.'

'Oh, no, they'll make sure of that,' said Salimba. 'They'll wait until the whole Chaka battle fleet is out, and they'll send you right into the middle. Those Chaka cruisers are mounted with the old heavy slashers. They'll rip you into pieces, all right.'

'Don't you care?' said Bowman, his eyes glistening.

Salimba looked at him, and then looked away, a little awkwardly.

'Well, it won't be good for you,' he said. 'I do see that. But –' he looked back, brightening – 'it'll be grand for us!'

Once he was gone, the twins puzzled over what to do.

'It's a strange thing,' said Bowman, 'but in spite of all this talk of hanging and killing, I have the feeling that they're quite gentle people really.'

'Whee-eee!' said Mumpo.

'Mumpo?'

'Yes, Kess?'

'Do you realise what's happening?'

'You're my friend, and I love you.'

His eyes looked a little odd, but she pressed on. 'We're going to be put in one of those land-sailers tomorrow morning, and attacked by a lot of other ones like it.'

'That's good, Kess.'

'No, it's not good. They have swinging knives that will chop us into pieces.'

'Big pieces or little pieces?' He started to giggle. 'Or very teeny-weeny pieces?'

Kestrel looked at him more closely.

'Mumpo! Show me your teeth!'

Mumpo bared his teeth. They were yellow.

'You're chewing tixa, aren't you?'

'I'm so happy, Kess.'

'Where is it? Show me.'

He reached into his pocket and showed her a bunch of tixa leaves.

'You are useless, Mumpo.'

'Yes, Kess, I know. But I do love you.'

'Oh, shut up.'

Bowman was staring at the grey-green tixa leaves.

'Maybe we can do it.'

'Do what?'

'When we were sheltering in the crashed wind-sailer, I worked out how its parts all went together. I think I understand it. If Mumpo was up on the mast, like when he was mud-diving, I think we could do it.'

The next morning, as the dawn light began to spread across the eastern sky, the lookouts high up in the watchtowers of Ombaraka sent the signal the navigators had been waiting for: Omchaka in sight! A second great craft, a mirror image of Ombaraka itself, was lumbering towards them over the plain, its sails and masts, its decks and towers, bristling against the pink and golden sky. A strong wind was blowing from the south-west, and the two rolling cities were each tacking at an angle to the wind, to come within range of each other by the time the sun was up.

Raka himself now took up his position on the command deck. Down below, the winches and gantries which held the attack fleet were being readied for action, and all over

Ombaraka men were preparing for the coming battle. The wind masters were in place on the outer galleries, their instruments held high; and in the command room, their stream of reports was being processed into ever more accurate predictions on the strength and direction of the wind. In battle, there were two crucial elements: wind direction, and timing of launch. The later the battle fleet was launched, the closer they were to their targets, and therefore the higher the degree of accuracy. However, if the launching was left too late, there was the danger that the fleet wouldn't have time to reach attack speed before the enemy craft struck them.

All this time the two great mother craft, Ombaraka and Omchaka, were lumbering into battle stations, each seeking the advantageous up-wind position. Inevitably, as happened every time, they ended up cross-wind to each other, where neither had the advantage. This was not a matter of great concern, since both battle fleets were designed, for this very reason, to run best in a cross-wind.

As the sun climbed over the horizon, sending dazzling rays across the surface of the plains, Raka gave the order for the battle horns to be sounded. The first horn boomed out high on the lead watchtower, and from there was picked up by the watchmen all over Ombaraka. One after the other, their long deep-throated notes overlapping each other, the horns echoed from deck to deck.

The children heard them in their prison cell, and knew what they meant. Soon there came running footsteps outside, and the door burst open. An escort of heavily-armed men seized them, and dragged them out into the passage. Roughly, without speaking a word, they hustled them across the yard, and down a ramp to the launch deck. Here, stretching as far as the eye could see in either direction, ranged the Baraka battle fleet: line upon line of wind-craft, each vessel suspended from gantries projecting from the high sides of the mother craft. Men were crawling all over the ships, aligning the propeller-like blades, hanging the nets, checking the belts and pulleys, and adjusting the sails. Each vessel in the fleet had its team of handlers, for whom this was a climactic moment. The machine they had so lovingly crafted, and were now preparing for battle with such precision, would soon be launched, never to return. It would carry with it their hopes of glory, and if they were fortunate would bring down a Chaka craft, before inevitably falling itself to the blows of the enemy or of the elements.

The children were marched down the line of battle cruisers and ordered to stop before the first of the lighter craft called corvettes. The soldiers of Baraka were everywhere, and whenever their eyes fell on the children they spat, and called out insults. 'Chaka scum! I'll be watching as your brains are spattered in the wind!'

By each gantry there were men with long hooked poles, which they used to pull the battle craft in to the side. Three such poles were holding the lead corvette close to the launch deck now, so that the children could be placed on board. The attack blades gleamed silver-sharp in the light of the rising sun, motionless until the corvette itself was in motion.

Counsellor Kemba now appeared, to oversee the fate of the Chaka spies. He nodded to the children in a friendly manner, and then issued an order to their escort.

'Tie the Chaka spies to the masts!'

'Please, sir,' said Kestrel. 'Didn't you say everybody would be watching?'

'What if I did?'

'Well, if you tie us up, it'll be over too quickly, won't it?'

'What are you suggesting?'

'I was thinking that if we were to run about in the corvette, it would be much more fun to watch.'

Kemba considered this suggestion, a little taken aback.

'But you might jump out altogether,' he pointed out.

'You could tether us loosely,' said Kestrel. 'And you could give us something to fight back with. Then we could put on a real show for you.'

'No, no,' said Kemba. 'No swords. Not for Chaka spies.'

'How about one of those poles?' said Bowman, pointing to the hooked poles that held the corvette to the deck.

'What do you want one of those for?'

'Maybe we can push the Chaka fleet away.'

'Push the Chaka fleet away? With a pole?'

The old counsellor smiled at that, and the men round him laughed out loud. They knew the overwhelming speed with which the battle cruisers bore down upon each other.

'Very well,' said Kemba. 'Give them a pole. We'll watch them push the Chaka cruisers away.'

Amid much mocking laughter, the children were carried on board the corvette, and each tethered by a long loop of rope to the centre mast. The ropes were slender, but extremely strong, and the knots were well and tightly made. A hooked pole was tossed in after them, and another laugh ran round the launch deck. The pole clattered into the well of the craft, and Bowman let it lie there. Kestrel murmured something to Mumpo. Mumpo nodded, and grinned, and picked up the pole.

All along the western flank of Ombaraka, the battle fleet now waited, tensed with readiness for the order to launch. From where the children stood, swaying in the lead corvette, they could count fourteen of the big battle cruisers ahead of them, and behind them, nine more corvettes. Much further away, they could see the looming bulk of Omchaka, silhouetted against the brightening sky, and they could hear the faraway sounds of the Chaka battle horns.

The two great mother craft moved steadily in the rising wind, narrowing the gap between them. The sails had not yet been set on the battle fleet, though the sailmen stood poised at the ready. Kestrel turned and looked upwards, up the towering decks and galleries above her, and saw hundreds of people, men, women and children, squeezed into every vantage point, staring silently across the plains. And higher above still, in the watchtowers, the watchmen trained their telescopes on the gantries of Omchaka, poised to cry out when the Chaka battle fleet began its launch.

It was a tense time for all, this waiting, with the enemy rolling nearer all the time; for all, that is, except Mumpo. Mumpo was swinging the long hooked pole round his head and laughing to himself. He seemed not to realise that the Baraka people hated him, and when they shook their fists at him and made gestures showing how he would be killed in the battle, he waved cheerily back and went on laughing. Bowman and Kestrel, by contrast, remained quiet, wanting to draw as little attention to themselves as possible. They were studying the sail mechanism, and the activities of the member of the launch crew whose task it was to set the craft on course.

Then at last there came the distant cry, followed by a nearer one, and then one nearer still.

'Prepare to engage!'

At once, a ripple of alertness ran through the teams on the launch deck, as they braced themselves to follow the expected commands. Ahead, a mile away across the plain, they could see movement on the launch decks of Omchaka. Then, distant but full, like the deep roar of a waterfall, there rose up the war-cry of the Chakas.

'Cha-cha-chaka! Cha-cha-chaka!'

At the same time, the sails on the Chaka battle cruisers unfurled, and the lead cruiser was lowered to the ground, sails straining in the wind. All eyes on Ombaraka watched as the Chaka craft was loosed, and its blades began to churn the air. All eyes followed it as it picked up speed, and began its charge.

'Launch one!'

The crisp order threw the launch deck into instant action. Smoothly the launch team by the lead battle cruiser ran through their practised routine: sails loosed, blades released, final wind-direction check, enemy locked in the sights, course set. A curt nod from the sightsman, and the launch leader gave the final command.

'Go!'

The holding clamps snapped open. The brisk wind pulled the heavy craft out from the launch deck, and it rolled away on its high wheels. The huge blades started to turn as the sails filled in the wind. Out from the lee of the mother craft, and the full force of the cross-wind hit the sails, howling through its mast-top horn, and the battle cruiser accelerated into its lethal charge. From every deck and gallery the war-cry of the Barakas rose up, urging it on its way.

'Raka ka! ka! ka! Raka ka! ka! ka!'

Now a second Chaka cruiser had been launched, and a third. As all eyes followed the lead craft, the orders echoed and re-echoed along the launch deck, and cruiser after cruiser was unleashed. All the time, the two great mother craft were closing in on each other.

The sightsmen had done their job well. The first two cruisers struck each other head on, their great blades interlocking, mangling each other, sending both craft spinning in a tumble of mutual destruction. A cheer went up from the onlookers, and across the plain, a similar cheer could be heard rising from the decks of Omchaka. The collision had taken place too far away to judge which craft had inflicted the most damage. The cheer was for the first hit of the battle.

Now the strikes were following thick and fast. The sightsmen and the wind masters on both sides were experts at their trades, and the battle cruisers closed in on their moving targets as precisely as if they carried living helmsmen. Soon the central area of the plains between the great mother craft became a graveyard of wrecked battle cruisers, their sails vainly tugging at their beached hulls.

The rate of launching was faster now, as the Chaka commanders piled on the pressure. Clearly their aim was to overwhelm the Baraka fleet with sheer numbers, leaving Ombaraka defenceless during the crucial final phase of the battle, when the two rolling cities were close enough for the attack fleets to inflict damage on the mother craft themselves. All the strategy of battle came down to this single decision: how long to hold back the last, fastest, most manoeuvrable craft in the fleet, the corvettes.

The battle cries never ceased, on either side; their steady roar mingling now with the splintering crashes of the cruisers as they piled into each other, or into already wrecked craft, and sprayed yet more wreckage up into the air.

Impossible to tell which side was gaining the upper hand, though the Chaka fleet seemed for the moment to be so huge that it covered all the plain.

Still the commands hammered out. 'Go! Go! Go!'

Craft after craft hit the dirt running, as the launch directors sweated to hurl their parrying punches out into the field. Up on the command deck, Raka prowled the observation window, in the midst of a pandemonium of shouting voices.

'Wind veering west two degrees!'

'Chaka launch thirty-one!'

'Hit! Full kill!'

'Closing distance twelve hundred yards!'

'Chaka launch thirty-two! Thirty-three!'

'How many more?' exclaimed Raka.

'Second fleet gone! Corvettes stand by!'

Tanaka, commander of the armed forces, hurried to the warlord's side.

'Do we commit the corvettes, my lord?'

'No! That's what they want!'

'Chaka launch thirty-four! Thirty-five! Thirty-six!'

'Closing distance one thousand yards!'

'We must launch, my lord! We can't block them without the corvettes.'

'Damn all Chakas!' exploded Raka. 'How many more are they holding back?'

'Chaka launch thirty-seven!'

'We must release the corvettes!'

'We're letting them dictate our strategy,' said Raka. 'It's what they want.'

'Chaka cruiser broken through! Chaka cruiser broken through!'

The cry sent a chill across the whole command deck. This was what they all dreaded: the first craft to evade the defending line of the Baraka battle fleet, and come speeding on its way towards Ombaraka itself.

'Track for point of collision!' barked Tanaka. 'Sound the danger alert!' And turning back to the warlord, his voice tense with urgency. 'My lord – the corvettes!'

'Go, then,' said Raka with a heavy heart. 'Send out the corvettes.'

On the launch decks the teams heard the horns as they sounded a new, shriller note: the danger alert. The war-cry faltered as the realisation spread from gallery to gallery: the Chaka fleet had broken through. But there was no time to wonder how or why, because right after the horns came the launch signals, and at last the corvettes were going into action.

'Go! Go! Go!'

Although the children were in the lead corvette, they found they were not to be the first on to the plain. Behind them, one after another, the slim but deadly craft were dropping down and racing away, in rapid-fire sequence, heading arrow-straight for the approaching line of Chaka cruisers. As they were unleashed, the single breakaway Chaka cruiser was already upon them, moving at overpowering speed. It hit the first corvette, sending the lighter craft flying, and roared on to smash like a flying hammer into the lowest deck of Ombaraka. A mighty cheer rose up from Omchaka, as the spinning fragments of the crashed cruiser rose high up the walls of Ombaraka, and the people ducked for cover.

The crews on the launch decks never flinched. Corvette after corvette went snaking out, to meet and halt the advancing Chaka cruisers.

'Go! Go! Go!'

The children waited in the one corvette that had been bypassed, watching the battle, Bowman and Kestrel intent and silent, Mumpo swinging his hooked pole and yelling with excitement.

'Smash! Smash! Hubba hubba! Here they come! Bang-crash-bash! Ya-ha!'

Then a new series of commands could be heard ringing out, and all over Ombaraka the sailmen could be seen furling their sails. Slowly the great rolling city came to a shuddering halt. Raka had chosen his ground for the last stand. Here they would fight to the finish.

For a few long minutes, Omchaka kept rolling towards them. Had they decided to fight the last phase of the battle at close quarters? Then Omchaka too could be seen to be furling its sails, and so the two juggernauts came to rest barely five hundred yards apart, to watch their battle fleets' last climactic clash.

On the command deck, Raka was in a frenzy of anguish.

'Do they have any more? I must know if they have any more!'

'No, my lord.'

'They've fired their last shots? I can't believe it.'

'Hit and kill! Hit and kill!'

'Wind veering south-west three degrees!'

'Three corvettes in reserve, my lord! Do we launch?'

'*Do they have any left?*'

'All Chaka gantries empty, my lord.'

'Then go! Go!'

He threw back his arms, and his eyes sparkled once more.

'They've thrown their last punch too soon! Now we'll see who can break through!'

The war-cries on both sides were at their height now, as the enemy tribes, close enough to see each other, competed to drown each other's voices.

'Cha-cha-chaka! Cha-cha-chaka!'

'Raka ka! ka! ka! Raka ka! ka! ka!'

The two battle fleets tangled and clashed, each collision throwing up a great roar from the onlookers. There had been no more breakthroughs on either side, and the Chaka launches had ended, when the Baraka reserve corvettes received the order to go.

The children's craft was third and last in line. Kemba's intention was that their destruction would form the grand finale of the battle. The children stayed calm as their sails were at last unfurled, and they felt the mast strain in the wind. The pulleys overhead squealed, as they were winched to the ground. The sightsman set his course, and strapped down the mainsail boom. Kemba gave one last amiable wave.

'Best idea I've ever had,' he called down to them. 'Give us a good show.'

'Go!' came the command. The holding clamps snapped open, and with a wild buck that tumbled all three children into the well, the corvette kicked into action, rocketing out into the open space. The blades on either side began to spin, and the mast-top horn let out its banshee wail.

The crowds ranged all along the decks of Ombaraka greeted the reserve corvettes with a howl of triumph. The last craft in the battle were sure to break through. Then, catching sight of the children in the last corvette, their howl became one of hatred.

'Chaka scum! Chaka spies! Die! Die! Die!'

Then suddenly the chant faded on their lips. Huge doors had swung open on the side of Omchaka, to reveal concealed gantries, cradling an entire new battle fleet.

On the command deck, Raka saw this with cold despair. There was nothing he could do. He had committed his last craft, they were under way and could not be recalled. Ombaraka lay at the mercy of the enemy.

'How many?' he said dully. But he could see for himself, as the gantries rolled out. Eight battle cruisers. At five hundred yards, they would never reach maximum speed, but they would still inflict terrible damage. Safe from attack themselves, the Chaka commanders could take their time releasing them, and he had no choice but to sit here and suffer the blows. Ombaraka would be crippled. It was a disaster.

All his people knew it. A stunned silence fell over the decks and galleries, as they watched their own corvettes collide with the last of the Chaka cruisers still in the battle. No cheers for a kill now. Only the wild war-cry of Omchaka carried to them on the wind.

'Cha-cha-chaka! Cha-cha-chaka!'

But then something odd started to happen. The third corvette, the one carrying the Chaka spies, was making a wide curving turn. Astonished, they followed its flight. Two of the children seemed to be working the set of its sails, one on the mainsail and one on the jib. The third had climbed to the top of the mainmast, where he was waving a pole. The wide turn took the corvette away from the battle, in a full circle, and back again.

In the corvette, racing at giddy speed, Bowman and Kestrel worked the sails with intense concentration, feeling the responses of the craft. On their first turn they took care to keep all four wheels on the ground, but on the second, they took the turn tighter, letting the craft tip a little. It performed beautifully. Communicating without words, they shared what they were learning.

Cross now! And over! Hold the turn! There she goes!

As they completed that second long turn, they knew they had control of the craft. They looked at each other, exchanging a flash of excitement at the speed of their movement, and at their power.

'You all right, Mumpo?' Kestrel called up to the mast top.

'Happy, happy, happy!' Mumpo carolled back, swinging the hooked pole round his head. 'Let's go fishing!'

The first of the hidden Chaka cruisers hit the ground. As it churned its way into action, set on a course that avoided the tangle of smashed craft, Bowman and Kestrel swung round and gave chase. Their course was designed not to collide with the Chaka cruiser, but to sweep round and run alongside it.

Round, Kess, round! Now let her run!

The people on Ombaraka watched this manoeuvre in bewilderment. The people on Omchaka were equally bemused, and their triumphant cry fell silent. What was going on? Was the corvette joining the Chaka cruiser in its attack? As the much lighter corvette swung alongside the lumbering cruiser, it certainly looked that way.

Nearer! Nearer! And nearer –

Kestrel at the prow, calling the turns, Bowman on the main boom, running the craft as close as he dared to the Chaka cruiser, without getting mangled by its huge spinning blade. Mumpo hung from the top of the mast by his knees, reaching out with his pole, yelling, 'Closer! Closer!' Steadily they closed in, until they were so near that they could feel the air-rush of the cruiser's blades.

'Fishy fishy fishy!' cried Mumpo.

'Now!' cried Kestrel.

Bowman jerked the mainsail to tip the craft on to two wheels as it raced along. Mumpo hung out from the mast and hooked the end of his pole into the top rigging of the battle cruiser.

'Pull away! Pull away!' cried Kestrel.

Bowman wrenched the mainsail boom, the corvette righted itself and veered sharply away from the battle cruiser, and Mumpo hung on tight. The Chaka craft lurched on to one side, Mumpo unhooked his pole, the corvette shot away, turning now on its other two wheels, and the battle cruiser came thundering down, to thrash itself to pieces with its own blades.

A wild stamping roar went up from all Ombaraka. The corvette righted itself again, crashing back on to four wheels, sweeping Mumpo vertical once more. He raised his arms like a champion.

'Hubba hubba Mumpo!' called Kestrel.

And round they raced, back into the attack. The light of battle was in their eyes, and the more they struck, the bolder they became. As the great cruisers were launched, they leaped on them, running them to ground like a hound harrying deer. Twice they missed, but so light were they on the turns that they were back round again for another strike before the heavy cruisers could build up the speed to outrun them. And with every kill, up went the echoing stamping roar from the decks of Ombaraka.

On the command deck, Raka watched in awe, his hands pulling convulsively at his beaded belt.

'These are no Chaka spies,' he said softly.

The disaster was turning into triumph before his eyes.

After the fourth of the brand-new battle cruisers had been destroyed, the Chaka high command launched no more. The doors to the secret launch decks closed again, and Omchaka set its sails for a retreat.

Raka of Baraka saw this, and ordered the victory call. The high horns began it, and the people of Ombaraka took it up, every man, woman and child. To the chanting of a thousand voices, Bowman and Kestrel steered the corvette back towards its mother craft, its attack blades still turning. As they came into the lee of the great structure, the sails slackened, and the craft coasted to a standstill. Mumpo came slithering down the mainmast, and the three children embraced each other, still trembling with the tension of the battle.

'Mumpo, you're a hero! Bo, you're a hero!'

'All heroes,' said Mumpo, happier than he'd ever been in his entire life. 'We're the three heroes!'

As they were hoisted back on board, they were cheered and cheered, all the way over the launch deck and up the walkway and through the pillared halls to the command deck, where Raka was waiting for them.

'After what I have seen today,' he declared, 'I know that you are not Chakas. And if you're not Chakas, you are Barakas! You are our brothers!'

'And our sister,' said Counsellor Kemba, smiling his most amiable smile.

Raka embraced each one of them, shaking with emotion.

'I and all my people are at your service!'

As a special sign of his gratitude, Raka of Baraka ordered that all three children should have their hair braided by the Master Braider. After some earnest discussions among his counsellors, it was agreed that the young heroes could have gold threads braided into their hair. This was the highest honour short of the blades worn by the warlord himself, and many eyebrows were raised at its granting. But as Counsellor Kemba pointed out, the children would not be staying long on Ombaraka, and once beyond the care of the Master Braider the gold threads would soon tarnish.

Mumpo was very excited at the prospect of golden hair; Kestrel and Bowman less so. But they sensed it would be discourteous to refuse. Once the elaborate process had begun, however, they found themselves enjoying it more than they had expected. First, their hair was washed three times, which at last removed from it the mud of the Underlake. Then skilled combers set to work drawing out the strands of hair into hundreds of slender tresses. The combing was both gentle and strong, which was an odd sensation, and made their scalps tingle. Then the under-braiders took over, working to the instructions of the Master Braider himself.

Each tress was plaited both with itself and with three lengths of gold thread, to form a fine criss-cross braid, ending in a little lumpy golden knot. Unlike Salimba's earlier work on Mumpo's hair, the plaits were worked carefully to hang perfectly straight, and this took a very long time. If the Master Braider saw the beginnings of a kink in a plait, he ordered it undone to the roots, and started again.

When this patient work was almost done, Counsellor Kemba joined them.

'My dear young friends,' he said, 'Raka of Baraka sends me to invite you to a dinner in your honour this evening. He also wishes to be informed if there is any way in which he can show his gratitude in a more lasting fashion.'

'We would just like to be helped on our way,' said Kestrel.

'And what way is that?'

'We have to find the road known as the Great Way.'

'The Great Way?' Kemba's pleasant voice suddenly sounded grave. 'What do you want with the Great Way?'

Kestrel met Bowman's eyes, and saw there the same suspicion.

'It's just the path we have to follow,' she said. 'Do you know where it is?'

'I know where it was,' replied Kemba. 'The Great Way hasn't been used for many, many years. That region is full of dangers. There are wolves there. And worse.'

'Wolves don't frighten us,' said Mumpo. 'We're the three heroes.'

'So we have seen,' said Kemba with a thin smile. 'But nevertheless, I think it would be best if we were to take you south, to Aramanth, which you say is your home.'

'No, thank you,' said Kestrel firmly. 'We have to go north.'

Counsellor Kemba bowed in what seemed like assent, and left them to their braiding.

The final results were spectacular. The three children gazed at themselves in the glass and were silent with awe. Their hair now haloed their faces in a shimmer of light, which danced this way and that with every move of their heads. The Master Braider beamed at them with pride.

'I knew the gold would set off your pale skins,' he said. 'We Barakas need stronger colours, to tell you the truth. Gold would be lost on me.'

He fingered his own red, orange, and acid-green plaits.

At the grand dinner, the children's entrance was greeted by a standing ovation. All down the long lines of tables gasps of admiration could be heard, at the gleam of their golden braids in the candlelight. Raka of Baraka beckoned them to sit on his either side. Thinking that he was pleasing them, he announced:

'We're sailing south! Kemba has told me that your one wish is to return to Aramanth. So I have given the order to sail south.'

'But that's not right,' cried Kestrel. 'We want to go north.'

The smile left Raka's face. He looked across the table to Kemba for an explanation. Counsellor Kemba spread his smooth hands.

'I consider it our duty, my lord, to look after our young heroes in every way we can. The road north is impassable. The bridge over the gorge is in ruins. No travellers dare go that way any more.'

'Well, we dare,' said Kestrel fiercely.

'There is another matter.' Kemba sighed, as if it hurt him to speak of it. 'My lord, as you know, although we have been at war with Omchaka for a long time, we have been spared a greater danger. I speak of – ' he hesitated, then murmured low –, 'the Zars.'

'The Zars?' said Raka, in his booming tones. And the word was repeated all down the lines of tables, like an echo. 'The Zars – the Zars.'

'Were the children inadvertently to wake – '

'Quite, quite,' said Raka hastily. 'Better to head south.' The twins heard this with dismay.

Leave it for now, said Bowman silently. So Kestrel said nothing more, and Counsellor Kemba, watching them closely, was satisfied.

At the end of the grand dinner, Bowman asked Raka for a special favour. He asked to speak to the warlord alone.

'Certainly,' said Raka, who had eaten and drunk well, and was filled with sensations of goodwill. 'Why not?'

But Kemba was suspicious.

'I think, my lord – ' he began.

'Now, now, Kemba,' said Raka. 'You worry too much.'

He took Bowman off into his private quarters, and Kemba had to content himself with standing close to the door in the next room, and listening to every word.

What he heard was not at all what he expected. For a long time, the boy and the warlord sat together in total silence. It even seemed possible that Raka had gone to sleep. But then the counsellor heard the boy's voice, speaking softly.

'I can feel you remembering,' he said.

'Yes . . .' This was Raka.

'You're a baby. Your father takes you everywhere. He holds you high, and he smiles. You're only little, but you feel his pride and love.'

'Yes, yes . . .'

'You're older now. You're a boy. You stand before your father, and he says, Head up! Head up! You know he wishes you were taller. You wish it too, more than anything in the world.'

'Yes, yes . . .'

'Now you're older still. You're a man, and your father never looks at you. He can't bear to see you, because you're so small. You say nothing, but your heart cries out to him, Be proud of me. Love me.'

'Yes, yes . . .' Raka was sobbing softly now. 'How do you know these things? How do you know?'

'I feel it in you. I feel it in me.'

'I've never spoken of it. Never, never.'

Counsellor Kemba, listening at the door, could endure it no longer. He was unclear quite how it would interfere with his schemes, but he was sure it was not healthy for the warlord of Ombaraka to be weeping like a baby. So, pretending agitation, he swept into the private meeting.

'My lord, what has happened? What's the matter?'

Raka the Ninth, Warlord of the Barakas, Suzerain of Ombaraka, Commander-in-chief of the Wind Warriors and Ruler of the Plains, looked up at his chief counsellor with tears streaming from red-rimmed eyes, and said:

'Mind your own business.'

'But, my lord – '

'Go and twiddle your hair! Out!'

So Counsellor Kemba retreated. And a little time later, the order went out to the helmsmen to set course for the north, and slowly the great mother craft lumbered round and began to roll towards the mountains.

As the sun came up on the new day, Kestrel climbed to the top of the highest watchtower on Ombaraka, and looked across the plains. It was a cool clear morning, and she could see for miles. There where the plains ended, she could make out the rising land, and the great forest that covered it. And not so far off now, on the horizon, the dark mass of the mountains.

As Kestrel stared at the land, she thought she saw beneath the dust of the plains and between the trees of the forest the outlines of a long-abandoned road, broad and straight, running towards the mountains. She had the map open before her, and there on it was the Great Way, broken by the jagged line called Crack-in-the-land. At the road's end, at exactly the point where the Great Way met the highest mountain, there were written the words that her father had told her said, *Into the Fire*.

The grateful people of Ombaraka gave their heroes a grand send-off; all but Counsellor Kemba, who was nowhere to be seen. Raka embraced them, one by one, with a specially close hug for Bowman.

'If ever you need our help,' he said, 'you have only to ask.'

Salimba came forward with three shoulder bags filled with food for their journey.

'I knew they weren't spies from the first,' he said. 'Didn't I do his braids?'

Then they were lowered to the ground, and all Ombaraka gathered to chant the victory call once more, as a final tribute. The cries resounding in their ears, the children headed for the nearby foothills, and the great forest. They turned back once, to wave farewell to their new friends, and stood for a moment watching as the great rolling city loosed its myriad sails and went creaking and rumbling back over the plains. A gust of wind tugged at their gold-braided hair, and made them shiver. The air was colder here, and ahead the land was dark.

17

THE HATH FAMILY FIGHTS BACK

'Where Bo?' said Pinpin. 'Where Kess?'

'They've gone to the mountains,' said Ira Hath, who did not believe in deceiving a child even as young as two. 'Lift up your arms.'

'Where Pa?'

'He's gone to study for his exam. Stand still while I do you up. It'll all be over soon.'

She examined the child with a critical eye. There had not been enough material in the bedspread to make complete robes for both of them, so for Pinpin she had just made a sleeveless tunic, which she put over her orange smock. Looking at them both now, she felt satisfied that this had been the right decision. To have mother and child in matching stripes would have been too much.

When they were both ready, she picked up the large

basket she had packed earlier, took Pinpin's hand, and went out into the passage. As they passed the doorway to the Mooths' room, she heard the door open a crack, and a sharp cry come from within.

'Oh! Look what she's done now!'

Three shocked faces appeared in the crack, to watch them make their way to the stairs.

Out in the street, their multi-coloured stripy appearance caused a sensation. The block warden, who happened to be passing, at once raised his hand high, blew his whistle, and called out:

'You can't do that!'

A man wheeling a cart laden with barrels turned to look, and not watching where he was going, wheeled the cart into a man carrying a basket on his head. The basket went flying, and the barrels tumbled off the cart. Out of the upturned basket fell a mass of small pink crabs, a delicacy much appreciated in White District. Two large women coming the other way, also staring at Ira and Pinpin Hath, fell over the runaway barrels, the larger of the two women crushing one barrel so completely that it burst open, spilling crude molasses on to the stone street. The block warden, hurrying forward to restore order, stepped into the molasses, strode on through the scurrying crabs, and fell headlong over the smaller of the large women. As he struggled to get up again, his flailing boots smeared her head with molasses, in which several small pink crabs had become stuck.

Pinpin saw all this with delight, as if it was a performance put on specially to entertain her. Ira Hath paid no attention whatsoever. Magnificently indifferent to the stares of her neighbours, the oaths of the warden, and the shrieks of the woman with crabs in her hair, she marched on down the street, and turned into the main avenue to the centre of the city.

As she strode along, her basket in one hand and Pinpin holding the other, she collected a little train of followers. They hung some way behind, and spoke to each other in whispers, as if afraid she would hear. Ira Hath found that she was almost enjoying herself. Being stripy gave her a kind of power.

As she passed into Maroon District, and then into her former home territory of Orange, her followers grew in number, until there were fifty and more people of various ranks trailing along behind her. As she entered Scarlet District she stopped unexpectedly, and turned to look at them. They all stopped too, and looked back at her in silence, like a herd of cows. She knew why they were following her, of course. They wanted to see her punished. There was nothing that excited people in Aramanth more than seeing fellow-citizens humiliated in public.

Something in those rows of sad blank eyes spoke to her, at an ancestral level, and the words rose to her mouth unbidden.

'O, unhappy people!' she cried. 'Tomorrow will bring

sorrow, but the day after will bring laughter! Prepare to mingle your colours!'

Then she turned and walked on, and they all came shuffling after her, murmuring among themselves.

Ira Hath walked tall, and felt the blood sing in her body. She liked being a wife and mother, but she had just discovered she liked being a prophetess more.

By the time she reached the plaza by the Imperial Palace, every idle person in Aramanth seemed to have joined the crowd. Strictly speaking, of course, there were no idle people in Aramanth, since the city made sure everyone had useful work to do. So the sight of the shuffling procession that trailed the brightly-striped mother and child past the College of Examiners was not a pleasing one to the city's governors.

On she strode, through the double row of marble columns, into the arena. Down the nine tiers she went, and the crowd followed her, to see what she would do next. In the centre of the great arena, at the foot of the wooden platform of the wind singer, she came to a stop. She hoisted her basket up on to the platform's base. Then she hoisted Pinpin after it. Then she clambered up herself. Once in position, she took a blanket out of her basket and spread it on the boards, and sat herself and Pinpin down. Out of the capacious basket came a bottle of lemonade and a bag of buns.

The crowd watched, all agape, for her next outrageous action.

'O, unhappy people!' cried the prophetess. 'The time has come to sit and eat buns!'

Which is what she did.

The crowd waited patiently, knowing there would be developments. After a while, a white-robed senior examiner appeared, followed by four marshals. The examiner, Dr Greeth, was responsible for the maintenance of order in the city. The sight of him stepping down the nine tiers, flanked by four huge marshals, sent shivers of anticipation through the crowd.

'Madam,' said Dr Greeth in his clear cutting voice. 'This is not a circus. You are not a clown. You will come down from there, and dress yourself in your designated clothing.'

'No, I won't,' said Ira Hath.

Dr Greeth nodded briskly to the marshals.

'Get her down!'

The prophetess rose to her full height and cried in her most prophetic voice.

'O, unhappy people! Watch now, and see that there is no freedom in Aramanth!'

'No freedom in Aramanth?' exclaimed Dr Greeth indignantly.

'I am Ira Hath, direct descendant of the prophet Ira Manth, and I have come to prophesy to the people!'

Dr Greeth signalled to the marshals to wait.

'Madam,' he said, speaking loudly so that all the people in the crowd could hear him. 'You are talking nonsense. You are fortunate enough to live in the only truly free society that has ever existed. In Aramanth, every man and woman is born equal, and has an equal chance to rise to the very highest position. There is no poverty here, or crime, or war. We have no need of prophets.'

'And yet,' cried the prophetess, 'you fear me!'

This was a clever move, as Dr Greeth at once realised. It would not look good if he were to overreact.

'You are mistaken, madam. We don't fear you. But we do find you a little noisy.'

The crowd laughed. Dr Greeth was satisfied. There was no need to use force, it would only bring the woman sympathy. Better to leave her on her perch until she grew cold and hungry, and came down of her own accord.

In the meantime, in order to reassert his authority, he ordered the marshals to disperse the crowd.

'Back to your work!' he cried. 'Let's leave her to prophesy what she's going to eat for dinner.'

Hanno Hath, shut away in the Residential Study Centre, did not learn of his wife's rebellion until the midday meal. The serving girls passed on the gossip in excited whispers, as they spooned vegetable stew into the candidates' bowls. A wild woman dressed as a clown was sitting on the wind singer, they said, telling everyone to be unhappy. Hanno recognised his wife's style at once, and felt a rush of pride and concern. He pressed the serving girls for more details.

Had the authorities tried to force the wild woman off the wind singer?

'Oh, no,' said the girl on the rice pudding. 'They come and have a good laugh like the rest of us.'

This both reassured Hanno, and hardened his resolve. The High Examination was now only two days away, and his own small act of rebellion was well advanced. Little by little, the other candidates had fallen in with his plan, until only one, a factory cleaner called Scooch, remained unconvinced. One accidental result was that the atmosphere of the Study Course had been transformed. The candidates who had stared so numbly at their revision books, and had listened to the Principal's lectures with defeat in their eyes, were now applying themselves eagerly to their exercises.

Principal Pillish too saw this with satisfaction. It seemed to him that the candidates were helping each other overcome their negative approach to examinations, and this augured very well for the results. He observed that the gentle soft-spoken Hanno Hath was the centre of this new enthusiasm. Curious to know what it was he had told his fellow-candidates, he called Hanno into his study for a private talk.

'I'm impressed, Hath,' he said. 'What's your secret?'

'Oh, it's very simple,' said Hanno. 'We have the time here to think about the real value of examinations. We've realised that what an examination does is test the best in us. So if we give it our best, well – whatever the result, we should be content to be judged by it.'

'Bravo!' cried Principal Pillish. 'This is a real turnaround. I don't mind telling you, Hath, that your file has you down as incurably negative in your attitudes. But this is excellent! Give it your best – quite so. I couldn't put it better myself.'

What Hanno Hath did not feel obliged to explain to the Principal was just how he and the other candidates proposed to give their best. The idea had come to Hanno while listening to Miko Mimilith talk about the different fabrics he handled. If Miko could only sit an exam on fabrics, he had thought, he would have no fears. This had been followed at once by a further thought. Miko's knowledge of fabrics is his special expertise, and his passion. Why is he tested on other subjects, at which he will only fail? Each of us should be tested on what we do best.

He had said as much to his new friends on the Study Course.

'That's all very well,' they said. 'But it's not going to happen.'

The High Examination contained over a hundred questions, of which they would be lucky to get even one on fabrics, or cloud formations.

'Ignore the questions on the paper,' said Hanno. 'Write about what you know best. Give them your best.'

'They'll just fail us.'

'They'll fail us anyway, even if we try to answer their questions.'

They all nodded. That was true enough. They were on the

Study Course precisely because they'd always failed before. Why should it be any different this time?

'So what's the point?' said Hanno, gently persisting. 'It's like giving tests in flying to fish. Let's each of us do what we're good at.'

'They'll hate it.'

'Let them. Do you want to sit in that arena and feel sick with panic for another four hours?'

That was what did it. Every one of them dreaded, almost more than the results, the long humiliation of the exam itself. Every hated detail had burned itself into their memories. The slow walk to the numbered desk. The scrape of a thousand chairs as they were pulled out. The rustle of a thousand exam papers as they were turned over. The smell of the fresh print. The dancing black letters on the paper, forming words that made no sense. The scratch-scratch-scratch of pens all round, as the clever candidates began their answers. The pad-pad-pad of soft shoes, as the supervising examiners passed down the rows. The panic need to begin writing, something, anything. The deep dull certainty that nothing you wrote would be right, or good, or beautiful. The slow drag of the hands on the clock. The spreading paralysis of despair.

Anything, anything, but that.

So one by one they joined Hanno Hath's secret rebellion. In their exercises, they practised writing papers on subjects of their own choosing. Monographs were in preparation on drainage systems, the growing of cabbages, and rope-jumping games. Miko Mimilith was working on the definitive classification of woollen weaves. Hanno Hath was tackling some problems in old Manth script. Only little Scooch wrote nothing. He sat hunched at his desk, staring at the wall.

'You must know something about something,' Hanno said.

'Well, I don't,' said Scooch. 'I don't know anything about anything. I just do what I'm told.'

'Isn't there something you like to do when your work is finished?'

'I like to sit down,' said Scooch.

Hanno Hath sighed.

'You have to write something,' he said. 'Why don't you just describe a typical day in your life?'

'How do you mean, describe?'

'Just start at the beginning, when you get out of bed, and write down what you do.'

'I eat breakfast. I go to work. I come home. I eat supper. I go to bed.'

'Right. Now all you have to do is add a little more detail. Maybe put down what you have for breakfast. What you see on your way to work.'

'It doesn't sound very interesting to me.'

'It's more interesting than looking at a wall.'

So Scooch settled down to describe his typical day. After an hour or so of steady work, he reached mid-morning in his description, and made a surprising discovery. When it was time for the candidates' own mid-morning break, he hurried over to Hanno Hath to tell him about it.

'I've found something I know about,' he said. 'I'm going to write about it in the High Examination.'

'That's wonderful,' said Hanno. 'What is it?'

'Tea-breaks.'

Scooch beamed at him, his face glowing with pride.

'I didn't realise till I started writing about my day, but what I love most in all the world is tea-breaks.'

He passed the next half-hour explaining to a patient Hanno Hath how he looked forward to his tea-break from the moment he started work. How his anticipation mounted as the time approached. How the laying down of his broom and the picking up of his flask of tea was a moment of almost perfect joy. How he breathed in the steam that rose from the flask as he removed its stopper, and poured the hot brown tea into his mug. How he unwrapped his three oat biscuits from their slippery greaseproof paper wrapping, and how, one by one, he dipped them into the hot tea. Ah, the dipping of the biscuits! This was the heart of the tea-break, the time of tension and gratification, the exercise of skill, and the encounter with the unknown. Sometimes, when he judged it right, he raised the sweet sodden biscuit to his mouth and consumed it intact, allowing it to crumble and melt on his tongue. Sometimes he dipped it for too long, or raised the biscuit too abruptly, or at too sharp an angle, and a large fragment fell off, and sank to the bottom of the mug. What made the tea-break so intense an experience was not knowing when or whether this would happen again.

'Really, you know,' said Hanno Hath thoughtfully, 'someone should find a way to make a biscuit that goes soggy when dipped in tea, but doesn't break.'

'Make a biscuit?' said Scooch, astonished. 'You mean, invent a different sort of biscuit altogether?'

'Yes,' said Hanno.

'Well, boggle me!' said Scooch; and he began to think. To be an inventor of biscuits! That would be something.

In this way, as in many others, with a mounting eagerness, inspired by Hanno Hath's gentle leadership, the candidates in the Residential Study Course prepared for the day of the High Examination. For the first time in their lives, whether it was wanted or not, they would be giving their best.

Ira Hath and Pinpin remained on the wind singer all night. It turned out that Ira had planned for this, and had brought extra food and blankets in the deep basket. She had even brought night clothes for Pinpin, and her special pillow.

When they were found to be still there in the morning, another crowd gathered, to laugh and jeer.

'Let's hear you prophesy, then!' they cried. 'Go on, say, O unhappy people!'

'O, unhappy people,' said Ira Hath.

She spoke rather more quietly than they liked, and

somehow it didn't sound so funny any more. Then again, soft and sad, she said:

'O, unhappy people. No poverty. No crime. No war. No kindness.'

This wasn't funny at all. The people in the crowd shuffled their feet and avoided each other's eyes. Then for a third time, most quietly of all, Ira Hath said:

'O, unhappy people. I hear your hearts crying, for want of kindness.'

No one ever said such things in Aramanth. The people heard her in shocked silence. Then they began to leave, in ones and twos, and Ira Hath knew she had proved herself a true prophetess, because none could bear to hear her speak.

The Board of Examiners raised the matter at their morning meeting. Dr Greeth continued to argue against intervention.

'The woman can't stay there much longer. Better to let everyone see how futile this kind of behaviour is. She'll realise it herself soon enough, and what will she do then? She'll climb down.'

Dr Greeth was rather pleased with this turn of phrase. It seemed to him to make the point with economy and precision. But the Chief Examiner didn't smile.

'I know this family,' he said. 'The father's an embittered failure. The mother is mad. The older children – well, one way or another they won't trouble us again. That leaves the infant.'

'I'm not quite clear,' said Dr Greeth, 'whether you are disagreeing with me or not.'

'I agree with your approach in principle,' replied Maslo Inch. 'In practice, we must have her out of there before the High Examination.'

'Oh, she'll be gone long before then.'

'And then there is the matter of reparation.'

'What exactly do you propose, Chief Examiner?'

'The conduct of this family has been an insult to the city of Aramanth. There must be a public apology.'

'She's a high-spirited woman,' said Dr Greeth doubtfully. 'A wilful woman.'

'High spirits can be brought low,' said the Chief Examiner, smiling his cold smile. 'Wilful spirits can be broken.'

18

CRACK-IN-THE-LAND

Now that the twins were on the ground, the Great Way, which Kestrel had seen so clearly from the high watchtower of Ombaraka, seemed to have hidden itself again. The low rising hills were scattered with mounds and ditches, and there were clumps of scrubby trees here and there, but no obvious broad avenue between them. Only the jagged mountains could still be seen on the horizon ahead, and it was towards these that they directed their steps.

Mumpo groaned as he walked. He had chewed too much tixa at the time of the battle, and now the inside of his head hurt and his mouth was dry, and he had that feeling where you want to be sick but never quite do it. Bowman and Kestrel were concerned at first, and very sympathetic. However, his complaining went on so long that after a while they became irritated, and Kestrel reverted to former habits.

'Oh, shut up, Mumpo.'

After that, as well as groaning, Mumpo started to cry. When he cried, his nose ran, and it was even harder to be sympathetic to him, because his upper lip was shiny with nose-dribble. Anyway, both Bowman and Kestrel had other matters on their minds. As the trees became more frequent, and their path lay more and more through shadowy glades, Kestrel was searching for signs of the Great Way, and Bowman was looking about him, fearful of possible danger. He knew he had an overactive imagination, and he didn't want to alarm the others if there was nothing there, but it seemed to him that they were being followed.

Then he saw something, or someone, ahead. He froze, pointing silently so the others could see. Through a clump of trees they could make out a huge figure, standing on some high perch, and staring towards them. Both Bowman and Kestrel had the same thought at the same time: giants. The Old Queen had said there were giants on the Great Way. For several long moments, they didn't move, and the giant didn't move. Then Mumpo sneezed, suddenly and loudly, and said:

'Sorry, Kess.'

The giant showed no signs of having heard. So they approached, cautiously at first, until as they cleared the clump of trees, their fears evaporated.

They were looking at a statue.

The figure was at least twice life-size, and very old, and very weather-beaten. It represented a robed man, raising one hand to point south: one arm, rather, for the hand was gone. As was the other arm, and much of the face. The figure stood on a high pedestal of stone, its edges worn smooth by wind and rain.

Not far off there was another pedestal, with another statue. Now that they understood what they were, they could make out more and more, forming a broad double line through the trees.

'Giants,' said Kestrel. 'To guide travellers down the Great Way. There must have been statues all down it, once.'

Confident now that they were on the right path, they pressed on towards the mountains. But soon Mumpo was snivelling and groaning again.

'Can't we sit down? I want to sit down. My head hurts.'

'Best if we keep moving,' said Bowman.

Mumpo started to howl.

'I want to go home,' he cried dismally.

'I'm sorry, Mumpo,' said Bowman, trying not to be too hard on him. 'We have to go on.'

'Why don't you ever wipe your nose?' said Kestrel.

'Because it just goes on running,' said Mumpo miserably.

When they had reached the forest proper, and there were tall trees on either side, they saw that they were indeed following what once had been a road. Some young saplings had seeded in the open space, but the really big old trees rose up high on either side of a broad avenue, just as they must have done in the far-off days of the Great Way. Satisfied that they were making progress, Kestrel said that they could stop for a short rest, and eat their food. Mumpo at once collapsed in a heap. Bowman divided up the bread and cheese, and they ate hungrily, in silence.

Kestrel watched Mumpo as they ate, and saw how his good spirits returned as his stomach was filled. It reminded her of Pinpin.

'You're just like a baby, Mumpo,' she said. 'You cry when you're hungry, like a baby. You sleep like a baby.'

'Is that wrong, Kess?' said Mumpo.

'Do you want to be like a baby?'

'I want to be whatever you want me to be,' said Mumpo simply.

'Oh, honestly. It's no use talking to you.'

'Sorry, Kess.'

'I really don't know how you managed to stay in Orange all these years.'

Bowman said quietly, 'That's because we've never asked him.'

Kestrel stared at her brother. It was true: she knew next to nothing about Mumpo. At school, he had always been the one who was odd, the one to avoid. Then when he had become her unwanted friend, she had found his affection irritating, and had not wanted to do anything to encourage it. In the course of their journey together she had come to think of him as a kind of wild animal, that had attached itself to her, and become almost a pet. But he was not an animal. He was a child, like herself.

'What happened to your father and mother, Mumpo?'

Mumpo was surprised at her question, but very happy to answer her.

'My mother died when I was little. And I haven't got a father.'

'Did he die too?'

'I'm not sure. I think I just haven't got one.'

'Everyone's got a father. At least for a while.'

'Well, I haven't.'

'Don't you want to know what happened to him?'

'No.'

'Why not?'

'I just don't.'

'If you haven't got a family,' said Bowman, 'how can you have a family rating?'

'How can you go to school in Orange District,' said Kestrel, 'even though – '

She caught Bowman's glance, and broke off.

'Even though I'm so stupid?'

He didn't seem at all offended.

'I've got an uncle. It's because of my uncle that I go to school in Orange District, even though I'm so stupid.'

Bowman felt a wave of sadness pass through him, and he shuddered as if it were his own.

'Do you hate school, Mumpo?' he asked.

'Oh, yes,' replied Mumpo simply. 'I don't understand

anything, and I'm always alone. So I'm always unhappy.'

The twins looked at him and remembered how they had laughed at him along with the others, and they felt ashamed.

'But it's all right now,' he said. 'I've got a friend now. Haven't I, Kess?'

'Yes,' said Kestrel. 'I'm your friend.'

Bowman loved Kestrel for saying that, even if she didn't mean it.

Love you, Kess.

'Who's your uncle, Mumpo?'

'I don't know. I've never seen him. He's very important, and has a very high rating. But I'm stupid, you see, so he doesn't want me in his family.'

'But that's horrible!'

'Oh, no, he's very good to me. Mrs Chirish is always telling me so. Only, if I was in his family, it would make his family rating much lower. So it's better that I lodge with Mrs Chirish.'

'Oh, Mumpo,' said Kestrel. 'What a bad, sad place Aramanth has become.'

'Do you think so, Kess? I thought only I thought that.'

Bowman wondered at Mumpo. The more he knew of him, the more, in a strange way, he admired him. There seemed to be no malice in him, or vanity. He accepted what each moment brought him, and never troubled himself with matters that were outside his control. Despite the unhappiness of his lonely life, he seemed to have been born incurably good-hearted: or perhaps the one had somehow led to the other, and the many cruelties he had known had taught him to be grateful for even the smallest kindness.

They had eaten now, and rested, and the day was wearing on, so they rose and continued on their journey. Mumpo was in much better heart, and it was in a new spirit of determination and fellow feeling that they marched up the ruins of the Great Way towards the mountains.

Their road ran straight enough, but all the time it was climbing, ascending the foothills of the larger mountain range ahead. Little by little, the trees grew taller on either side, and closer together, and as the sun dropped in the sky, the shadows deepened round them. They began to see or to imagine shapes moving between the trees, and the glint of watching eyes. They kept close together, and walked faster, and it seemed that the shapes loped alongside them, always just out of sight.

When dusk began to gather, they realised they would have to pass at least one night in the forest. They kept moving, but now as they went they looked about them for a suitable place to make camp. Mumpo was becoming tired, and cared very little where he lay down, so long as it was soon.

'What about here? Here's good.'

'What's good about it?'

'Between these big trees, then.'

'No, Mumpo. We need somewhere where we can't be seen.'

'Why? Who's looking for us?'

'I don't know. Probably nobody.'

But Mumpo got nervous after that, and kept jumping and looking round. Once he saw something, or thought he saw something, in the trees, and started to run round and round in a panic. Bowman had to catch him and hold him until he became quiet again.

'It's all right, Mumpo.'

'I saw eyes watching us! I did!'

'Yes, I've seen them too. So whatever it is, we mustn't let it hurt Kess.'

'You're right, Bo.' He became calmer at once. 'Kess is my friend.'

He still went on looking nervously into the trees, but after that, whenever he saw a shape moving, he shook his fist at it and cried:

'Come any nearer, I'll bash you!'

So they trudged on into the twilight, determined to cover as much ground as they could. And just when they had decided the time had come to stop, whether there was a suitable camping place or not, they saw looming ahead of them between the trees two tall stone pillars.

The pillars stood on either side of the old Great Way, marking the beginning of a long stone bridge across a ravine. On the far side, two more pillars stood, where the land began again: far away, two hundred yards or more. The bridge was in ruins. Its two walls, each one capped with a parapet, crossed the ravine on two lines of immense stone arches, twenty yards apart: but the entire middle of the bridge, what had once been the roadway, was gone. How had these twin rows of soaring arches survived without the support they had once given each other? For the gorge they had been built to cross was stupendous.

The three children came to a stop by the pillars, and gazed into the canyon. The ground dropped away before them in a series of steep rock faces, down and down into the twilight shadows, to a river far below. They could see it glinting as it rushed along, passing between the two centre arches that held the high bridge. The further side of the canyon rose up before them, higher than any sea cliff, its fissures sprouting grasses and scrubby bushes, and crazed and riven with fault lines. To either side of them, the jagged edge of the gorge ripped through the forest as far as the eye could see, like a great knife-wound in the world.

'Crack-in-the-land,' said Kestrel.

There was no way across the great rift except by the bridge: and the more they looked at the bridge, the less they wanted to cross it.

'It's crumbling,' said Bowman. 'It won't hold us.'

Eroded by a hundred winters, the masonry had crackled and broken away, leaving sloping shoulders of stone that looked friable and treacherous. Only the two parapets, cut from a more enduring stone, stood unbroken, forming a narrow but level cap to the remaining walls.

Kestrel went up to one parapet and felt its surface. It was firm to the touch. The top of the wall was about two feet wide, and it was flat. She looked along its length, all the way to the far pillars. It ran straight and level all the way.

'We can walk on the wall,' she said.

Bowman said nothing, but he was filled with terror at the narrowness of the parapet, and the dizzying drop below.

'Just don't look down,' said Kestrel, who knew what he would be thinking. 'Then it'll be no different from walking along a path.'

I can't do it, Kess.

'What about you, Mumpo? Can you walk on the wall to the other side?'

'If you go, Kess,' said Mumpo, 'I'll go too.'

I can't do it, Kess.

But even as he was sending his sister this fear-filled thought, there came a shuffling sound behind them, and an icy chill went through him. He turned slowly, dreading what he knew he would see. There they were, in a line, holding hands all across the Great Way. They advanced slowly and carefully, snickering as they came, like children playing a secret game; except that their laughter was deep and old.

'You have come a long way,' said their leader. 'But here we are again.'

Mumpo began to whimper with fear. Kestrel took one look at the line of old children, another at the long parapet, and said:

'Come on! Let's go.'

She jumped up on to the parapet and set off towards the far side. Mumpo followed her, calling out:

'Don't let them touch me, Kess!'

Bowman hesitated a little longer, but he knew he had no choice. So he drew a long breath, and climbed up on to the parapet. Moving with tense and careful steps, he followed after the other two.

For a few yards, the bridge wall ran over the broken edge of the gorge, and the drop below wasn't far at all. But suddenly the land fell away in a sheer cliff below them, and after that it was as if they were walking in mid-air. The daylight was now fading fast, but not fast enough, and when Bowman looked down, as he had sworn he would not, he could see the gleam of the river running like a silver thread so far below that it made his head go faint, and his body started to shake.

Kestrel stopped to look back, and saw that the old children had clambered up on to the parapet and were following them.

'Just keep walking,' she said. 'Remember, they're old, and can't go as fast as us. We'll be on the other side long before them.'

She pressed on, drawing the other two after her by sheer determination. Bowman, looking back, saw that she was right, and they were crossing the long bridge much faster than the old children. Several of them were now on the parapet, coming one behind the other, picking their way with slow care.

Kestrel stepped steadily on, one foot in front of the other, not looking down, not thinking about the gorge below, thinking, Halfway there, not much longer now, when she saw on the far side a sight that made her heart jump. Beside the pillars that marked the end of the bridge stood more old children, dozens of them. And as she came to a stop, and stared, they climbed up on to the parapet ahead and began to shuffle towards her.

Bo! They're at the other end!

Bowman looked, and saw, and understood, in a single flash of knowledge. This time there was no escape. The old children were advancing slowly from either end. Once they reached the middle, there was no way of fighting them off, because every touch brought weakness. He looked over the side, at the immense drop into the gathering darkness, and wondered what it would feel like to fall and fall, and then *smash!* to hit the rocks. Would the dying be quick?

Bo! We have to fight!

How?

I don't know. But I'm going to fight them.

He felt the familiar fury in her thoughts, which was oddly reassuring. He tried to think what they could do, but all the time the old children were shuffling nearer and nearer. At this point, Mumpo realised what was happening, and began to panic.

'Kess! Bo! They're coming to get us! Don't let them touch me! What shall we do? I don't want to be old!'

'Don't jump about, Mumpo! Stay still.'

'It's all right, Mumpo. They won't get past us.'

Remember, said Kestrel, *they're old and weak, and they can only come one at a time. All we have to do is keep them out of reach.*

'Without touching them,' said Bowman, answering aloud.

'Keep them away from me!' cried Mumpo, jerking from side to side in his fear. He tried to grab hold of Kestrel, and was threatening to unbalance them all.

'Stop it, Mumpo!'

How can we calm Mumpo down?

Feed him, replied Bowman.

Kestrel then realised she was still carrying her nut-socks round her neck, and that in one of the socks there was one mudnut remaining. She unhooked it and reached it out to Mumpo.

'Here you are, Mumpo.'

As she swung it towards him, she felt the weight of the mudnut, and letting it swing back, she set it circling round and round at the end of the sock. Her eyes followed the swinging weighted end.

'Bo!' she cried out. 'Have you got any mudnuts left?'

Bowman felt the nut-socks round his neck. One mudnut left in each. He had distributed the last two that way, for balance.

'Two,' he said.

'Here's how we keep them away from us,' said Kestrel, and she swung her weighted nut-sock through the air before her.

'Mudnuts won't hurt them.'

'They don't have to. All we have to do is knock them off balance.'

'Or us.'

'Remember, we're young and bendy. They're old and stiff.'

Not at all convinced, Bowman tried swinging his nut-sock round and round, and nearly fell off the wall. Heart pounding, sweat streaming down his body, he righted himself.

'It won't work. I can't do it.'

'You've got to,' said Kestrel.

'I'm hungry,' said Mumpo. In all this talk of mudnuts, he had forgotten his fear.

'Shut up, Mumpo.'

'All right, Kess.'

All this time, the two leading old children were still creeping towards them across the parapet, from either end of the bridge. Others followed steadily behind them. The ones on Bowman's side were the nearest, and would have to be fought off first.

'Swing it round, Bo,' called Kestrel. 'Get your balance.' Bowman looked down and saw beneath him now only inky blackness. I wouldn't mind, if there wasn't that great drop below, he thought. And as he stared down, a simple idea popped into his head. It's all dark down there. It can be anything I want. So he stopped imagining the great drop, and built a new picture in his head. There's no Crack-in-the-land, he told himself. Just a little way below me there's soft meadow grass. He added some details to this picture: clover, and poppies, and, to be real, a clump of stinging nettles, and he found to his surprise that his fear of falling was gone. That left the old child, shuffling ever closer on the wall.

He swung his nut-sock round, holding it above his head so that it made horizontal circles in the air. He swung it faster, giving it extra power each time it passed in front of him. He imagined the position of the old child's head, and he swung the mudnut through the air just where it would soon be.

Soft grass, soft meadow grass, he said to himself. Soft cushiony grass.

'Be careful, boy,' said the old child, in his creaky voice. 'Here, take my hand.'

He reached out his withered hand and snickered. But he wasn't close enough yet.

Kestrel was facing the other way, her nut-sock in her hand, watching the leading old child approaching from her side.

It's going to be you first, Bo. Can you do it?
I'll try.
Love you, Bo.

No time to answer, not even in the silence of his head. The old child was close now, his hand patting the air between them. Bowman swung his mudnut, still holding his arm back, and it hissed through the air some way from his attacker.

'Why struggle?' said the old child. 'It's as the Morah wills. You know that.'

Bowman said nothing. He flexed his legs, and tested his balance on the narrow parapet. He swung the weighted nut-sock faster and faster, and gauged the distance between them.

'You mustn't be afraid to be old,' murmured the old child. 'It's only for a little while. And then the Morah will make you young again, and beautiful.'

He kept shuffling forward as he spoke, and now Bowman calculated he was within range. But he had to be sure.

'There, there,' said the old child. 'Come and let me stroke you.'

Bowman swept his arm forward over his head, swung the mudnut at full power, and aimed for the grizzled head.

Wheee!

It whistled harmlessly past, meeting no resistance. Bowman tottered and almost fell. The old child had ducked.

'Oh, dear, dear,' the deep voice sniggered. 'Be careful, boy. You wouldn't want to – '

Bowman swung again, made bold by anger, and hammered the weighted sock *smack!* into the old child's face, catching him full on the cheek, just below the ear.

'Yow! Yow-ow-ow!'

Clutching at his face, the old child rocked on the wall, and lost his balance. His arms reached for support, but there was nothing. He beat the air, as if to hold himself up, but even as he did so, he fell.

'Aaa-aaah . . .'

The thin voice, keen with terror, shrieked as he fell, and went on shrieking, down and down and down. And still they could hear that ghastly scream, dropping and dropping, until at last it ceased.

Hubba hubba hubba Bo! cried Kestrel.

Nut-sock flying, she ran at her own attacker, and swept him too off the parapet and into the great gorge.

This galvanised the old children, and uttering creaking cries of vengeance, they pushed in on Bowman and Kestrel from either side. But only one could come forward at a time, and as Kestrel had foreseen, their reactions were slower and their joints were stiffer, and the twins sent them tumbling, one after another, into the inky darkness.

Kestrel exulted as she swung her weapon.

'Come on, you wrinkly old pocksicker! You want to practise sky-diving too?'

'Hit him, Kess!' cried Mumpo, bouncing with excitement. 'Knock him off!'

Kestrel lunged forward and struck, and another old child fell shrieking into the void. Mumpo called after him.

'You're going to go smash! Smish-smosh-smash and bashed flat, yah-de-dah, stupid stinky no-friends!'

After seven of the old children had been sent tumbling from the wall, they stopped shuffling forward, and murmured among themselves. Then turning with nervous care, they faced the other way, and shuffled back to their companions on either side of the gorge. They had retreated.

The twins saw this, and raised their arms in the air and cheered in triumph. Bowman especially was flushed with a fierce and unaccustomed pride.

'We did it! We beat them!'

'They won't come near us again!' cried Mumpo.

But the old children hadn't gone far. They climbed down from the parapet at either end, and there they stayed. Mumpo may have believed that their victory made them safe, but Kestrel and Bowman knew otherwise. They knew that on the land, where the old children could cluster round them as they had done before, a swinging nut-sock would never save them.

Once again, they were trapped.

'Chase them, Kess!' cried Mumpo. 'Bash them again!'

'I can't, Mumpo. There's too many.'

'Too many?'

He looked one way across the long bridge, peering into the night; and then the other.

'We have to stay here,' said Kestrel. 'At least until morning.'

'What, all night?'

'Yes, Mumpo. All night.'

'But Kess, we can't. There's no room to sleep.'

'We're not going to sleep, Mumpo.'

'Not sleep?'

To Mumpo, sleeping was as necessary and as unavoidable as eating. He wasn't so much dismayed as bewildered. How could he not sleep? Sleep wasn't something you chose. Sleep came upon you, and closed your eyes for you.

The twins knew this as well as Mumpo.

'Come on, Mumpo,' said Bowman. 'We'll sit either side of you, and if you want to sleep, you can.'

They sat down on the wall in a row, and Bowman and Kestrel held hands round Mumpo, who sat between them, and they both leaned inwards, to hold him in a double hug, just like a wish huddle. That way if he fell asleep they could stop him from rolling off the wall. Mumpo felt the close warm embrace of the twins, and was deeply happy.

'We're the three friends,' he said. And so great was his trust that he actually did fall asleep, sitting on two feet of stone wall, balanced half a mile above the granite gorge.

The twins did not sleep.

'We can't get away from them, can we?' said Bowman.

'I don't see how.'

'One of them said to me, Don't be afraid to be old. The Morah will make you young again.'

'I'd rather die!'

248

'We'll go together, won't we, Kess?'

'Always together.'

They fell silent. Then, after a while,

'What about ma and pa and Pinpin?' said Bowman. He was imagining what they would think if they never returned. 'They wouldn't know we were dead. They'd go on waiting for us.'

Somehow this picture of his parents still hoping, after they were dead, upset him more than the prospect of dying. Because they were in a kind of a wish huddle, he turned his dismay into a wish.

'I wish pa and ma could know what's happening to us.'

'I wish we could escape the old children,' said Kestrel, 'and find the voice of the wind singer, and get safely home.'

After that they were silent. The only sounds were Mumpo, snuffling in his sleep, and the sighing of the wind through the great gorge below.

And distant thunder.

'Did you hear that?'

A red flash lit up the sky, and faded away.

'Is it a storm?'

Again the roll of thunder. Again the burst of red light. This time they saw it: a jet of fire, far off, streaking skywards, and then curving down to earth.

'It's coming from the mountains.'

'Look, Kess! Look at the old children!'

Crash! went the thunder, and *flash!* went the fireball,

and as the arc of burning red was traced across the sky, and another, and another, the old children on both sides of the gorge were calling, and running about, and watching the falling fire.

Now the thunder was rolling all the time, and the fireballs were shooting skywards in all directions. Some of the burning fragments were falling close by. The twins saw one pass within a few yards of them, and drop down and down, a glowing ember, into the ravine below. Another fell to earth on the ground ahead, and burned for a moment, before fading into the night.

The old children were going wild. At first the twins thought it was fear, but then they saw how they were reaching their arms to the sky, and hurrying towards the fireballs as they sank to earth.

'They want to be hit!'

As Kestrel spoke these words, a fireball landed directly on one of the old children, and at once exploded in a gush of orange flame. The brilliant light faded as quickly as it had come, leaving behind – nothing.

The old children became frantic, running about, stretching up their arms, crying:

'Take me! Take me!'

And here and there, more by luck than by judgement, a fireball would fall on one of them, and he would be consumed.

The sky was now bright with fire, and the thunder

was unceasing. So many fireballs rose up that they could distinguish their source, which was the highest of the mountains in the northern range. The twins gazed at it, too awed by the spectacle to be frightened, and Mumpo slept stolidly on.

'That's where we have to go,' said Kestrel, looking at the mountain. 'Into the fire.'

The fireballs fell all around them, and they never moved, because they had nowhere to go. Somehow they knew they would be safe. This wasn't for them, this shower of death, they were only accidental witnesses. This was for the old children.

'Take me!' the old children cried, reaching for the fire. 'Make me young again!'

But when the flame took them, it left nothing.

Then the thunder began to fade, and the sky grew darker, as the fireballs came less and less frequently. The last few rose only a little way into the night, and fell far off. The remaining old children, crying pitifully, ran off towards them, as if they could cover the many miles before the flaming fragments fell to earth. And after a while, the mountain was silent, and the twins realised they were alone again.

They woke Mumpo gently, not wanting him to get up with a bounce and fall off the parapet. In fact, he remained half asleep, and did as he was told without really knowing where they were going. So feeling their way with care, they crossed to the other side of the gorge, and stepped down from the narrow parapet to the safety of solid ground.

Here Mumpo simply curled up and went back to sleep. The twins looked at each other, and realised how exhausted they were. Kestrel lay down.

'What if they come back?' said Bowman.

'I don't care,' said Kestrel, and she too fell asleep.

Bowman sat down on the rough scratchy ground and decided he would keep watch over the others. However, within moments he too was asleep.

19

MUMPO GOES WRONG

When the twins awoke, it was full daylight. There were no signs of the old children of the night before. They were lying close to the edge of the great gorge that they had only seen before in the half light of dusk. Now as they rose and stretched their aching limbs they saw the fearsome depth of the gorge, and the fragile thread of wall by which they had crossed it, and they were amazed.

'Did I really walk on that?' said Bowman.

Kestrel was looking down at the great stone arches that carried the bridge across the gorge. She could see now what had not been obvious the night before, that the supporting stonework was crumbling at many points. One of the columns that held up the arches was so worn at its base by the floodwaters of the river that it seemed to stand on a pin-point. But Kestrel said nothing to Bowman about this, knowing that they would have to return this way.

Mumpo now awoke, and announced that he was hungry.

'Look, Mumpo,' said Kestrel, showing him the spectacular sight of Crack-in-the-land. 'We crossed that great bridge!'

'Did we bring anything to eat?' said Mumpo.

Bowman found the nut-sock that he had used as a weapon against the old children, and pulled out the mudnut. It was heavily bruised, but better than nothing.

'Here you are.'

He tossed it towards Mumpo, but Mumpo missed it. It rolled over the sloping ground to the edge of the gorge. He chased after it, and saw where it disappeared over the edge. Kneeling on the edge, he peered down.

'I see it!' he cried. 'I can get it.'

'I've got another one,' said Bowman.

'Let him get it if he can,' said Kestrel. 'We need all the food we've got.'

They joined Mumpo at the edge, and saw where the mudnut was caught in a tussock of springy grass growing from the rock face. Just below it was a clump of bushes. Bowman backed away, made giddy by looking down the immense drop. Mumpo lay on his stomach and reached over the edge for the mudnut. He could almost touch it, but not quite. So he started to wriggle forward.

'Careful, Mumpo.'

But Mumpo was hungry, and his only thought was for the mudnut that lay before his eyes. He wriggled a little further, and his fingers touched it. But still he couldn't grasp it.

'Just a bit more,' he said, and wriggled again. His hand reached for the mudnut, just as his body started to slither over the edge.

'He-e-elp!' he cried, realising he couldn't stop himself.

Kestrel threw herself on to his legs, and wrapped herself tight round them.

'That's better,' said Mumpo, and dangling over the edge of Crack-in-the-land, his mind was back on his breakfast.

'Climb back!' called Kestrel. 'Back!'

'I'll just get the – '

His fingers were closing over the mudnut, when a withered bony hand shot out of the bush below, and seized his wrist.

'Aah! Aah! Help me!'

Mumpo jerked in terror, and Kestrel nearly lost hold of his legs.

'Bo! What's happening?'

Bowman forced himself to look over the edge, and saw there one of the old children, half supported by the bush, gripping tight to Mumpo's arm.

'Bash him, Mumpo!' Bowman screamed. 'Bite him!'

'What is it?' cried Kestrel, struggling to hold Mumpo, feeling the extra weight pulling him down.

'Help me,' came Mumpo's pitiful voice, changing as he spoke, growing deeper. 'Help me . . .'

'It's one of the old children,' said Bowman. He unhitched his second nut-sock, and trying not to look down at the giddy-making drop, he swung it over the edge. The weighted end brushed the old child harmlessly on the shoulder. At once he turned to look up at Bowman, and his wrinkled face contorted with hatred and rage.

'Babies!' he hissed. 'Silly little babies!'

That made Bowman look at him properly. He saw the thinning grey hair, the wizened cheeks, the scrawny neck: and he felt the hard dry longing in him, to hurt and to destroy. He raised the nut-sock high and he swung it hard, and he brought it down on the old child's upturned face.

'Aaah!' cried the old child, and released his grip on Mumpo's arm. Losing his hold, he slipped down into the bush. The bush juddered under his weight and gave way, and down he fell.

'Aaa-aa-aa-aa . . .'

They heard his cry all the way to the bottom, and they heard the distant sound as he struck the rocks.

Kestrel dragged Mumpo back from the edge, and then let go of him. Holding him made her feel weak. He lay there, not moving, groaning a little.

'Are you all right, Mumpo?'

His reply came in a deep cracking voice.

'I hurt all over.'

He tried to stand, but the effort was too much for him. He sat down again, breathing heavily.

'I've gone wrong, Kess.'

Kestrel and Bowman stared at him, trying to conceal their horror at what they saw. Mumpo's braided hair had gone grey, with the golden threads still plaited into it. His skin had gone wrinkly and baggy. His body was bent. He had turned into a little old man.

'It'll be all right, Mumpo,' said Kestrel, fighting back an impulse to cry. 'We'll make you all right again.'

'Am I ill, Kess?'

'Yes, a little. But we'll make you well again somehow.'

'My body hurts all over.'

He started to cry. Not the noisy howls of the Mumpo they knew, but a silent weary weeping, a few thin tears creeping down the deep wrinkles that had formed in his face.

What can we do?

We have to go on, Bowman replied. Aloud, he said to Mumpo, 'Can you walk?'

'I think so.'

He got up, more carefully this time, and took a few steps.

'I can't go fast.'

'That's all right. Just do your best.'

'Could you help me, Bo? If I could lean on you just a little, I could go faster.'

'You mustn't touch us, Mumpo. Not until you're better.'

'Not touch you? Why not?'

They realised then that he hadn't understood what had happened to him.

'So we don't catch your sickness.'

'Oh, I see. No, we don't want that. Will I be better soon?'

'Yes, Mumpo. Soon.'

So they turned their backs on Crack-in-the-land, and set off up the Great Way to the mountains.

It was pitifully slow going. Try as he might, Mumpo couldn't walk at a normal pace. He shuffled along, and then he had to stop and rest for a few minutes. Then he shuffled along again, making no complaint, so clearly trying as hard as he could. But it was plain to both the twins that they would never make it to the top of the mountain like this.

Mumpo was not their only concern. The forest on either side was changing. The route they were following, the overgrown avenue that had once been the Great Way, was itself clear of trees, but it was flanked by an ever-denser wall of deepening forest. And through the trees, just out of the light, there sometimes seemed to be shapes accompanying them, loping silently alongside, never running ahead, never falling behind. Bowman sensed their presence out of the corners of his eyes, but whenever he turned to look, there was nothing there.

Then there were the shadows overhead. They could see now that they were birds, circling high above the trees. At first they paid them no attention; but all the time they were descending, gliding noiselessly on great outreached wings. For a while there were no more than five or six of them, but when Bowman next looked up, he counted thirteen. When he looked up again, barely half an hour later, there were too many to count: a streaming flock of ominous black shapes trailing away into the high distance. Dim tales surfaced in his mind of wild animals following travellers, watching for stragglers, waiting for their strength to fail. He pressed on faster, increasing the pace.

'This is too hard for Mumpo,' said Kestrel. 'We have to slow down. We should rest.'

'No! We mustn't stop!'

Kestrel looked round sharply, hearing the fear in his voice.

'It's – all right,' said Mumpo. 'I'll – keep – up.' But he could hardly find the breath to speak these few words.

Bo, we can't do this.

What else can we do?

So they struggled on. The slower they went, the bolder the birds became. They were sailing lower now, at tree-top level, their great black wings casting shadows on the ground. They looked like eagles, except that they were black, and far bigger. Hard to judge just how big they were, up there above the trees.

Then Mumpo stumbled on some loose stones, and fell. He lay there, making no attempt to get up. Kestrel knelt down beside him to make sure he wasn't hurt; but he was only exhausted.

'He has to rest, Bo. Whether we want it or not.'

Bowman could see that she was right.

'He'll feel better after he's had something to eat.'

He swung down his nut-socks and took out his last remaining mudnut. He was reaching it out to Kestrel to give to Mumpo, when he felt a sudden rush of wind, a swish of darkness, and a sharp painful blow to his hand.

Bowman cried out, more in surprise than pain, and clutched his hand. Blood trickled out between his fingers. The black eagle was already powering away, beating its immense wings, the mudnut clutched in the razor-sharp talons that had sliced his skin in four clean shallow lines. He looked up in sheer shock at the size of the bird. There were three more of them, hovering low above them, waiting for more food to come out of the sock. Their wingspan was so huge that the three of them, side by side, shaded the whole broad avenue.

Mumpo lay staring up at the giant eagles, his eyes wide with terror, his heart pumping. Instinctively, Kestrel had put her arms over him, as if to protect him. The birds were dropping ever lower, looking for food.

'Throw it away, Bo!' shouted Kestrel.

Bowman hurled the nut-sock as far away as he could. At once, a giant eagle swooped, and snatched up the sock, and sailed up to the tree-tops. And the others, so many of them, went on circling silently overhead, watching, waiting.

Because the children's eyes were on the sky, they didn't see the first beast come padding silently out from between the trees; or the second. The beasts could smell Bowman's blood: the smell of wounding, and weakness. They came quietly out of the forest, one by one, and stood there, yellow eyes staring. It was Mumpo who saw them first.

He screamed.

Bowman turned quickly: and froze. All round them, some twenty yards away, stood a ring of huge grey wolves. Lean and shaggy-coated, as big as deer, their immense jaws hung open, their tongues lolling out, as they panted softly, and stared.

'It's all right, Mumpo,' said Kestrel, hardly thinking what she was saying, just to stop him screaming.

The black eagles circled lower once more, expecting a kill. Their great wings, overlapping each other, cast all the broad avenue now into shadow, as if night was falling. The wolves padded nearer, and stopped again. Waiting to see if their prey would turn and fight.

Mumpo's scream became his familiar fearful whimpering; only now he sobbed with an old man's voice.

'Don't let them get me,' he croaked.

Now they could feel the rush of the air as the eagles swept by overhead, and they could smell the hot wet smell of the wolves' pelts. Motionless, huddled together in their terror, the children saw the wolves bare their teeth, slick and sharp and creamy-white, and pad closer still.

Then there came a sound from the trees, a long baying call. At once the wolves came to a stop. The great eagles, who had been dropping lower with each circling pass, began to climb again. The baying call sounded once more, mournful and strong, and the wolves turned and looked expectantly into the forest.

Out of the trees, stepping slowly, came a huge grizzled old wolf, the biggest of them all. His every movement spoke of power and authority, but he was old now, and with each breath there came a low sighing rumble from his broad chest. As big as a stag, but lean and sinewy for all his age, he came stepping out of the trees, and his yellow eyes were on Bowman all the way.

Bowman never flinched. The other wolves parted to make way for their leader, and the father of the pack padded forward until he was towering over the boy. Then his long shaggy body rippled, and he sank down on to his haunches; and from there into a prone position. He laid his head on his outstretched paws, and his eyes gazed steadily at Bowman. The other wolves followed their leader's example, until the entire pack was lying down, all round the three children, panting softly.

Bowman then realised he knew what it was he must do. He held out his bleeding hand, and the father of the wolves lifted his grey muzzle, and smelled it. Then out came the long pink tongue, and licked away the blood.

Bowman sat himself slowly down on the ground, with his legs crossed, and the wolf rested its head in his lap. Its eyes looked up at the boy, and as much as man and beast can, they understood each other.

'They've been waiting for us,' said Bowman, wondering how he knew the wolf's mind.

'What for?'

'To fight the Morah.'

As he spoke this name, a ripple ran through the wolves, like a cold wind passing, making their shaggy fur shiver. The father of the pack rose up on to his haunches, and all the others followed suit. The old wolf then lifted up his head high and gave another mournful baying call.

The great eagles circling overhead heard the call, and they began to descend, lower and lower, until they were passing so close that their wing-tips seemed to brush the children's heads. Then one by one they landed, to stand round the wolves in a second guardian ring.

Bowman looked into the black eyes of the eagles and the yellow eyes of the wolves and saw their pride and their courage.

We have waited a long time. Now we will face the ancient enemy at last.

'They'll help us,' he said. He rose to his feet, and all the wolves rose.

'Now it's time to go.'

Kestrel and Mumpo obeyed him without question, accepting that he knew things they could never know. The eagles unfurled their wings and took to the air; and children and beasts continued up the Great Way towards the mountains.

Mumpo moved slowly, his weary old bones dragging him down. The twins kept to his pace, knowing how afraid he was of being left behind. But after a little while, the time came when he knew he could go no further. He sat down on the ground, and began to cry.

'Don't leave me,' he said as he wept.

The father of the wolves saw and understood. Shortly a strong young wolf was loping forward to lie beside Mumpo.

'Climb on his back, Mumpo. He'll carry you.'

They dared not help him, but after an awkward scramble, Mumpo got himself up on to the wolf's back, and there gripped on tight to the shaggy coat. The journey was now resumed at a good steady pace, and they began to make progress towards the distant mountain.

In time the twins too became tired, and the wolves took them on their backs. Now for the first time they were free to leave the open track of the Great Way, and follow the wolf-trails through the trees. And so, all three riding, they covered the ground far more swiftly, while the great eagles flew overhead, and their escort of wolves ran on either side, and all they could see round them were the shadowy vaults of the forest.

They were now on the higher slopes of the mountains, where the air was cold, and a mist lingered in the topmost branches of the tall pines. The trees became sparser, and when they looked back they could see the great number of wolves that had joined them, streaming away behind them as far as the eyes could see; while overhead flew hundreds and hundreds of eagles.

Ahead now loomed the mountain towards which they had been journeying. It seemed so immense, its flattened peak so impossibly high, that they couldn't see how they could ever reach it, even at the speed of the running wolves. What was worse, it proved to be even further away than they supposed, for as they came over a ridge they saw a tree-covered valley dip away before them, and realised they hadn't even begun to ascend the main peak.

The trail curved here as it descended, and passed out of sight round the ridge. The wolves carrying the children ran slower now, and then walked, while the eagles above began dropping down, circling to land. As they reached the bend in the trail, the wolves came to a complete stop, and lay down. It was evident that they wanted the children to dismount. As they did so, the eagles landed in their hundreds, all over the ground and in the trees.

Kestrel looked to Bowman to know what they were to do next, but he had no idea. It was Mumpo who now took the lead.

To the surprise of the twins, as soon as he was standing, he started to move, shuffling down the trail as fast as he was able, impelled by some inexplicable urgency.

'Mumpo! Wait!'

He didn't hear them. He was reaching his arms forward as he went, as if to come all the sooner to whatever it was that drew him on. Bowman turned to look at the great army of the wolves. They sat or lay, tongues out and panting, eyes on the father of the pack. He for his part sat with raised head, sniffing the wind, waiting. Bowman smelled the air.

'Smoke.'

'We can't lose him.'

So they set off after Mumpo, who was now out of sight. And as they too rounded the bend in the trail, they saw before them an extraordinary sight. There below them lay the Great Way once more, broad and open, and down it were moving many figures, Mumpo now among them. Like Mumpo, they had their arms outstretched, and they were stooping, and they hobbled as they went. Mumpo was some way ahead of them, and almost running. He groaned and panted as he ran, calling out in his old man's voice.

'Take me!' he cried. 'Take me!'

He was running towards the source of the smoke, where the Great Way ran into the mountainside: into a rift as wide as the road, that was filled with fire. The flames climbed high and became smoke, and the smoke streamed out into the open air above. Down the Great Way towards this gate of fire, ahead of Mumpo and behind him, moved the other stooping figures, their arms outstretched like his, not all children, but all old; and from their mouths came the same cry, as they neared the flames.

'Take me! Make me young again!'

Mumpo was truly running now, jerkily and with difficulty, but as if his life depended on it.

'Mumpo! No!'

Kestrel started after him, but he was too far ahead, and he didn't seem to hear her. He was running directly towards the fire. The other old people were all doing the same: the nearer they got to the flames, the faster they hurried, as if eager for death. When they reached the fire, they let their outreached arms drop, and they walked into the flames, without visible fear or pain. What happened to them then Kestrel couldn't see, because they were lost in the brightness of the fire.

Bowman caught up with her, and stood by her side. In silence, they stared at the towering crack in the mountain, and the belching smoke. They stared as Mumpo ran stumbling and calling towards the flames.

'Take me! Make me young again!'

Then the pitiful cry fell silent, and his clumsy gallop was slowed to a hobbling walk, and he too was swallowed by the fire.

For a moment longer, the twins were silent, in shock. Then Kestrel felt for her brother's hand.

We must go into the fire.

We go together, he said, knowing this was how it had to be.

Always together.

So hand in hand they walked down the last of the Great Way towards the flames.

20

INTO THE FIRE

As they approached the great rift in the mountain, the twins felt the fierce heat of the fire, and smelled its acrid rising smoke. Why did the old people have no fear? How could they step so eagerly into its very heart and never cry out? But on they walked towards the fire, only revealing their fear by the tightness with which they held hands.

When the glare was too bright, they closed their eyes. The heat was strong, but not burning. The sounds of the outer world, of the mountains and the forest, were slipping away into silence. Even their own shoes, resolutely treading towards the furnace, seemed now to make no sound.

No going back now. Just a few more steps . . .

All at once, the heat faded away, to be replaced by a soft coolness that seemed to lick about them. The brightness was still dazzling, blinding their closed eyes with blood-red light.

But even without seeing it, they knew they had entered the fire, and were being bathed in cool flame.

On they walked, unharmed, and the dazzling light became less intense, and the cool caress fell away. Then little by little they sensed that the light was fading. Opening their eyes, they saw that the flames were fainter now. And within a few more paces, they were out of the fire entirely, and into a realm of shadow. Though where they were was hard to say.

As their eyes adjusted to the darkness, they made out the walls of a broad passage, with doors at its far end. The walls were timber panelled, and the floor was tiled. They seemed to be in the hallway of a grand mansion.

Looking back, they had another surprise. There was the fire behind them, but it was no more than a coal fire, burning in a well-kept grate, within a carved stone fireplace. Had they just walked out of that?

The long hallway ran from the fireplace at one end to the doors at the other. It had no windows. There was only one way to go.

Still hand in hand, beyond amazement, they made their way down the hallway to the closed double doors at the far end. Bowman tried the handles, and found the doors were not locked. He eased one open a crack, and looked through. Another hallway.

This hallway, an extension of the first, had many rooms opening off it on either side. It was candle-lit, and more ornately decorated. The dark wood panelling was carved in patterns of leaves and flowers. There were tapestries hanging between the many doors, faded scenes of hunting, and archery. Down the centre of the passage ran a finely woven carpet.

The twins made their way down this carpet, looking through the open doors to the right and left as they went. They caught glimpses of darkened sitting-rooms, the furniture all draped in dust sheets.

They moved as quietly as they could, fearful of what they might find. Although there was nothing to tell them so, they were directing their steps towards the far end of the hallway, which as before was closed with double doors. As they drew closer, they saw that unlike the other rooms they were passing, which were dark, there was a glow of light beneath the end doors.

They heard nothing as they went but the beating of their own hearts. The mansion, if mansion it was, seemed to be deserted. Yet candles burned in sconces along the passage walls, and the carpet over which they walked was well swept.

When they reached the end doors, they stood close by them and listened. There were no sounds. Softly, Kestrel turned one handle, and opened one door. The hinges gave a slight creak. They froze. But nothing happened, no footsteps, no calling voices. So she opened the door all the way, and they entered the room beyond.

It was a dining-room, and it was laid for dinner. A handsome dining-table stood in the middle of the room, gleaming with silver and crystal. Places were set for twelve. The candles on the two branched candelabra were burning, as were the candles in the great chandelier that hung above. There was water in the crystal water jugs and bread in the silver bread baskets. Coal fires burned in two elegant fireplaces, one on each side of the room. Portraits hung on the windowless walls, haughty images of lords and ladies of the distant past. There was only one other door, and that was facing them, at the far end. It was closed.

None of this was as the twins had imagined. They had hardly known what to expect, except that it would make them feel fear. This strange deserted grandeur was frightening, but not because it felt dangerous. The fear lay in not understanding. Because nothing they were now seeing made any sense, anything could happen. And there was nothing they could do to prepare themselves for it.

Stepping softly, they crossed the room, past the brocaded chairs lined up before the long glittering table, to the far door. Once again Kestrel paused, listened, and heard nothing. She opened the door.

A lady's dressing-room, lit by two oil lamps. Tall closets, their doors open, filled with beautiful gowns. Stacks of drawers, also pulled open, in which lay chemises and stockings and petticoats, all beautifully pressed and folded. And shoes, and slippers, and boots, in numberless array. On a dressmaker's dummy hung a ballgown in the process of being made, its seams held together by pins. Bolts of fine figured silk lay partly unrolled over a day-bed, and on an inlaid table were arranged all the tools of the dressmaker's art, the scissors and needles, the threads and buttons and braids. There was a tall pier-glass, in which they caught sight of their own reflections, pale-faced and nervous, eyes wide, hand in hand.

Two doors led out of the dressing-room, and both were open. One was to a bathroom: unlit and empty. The other led to a bedroom.

They stood very still in the dressing-room doorway, and looked into the bedroom. A lamp burned here too, on a low table beside a bed. The room was large and square. Trophies hung from its panelled walls: swords and helmets, flags and pennants, as if this were the mess-room of a regiment, proud of its battle history. But instead of leather club chairs and tables spread with newspapers, there was only the high ornate canopied bed, set right in the middle of the polished floor. The canopy was of gauze, suspended from a centre-ring in the ceiling, spread out like a diaphanous skirt to cover the entire bed. On the bedside table, beside the softly glowing lamp, stood a glass of water, and an orange on a plate. Beside the orange, a little silver knife. And in the bed, just visible through the gauze, beneath lace-edged linen sheets and embroidered coverlets, propped up in a sitting position by a mound of pillows, lay an old, old lady, fast asleep.

Very slowly, hardly daring to disturb the still air in which the old lady slept, the twins entered the bedroom. The wide boards made no sound beneath their feet, and they forced themselves to breathe in low even breaths. So, little by little, they came up to the bedside, and stood gazing at the old lady through the gauze; and still she slept.

Her face was calm and smooth in sleep, the outline of the bones showing clear through the papery skin. She looked as if she had been beautiful once, many years ago. Bowman gazed on her, and felt an almost unbearable longing, though for what he did not know.

Kestrel's eyes were darting round the room, to see if there was a cupboard or box that might contain the voice of the wind singer. It wasn't big, it could be anywhere: in this room, or one of the other rooms, or in some place they had not yet entered. For the first time Kestrel allowed herself to believe, with a deep dark lurch of fear, that they might fail. They might never find it. Her brother sensed the terror in her mind. Without taking his eyes off the sleeping old lady, he spoke silently to his sister.

It's there. In her hair.

Kestrel looked, and saw it. Holding back the old lady's fine white hair was a silver clasp, in the shape of a curled-over letter S: the shape of the outline etched on to the wind singer, and drawn on the back of the map. An intense relief, as sudden as the terror, streamed into her, bringing with it a renewal of strength and will.

Can you get it without waking her?

I'll try.

Bowman seemed to have lost his usual timidity; or to have forgotten it, in his fascination with that old, old face. Gently he reached out one hand, and with sure untrembling fingers took hold of the silver clasp. Holding his breath, so that his whole body was still, he drew the clasp slowly, slowly, out of the thinning white hair. Still the old lady slept on. Now, with the faintest shudder, the clasp came free, and in the glinting of the lamplight Bowman saw that across the curve of the S ran many fine threads of taut silver wire. He released his held breath, and lifted the clasp away. As he did so, he felt a sudden tug. A single white hair was snagged in the clasp, and as he lifted it, the hair strained tight, and snapped.

Bowman froze. Kestrel reached for the silver clasp that was the voice of the wind singer and took it from his outstretched hand.

Let's go!

But Bowman's eyes were on the old lady. Her eyelids were flickering and opening. Pale, pale blue eyes gazed up at him.

'Why do you wake me, child?'

Her voice was low and mild. Bowman tried to look away from those eyes, but he could not.

Bo! Let's go!

I can't.

As Bowman gazed into those watery blue eyes, he saw

them change. In her eyes there were other eyes, many eyes, hundreds of eyes, staring back at him. The eyes drew him in, and in each he saw more eyes, and more, so that there was no end to them. As he looked, he felt a new spirit flood his body, a spirit that was bright and pure and powerful.

We are the Morah, said the million eyes to him. *We are legion. We are all.*

'There, now,' said the voice of the old lady. 'Not afraid any more.'

As she spoke the words, he knew they were true. What was there to fear? So long as he looked into the million eyes, he was part of the greatest power in existence. No more fear now. Let others fear.

From far off he heard the sound of distant music: drums, pipes, trumpets. The unmistakable sound of a marching band, accompanied by the tramp of marching feet.

'Bo!' cried Kestrel aloud in her fear. 'Come away!'

But Bowman could not remove his gaze from those pale blue eyes in which he was joined to the legion that was the Morah; nor did he want to. The sound of marching feet was coming nearer, led by its jaunty band.

'They're coming now,' said the old lady. 'I can't stop them now.'

Kestrel took his arm and pulled at it, but he was unexpectedly strong, and she couldn't move him. 'Bo! Come away!'

'My beautiful Zars,' murmured the old lady. 'They do so love to kill.'

To kill! thought Bowman, and felt a thrill of power course through him. *To kill!*

He looked up, and there before him on the wall hung a fine curving sword.

Tramp! Tramp! Tramp! came the sound of the approaching marchers.

'Take the sword,' said the old lady.

'No!' cried Kestrel.

Bowman reached up and took the sword from the wall, and the handle felt good in his right hand, and the blade felt light but deadly. Kestrel stepped back from him, frightened, and it was well that she did, for all at once he turned, smiling a smile she had never seen before, and slashed with his sword across the space where she had stood.

'Kill!' he said.

Oh my brother! What has she done to you?

Tramp! Tramp! Tramp!

The beat of the drums, the blare of the trumpets. Kestrel looked and in her terror saw that the bedroom walls were fading away into darkness. The dressing-room door, the trophy-laden walls, were disappearing, until all that was left was the canopied bed, and the table beside it, and the lamp, reaching out its soft light in a circle of illumination. Beyond that, a black void.

Tramp! Tramp! Tramp!

'No more fear,' said the old lady. 'Let others fear now.'
Kestrel was backing away from Bowman, terrified, even as
she called out to him.

My Bo! My brother! Come back to me!

'Kill!' he said, slashing the air with his sword. 'Let others
fear now!'

'My beautiful Zars march again,' said the old lady. 'Oh,
how they love to kill.'

'Kill, kill, kill, kill!' said Bowman, singing the words to
a jaunty tune: the tune played by the marching band. 'Kill,
kill, kill!'

My dear one, called Kestrel, her heart breaking, *don't
leave me now, I can't live without you –*

And now at last, out of the darkness they came. In the
lead, twirling a golden baton, high-stepped a tall beautiful
girl in a crisp white uniform. Long golden hair flowed
freely over her shoulders, framing her lovely young face.
She looked no older than fifteen, and as she marched and
twirled her baton, she smiled. How she smiled! The white
jacket was square-shouldered and tight at the waist, with
big golden buttons. She wore spotless white riding britches,
and gleaming black boots. On her head, set at a jaunty
angle, was a white peaked cap, braided with gold, and over
her shoulders flowed a long white cape, lined with gold. She
gazed straight ahead of her, into the high distance, and she
smiled as she marched.

Behind her, out of the darkness, came a line of bandsmen,

all uniformed in white. They too were young, boys and girls of thirteen, fourteen, fifteen, and every one of them was beautiful, and every one of them was smiling. They marched briskly, keeping excellent time, playing their instruments as they came. Behind them were more bandsmen, followed by a rank of drummers. And behind them, singing as they smiled and swung along, came rank upon rank of youthful soldiers.

Kestrel heard the singing voices, and slowly the shape of the words penetrated her shocked senses. These beautiful boys and girls, this army of white and golden youth, were singing the same song as Bowman, the song that had only one word.

'Kill, kill, kill, kill! Kill, kill, kill!'

The tune was martial but melodic, and the melody, once heard, was impossible to forget. It swung up and down, and back up to its climax; and then round it came again, relentless.

'Kill, kill, kill, kill! Kill, kill, kill!'

The ranks of soldiers came on, line after line, out of the darkness. How many were there? The numbers seemed limitless.

'My beautiful Zars,' said the old lady. 'Nothing can stop them now.'

The baton-twirling band leader now came to a stop, but continued marching on the spot. Behind her the band, still playing, formed up in broad ranks, also marching on the spot. And behind them, the soldiers. The singing ceased, but the music and the steady tramping went on: though now the great army did not advance. At the rear, far away in the darkness where the lamplight didn't reach, more lines of soldiers were coming forward all the time, to join the waiting ranks. All were young, all were beautiful, and all were smiling.

Kestrel was backing further and further away all the time, in the direction of the passages and the fire. She still clutched the silver voice tight in one hand, but she had forgotten it entirely. She was weeping, also without knowing it. For her eyes were on her beloved brother, who she loved even more than she loved herself, and her young heart was breaking.

My brother! My love! Come back to me!

Bowman didn't hear her, or look at her, he was so changed. He was moving into position in front of the great army, and his sword was sweeping the air, and on his face was the same terrible smile that was on all their faces. Then in the ranks behind, even as she wept, Kestrel saw another familiar face transformed. It was Mumpo, wearing the white-and-gold uniform of the Zars, and he wasn't old any more, and he wasn't dirty. He was young, and handsome, and smiling with pride. As she stared at him, he caught her eyes and waved at her.

'I've got friends, Kess!' he called to her joyously. 'Look at all my friends!'

'No!' screamed Kestrel. 'No! No! NO!'

But her screams were drowned, as Bowman raised his sword high, and with a long rippling flash all the Zars drew their swords, and the army began to march. The beautiful baton-twirler came high-stepping behind Bowman, and the bandsmen and the drummers played, smiling into the distance, and the soldiers sang as they marched.

'Kill, kill, kill, kill! Kill, kill, kill!'

Kestrel turned and weeping, she ran for her life. When the column of Zars reached the canopied bed, they parted to either side of it. Their drawn swords flashed as they marched, slicing the orange on its silver plate, slashing the canopy to ribbons, sending fragments of gauze floating in the air. One fragment landed in the bowl of the lamp, and caught fire. In a moment, the whole bed was ablaze. Still the Zars marched on, unswerving, their handsome young faces briefly illuminated by the burning bed. And in the bed, the old lady lay motionless, raised on burning pillows, and watched the army pass in pride.

Kestrel ran weeping down the Halls of the Morah, the silver voice in her hand. Behind her came the Zars, destroying everything in their path. The elegant clothes laid out in the dressing-room, the dining-table laid for company that never came, all fell to the flashing swords and turned to dust.

Oh my brother, my dear love, my own!

Kestrel cried out in her heartbreak as she ran in her terror, until she saw before her the stone fireplace, where burned the fire in its grate. Behind her the marching tramp of a million feet, the singing of a million voices. No time to question or to understand. Without slowing down in her headlong flight, she hurled herself into the fireplace, and –

Silence. Cool columns of flame. Dazzling brightness. Panting, shaking, she forced herself to stop. The eerie cold of the fire cleared her head, and she knew this was not what she wanted to do. Why was she running from her twin? For her, there was no life without him. If he was changed, then she would change too.

Not like this, she thought. *We go together*.

She turned, and there in the white light she saw her beloved brother coming towards her, at the head of the army of the Zars. He was moving slowly, and the sound of the music seemed far away, but he was still singing softly, as were they all, a smiling whisper as they came.

'Kill, kill, kill, kill! Kill, kill, kill!'

Kestrel raised her eyes to meet his, and opened her arms wide, so that his sword, which rose and fell before him as he marched, would strike her across the breast.

We go together, my brother, she said to him. *Even if you have to kill me*.

His eyes found her now. He was still smiling, but the words of the song faded on his lips.

I won't leave you, she said to him. *I'll never leave you again*.

He was closer now, the sword still rising and falling before him.

I love you, she said to him. *My beloved brother*.

Now the smile too was fading, and the sword rising and falling more slowly. He was very close to her, and could see the tears on her cheeks.

Kill me, dear one. Let's go together.

His eyes filled with confusion. His sword was raised now, and he had reached her. One more downward stroke would cut her through. But the blow never fell. He stopped, and stood there, motionless.

The beautiful band leader came high-stepping right past them without so much as a sideways glance. So too the lines of bandsmen and drummers, playing away, smiling into the chill of the flames. Bowman's eyes were locked on Kestrel's, and she could see him returning, the brother she had lost, like a diver rising from the deep.

Kess, he said, recognising her. And the sword fell from his hand. He took her in his arms and hugged her, as the army of the Zars marched singing past them.

Oh, Kess . . .

He was shaking now, and weeping. She kissed his wet cheeks.

There, she said, *there. You've come back*.

21

THE MARCH OF THE ZARS

Seizing his sister's hand, Bowman ran through the cool white flames, and Kestrel ran with him. There was no time to talk of what had happened. They overtook the leader of the band, who still paid them no attention, as if the fire through which they passed held everything in suspension. Then suddenly they were out of the fire, and there were the forest-clad mountains rising on either side, and the wind in their faces, and the broad sweep of the Great Way before them, and dark clouds above.

Not clouds: Kestrel looked up and saw them. The eagles were circling in their hundreds, darkening the sky. She pulled Bowman off the road, into the trees.

'They're going to attack!'

The great eagles swept lower and lower, the beat of their powerful wings shivering the branches of the trees. And there, standing silently between the trees, yellow eyes on the gate of fire, were line upon line of grey wolves.

The beautiful young band leader came strutting out of the fire, her baton flying high, and after her the band, playing their jaunty music. As the columns of the Zars followed them eight abreast on to the Great Way, the eagles folded their wings and dropped like thunderbolts, screaming out of the sky. They spread their wings again at the last moment, as the giant talons struck. The claws took hold, and up they powered, white-and-gold bodies twitching beneath, to release their victims high above the tallest tree-tops. Never once did the raptured Zars utter a single cry; never once did their comrades look up, or show fear. Eagle after eagle, wave after wave, ripped into the marching column, but each hole they tore in the ranks was immediately filled from behind, and still the Zars marched on. Their long swords were out, flashing and deadly, and many an eagle made its dive and never rose again. But more terrifying than the blows the Zars struck was their disregard of the blows they received. Not for one instant did they cease to smile as their comrades were hurled into oblivion. Not once did they miss a step. And still, unending, they marched out of the tunnel, a long unbroken line of white and gold.

Now the eagles were peeling away, and it was the turn of the wolves. The old wolf lifted up his head and gave a savage cry. From out of the trees, howling with blood-lust, the first lines of wolves fell on their enemy. The great jaws ripped into the Zars, rending bloody holes in the column, but the long swords were fast and deadly, and not one of the beasts rose up to attack again.

And so the battle raged. Now the eagles returned to the attack, and now the wolves: but always the marching lines reformed from behind, and the shining white-and-gold soldiers marched steadily onwards to the music of the band, tramping over the bodies of eagles and wolves, and the bodies of their dead and wounded comrades alike.

Tramp! Tramp! Tramp!

'Kill, kill, kill, kill! Kill, kill, kill!'

They never even stopped singing.

Bowman watched them with horror and fascination.

'They're marching to Aramanth,' he said. And turning to Kestrel, with fierce urgency, 'Do you have the voice?'

'Yes. I have it here.'

'We must go! We must get to Aramanth before them!'

He was ready to go there and then, to try to outrun the tireless Zars all the way home, but Kestrel held his arm.

'Look! There's Mumpo!'

In the midst of the battle, radiant with returned youth, his white-and-gold uniform spattered with blood, Mumpo marched with the Zars, smiling at the carnage on all sides.

'Go!' cried Bowman. 'We must go!'

'We can't leave him,' said Kestrel.

As he marched past, she dashed into the fray and caught hold of his arm, and dragged him out to the side. Half hypnotised by the music and the marching, he didn't at first realise what was happening.

'Kess! Look at all my friends, Kess!'

Kestrel and Bowman took him between them, and ran with him deeper into the trees. As they ran, a detachment of Zars broke away from the column in pursuit.

They ran until they were exhausted. Then Kestrel rounded on Mumpo.

'Listen to me, Mumpo. The Zars aren't your friends, they're your enemies. We're your friends. Either you go with them, or you go with us.'

Mumpo stared at her in confusion.

'Why can't we all go together?'

'Can't you see – 'In her frustration, she almost shook him.

'It's all right, Kess,' said Bowman. He took Mumpo's hands in his, and spoke to him softly.

'I know what it feels like, Mumpo. I felt it too. It feels like you're not alone and afraid any more. Like no one can ever hurt you again.'

'Yes, that's right, Bo.'

'We can't give you that feeling. But we've stood by you, and you've stood by us. Don't leave us now.'

Mumpo looked into Bowman's gentle eyes and slowly the dream of glory faded.

'Am I to be alone and afraid again, Bo?'

'Yes, Mumpo. I wish I could tell you we'll keep you safe, but I can't. We're not as strong as they are.'

Kestrel watched her brother speaking, and she marvelled at him. He sounded older, sadder, surer. Mumpo too, she saw it now, had been changed by all that had happened to him. He was confused, but he was no longer foolish.

'You were my first friends,' he said simply. 'I'll never leave you.'

The twins took him in their arms, both together, and there was just time for a hug of comradeship, before they saw the glint of white uniforms approaching through the trees. The Zars had not just followed them, as they very soon saw: they had encircled them. A dozen and more now closed in on the spot where they stood.

'Climb!' said Kestrel.

She jumped up into the spreading branches of the tree above, and started to climb. Bowman and Mumpo followed her. They climbed up and up, until they came out on to the topmost branches. From here they could see the Great Way, and the still-raging battle. The eagles were fewer now, and the wolves almost all exhausted. On a high rock, the grizzled father wolf stood, his long baying howl sending the last lines of wolves into the attack.

From their high tree, the children watched helplessly as the wolves made their charge. The few remaining wolves stood tall and proud among the trees, waiting their turn, and when the order came, they knew they too would meet their death at the edge of those merciless swords. But in they went, crying their deep-throated war-cries, to bring down as many Zars as they could before falling themselves. Against any natural enemy, the power and the savagery of the wolves would have been devastating. But the Zars were numberless, and however many were brought down, there were always more.

'Stop!' cried Kestrel from the high branch, in pity and horror. 'Stop! It's no good!'

But if the old wolf heard her, he paid her no heed. He shook his shaggy mane, and called once more, and the very last line of wolves threw themselves into the battle. As he watched them fall, one after the other, the pride of the mountains laid low, he stilled his aching heart.

We face the ancient enemy at last. What can we do but die?

Then he lifted his old head high, and howled his own war-cry, his death-cry, and gathering all the power remaining in him, he hurled himself into the fray. One down, his killer teeth ripping, tossing; two down, turn on a third, and for a second he saw the bright gleam before the blade passed through his shoulder and into his bursting heart.

And still the Zars marched singing onwards. Behind them they left a grisly litter of corpses, above them the great eagles still swooped and struck, but the column swung gaily along, unbroken, the only sign of their losses the blood that spattered their billowing white cloaks.

Meanwhile, below the children, their pursuers surrounded the base of the tree. Laughing like young people at play, they threw off their caps and their cloaks and began to climb.

They were astonishingly agile, and seemed able to cling to the side of the broad trunk itself. Soon the leader, a sunny-faced boy who could not have been older than thirteen, had reached the higher branches, and was gazing up to where the children were perched.

'Hallo!' he called up to them in a friendly voice. 'I'm coming to kill you!'

And as he began the next stage of his climb, he hummed the tune of the marching song under his breath.

'Kill, kill, kill, kill! Kill, kill, kill!'

Behind him came a lovely ash-blonde girl, catching him up fast.

'Leave one for me!' she called to her comrade. 'You know how I love killing!'

The children shuffled further out along their branch. That way, the Zars would have to come after them one at a time. Kestrel looked down. Too far to jump. Bowman looked up, knowing there was now only the one way of escape. He called, a long wordless cry, and they heard him, and came beating fast across the sky towards them, the great eagles.

The leading Zar was just one layer of branches below them now, and as they watched, he came climbing up to support himself on their branch.

'Doesn't take long, does it?' he said, smiling. And drew his long sword.

'Leave one for me!' called the girl below. 'I want the girl.'

'I want the girl for myself,' said the young Zar, stepping

out on to their branch. 'I've never killed a girl.'

A flash of darkness, a shuddering blow, and he was seized by the talons of a diving eagle, and ripped into the air. Before the children could quite absorb what had happened, there were three eagles hovering above them, and they knew what they had to do. Bowman raised his hands high.

'Hands up!'

Mumpo copied Bowman's gesture. An eagle dropped down, gently clasped his wrists in its great claws, and carried him up and away. Bowman followed. Kestrel hesitated, staring at the girl Zar coming along the branch towards her, her sword snicking the air. She raised her arms too, seeing the eagle approaching. The sword flashed, forcing the eagle to swerve, just as Kestrel sprang off the branch into nothingness. Her arms outreached, she fell, and the eagle fell with her, its wings hissing. Then she felt its sudden rushing closeness, and the swooping claws closed about her wrists, and she was falling no more.

The great wings beat strongly, carrying them over the marching ranks of Zars, and on down the Great Way. The wind on her face, the wide wings above shielding her from the sun, Kestrel allowed herself to feel hope. She looked back and down. The Zars seemed small and far away now; though the end of the marching column was still not in sight. Then she became aware that her eagle was straining to maintain its height. Ahead she could see Bowman's eagle was already flying more slowly, and losing altitude. Big though the eagles were, the children were too heavy for them to carry far. What now? If they were put down, the Zars would overtake them soon enough.

She looked back to see how much of a lead they had, and there behind her, keeping pace with them, were three more eagles. As she watched, she saw them separate and glide silently into position.

It happened so quickly she had no time to be afraid. One moment she became aware that an eagle was passing beneath her. The next moment she felt the talons holding her wrists open wide, and she was dropping like a stone. And barely a moment later, the eagle below had banked, turned on its back, and its talons had locked on to her wrists. The great wings beat once, and she was in flight again, sailing up over the trees.

Twisting about, she was able to watch the entire manoeuvre take place with Mumpo. He lost control when he was let go, and thrashed his arms in the air, but the eagle waiting for him was still able to catch his wrists and swing him the right way round.

Bowman was already on to his second eagle, streaming through the air on her left. She turned and looked back, and there in the far distance she could see the column of the Zars, marching steadily down the Great Way, harried by the few eagles now left to fight the lost battle. Turning again, she saw ahead the jagged rift called Crack-in-the-land, and the high arches of the ruined bridge that was its only crossing.

There were no more eagles to carry them when these three tired, and Aramanth was still far away. She knew they had only the one chance.

'Bo!' she called out. 'We have to smash the bridge!'

Bowman too had been looking ahead, and he understood all that his sister was thinking. He tugged on his eagle's legs, and the great bird, glad to rest, circled down to the ground.

They landed on the south side of the ravine, near the high pillars which marked the start of the bridge. Once they were safely on the ground, the eagles took off again, to return to the battle; as if it was understood that all must die before it was over.

Bowman started gathering up stones at a frantic pace. 'We have to make an avalanche,' he said.

'We have to bring down the bridge.'

He rolled stones down the slope, following them to the very edge of the gorge to watch where they fell. When at last one of the stones rattled against the base of the most fragile supporting column far below, he marked the spot.

'Mumpo, give me your sword!' he cried.

Mumpo drew his sword from its scabbard, and Bowman drove it firmly into the ground.

'All the stones we can find, here!' he said; and started to form a pile of stones against the blade.

Mumpo meanwhile was unbuckling his sword-belt, and unbuttoning his gold buttons and peeling off his white jacket. Off came the high black boots and the white riding britches with the gold braid down the outside seam. Underneath were his old faded orange clothes. When all of the uniform of the Zars was off, he pulled the boots back on, because he had left his own shoes behind. Then he took the little pile of white blood-stained clothes, and threw them into the ravine.

'That's over now,' he said.

Then all three of them worked as fast as they could, building their mound of stones. They laboured on as the light faded in the sky, until the pile was higher than their own heads. And all the time, the marching Zars were getting nearer. Every now and again, some of the stones broke free from the pile, and skittered down the slope into the gorge. Each time Bowman ran ahead to follow the stones' fall. Each time he came back saying:

'More! We need more!'

The sun turned red and began to set. Across the great ravine the vanguard of the Zars was near enough now for them to make out the baton-twirling band leader, high-stepping at the front. There was no way of knowing whether they had gathered enough stones to do what they wanted, but Bowman knew that now they had run out of time.

'Let's do it!'

All three of them positioned themselves against the high mound of stones, and braced themselves. The sounds of the band came floating through the sunset air towards them, and with it that ceaseless beat of marching feet.

Tramp! Tramp! Tramp!

'Now!' said Bowman, and he pulled away the sword, and they all pushed. A part of the pile slithered and went crashing down into the ravine.

'Push! Harder! We have to get it all moving at once!'

They pushed again, straining with all their might, and suddenly the pile gave way. With a slow rumble, it started to slide. The thousands of stones they had gathered poured down the slope, gathering speed, throwing up a cloud of dust and other fragments, until they leaped out into the emptiness of Crack-in-the-land. Down fell the spill of rubble, down and down in a ribbon of smoky debris, as the children watched and listened, holding their breath. The shadows in the gorge were too deep now to see where their avalanche fell, but after a longer time than they had thought possible, at last they heard it: the fusillade of cracks and rattles as the stones struck – what? The supporting columns? The sides of the gorge? Then there followed the sound of more falling fragments, but they had no way of knowing whether this was the avalanche they had triggered from above, or the breaking masonry of the tall slender arches. They watched the upper sections of the bridge, that same narrow parapet on which they had fought the old children, but nothing was moving. And on the far side of the gorge, the Zars were in view now, their white-and-gold uniforms glowing red in the low rays of the setting sun.

'It didn't work.'

This was Kestrel, gazing at the bridge.

'We must go,' she said. 'We have to keep ahead of them.'

'No,' said Bowman, his voice steady and low. 'They'll overtake us long before we get to Aramanth.'

'What else can we do?'

'You go on, with Mumpo. I'll stay here. Only one of them can cross the bridge at a time. I can hold them.'

Now the Zars had reached the edge of Crack-in-the-land. The band leader was marching on the spot, the golden baton still rising and falling; and behind her the band was formed up, still playing. Then even as Kestrel was finding words to tell her brother there had to be another way, the band leader caught her baton, pointed it forward, and stepped up smartly on to the parapet of the bridge. Behind her, while the band played along the lip of the gorge, came the Zars, in single file.

Bowman stooped and picked up the sword.

'No!' cried Kestrel.

He turned and gave her a curious smile, and spoke in a voice she had never heard him use before: quiet, but very strong.

'Go on to Aramanth. There's no other way.'

'I can't leave you.'

'I've felt the power of the Morah. Don't you see?'

He turned and ran towards the bridge. The band leader was already halfway across, high-stepping as calmly as if she was still on the Great Way itself, and behind her came the long line of smiling Zars. Bowman raised the sword high as he ran, and he shouted, a wordless howl of fury, unaware that as he cried out, the tears were streaming down his cheeks.

Kestrel started to run after him, calling with all her might. 'Don't go! Don't go without me!'

Only Mumpo stayed staring at the slope, and so it was he who saw the first signs of what was about to happen.

'The bridge!' he called out. 'It's moving!'

Bowman had just reached the start of the stone parapet, when the central arch gave a slow ripple, like a tree in a strong wind, and there came the sound of cracking masonry. Then, still slowly, the thin line that joined one side of the ravine to the other snapped like an over-stretched string, and the wall and the parapet shivered and started to fall. It fell first from the children's end, unravelling faster and faster towards the middle, where the Zars were high-stepping across. Then the parapet on which they marched was curling down and away, and the band leader was falling, and the line of Zars was falling, out of the region of sunset light and into the well of darkness. They neither cried out nor made a sound. And behind them as they fell, their comrades marched on, to fall in their turn.

Bowman had come to a stop, staring in shock at the sight. Kestrel now joined him, and put her arms round him. Hugging each other, they watched as the Zars marched on, now in their column formation, eight abreast, over the edge of the gorge, to plunge to their doom. Line after line, to the beat of the band, over they went.

'We stopped them, Bo. We're safe.'

Bowman stared at the fallen bridge.

'No,' he said. 'We're not safe. But we've got time now.'

'How can they cross Crack-in-the-land, with the bridge gone?'

'Nothing can stop the Zars,' said Bowman.

Mumpo came to join them, awed by the sight of the Zars marching so blithely to their deaths.

'Don't they mind dying?' he said.

'Don't you remember how it felt, Mumpo?' said Bowman. 'So long as one Zar lives, they all live. They live through each other. They don't care how many die, because there's always more.'

'How many more?'

'There's no end to them.'

This was the horror the Old Queen had seen. The Zars could be slain, they could be defeated, but they could never be stopped. There were always more.

'That's why we have to get to Aramanth before them,' said Bowman.

He turned as if to set off then and there; but his last charge, in which he had expected to die, had drained him of all his remaining strength; and after taking a few steps, he folded slowly to the ground. Kestrel dropped to his side, alarmed.

'I can't go on,' he said. 'I have to sleep.'

So Kestrel and Mumpo curled up on either side of him, where he had fallen, and the three of them slept in each other's arms.

22

THE HATH FAMILY BROKEN

On the day before the High Examination, Principal Pillish assembled all the candidates on his Residential Study Course to give them his customary day-before talk. He was proud of this talk, which he had given many times, and knew by heart. He believed it steadied the nerves of the candidates in a specially valuable way. It was true that year after year every member of his little group, without exception, went on to fail the High Examination. But who was to say they would not have failed even more dismally, but for his day-before talk?

The truth was, Principal Pillish had a secret dream. He was an unmarried man, devoted to a job that offered little in the way of rewards. His secret dream was that one year one of his failing group of candidates would surprise himself, and all Aramanth, by winning top marks in the

High Examination. In his secret dream, this happy candidate would then come to him, Principal Pillish, with his wife and children accompanying him, and weeping tears of joy would thank him for transforming his life. Then the candidate's wife would bow humbly before him and kiss his hand, and the candidate's children would step forward to present him, shyly, with a little posy of flowers they had picked themselves, and the candidate would make a clumsy but heartfelt speech, in which he would say that he owed it all to those few shining words in that precious day-before talk. After that, felt Principal Pillish with a sigh, he could retire happy, knowing his labours had not been in vain.

This year, he told himself as he surveyed the faces of his candidates, this year, surely, there really was a chance. Never before had he known such high morale. Never before had he reached this stage in the Study Course without a single nervous breakdown. This year, surely, at long last, he would have his winner.

'Candidates,' he began, beaming at them to infuse them with vital confidence. 'Candidates, tomorrow you sit the High Examination. You are nervous. That is natural. All candidates are nervous. You are not at a disadvantage because you are nervous. In fact, your nervousness will help you. Your nervousness is your friend.'

He beamed at them again. He believed this to be one of the transforming insights of his day-before talk. In his secret dream, the successful candidate would say to him,

'When you told us, Your nervousness is your friend, I saw everything differently. It was as if a blindfold was removed from my eyes, and everything became clear.'

'An athlete is nervous before the start of the race,' he went on, warming to his theme. 'That nervousness brings him to the highest pitch of readiness. The starting signal is given, and off he goes! His nervousness has become his power, his speed, his victory!'

He had hoped at this point to see an answering glow of excitement in their eyes. Instead, they seemed to be smiling. This was unusual. By this stage in the Study Course, in all former years, the candidates wore a sullen defeated look, and avoided meeting his eyes. This year they were positively cheerful, and somehow he had the feeling that they weren't really listening to him.

He decided to break off from his day-before talk, if only briefly, to check their responses.

'Candidate Hath,' he said, picking out the one on whom his highest hopes rested. 'Do you feel well prepared for tomorrow?'

'Oh, yes, I think so,' said Hanno Hath. 'I shall give my best.'

'Good, good,' said Principal Pillish. However, there was something about Candidate Hath's reply that didn't feel quite right.

'Candidate Mimilith. How are you feeling?'

'Not so bad, sir, thank you,' said Miko Mimilith.

There it is again, thought Principal Pillish. Something isn't right here. Instinctively he turned to the weakest candidate on the course.

'Candidate Scooch. One day left. Raring to go, I trust?'

'Yes, sir,' said Scooch cheerfully.

This was downright odd. What is it that's wrong here? Principal Pillish asked himself. Back came the answer: they're not nervous.

At once he was overcome with a sensation of outrage. Not nervous! What right did they have not to be nervous? What use was his day-before talk if they weren't nervous? It was disrespectful. It was insolent. It was – yes – it was ungrateful. And worst of all – yes, this was undoubtedly true – if they were not nervous, they would perform poorly in the High Examination, and that would damage their family ratings. Nervousness was their friend. It was his duty, as their teacher and guide, to reintroduce nervousness to this inappropriately confident group. He must do it for their sakes, and for the sake of their families.

'Candidate Scooch,' he said, no longer smiling. 'I'm delighted that you feel so eager for the fray. Why don't we sharpen our mental swords for battle by trying a few questions here and now?'

He reached for one of the study books and opened it at random.

'What is the chemical composition of common salt?'

'I don't know,' said Scooch.

Principal Pillish turned pages at random. 'Describe the life cycle of the newt.'

'I can't,' said Scooch.

'If sixty-four cube-shaped boxes are stacked in a cube-shaped pile, how many boxes high is the pile?'

'I don't know,' said Scooch.

Principal Pillish closed the book with a sharp snap.

'Three typical questions from the High Examination, Candidate Scooch, and you can't answer any of them. Does that make you feel just the smallest bit nervous about tomorrow?'

'No, sir,' said Scooch.

'And why is that?'

'Well, sir,' said Scooch, unaware that Hanno Hath was trying desperately to catch his eye, 'I won't be answering those sorts of questions, sir.'

'What then, Candidate Scooch, will you be writing about on your examination paper?'

'Tea-breaks,' said Scooch.

A faint pink mist seemed to form before Principal Pillish's eyes. He felt for the edge of the table beside him.

'Tea-breaks?' he repeated faintly.

'Yes, sir,' said Scooch, all unaware of the effect he was producing. 'I think I may be a bit of an expert on tea-breaks. Not everybody has them, it turns out. I've been talking it over with the other fellows on the course. How can mortal man last from breakfast until lunch, sir, without a little something that's both restful and stimulating? For the first part of the morning you can look forward to it, sir, and for the second part of the morning you can remember it – '

'Be quiet,' said Principal Pillish.

He glowered at the assembled candidates. His secret dream, that had seemed so close, lay shattered at his feet. His heart was filled with bitterness.

'Does anyone else propose to write about tea-breaks?'

No one answered.

'Will someone please tell me what's going on?'

Hanno Hath raised his hand.

Principal Pillish listened to Hanno Hath's explanation in the privacy of his office. Hanno delivered a passionate defence of his novel system, but none of it made any sense. When Hanno said, 'You might as well test fish for flying', Principal Pillish passed a hand over his brow and said, 'The candidates on my course are not fish.' When Hanno was done, the Principal sat in silence for a while. He felt betrayed. He had not understood the flow of eager words, but he had heard, loud and clear, the underlying note of rebellion. This was not a case of laziness, or exam nerves. This was mutiny. Under the circumstances, his duty was clear. He must inform the Chief Examiner.

Maslo Inch listened to the whole unhappy tale, and then shook his head slowly from side to side, and said:

'I blame myself. The man's a rotten apple, and now he's infected the whole barrel.'

'But what should I do, Chief Examiner?'

'Nothing. I will deal with him myself.'

'The difficulty is, he's not sorry. He thinks he's right.'

'I'll make him sorry.'

The Chief Examiner spoke these words with such forceful conviction that Principal Pillish's wounded pride was soothed somewhat. He wanted to see Hanno Hath's smile crumple into an expression of fear and need. He wanted to see him humbled. For his own good, of course.

This new development decided the matter for Maslo Inch. He sent for the captain of the marshals, and gave him his orders. That night, two hours after sundown, a troop of ten specially picked men moved quietly into the arena and surrounded the wind singer, where Ira Hath was sleeping with Pinpin in her arms.

They achieved complete surprise. Ira Hath knew nothing until she felt her arms gripped tight, and awoke to find the warm weight of her child being lifted away from her. She started to cry out, but a strong hand clamped over her mouth, and a blindfold was pulled tight round her eyes. She could hear Pinpin calling pitifully, 'Mama! Mama!' and she kicked and struggled with all her might, but the men who held her knew what they were doing, and she could not free herself.

Then Pinpin's cries faded out of hearing and, exhausted and gagging for breath, she fell still. A voice close to her ear said:

'Are you done?'

She nodded.

'Do you come with us, or do we drag you?'

She nodded again, meaning she would come. The rough hand was removed from her mouth. She drew a long gasping breath.

'Where's my daughter?'

'Safe enough. If you want to see her again, you do as you're told.'

After that Ira Hath knew she had no choice. Still blindfolded, she let them lead her down from the wind singer, and out of the great arena. They went across the plaza, and into a building, through doors and down corridors, into one room and then another, until she and her escort at last came to a stop.

'Let her go,' said a voice she recognised. 'Take off the blindfold.'

There in front of her, seated at a long table, was Maslo Inch. And on her right, not quite close enough to reach out and touch, stood her husband.

'Hanno!'

'Silence!' barked the Chief Examiner. 'Neither of you will speak until I've said what I have to say.'

Ira Hath was silent. But her eyes met Hanno's, and they

spoke to each other in looks, saying, *We'll get through this together somehow.*

A warden entered the room carrying a small pile of neatly-folded grey clothes.

'Put them on the table,' said Maslo Inch.

The warden did as he was told, and left.

'Now,' said Maslo Inch, looking up at them with steady eyes. 'This is what you will do. Tomorrow is the day of the High Examination. You, Hanno Hath, will sit that examination, as is your duty to your family, and you will acquit yourself as best as you can. You, Ira Hath, will attend the High Examination, as a dutiful wife and mother, to show support for the head of your family. You will of course be wearing your designated clothing.'

He nodded at the pile on the table before him.

'When the examination is over, and before the people leave the arena, I will call upon each of you to make a short public statement. Your statements are written here. You will learn them by heart overnight.'

He held out two sheets of paper, and the captain of the marshals passed them on to Hanno and Ira.

'You will be spending tonight in detention. You will not be disturbed.'

'Where's my daughter?' broke in Ira Hath, unable to stop herself.

'Your child is in safe hands. The good woman who has charge of her will bring her to the arena tomorrow, where

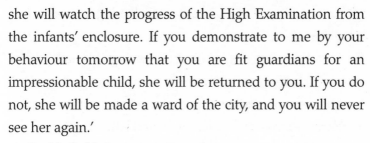

she will watch the progress of the High Examination from the infants' enclosure. If you demonstrate to me by your behaviour tomorrow that you are fit guardians for an impressionable child, she will be returned to you. If you do not, she will be made a ward of the city, and you will never see her again.'

Ira Hath felt hot tears rise to her eyes.

'Oh, monster, monster,' she said in a low voice.

'If that is your attitude, ma'am – '

'No,' said Hanno. 'We understand. We'll do as you say.'

'We shall see,' said Maslo Inch evenly. 'Tomorrow will tell.'

Left alone in their detention room, Ira and Hanno Hath fell into each other's arms and broke into bitter sobs. Then after a while Hanno wiped away his wife's tears and his own, and said,

'Come, now. We must do what we can.'

'I want Pinpin! Oh, my baby, where are you?'

'No, no. No more of that. Just one night, that's all.'

'I hate them, I hate them, I hate them.'

'Of course, of course. But for the moment, we must do as they say.'

He unfolded his sheet of paper and read the statement he was to learn and repeat in public:

My fellow citizens, I make this public confession of my own free will. For some years now I have not striven to do my best.

As a result, I have failed my family and myself. To my shame, I have sought to blame others for my failure. I now see that this was childish and self-centred. We are each of us responsible for our own destiny. I am proud to be a citizen of Aramanth. I promise today to do all in my power, from now on, to make myself worthy of that honour.

'I suppose it could be worse,' said Hanno with a sigh, after he had finished reading it.

Ira Hath's statement ran:

My fellow citizens, you may know that recently I have lost two of my children. The strain of this loss led to a mental breakdown, in the course of which I acted in ways of which I am now ashamed. I ask for your forgiveness and understanding. I promise in future to behave with the modesty and decency that befits a wife and mother.

She threw the paper to the floor.

'I won't say it!'

Hanno picked it up.

'It's only words.'

'Oh, my babies, my babies,' cried Ira Hath, starting to weep again. 'When will I hold you all in my arms again?'

23

THE SCOURGE OF THE PLAINS

When the light of dawn woke the three children, the first sound they heard was the music of the band, and looking across the great gorge they saw the Zars still marching, and still falling. Horrified, they went to the edge of the gorge and looked down. There far below, the river-bed was white, as if with a drift of snow, except that in the white there glittered points of gold. Into this whiteness fell the beautiful young Zars, and little by little the whiteness was reaching further and climbing higher. There would come a time, who knew how soon, when the Zars would walk across a mountain of their own dead, to the other side.

Without further words, the three friends turned and rejoined the Great Way, and strode off in the cool of the morning towards Aramanth.

The silver voice of the wind singer hung round Kestrel's

neck, inside her shirt, tied by a gold thread she had unplaited from her hair. It lay against her bony chest, made warm by her own warmth, and as they walked she felt it tickling her skin. Already, because they were on the homeward journey, her thoughts were reaching ahead to Aramanth, and her father and mother and little sister. This gave needed strength to her legs, for Bowman was keeping up a relentless pace.

'We must get to Aramanth first,' he said.

The Zars were no longer pursuing them, but as they hurried on down the Great Way, they faced a different problem, about which none of them spoke. It was a sign of the great change that had taken place in Mumpo that he too said nothing, though the ache in his stomach was growing stronger with every hour. They were hungry. They had eaten nothing for a day and a night, and now half another day. Their food bags were empty, and the trees they were passing bore no fruit. Here and there a wayside stream provided water, but even this refreshment would end, they knew, when they reached the great desert plains. How far did they then have to go? They couldn't tell, because they had been carried across the plains by the thousand sails of Ombaraka. They guessed three days, maybe more. How could they make the long crossing without food?

The Great Way was broad, and sloped gently downwards, and now they could see the plains lying before them as they went. By noon, their hunger was slowing them down, and feeling their growing weakness, they began to be afraid.

Even Bowman was becoming weary. So at last he gave in, and called a rest stop. Gratefully they sank to the ground, in the shade of a broad-leafed tree.

'How are we going to get home?' said Kestrel. She realised as she spoke that she was turning to her brother now, as their natural leader.

'I don't know,' he answered simply. 'But we will get home, because we must.'

It was no answer, but it comforted her.

'Maybe we could eat leaves,' she said, tugging at the branch above.

'I know!' said Mumpo. He reached inside his pocket, and brought out the last of the tixa leaves he had carried with him all the way from the Underlake. He tore them into three, and gave a share to each of the others.

'It's not real food,' he said, 'but it makes you not mind about food.'

He was right. They chewed the tixa leaves, and swallowed the sharp-tasting juice, and though it did nothing to fill their empty bellies, it made them feel it didn't matter.

'Tastes bitter,' said Kestrel, pulling a face.

'Bitter bitter bitter,' said Mumpo in a sing-song voice.

Up they got and on they went, loping and rolling, and all the insuperable problems ahead seemed to dwindle away. How would they cross the great plains? They would fly like birds, carried effortlessly on the wind. They would drift like clouds over the land.

As they danced down the Great Way, borne in the arms of tixy, they found themselves speaking their fears out loud, singing them, laughing at them.

'Ha ha ha, to the Zars!' sang Mumpo.

'Ha ha ha, Zar Zar Zar!' sang the twins.

'Mumpo was an oldie!' chanted Kestrel.

'Oldie, oldie, oldie!' they all sang.

'What was it like being old, Mumpo?'

Mumpo danced an oldie dance for them, moving with exaggerated slowness.

'Slow and heavy,' he sang as he pranced gravely before them. 'Slow and heavy and tired.'

'Tired, tired, tired,' they sang.

'Like when we were all covered with mud.'

'Mud, mud, mud!'

'Then the mud fell off, and – ' he sprang into the air and waved his arms wildly – 'Zar, Zar, hurrah!'

'Zar, Zar, hurrah!' they echoed.

Linking arms, all three fell into the high-stepping march of the Zars, making their own band music with their mouths.

'Tarum-tarum-taraa! Tarum-tarum-taraa!'

In this fashion, marching and singing, they came out of the forest and on to the plains. Here they came at last to a stop. Then, as they gazed across the arid wastes at the distant horizon, the effects of the tixy wore off, and they knew once more that they were hungry, starving hungry, and far, far from home.

It would have been easy then to lie down and sleep and never get up, because their singing and dancing had taken the very last of their strength. But Bowman wouldn't allow it. Stubbornly, relentlessly, he insisted their journey must go on.

'It's too far. We'll never get there.'

'It doesn't matter. We have to go on.'

So they went on, keeping the sun on their right side as it slowly descended in the sky. A keen wind was whipping up, and they went slower and slower, but they didn't stop. They stumbled in their weariness, but on they trudged, driven by Bowman's will.

Dusk was falling, and heavy dark clouds scudding across the sky, when Kestrel at last came to a stop. She drew the gold thread over her head and handed the silver voice to Bowman, saying quietly:

'You go on. I can't.'

Bowman took it, and held the fine silver clasp tight in his hand, and his eyes met hers. He could see there her shame that she could do no more, but deeper and stronger than the shame, the weariness.

I can't do it without you, Kess.

Then it's over.

Bowman turned and saw Mumpo watching him, waiting for what he would say that would make them believe there was hope: and he had no words left. He closed his eyes.

Help me, he said silently, not knowing to whom or what he was appealing.

As if in answer, there came a half-familiar sound: a distant creaking and groaning, carried on the wind.

He opened his eyes, and all three of them turned to look. There, rising slowly above the swell of the land, was a pennant snapping in the wind, silhouetted against the twilight sky. Up over the rim of land rose the masts and sails, the lookout towers and the topmost decks. Then the main decks, crowded on all sides by full-bellied sails, and the whole vast bulk of the mother ship grinding slowly towards them, rolling out of the dusk.

'Ombaraka!' cried Kestrel.

Energised by hope, the children set off running towards the immense moving city, waving their arms and calling out as they ran, to attract the attention of the lookouts. They were seen. The great craft lumbered to a slow halt. A boarding cradle was winched down. They clambered into it, hugging each other, weeping tears of relief. Up creaked the cradle, past the lower decks, to judder to a halt at the command deck. The gates were thrown open, and there before them stood a troop of heavily armed men, their hair shaved close to the skull. 'Baraka spies!' cried their commander. 'Lock them up! They'll hang at first light!'

Only then did they realise they were prisoners of Omchaka.

The children were thrown into a cage that was just big enough for the three of them to sit in, side by side, their knees drawn up to their chests. Once locked in, the cage was winched several feet into the air, and there they were left to dangle, twisting in the wind, jeered and spat at by the guards set to watch over them.

'Baraka scum! Got up like dolls!'

'Please,' pleaded the children. 'We're hungry.'

'Why waste food on you? You'll hang in the morning.'

The Chaka people seemed to be fiercer than the Barakas, perhaps because of their way of shaving their heads; but in all other respects they were strikingly similar. The same sand-coloured robes, the same warrior-like swagger, the same festoons of weapons. When the children were heard to be crying, they laughed, and reached up to poke them through the bars.

'Snivelling girlies!' they taunted. 'You'll have something to cry about in the morning.'

'We won't live till morning,' said Kestrel in a faint voice. 'We haven't eaten for days.'

'You'd better live,' cried the biggest of their guards. 'If I find you dead in the morning, I'll kill you.'

The other guards laughed tremendously at this. The big guard went red.

'Well, what's your brilliant idea, then? Do you want to tell Haka Chaka there'll be no public hanging?'

'Kill them again, Pok! That'll scare them!'

They laughed even more. The big guard they called Pok scowled and fell to muttering to himself.

'You all think I'm so stupid, well, you're the stupid ones, not me, you'll see all right, just you wait . . .'

As night descended and the wind grew stronger, the guards decided to take it in turns to stand watch. Big Pok volunteered to go first, and the others departed. As soon as they were alone, Pok approached the cage and called up in a hoarse whisper,

'Hey! You Baraka spies! Are you still alive?'

No answer came from the cage. Pok groaned aloud. 'Please talk to me, scum. You're not to die.'

Kestrel spoke, in a tiny croaking voice.

'Food,' she said. 'Food . . .'

The word faded on her lips.

'All right,' said Pok nervously. 'Just wait there. I'll get you food. Don't do anything. I'm going to get you food. Don't die, all right? Promise me you won't die, or I won't go.'

'Not long now . . .' said Kestrel faintly. 'Slipping away . . .'

'No, no! That's what you're not to do! Don't do that or I'll – I'll – '

Realising he had no effective way to threaten them, he resorted to pleading.

'Look, you're going to die anyway, so it doesn't matter to you, but it does matter to me. If you die on my watch, they'll blame me, and that's not fair, is it? You've got to admit, it wouldn't be my fault, but I can tell you now how it'll be. Oh, Pok again, they'll say. Trust Pok to make a mess of it. Poor old Pok, thick as a rock. That's what they say, and it isn't fair.'

Silence from the children. Pok panicked.

'Just don't die yet. That's the thing. I'm going. Food's on its way.'

He galloped off. The children stayed still and quiet, in case someone else was watching, although by now the night was very dark, and the roaring wind kept the people indoors. Shortly Pok reappeared, his arms full of bread and fruit.

'Here you are,' he said, panting, poking loaves through the bars. 'Eat it up! Eat it up!'

He watched anxiously, and when he saw the children begin to eat, he let out a sigh of relief.

'There! That's better. No more dying, eh?'

The more the children ate, the happier Pok became.

'There! Old Pok's not made a mess of it after all! You'll be chirpy as sparrows in the morning, and Haka Chaka can have a fine hanging. So all's well that ends well, as they say.'

The food brought strength back to Bowman, and with strength came hope. He began to think of how to escape.

'We're not really Baraka spies,' he said.

'Oh, no,' said Pok. 'Oh, no, you can't fool me that easily. Even old Pok can see you're not Chaka, and if you're not Chaka, you're Baraka.'

'We're from Aramanth.'

'No, you're not. You've got Baraka hair.'

'What if we were to unbraid our hair?' said Kestrel.

'What if we were to shave it all off, like you?'

319

'Well, then,' said Pok uncertainly. 'Well, then, you'd be . . . You'd look like . . .'

He found the whole idea deeply muddling.

'We'd look like you.'

'That's as maybe,' he said. 'But you can't shave your hair off tonight, and in the morning you're going to be hanged. So that's that.'

'Except you wouldn't want to hang us and find out afterwards it had all been a mistake.'

'Haka Chaka gives the orders,' said Pok contentedly. 'Haka Chaka is the Father of Omchaka, the Great Judge of Righteousness, and the Scourge of the Plains. He doesn't make mistakes.'

The children did sleep that night, for all the cramped conditions in the cage, and the howling of the wind. The food in their bellies and the weariness in their bones was stronger than their fear of the morning, and they slept deeply until the light of dawn awoke them.

The wind had fallen, but the sky was leaden grey, heavy with an approaching storm. A squad of Chaka guards marched up, and formed a circle round the cage. The cage was winched down on to the deck, and the gate unlocked. The children stumbled out. The squad formed up round them, and they marched across a causeway to the central square of Omchaka. Here a great crowd was waiting, packed tight round the sides of the square, and hanging from the rails of the decks above. As soon as the children came in sight, the crowd began to hiss and call out insults.

'Hang them! Baraka filth! String them up!'

In the centre of the square there stood a newly-built scaffold, from which hung three rope nooses. Behind the scaffold stood the commanders of the Omchaka army, and a line of drummers. The children were led to the scaffold, and stood on a bench, each one before a rope noose. Then the drummers beat their drums, and the Grand Commander cried out:

'All stand for Haka Chaka, Father of Omchaka, Great Judge of Righteousness and Scourge of the Plains!'

No one moved, since they were all standing anyway, and into the square strode Haka Chaka, followed by a small entourage. He was an old man of imposing stature, his grey hair shaved close to his skull. But it was not at him that the children gazed in amazement. Behind him, hair also shaved, walked Counsellor Kemba.

'He's a Baraka!' cried Kestrel, pointing at him accusingly. 'His name's Kemba, and he's from Ombaraka!'

Kemba smiled, seemingly unconcerned.

'They'll be saying you're a Baraka next, Highness.'

'They can say what they like,' said Haka Chaka grimly. 'The talking will end soon enough.'

He gave a sign to the men holding the three children,

and the nooses were placed round their necks. Mumpo didn't cry, as he would have done once, but he did make a small choking noise.

'I'm sorry, Mumpo,' said Kestrel. 'We've been no good for you after all.'

'Yes, you have,' he said bravely. 'You've been my friends.'

Haka Chaka climbed up on to a high speaking-platform to address the crowd.

'People of Omchaka!' he cried. 'The Morah has delivered our enemies into our hands!'

All at once Bowman saw the way out.

'The Morah has woken!' he called out.

A surprised silence fell over the crowd. From the grey sky above came the low rumble of the approaching storm. Kemba's eyes turned on Bowman, burning intensely.

'The Zars are on the march!' cried Bowman.

This caused consternation in the crowd. A buzz of agitated chatter broke out on all sides. Haka Chaka turned to his advisers.

'Can this be true?'

'They're marching after us,' cried Bowman. 'Wherever we are, they'll find us.'

Now on all sides there were voices raised in fear, intensified by the sudden gusts of wind that rattled the rigging above.

'Nothing can stop the Zars!'

'They'll kill us all!'

'Tell the sailmen! We must set sail!'

'*Fools!*'

It was Kemba who took control of the panic. He spoke loudly, but in tones that were calm, even soothing.

'Can't you tell a Baraka trick when you see one? Why would the Morah have woken? Why would the Zars march? He lies to save his own miserable skin.'

'I woke the Morah myself,' said Bowman. 'The Morah said to me, We are legion.'

These words chilled the hearts of the crowd. Kemba looked at Bowman with hatred, but mingled with the hatred was fear.

'He lies!' he cried. 'These are our enemies! Why do we listen? Hang them! Hang them now!'

The crowd fell on this proposal, echoing it wildly, their newly aroused fear streaming out of them as hate-charged anger.

'Hang them! Hang them!'

The nooses were pulled close round the children's necks. Two guards stood at either end of the high bench, ready to knock it away from the children's feet. Haka Chaka raised his arms to still the baying of the crowd.

'What have we to fear?' he cried. 'We are Omchaka!'

A great cheer greeted this call.

'Let Ombaraka tremble! This is how we deal with all enemies of Omchaka!'

But in the moment of silence before he dropped his arms,

which was to be the signal for the hanging, a new sound came to them, carried by the storm wind: the tramping of marching feet, the music of a marching band, the singing of a multitude of young voices.

'Kill, kill, kill, kill! Kill, kill, kill!'

The people of Omchaka looked at each other in silent horror. Then the words that all dreaded formed on their lips.

'The Zars! The Zars!'

Counsellor Kemba was galvanised into action.

'Highness,' he said urgently. 'Release the spies! Put them in a land-sailer and send them south. The Zars will follow them. Omchaka must set course for the east at once.'

Haka Chaka understood, and the orders were given. As the crowd broke up, and the people of Omchaka hurried to their action stations, Kemba approached the children and addressed them in a savage whisper.

'Forty years of peace and you ruin everything! My life work destroyed! My only consolation is that you won't escape the Zars, nor will your precious Aramanth!'

The children were released, and bundled into a land-sailer: not one of the sleek manoeuvrable corvettes, but a heavy low-bottomed provisions craft, with a single fixed sail. It was winched hurriedly over the side, while the great city of Omchaka echoed with frantic activity. On every deck the sailmen were unfurling sails and yelling out instructions, and the ever-strengthening wind was bellying out the myriad canvases and tugging the immense mother craft into juddering movement.

As the little land-sailer banged on to the ground, the Zars could be seen far off, marching in their column, eight abreast, led by the band, high-stepping across the plains. The storm wind sweeping down from the north caught the sail and jerked the land-sailer out of the lee of Omchaka. Here, hit by the full force of the wind, the craft picked up speed. And all at once, with a roll of thunder across the iron sky, the storm overtook them, bringing with it drenching rain.

Faster and faster ran the land-sailer, crashing over the stony ground, and the children could do nothing but cling tight to the mast and hurtle through the storm. The wind became a gale, the rain became a torrent, through which they could see nothing. Again and again, lightning crackled across the livid sky, and the long booming explosions of thunder rolled over their heads. Water was filling up the well of the craft, slopping over their feet, but all they could do was hold tight as they charged on, bucking and bouncing, out of all control.

Then one wheel struck a rock, and two of its spokes snapped. For a few moments longer the wheel spun on, then the rim buckled, and almost at once the wheel imploded. The craft lurched to one side. The pitiless wind hammered into the sail, spinning them round, and a second wheel burst into fragments. The land-sailer went over on to its side, skated a little way under its sheer momentum; and then skidded to a stop.

Still the storm raged round them. They could do nothing, so they huddled together in the shelter of the broken hull, and waited for the pelting rain to pass. Bowman felt the silver voice of the wind singer, still hanging round his neck, and he thought how close they had come to death, and it seemed to him that someone or something must be looking after them. Someone or something wanted them to make their way home; though who or what it might be, he had no idea.

'We're going to do it,' he said.

Kestrel and Mumpo felt it too. They couldn't be far from Aramanth now.

In time, the heavy rain gave way to intermittent showers, and the wind dropped. The children crawled out from under their shelter, and looked round them in the light of the brightening sky. The storm was passing to the south, and there on the near horizon, unmistakable even through the veil of falling rain, rose the high walls of Aramanth.

'We're going to do it,' said Bowman again, exultantly.

Tramp! Tramp! Tramp!

Through the showers, soaked but smiling, singing as they marched, came the unstoppable Zars.

'Kill, kill, kill, kill! Kill, kill, kill!'

Without another word, the children set off at a run towards the city walls.

24

THE LAST HIGH EXAMINATION

Today was the day of the High Examination. The unseasonal rainstorm had delayed the start of the session, which was most unusual, but now the rows of desks that filled the arena terraces had been wiped dry, and the examination was well under way. Seated at the desks were the heads of every family in the city, at work on the papers that would determine their family rating for the coming year. Each circular terrace held three hundred and twenty desks, and there were nine terraces: nearly three thousand examinees all sitting in utter silence, but for the scratching of pens on paper, and the soft padding of the examiners as they patrolled the arena.

All round the main terraces, and crowded into the steeply-raked stands on either side, sat the families of the examinees. Everybody except those engaged in essential occupations had to be present on the day of the High Examination, partly to lend support to their family head, and partly to demonstrate that the examination ranked the family as well as the individual. The families sat in segregated sections, according to their colours. The few whites and the many more scarlets at the palace end; the broad middle taken up by orange on one side and maroon on the other; the end by the statue of Creoth a sea of grey. Maslo Inch, the Chief Examiner, sat on a podium raised on a stone plinth, on which was carved the Oath of Dedication.

> I VOW TO STRIVE HARDER, TO REACH HIGHER,
> AND IN EVERY WAY TO SEEK TO MAKE
> TOMORROW BETTER THAN TODAY.
> FOR LOVE OF MY EMPEROR
> AND FOR THE GLORY OF ARAMANTH.

He looked at his watch, and noted that one hour had passed. Rising, he stepped down from the podium, and made a slow circuit of the arena, letting his eyes roam at random over the bowed heads of the examinees. For Maslo Inch, the High Examination was always a time for satisfying reflection; and today, after the recent disturbances, more so than ever. Here were the people of Aramanth, ranked and ordered, going about the business of being tested in a manner that was fair and just. None could complain of favouritism, or of secret grudges against them. All sat the same exam, and all were marked in the same way. The able and the diligent came to the fore, as was right and proper, and the stupid and the idle slipped down the rankings, as was also right and proper. Of course it was unpleasant for those who performed poorly, and had to move house to a poorer district, but it was fair, because always it meant that some other family that had worked hard and done well was being rewarded. And never forget – in his mind he rehearsed his end-of-exam speech – never forget that next year, at the next High Examination, your chance will come round again, and you can win back all you have lost. Yes, all things considered, it was the best possible system, and no one could deny it.

His wandering eyes fell on the group from the Residential Study Course, who sat together because they were subject to extra supervision. He saw on their faces the looks of panic and despair that he saw every year, as they struggled with questions for which they had failed to prepare themselves, and he knew that all was as it should be. Why is it, he thought, that some people never learn? All it takes is a little effort, a little extra push. And there in the midst of them sat Hanno Hath, with his head in his hands. Truly that man was a disgrace to Aramanth. But he was under control now.

His eyes swept across the arena to the area where the families from Grey District sat. There was the Hath woman, sitting dressed in grey, her hands folded in her lap, as docile as you could wish. His eyes moved on to the infants' enclosure, where that dependable woman Mrs Chirish sat with the Hath child in her lap. He had expected the child to cause trouble, but it seemed to be quiet, no doubt awed by the great studious silence that hung over the arena.

Well, that's a good job well done, said Maslo Inch to himself. The pride of the Hath family was well and truly broken.

High in the tower above the Imperial Palace, the Emperor stood moodily eating chocolate buttons, looking down on the deserted streets of the city. He had watched the examinees and their families arrive earlier, and had sensed their feelings of anxiety and dread. He hated the annual day of the High Examination. He had heard the thousands of voices chanting the Oath of Dedication, and when it came to the part that said 'for love of my Emperor', he had blocked his ears. But for the last hour, all had been silent. It was as if the city had died.

But now he began to imagine he could hear a new sound: far away, faint, muffled, but – could it be a band playing? He strained his ears to catch it more clearly. Who would dare to play music on the day of the High Examination?

Then as he stared down at the streets below he saw the strangest sight. A manhole opened up in the road, and a muddy child burst out, followed by two more. They looked round them, seemed confused for a moment, and then set off at a run towards the arena. The Emperor watched them run, and it seemed to him he knew one of them. Wasn't it the girl – ?

Suddenly out of the manhole popped a handsome young lad in a white-and-gold uniform. After him came another, and another. Then from behind them, down the long street, came a whole column of them, led by a marching band. The Emperor's eyes stood out in his head, and he was rooted to the spot. He needed no telling. This was the army of the Zars.

More and more of them came marching out of side streets and clambering out of sewers to join the main column. And now as they marched they started to sing, a song made of only one word:

'Kill, kill, kill, kill! Kill, kill, kill!'

The Emperor knew he must stop them. But how? He couldn't even move. He took a handful of chocolate buttons from the bowl, unaware that he was doing so, and ate them without tasting them, and wept as he ate.

The children raced past the statue of Creoth, burst through the pillared entrance to the arena, and came to a stop, panting, on the topmost terrace. Somehow, urgent though the danger was, the sight of the thousands of examinees bent over their desks in silence awed them, and for a few crucial moments, regaining their breath, they hesitated.

In these few moments, Maslo Inch had seen them, and was outraged. Nothing was permitted to break the sacred silence of the High Examination. He did not recognise the three bedraggled urchins, with their ridiculous stringy hair and their muddy feet. It was enough that they were intruders. He signed sharply to his assistants to deal with the matter.

The children saw the scarlet-robed examiners moving grimly towards them. Down in the centre of the arena, the wind singer stood turning silently this way and that in the breeze. Bowman drew the silver voice out of his shirt, and unlooped the string from round his neck. He spoke silently to his sister.

Stay close. If they get me, you take it.

The children spread out, staying in reach of each other, and started down the terraces towards the wind singer. By now the examinees were beginning to notice the disturbance, and a buzz of low voices came from the stands. This is intolerable, thought Maslo Inch to himself, moving instinctively back to his podium.

The examiners closed in on the children from above and below, thinking at first that it would take no more than stern whispers to remove them. But as they came close, the children suddenly bolted in three different directions, sprinting round the terraces, past the examinees.

'Get them!' roared the Chief Examiner to the marshals, no longer caring that the examination would be disrupted. 'Stop them!'

As he shouted, he heard an impossible sound from outside in the street: a marching band, and marching feet.

Tramp! Tramp! Tramp!

Bowman zigzagged through the desks, knocking over

piles of papers here and there, jumping down from terrace to terrace. To his left he saw Kestrel, keeping up with him. He raced past Hanno Hath without even noticing, but his father recognised him, and his heart pounding with joy, he rose up in his seat –

A marshal caught Kestrel, but she buried her face in his arm and bit him so hard that he let her go. No one was working at their papers now: all heads raised, gazing in astonishment at the children, and the pursuing marshals.

In the Grey stand, Ira Hath rose to her feet, staring. She was almost sure – only their hair was so different – but surely it was –

'Hubba hubba Kestrel!' she yelled, wild with excitement. And Hanno Hath, on the far side of the arena, also standing, his heart hammering, cried out:

'Hubba hubba Bowman!'

Turning to wave to him, Bowman ran into two marshals, and between them they caught him fast by the neck and legs.

'Kess!' he yelled, and threw the silver voice high in the air.

She heard, and saw, and was there: scrabbling for the voice where it had landed, racing down the next terrace towards the wind singer, Mumpo by her side.

In all this excitement, Mrs Chirish let go of Pinpin, who at once seized the opportunity to jump off her lap and run away.

'Hey!' cried Mrs Chirish. 'Stop that child!'

But Pinpin was gone, wriggling under benches and between legs, towards the funny brown figures she had instantly recognised as her brother and sister.

Kestrel hurled herself down from the last terrace and ran for the wind singer, with two big marshals close behind her. She got as far as the base of the wooden tower, when their hands closed about her and dragged her down.

'Mumpo!' she yelled, and threw the silver voice towards him. Maslo Inch saw it as it fell, and suddenly and completely understood what was happening. He strode across the floor to seize it. Mumpo got there just before him.

'Give that to me, you dirty little brat!' commanded the Chief Examiner in his most authoritative voice, seizing Mumpo in his powerful hands. But as he spoke, his eyes met Mumpo's, and something happened inside him that he couldn't control. He gave a low gasp, and felt a hot rush in his throat and face.

'You!'

He let go, and Mumpo broke away, and raced towards the wind singer, the silver voice in his hand. Outside, the marching Zars were closer now, and the crowd in the arena could hear the band, and were straining to see who it was that dared to play music on this day of days. Bowman and Kestrel, each held tight by their captors, watched as Mumpo reached the wind singer, and started to climb.

Go, Mumpo, go!

Agile as a monkey, Mumpo shinned up the wooden

tower, the silver voice in his hand. But where was it to go?

'In the neck!' shouted Kestrel. 'The slot in the neck!'

Now the music of the Zars was coming clear from the street, and the tramp! tramp! tramp! of their marching feet. Mumpo searched frantically for the slot, his hands feeling the rusty metal of the wind singer's neck.

Hanno Hath watched him, his heart in his mouth, willing him with all his being.

Go, Mumpo, go!

Ira Hath watched him, trembling uncontrollably.

Go, Mumpo, go!

All at once his fingers felt it, higher up than he had expected. The silver voice slipped into the slot with a slight springy *click!*, just as the leading Zars burst through the pillars, their swords drawn and flashing, their song on their lips.

'Kill, kill, kill, kill – '

The wind singer turned in the breeze, the air flowed into its big leather funnels, and found its way down to the silver voice. Softly, the silver horns began to sing.

The very first note, a deep vibration, stopped the Zars dead in their tracks. They stood as if frozen, swords raised, faces bright and smiling. And all round the arena, a queer shivery sensation ran through the people.

The next note was higher, gentle but piercing. As the wind singer turned in the wind, the note modulated up and down, over the deep humming. Then came the highest note of all, like the singing of a celestial bird, a cascade of tumbling melody. The sounds seemed to grow louder and reach further, taking possession of the arena terrace by terrace, and then of the stands, and then of the city beyond. The marshals holding Bowman and Kestrel released their grip. The examinees looked at the papers on their desks in bewilderment. The families in the stands stared at each other.

Hanno Hath left his desk. Ira Hath left the Grey stand. Pinpin crept out from the lowest benches and toddled into the open space, and started to chortle with joy. And all the time, the song of the wind singer was reaching deeper and deeper into the people, and everything was changing. Examinees could be heard asking each other, 'What are we doing here?' One examinee took the papers off his desk, tore them up, and threw the pieces into the air. Soon everyone was doing it, laughing like Pinpin, and the air was thick with flying paper. The families in the stands began to intermingle, and there was a great mixing of colours, as maroon flowed into grey, and orange embraced scarlet.

The Emperor up in his tower heard the music of the wind singer, and opened his window wide, and hurled out his bowl of chocolate buttons. They scattered as they fell, and landed all round the column of the frozen Zars. Then the Emperor turned and strode out of one of his many doors, and down the stairs.

In the arena, Ira Hath moved wonderingly down the

tiers, through the crowd, where people were now swapping clothes, trying out combinations of colours, and laughing at the unfamiliar sight. She saw Hanno coming from the other direction, his arms outstretched. She reached the centre circle and took Pinpin in her embrace, and hugged her and kissed her, and turning found her dear Bowman before her, his arms reaching for her, his lips kissing her cheeks. Then Hanno joined them, and Kestrel was in his arms, and there were tears streaming down his kind cheeks, and that was when Ira Hath too started to weep for pure joy.

'My brave birds,' Hanno was saying as he embraced them all, kissing them over and over again. 'My brave birds came back.'

Pinpin jumped and wriggled in her mother's arms, beside herself with excitement.

'Love Bo!' she cried. 'Love Kess!'

'Oh, my dear ones,' said Ira Hath, as she put her arms round them all. 'Oh, my heart's darlings.'

Not far away, unnoticed in the confusion and the laughter of the crowd, Maslo Inch made his way to Mumpo, and slowly sank to his knees before him.

'Forgive me,' he said, his voice trembling.

'Forgive you?' said Mumpo. 'Why?'

'You're my son.'

For a few long moments, Mumpo stared at him in astonishment. Then, shyly, he held out one hand, and the Chief Examiner took it, and pressed it to his lips.

'Father,' said Mumpo. 'I've got friends now.'

Maslo Inch began to weep. 'Have you, my boy?' he said. 'Have you, my son?'

'Do you want to meet them?'

The Chief Examiner nodded, unable to speak. Mumpo led him by the hand to where the Hath family stood.

'Kess,' he said. 'I have got a father, after all.'

Maslo Inch stood before them, his head lowered, unable to meet their eyes.

'Look after him, Mumpo,' said Hanno Hath in his quiet voice, his arms still tight round his children. 'Fathers need all the help their children can give them.'

The Emperor passed between the double row of pillars on to the top terrace, and stood gazing at the chaotic scene in the arena. The song of the wind singer flowed on, and he felt its warming loosening power like sunshine after a long winter. He spread his arms wide, and smiled happily and called out:

'That's the way! Ha! A city needs to be noisy.'

As for the Zars, from the moment that the wind singer had begun to sing, they had started to age. Standing still as statues, the beautiful features of the golden youths crinkled and sagged, and their fanatic eyes grew dim. Their backs began to stoop, and their golden hair thinned and went grey. Years passed by in minutes, and one by one the Zars crumpled to the ground, and there they died. Time and decay, held at bay for so long, now overwhelmed them. The flesh rotted on their bodies, and turned to dust. Out in the streets of Aramanth, the wind that sang in the wind singer blew the dust from their bones, and swirled it away into gardens and gutters, until all that was left of the invincible army of the Morah was a long line of skeletons, swords at their sides, glinting in the sun.

THE
WIND
SINGER

Turn the page for special bonus material . . .

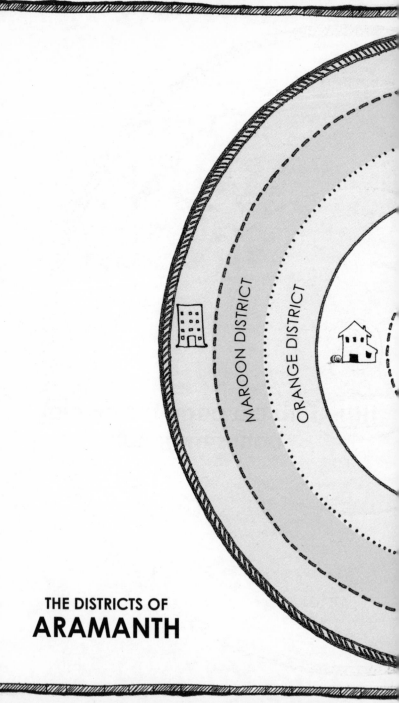

MAROON DISTRICT

ORANGE DISTRICT

THE DISTRICTS OF
ARAMANTH

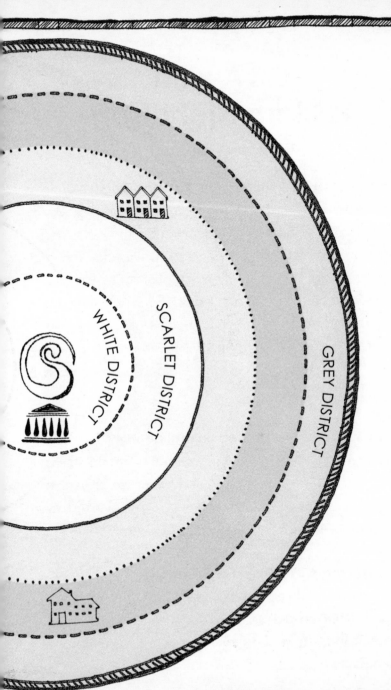

Q&A with William Nicholson

What first inspired you to write *The Wind Singer*?

I wanted time off my film writing to do something that was just from me, without anyone leaning over my shoulder telling me what to write. I decided to write for young readers so that I could let my imagination loose, with the only requirement being: don't get boring. So I thought: what really makes me angry? Anger is always a good driver for a story – look at Roald Dahl. The answer, then, was the over-testing of my children, and all children, in schools. So I began . . .

Are your characters based on real people?

I never meant them to be. But now that I read my stories I can see that my own mother and father are present in Ira and Hanno Hath, and a combination of myself and my children in Kestrel, Bowman and Pinpin.

Are you more like Kestrel or Bowman?

I'm definitely both, which may seem odd, given that I'm male. But I really did feel I was Kestrel when I was writing her. But that's how writing works – you become all the characters.

It seems like the book's concerns about too many tests and the threat to creativity is now more relevant than ever. Do you think that stories can play a part in combating this?

I hope so, if students are ever allowed to come across stories. I hate what's happening to schools and education, which seems now to be viewed as one long job application. When you're still at school you should be free to roam this world and all other worlds. When you're grown up, the walls close in round you.

If you were going to defy the examiners of Aramanth and write about what you know best, what would that be?

Building a fire. I'm very good at it, and feel a strong urge to explain to everyone how to do it properly. In essence what you have to do is build a small house where the fire can be sheltered and protected as it grows up.

When writing fantasy, what are the things you find more enjoyable and what presents more of a challenge than when you are writing historical or contemporary stories?

The joy of writing fantasy is that things pop into your head that seem to come from nowhere (though of course they don't), which is very liberating. The challenge is to create a world of rules. Even fantasy must have rules. If anything can happen at any time then it becomes boring.

How did you find the process of writing these novels compared to writing a film script?

Writing the book stories is far more personal, far more purely me. Film writing is very collaborative. You work with many people, and rightly have to consider their views. This teaches me a lot. So moving back and forth between books and films is ideal.

Did you enjoy coming up with Aramanth's rude words? Which one is your favourite?

The Wind Singer was originally called *The Book of Oaths,* and the climax was going to be achieved by the reciting of an enormous oath. That all got changed, but I did keep in some part of my invented swear words. I think I like 'Pompaprune' best. It's so silly.

Which books would you nominate to be modern classics?

The Just William books. I grew up on them and still adore them.

'The song of the wind singer will set you free'

Music can often be said to cast a powerful spell, and the wind singer is no exception. Its song allows Kestrel and Bowman to free the city from tyranny, as well as keeping it safe from the evil forces outside. Here are some other moments from stories where music exerts a magical power.

The Egyptian sistrum

(origin: Egyptian mythology)

The name 'sistrum' comes from a Greek word that means 'that which is being shaken' and this instrument consists of a metal U-shaped frame with moveable crossbars, which have small rings. The sistrum was a sacred instrument in ancient Egypt and it was believed that shaking it could prevent the Nile from flooding and also scare away the evil Set, god of storms, chaos and war. The Egyptian mother god, Isis, was often depicted holding a sistrum.

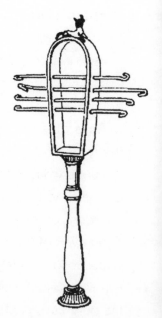

The sirens' song

(origin: Greek mythology)

The sirens were beautiful yet deadly creatures in Greek mythology. Their captivating song would lure sailors to their deaths, as ships crashed on the rocks around the sirens' island. In Homer's *Odyssey* Odysseus makes his crew stuff their ears with wax so they won't follow the sirens' call. He also gets them to tie him to the mast, so he can hear what the song sounds like. And in the story of Jason and the Argonauts, the siren song is drowned out by even more powerful music – Orpheus and his lyre.

Orpheus's lyre (origin: Greek mythology)

The lyre (which is a small, U-shaped harp) was a popular musical instrument in ancient Greece, and in Greek myth Orpheus was its most famous player. He was given his golden lyre by the god Apollo and his music was supposed to have able to charm all living things, and even cause the rocks and trees to dance. When Orpheus travels to the underworld, torn apart with grief after the death of his wife Eurydice, his song of mourning softens the heart even of Hades, the god of the underworld. Hades agrees to let Eurydice return with Orpheus. (But the story doesn't end there . . .)

Panchajanya

(origin: Hindu mythology)

The Shankha or conch shell is a sacred object in Hinduism and Buddhism and is one of the objects the Hindu god Vishnu carries in his four hands. Blowing the Shankha is said to purify the environment of any negative energy. In the past it was used as war trumpet and it is still used as a trumpet in Hindu ritual. Vishnu's own Shankha was named Panchajanya and, according to one story, this is a because a sea monster with this name lived in the shell before Vishnu defeated him.

Tristan's harp

(origin: Celtic mythology)

The epic love story of Tristan and Isolde was a Celtic legend that is said to have influenced the forbidden love of Guinevere and Lancelot in the stories of King Arthur. Tristan was a knight sent to fetch princess Isolde so she could marry his uncle, King Mark. But on the journey Tristan and Isolde fall madly in love.

The association of love and music is a strong theme and Tristan's harp plays a significant role in the story. When he first meets Isolde he is disguised as a musician and she is so struck by the beauty of his harp-playing that she asks him to teach her. This is when they begin to fall in love. Later, when Isolde is kidnapped by another knight, Tristan uses his harp to enchant the knight and rescue her.

The Pied Piper's pipe
(origin: medieval German fairy tale)
The town of Hamelin is overrun with rats and the inhabitants are getting desperate. Then a stranger wearing multi-coloured clothes arrives, claiming that he will solve the problem. The mayor agrees that he will pay the man handsomely if he can indeed get rid of all the rats (thinking this is unlikely). The stranger produces a pipe and starts to play, and the rats start to follow him. He leads them out of the town and to the river, where they drown. However, the mayor goes back on his promise to pay the piper. And this is something the town will regret when the piper starts to play another song . . .

Bad words
said loud

Aramanth has its own set of rude words, most of which are shouted by Kestrel Hath from the top of the wind singer. You can use the generator below to create your own made-up oath!

The first letter of your first name

A Saga		**N** Looni
B Gruna		**O** Ticka
C Banga		**P** Udder
D Hollo		**Q** Rool
E Pompa		**R** Eggsa
F Gurt		**S** Silla
G Dumpa		**T** Pooa
H Crag		**U** Cobler
I Ratta		**V** Hasta
J Pongo		**W** Zippi
K Flib		**X** Grup
L Pock		**Y** Stupa
M Yollo		**Z** Frago

The first letter of your second name

A Grub	**N** Sicker
B Prune	**O** Drop
C Crump	**P** Dog
D Frog	**Q** Nub
E Pip	**R** Jig
F Boot	**S** Plop
G Hog	**T** Pip
H Hickle	**U** Ding
I Mog	**V** Sock
J Bib	**W** Rat
K Bug	**X** Trill
L Moon	**Y** Pop
M Gull	**Z** Cat